NEBULA AWARDS 20

NEBULA AWARDS 20

*SFWA's Choices for the Best
Science Fiction and Fantasy 1984*

Edited by GEORGE ZEBROWSKI

HARCOURT BRACE JOVANOVICH, PUBLISHERS

SAN DIEGO   NEW YORK   LONDON

The Library of Congress has cataloged this serial publication as follows:
The Nebula awards.—No. 18-—San Diego [CA]: Harcourt Brace Jovanovich, Publishers,
   c1983-
     v.; 22 cm.
   Annual.
   Vols. for 1983-   published for the Science Fiction Writers of America.
   Continues: Nebula award stories (1982)
   ISSN 0741-5567 = The Nebula awards.
     1. Science fiction, American—Periodicals.   I. Science Fiction Writers of America.
   PS648.S3N38   83-647399
                              813'.0876'08—dc19
                                                                      AACR 2   MARC-S
   Library of Congress
   ISBN 0-15-164927-8
   ISBN 0-15-665477-6 (Harvest/HBJ:pbk.)

Designed by G.B.D. Smith
Printed in the United States of America
First edition
A B C D E

In Memory of

Theodore Sturgeon: 1918–1985

Contents

Introduction

GEORGE ZEBROWSKI

Throughout the year the members of the Science Fiction Writers of America read and recommend stories and novels for the annual Nebula Awards. These recommendations are recorded in a newsletter, and toward the end of the year the recommendations are counted. A preliminary ballot is then drawn up and circulated to the membership. The top five novels (40,000 words or more), novellas (17,500–39,999 words), novelettes (7,500–17,499 words), and short stories (fewer than 7,500 words) are placed on the final ballot, which is then sent to members for their votes. A Nebula Awards jury may add one additional nominee to each category.

The results of this process can scarcely be expected to please everyone. Awards systems are by their very nature imperfect. Happily, the annual Nebula anthology lets the editor do something that no awards system allows: he or she can give an indication of the larger process of selection by presenting to readers the winners, nominees, and other contenders—as much as the size of the anthology will allow and as much as the concept of selectivity will permit. Inevitably, there will be some overlap between the Nebula anthology and other best-of-the-year collections; this perhaps argues for a prevalence of good taste, or bad, but that will have to be decided by posterity.

What this collection illustrates is that each contender is as worthy as any other in the group. The actual winner must exclude other worthy choices. Writers probably debate this fact about excellence more than most readers. Critics and reviewers do it still more, and more confusedly. The special pleasure of a Nebula collection is that here the winners are seen in context, jostling other worthies, proclaiming that no work exists in isolation; they nourish one another and enlarge the growing ground of accomplishment. Writers know that good work is individual work, but in this collection they can show solidarity with other achievers.

All this is well understood by the thoughtful, but at a time when other considerations seem overwhelming, when the flowers of achievement are cut down by misguided commerce, we need to remember the love, dedication, and skill that go into the writing life. Science fiction and fantasy are still too often judged by their worst—a startling form of bigotry that is not directed at contemporary general fiction, even though as much, if not more, bad work is produced elsewhere. I believe that it is the very vitality of SF that makes it suspect—the fact that its life exists over such a great range, from popular entertainments in film and television, stage works, poetry, and musical works to novels of ideas and cautionary concern about the human future. All creative endeavor is tied to commerce in some degree; no one is immune. What is surprising is that so much good work gets done at all, delighting discerning perceivers who do not judge by outward appearances and received opinions.

The clear fact is that science fiction and fantasy constitute *the* major area of activity in English-language short fiction, and this is increasingly being recognized by literary movers and shakers. Consider: what will the fiction of a rapidly changing, technically based civilization be like even a few decades from now? If a work from 2050 were to be transported back to us, what would we make of it? I say that to us it would appear science fictional, if it were true to its time. The very nature of the relationship between forms of fiction and their times belongs to the speculative ways of thinking beloved by science fiction writers. Science fiction is both a fiction of its times and a varied metafiction.

Of course, there will be no pleasing the insular zealots of mandarin taste, the critics of awards, or all popular appetites. What counts is that intelligent readers (those who at least know and practice the principle that reading is not entirely a passive activity) continue to respond to the various efforts of writers. What is good, and how can we tell? As Algis Budrys has written: "A book should be good. A bird should fly." And while we can all agree that this is true, it is, again happily, difficult to get general agreement in specific cases.

Somewhere, perhaps, there are readers and judges with minds like lamps, where what is good is clearly demonstrable, but this can never be in our own, open-ended Gödelian universe. Maybe there's a story in that—and one that might win all the prizes. "The Aliens Who Came to Give Out Awards—Because They Could Be Objective" strikes me as a perfect title.

Johnson City, New York
1 July 1985

1984 or Against

ALGIS BUDRYS

Algis Budrys is the author of the now-classic novels Rogue Moon, Who?, *and* Some Will Not Die. *His most recent novel is the highly acclaimed* Michaelmas. *He is also the author of many stories and writes a regular critical column for* The Magazine of Fantasy & Science Fiction. *Budrys is a member of the SFWA Hall of Fame and received a Special Award from the Mystery Writers of America. He is quite simply the best American critic of science fiction and fantasy.*

A young man won the 1984 Nebula Award with his first science fiction novel, and two others damned near did. That was the signal: discomfitingly, 1984 was a year in which things in the world of speculative fiction had turned upside down once more.

Where had things been, and what is "speculative fiction"?

The one answer depends on the other. For years, "sf" had plainly meant "science fiction," and, operationally, "science fiction" (which tacitly meant "newsstand-derived technology romances") had often also meant "newsstand-derived fantasy," though many serious students of the literature would have disputed that. (They would have disputed it on any of several opposing sets of grounds.) These terms were not anywhere near as much literary denominators as they were marketplace categorizations; touch them with an inquiring mind and they shivered, shattered, and evanesced. Meanwhile, however, the wholesale distributors knew what cartons to put on the trucks, quite different from the air-war pulps, the westerns, the sports, and the crime.

By exactly the same sort of operation of necessary convenience, over the past fifteen-odd years there has come to be this newer usage, speculative fiction, or SF (as distinct from sf), which is a basket designed to contain both science fiction and fantasy. In this case, the academics were a little ahead of the warehousemen, but they were responding to a necessity as practical as a length of pipe; the marketplace was emphatically demonstrating that there is no essential difference in the readerships, and that where a "science fiction" reader differs from readers of other generic fictions is the same place where only a "fantasy" reader also differs. They, their writers, and their publishing programs are essentially one particular universe, and apparently what is academically true of the one is almost entirely true of the other.

This discovery was the discovery of a revolution. There had been this long time, from approximately the Battle of Midway to the Tet Offensive, when SF authors wrote science fiction, and perhaps a little fantasy as an act of self-indulgence. Perhaps because so many came to perceive science fiction as an isolated form, cut off nearly entire from the Main, attempts raged to "define" science fiction. Some, espousing the view that science fiction was "the mythology of The Machine Age," tried to prove its existence as a totally new entity, quite different from "fantasy," a form viable only with the dwindling few who didn't know how radios worked. Others, equally strenuous in their feelings, saw science fiction as a subordinate form of fantasy, that classic literature whose innate power had made a fantasy magazine editor even out of John W. Campbell, Jr., erstwhile Technocrat. But whatever the art and eschatology of it all might be, fantasy as a thing that came in cartons was nearly nonexistent in commerce, its budgets entirely impoverished even by the standards of the science fiction markets.

It was during this time that the Science Fiction Writers of America was founded as a tough craft guild to represent science fiction (and fantasy) authors. As it now is, it performs this function throughout the English-speaking world and a little bit beyond, and performs it in a market where at least an assiduous and clever few can make quite decent fortunes at it, and many can make a respectable middle-class living. Its evolution toward that point proceeded unhampered by the fact that in the 1970s, a great many SFWA members were plunged into the booming fantasy market and most new recruits were establishing their professional credentials via that route. It made no operational difference to the SFWA, any more than it did to bookstores that stacked an increasing proportion of fantasy titles on shelves still marked "science fiction," or to publishers, who similarly lumped the two things together and tacitly assumed they were hiring fantasy *and* science fiction specialists when they hired people called science fiction editors.

No one now can swear unflinchingly to what caused the fantasy boom. There is a theory that a generation of Tolkien readers had come to fruition, but with only a few exceptions the new fantasy was not particularly imitative of the *Rings* trilogy. Rather, some of it, like the *Rings*, tended to repeat classic archetypes of the "quest" romance. And some of it was quite different—for instance, was fueled by, or quickly seized upon, a Conan revival that had hitherto been trying to get itself started since the late 1940s. Nor does any of this explain the parallel phenomenon of the horror-fiction floreat perhaps initiated by Blatty's *The Exorcist* or by Thomas Tryon's earlier *The Other*.

It is less productive of future obfuscation to simply declare that fantasy time had come round again, and noteworthy to recall that it came at the hands mostly of new writers or of old writers who had abruptly abandoned what had been patient mediocre careers in other styles of SF. That is, it was an invasive rather than a pervasive revolution, it apparently had the sanction of a broad social readiness, and it proceeded at the implosive speed with which vacuums usually fill.

This transition had thus proceeded glibly in the marketplace, smoothing its progress with cash flow. Only the theorists of the genre—was it a genre at all, was it two genres, what was it?—had to scramble to catch up, but as usual they had accomplished this in little more than a decade. We now have the academic apparatus with which to know where we are. More and more people now speak of speculative fiction, sometimes *a* speculative fiction, and sometimes understand what is meant by SF as distinguished from sf, and certainly as distinguished from "sci-fi," a term that has come to mean only the sort of science fiction suitable for special-effects movies, and grates.

With the advantage of this perspective, it has now been possible to once again reinterpret the significance of the fact that quite a few top-rank science fiction writers of the 1940s either entered the field as writers of newsstand fantasy for *Unknown Worlds* magazine or else contributed with equal ease to *Unknown* and its sister publication, *Astounding Science Fiction*. The latter, also edited by Campbell, was, despite its title, the most serious, thoughtful, and influential sf medium of its time. These individuals then stayed with *ASF*, and the other newsstand science fiction media, when *Unknown* was killed for its paper allocation in the midst of World War II, leaving behind it the firmly held wisdom that fantasy didn't sell. And the equally beloved legend that science fiction, as defined during the "Golden Age" of the 1940s, was entirely a literature for engineers by blindered engineers, narrowly technist and studded with rivets.

When the idea about fantasy was disproved a quarter century later, disproof coincided with another trend. Many of the new fantasy writers were female. Some, one could say inevitably, also produced science fiction. In many prominent cases—Anne McCaffrey, Marion Zimmer Bradley, Kate Wilhelm, Joanna Russ, Ursula K. Le Guin—it was altogether impossible to decide whether these were fantasy people or sf people, and it was at this time, and largely because of the work of these minds, that "SF"—a once-idiosyncratic usage by 1960s critic and anthologist Judith Merril—was increasingly adopted into continuing and useful service.

It was not altogether clear, even so, what had peppered the fantasy boom with females. What was clear was that SF would never be the same. What was thought to be clear was that SF, arguably not in itself small enough or particular enough to be a genre, was rapidly labeling a notable number of genres within itself and might, like the expanding physical universe, attain a point at which the components of a once densely packed core, now flying outward in their infinite variety, might come to be light-years apart from each other.

Where things SFnal were, as recently as 1980, was here:

Fantasy accounted for over half the SF titles on sale in the popular market. It accounted for an even larger proportion of the total wordage, because one genre—the "heroic" or sword-and-sorcery quest métier—appeared to be most viable in extremely long forms, engendering "sagas" embodied in multivolume books, and thick volumes at that.

Science fiction had adapted this form to its own uses. Such novels as Robert Silverberg's massive *Lord Valentine's Castle*, which has since, as expected, yielded sequelae, or Gene Wolfe's *Book of the New Sun* tetralogy, are quest novels set in a science fiction milieu in many respects indistinguishable from the venues of fantasy. Julian May's "Pliocene Saga," which began with a huge book, *The Many-Colored Land*, and prospers on through successor after successor, launched a science fictional attempt to create a thoroughgoing fantasy universe by calling in time travel and exotic alien spacefarers to account for all our ancient legends and magicks. And though it is stretching a point to call Frank Herbert's evolved *Dune* series a heroic fantasy pastiche, it is not stretching it very far.

Science fiction was not only assimilating technical aspects of fantasy, it was developing a fantaisiacal turn of mind. Robert A. Heinlein, for instance, a stalwart of the *ASF* Golden Age, brought out *The Number of the Beast*, a novel toward which he had obviously been pointing for some time. In it, a machine enables people to enter fictional fantasy universes—for instance, the Land of Oz—but, even more noteworthily, it is a painstakingly worked-out vehicle for the proposition that there is no reality.

At the very same time, editors like Ben Bova at *Omni* and Stanley Schmidt at *Analog* (*Astounding* with a changed title) and

writers like Bova, James P. Hogan, Charles Sheffield, and Jerry
Pournelle (alone and with Larry Niven) were leading a clear evolution toward a "space fiction" genre, wedding science fiction directly to technological progress and in many cases using it as a
vehicle for lobbying legislators and industrialists as well as the elec-
torate. Close observers might have felt that this neotechnic f out-
hardwired anything promulgated during the Golden Age or even in
the founding days of Hugo Gernsback, when "scientifiction" was
frankly addressed to the same sort of technology hobbyist that sub-
scribes to *Popular Mechanics* today.

At the very same time, Gregory Benford, an important physicist
and a lifelong SF fan, in his teens a prolific publisher and writer
in the SF amateur press universe, set out to revive the midcentury
science-poetic visions of Arthur C. Clarke. Clarke's archetypal title
was *Against the Fall of Night*. Benford's ongoing series of powerfully
evocative novels and novellas began with *In the Ocean of Night* and
currently has advanced up to *Across the Sea of Suns*, which received
a number of 1984 novel Nebula nominations.

At the same time, giants returned. Over the past few years, the
present Arthur C. Clarke, with *2010*, and Isaac Asimov, with *Foundation's Edge* and other novels published or in progress, had launched
a significant effort to reestablish themselves as current science fiction
bylines. L. Ron Hubbard, suddenly doubling back into a field he
had forsaken in the 1940s, produced a hefty new action novel,
Battlefield Earth. All three efforts were marked by self-indulgence
and prolixity—no editor dares lay on these writers the hand no
author should evade—that is, by the literary effects of too much
money. Clarke's next project—he had ostensibly retired at the end
of the 1970s—is imponderable, though few doubt there is one, with
advances of well over a million dollars instantly available to him.
Asimov is busy reconciling his two major canons—his robot stories
and his Foundation series—into one. This will take several volumes
and some time. Hubbard in 1985 will bring out the first volume in
his new ten-book work, *Mission Earth*. All of this may or may not
have some literary merit—Hubbard's will at least have verve—but
that will not be relevant. It is as if all the elephantiasic exercises in

SF merchandising that have been invented and executed over the past ten years were merely a tune-up. These new books are the Great Sphinx brought to market. Conscious of this, the SF community has been preparing to live for years to come under the loom of the cyclopean point-of-sale gantries and propulsive gases required to get such megalithic properties into the air and sustain them in flight.

This is the picture that the SF community has been seeing. With all its hurtling parts—and with many others like them that have mercifully not been cited here—no two persons within that community could possibly have resolved the same mosaic from them. But it may be that in some Jungian sense in which details do not matter, down in the subconscious labyrinths where move things not to be borne forever, the community has come up with a collective reaction. How else to explain the good fortune that has befallen William Gibson?

William Gibson's novel, *Neuromancer*, won the Nebula Award. Close behind it on the final ballot was Kim Stanley Robinson's *The Wild Shore*, and close behind them in the nominations, though it was not on the final ballot, was Lucius Shepard's *Green Eyes*. All three men were first novelists, competing for best-of-the-year honors with the impeccable likes of Heinlein and Niven, each in his own way an institution.

Shepard, in fact, scored a singular honor; he lost in every one of the four Nebula categories. To accomplish that, he had to have been prolific throughout the year at every fiction length, and, more tellingly, to have done work exciting the broad admiration of his fellow practitioners. To win, and to come very near winning, Gibson and Robinson had to accomplish parallel feats.

All three writers had for some years been producing well-received short fiction, but those were few years; to most intents and purposes, Gibson, Robinson, and Shepard are the instigators of overnight success. Additionally, they had, a month prior to the Nebula Awards announcement, finished in the same way vis-à-vis the Philip K. Dick Memorial Award for the best American original paperback of speculative fiction in 1984. (Both elections were actually concluded at about the same time. But while Nebula winners are determined by nomination and then by ballot counting throughout the active guild membership of the Science Fiction Writers of America, the Dick Award is conferred by a small jury of professionals drawn from the SFWA and from among SF academics, who have their own Science Fiction Research Association.) It happened that all three books were Ace Specials softcovers, part of a newly launched experimental program done by a small division of the colophon-ridden Berkley-Putnam publishing agglomerate.

The Ace Specials are edited by Terry Carr, a notable talent scout whose outstanding reputation over the years must have attracted knowledgeable attention to these candidates. Too, the accessibility of rack-size paperbacks, as distinguished from the hardback bookstore editions in which most of the competition appeared, must have been of some advantage in getting the work into the hands of the voters. But no quibble can stand up to the sheer impact of what has happened—that is, a strikingly swift redefinition of what SF writers will consider to be the best SF.

A look at the winners and runners-up in the shorter categories will discover more reflections of the same phenomenon. The smart money would have bet against it. Given their druthers, most SFWA members would rather not have had anything particular happen in a year that every pop sociologist from Ronald Reagan and the BBC documentarists on down had raked over for Orwellian resonances. Professionals try not to compete with amateurs. Nevertheless, something special did happen, although fortunately not where Ted Koppel or even Geraldo Rivera do a great deal of looking; that is, it happened in an art form.

What happened in essence is that the SFWA, which has set the standard for labor-publisher negotiations on the basis that writing is a trade, declared speculative fiction to be an art form. It did it in the best way—unconsciously, via a cumulative process, so that each bearer of the individual stone to the pile had little idea there would be an odeon standing in that place at the conclusion. Yet there it is.

Evidently not yet content, it also reversed itself on what the most popular speculative fiction form was, and reversed a trend in the sex of its forefront authors. Of the twenty-four pieces on the final Nebula ballot, only two were by women and very few were what the SF community calls fantasy as distinguished from science fiction.

Those newly on the scene, or those aware that there are separate, juried, awards conferred at the annual World Fantasy Convention, might not raise an eyebrow. Why should there be fantasy among science fiction awards nominees? Obversely, those who have not looked at speculative fiction since the demise of *Planet Stories* may still be clinging to the once altogether valid notion that SF is a man's game dominated by science fiction. And of course, as many yet another sort of educated person of taste can tell you, any pretensions to art within a commercial form are by definition pathetic.

All these people are right, but insufficiently so. And to understand what happened in 1984, those insufficiencies require some looking at. So we plunge our attention again backward from our time into the days when the core exploded. Or possibly formed. In some cosmologies, they are the same moment and always will be.

In 1926, when Hugo Gernsback founded the first newsstand magazine devoted to what he at first called scientific fiction—the swiftly imitated *Amazing Stories*—he created two mighty precedents. One was to enter the world of chain-published pulp media, where almost at once he found himself competed with by a flurry of *Astoundings*, *Astonishings*, *Startlings*, and *Thrillings*, their contents written by people whose first qualification was an ability to translate the storytelling tricks of cheap six-gun westerns into cheap ray-gun melodrama. The other precedent was to develop his own community: to create an enclave within which an irreducible number of captive readers would be nurtured, with future generations of artists, writers, editors, and even publishers to be drawn from among them. If there were to be additional readers—walk-ins; invasive readers—so much the better, but there would always be the dependable inner group. Thus was born the Science Fiction League with its various (and sporadic) chapter activities in various major population centers. What Gernsback had done with his paper charters, membership insignia, club news pages in his magazines, and his encouragement of science as well as the purchasing of Gernsback magazines was to found SF fandom. (From the very first, it included fantasy readers as well as scientifictionists.) And fandom has, over the generations since the late 1930s, furnished the bulk of SF creative personnel. It has also produced the influential readers who, through activity and articulation, endorse or attempt to expunge various features of its creative evolution as they come along.

No one has yet given a believable account of how it worked as well as it did. It didn't work for Gernsback commercially; he was forever going broke faster than his readership could stabilize. But it worked for the field as a whole, and it continues to work, in an evolved international ad hoc structure supporting all sorts of amateur and in effect professional fannish activities. It permanently bonds thousands of individuals who apparently have nothing else in common and who may be thousands of miles apart geographically, and it elaborately conditions its young. There is thus in fact a collective consciousness in SF, not necessarily Jungian but certainly operational.

This is quite different from anything having to do with the other pulp-derived fictions to which SF was a very late comer. Quite possibly it is not of their ilk at all. Many critics within the field point out that all other fictions are descriptive (they tend to call them "mundane" when in private), dedicated to exploring the world as it is or is said to be, many of them tacitly endorsing the idea that what exists is all that will ever exist, probably more than should exist. SF, on the other hand, in its two branches and to its fingertips, is the literature of suppositional existences, tacitly endorsing the idea that change is inevitable and in any case desirable, that there is not yet enough in the universe. Science fiction is the literature of belief in the efficacy of science as the agency of change, and fantasy is the literature of belief in the efficacy, instead, of magic; the ultimate psychic fulfillment for the reader is the same. Ultimately, SF is the literature of people who will not go gentle into that good night.

One cannot believe that Gernsback inseminated the world with such people. One must believe that he tapped into the existence of such people, gave them, with mass-market media, a universe of their own—a place that, once found, they will never surrender and can shape, or at least contend with only their own kind in shaping.

Not through overt conspiracy but simply through the generational development of an intensely recomplicated vocabulary of speech and concept, the SF community—distinct from the ready accessibility of SF reading matter—is now very difficult for strangers to enter. They have to invent their own genres—*Star Trek* and *Star Wars* fandom, the writing and performing of SF folk songs, the collecting of books and SF-oriented objects, the Society for Creative Anachronism—which then act as conveyances into the inner sancta.

Very few outsiders ever create anything that the community will accept as being SFnal, and even the marketplace has difficulty sustaining long-term interest in their work. They simply don't speak the genuine language. Except when some genre population burgeons larger than the core group, SF creativity is pervasive—it emanates from the core, drawing inspiration and surface detail as it comes up through the successive layers of generational accretion around that core. In doing so, it binds the latest accretions to itself, and they in turn become part of the speculative fiction universe, so that a careless glance sees only the one thing. Thus, too, the core always wins; the genres assimilate into it as surely as the universe will someday reverse its flights.

At that core, each successive generation impresses its successors. The teenagers who were reading the inept work in the early magazines did not know it was ludicrous and bad; by definition, it spoke to them and they thought it perceptive, poignant, and relevant. When they grew sufficiently older to begin creating or endorsing new work, they strove to make it as effective as the reading of their youths had been. To that effort, they brought of course as much as they could of what their high schools and colleges had since convinced them was good in literature and in the mind of the artist. And so there have been clear-cut spurts of energy in the evolution of newsstand-borne SF; there are detectable five-year generations to which we can point—"schools" of SF, each driven toward excellence, each defining excellence with all the sophistication it could gain between the time it was fifteen and the time it was twenty. As we look back down along the history of SF, the half-decade ripples come up from 1929 as regular as anything in nature, still spreading from Gernsback's flung stone or whatever it was.

This generational phenomenon proceeds without ever wiping out its past. Every idea and technique ever published in SF remains viable and is freely accessible to even the youngest SF writer. It may be that this is simply because the entire history of mass-market SF is only one lifetime old; 1984 saw the publication of new novels—excellent new novels—by Jack Williamson and Lloyd Arthur Esbach, both of whom were readers of the first issues of *Amazing* and whose professional careers are well over half a century long. But it will probably never be possible to be a noteworthy new writer of SF without having assimilated the core material either directly or, more likely, because the sense of the core has perfused even the outermost shells of the core. In a sense, it *is* all one thing, and even a shallow bite of the apple, taken in the proper mindset, in a moment of relevation dooms the youngster to a lifelong knowingness, and, of course, the impulse to amplify and transmit the terrible thrill of that transfiguring contact. So in SF, the past is never finished. There is no operational distinction between what was then and what is now. It is all one moment and it is lived in forever, changing.

In this volume, you can see some of the top shorter works of 1984 for yourself. They do, indeed, represent the state of the art and can speak to you for themselves. Let me describe *Neuromancer*, *The Wild Shore*, and *Green Eyes*.

All three are short by 1980 standards. Their language is direct, not "heightened" in the way of heroic fantasy or of science fiction set in faraway milieux where the use of the contraction would be rude. They are set on Earth, either contemporaneously with our time or in what we all expect will shortly be our time, and by today's standards they are pronouncedly science fiction, extrapolating their milieux from electronic physics, *realpolitika*l terror-war, and biology as we know them all too well and perhaps fear them. And they are frightening, but they are not fearful, reversing yet another trend.

They do not appear to be as similar to each other as they are.

Neuromancer's hero, with his built-in direct couplers to electronic devices, is a specialist in subjectively exploring and manipulating the objective reality of the electronic data world. The speech in which Gibson describes his events is full of neologisms and cascading social concepts, reflecting a hectic, machine-ridden culture. It is a place where inputs come hard, fast, and unpreambled; an eye blink represents catastrophic lag. Yet Gibson finds technical ways to take the reader directly to what is happening.

The Wild Shore is a coming-of-age novel set in what remains of coastal southern California after terrorists with nuclear car bombs destroy the urban structure of the United States and America is quarantined and repressed by the rest of the world. Played against that background is a young man's story much resembling what Steinbeck might have done; it is ultimately concerned with the endurance of human dignity under repression.

If we look for resemblances to famous descriptive writers of recent past generations, then *Green Eyes* is in a sense like what Tennessee Williams might have done if he had gotten the central idea, which seems unlikely even for someone whose first sale was to *Weird Tales*. Set in the Louisiana bayou country, it begins with an ethically dubious project—the induction of new personalities into the recently dead. Infecting their brains with a bacterium that Doctor Frankenstein would have given his soul to possess, the Institute sometimes creates wild geniuses whose technical discoveries or works of art can be lucratively marketed. Shambling, sometimes wheelchair-ridden, lied to, they rarely suspect how short their lives are, for the bacteria are destroying the tissues in which they proliferate. The story of *Green Eyes* is the story of one of them, who does suspect, who escapes, and who in the climactic scene strides and utters among giant magnets intended to divert the coursing bacteria from his most vital centers, who will not surrender to his doom, who will speak of what he is and what he thinks.

If the bacteria derive straight from our ancestress Mary Wollstonecraft Shelley, the ethical climate of the research is altogether modern and so is its victim, who at one interim becomes a commercial faith healer. His situation, however, would have spoken to Aeschylus, and vice versa. The major point, I think, is that this book, like the other two and like some others published during 1984 and early 1985, can be described in such a way as to resemble previously existing art. Lacking the facility to show their entire texts, that's the most convenient thing for a critic to do. But if they were in fact slavishly like prior art, they would be the less for it. These books do have flaws in them—all work has flaws in it—but they are never lesser than other works; they are successes on their own terms, and that makes them forever unique and forever available for the next art to learn from.

As it happens, they are describable as quest novels. So were most of the nominees in that category, Heinlein's being an indubitable piece of science fiction about the quest for the God of the Masonic Order. But these three are about the quest for self, not the talisman of power or the magic city. These writers have taken everything that SF makes available—all the trappings, all the technical heritage, most important the essence of what SF does in the psyche—and they have, independently but in communion, made superb new things.

Their storytelling is more than competent, their prose is often elegant, their choices of technique are excellent and often deftly handled. Their ideas are striking, even if one is not a lifelong SFnist. But we have seen all that many times before in newsstand-borne SF, even on occasion in its earliest days; that is the stuff of craftsmanship. There is more than that in these books, as there is in many of the nominated shorter stories.

We have from time to time seen examples of art in this field. In a sense, of course, every human expression is art. But then, in a sense, everything is anything. More directly, literature is that worded vehicle whereby we speak purposefully of ourselves and our world, and fiction is the literature of the heart. As the heart endures its rewards from the vicissitudes of passing time, the fiction evolves. Up to now, what art there was in SF was occasioned by bursts of individual good fortune, and for a variety of rationally founded reasons the community tended to be suspicious of such things. The principal reason, I think, was that such art—Ray Bradbury's, for instance—proved not to be transferable. The world did not see SF as a source of art but Bradbury as an artist who obviously could have nothing really in common with a form published behind three-color paintings of seminude women. Theodore Sturgeon died agonizingly as an artist in an attempt to bridge that chasm of perception, and he was not the only one.

But what we have now is something quite unique in the history of SF. A certified SF bellwether—operating a program specifically designed to locate the most promising and interesting commercially viable first novelists—produced an immediate cluster of young artists. Having put them to the judgment of the community's creative individuals, those works have won immediate, overwhelming endorsement. And a look at the shorter works reveals the depth and extent of this frame of mind that has suddenly (?) unfurled itself and declared that *this*—and this is art—is what SF now is.

There is, of course, only illusory suddenness in it; this has been coming since 1929. But the totality with which it has burst out, the sweep with which it has set aside the primacy of other SF genres— at least for a few years—speaks of how energetically driven it is.

These will be interesting, these next years.

Bloodchild

OCTAVIA E. BUTLER

Octavia E. Butler slipped quietly into the science fiction field with several very impressive novels, the latest of which is Clay's Ark. *The others include* Kindred, Wild Seed, *and* Survivor. *A short story, "Speech Sounds," won a Hugo Award in 1984. Born in Pasadena, California, and a writer since the age of ten, Butler is clearly one of science fiction's originals and an American writer of growing distinction.*

"Bloodchild," this year's winner of the Nebula Award in the novelette (and also a Hugo Award winner), is a powerful story that illuminates—in a terrifyingly alien setting—the currents of feeling that exist in all human families. The story exhibits Butler's ability to combine an overpowering sense of shared, common realities with science fictional situations of striking imagery.

M y last night of childhood began with a visit home. T'Gatoi's sisters had given us two sterile eggs. T'Gatoi gave one to my mother, brother, and sisters. She insisted that I eat the other one alone. It didn't matter. There was still enough to leave everyone feeling good. Almost everyone. My mother wouldn't take any. She sat, watching everyone drifting and dreaming without her. Most of the time she watched me.

I lay against T'Gatoi's long, velvet underside, sipping from my egg now and then, wondering why my mother denied herself such a harmless pleasure. Less of her hair would be gray if she indulged now and then. The eggs prolonged life, prolonged vigor. My father, who had never refused one in his life, had lived more than twice as long as he should have. And toward the end of his life, when he should have been slowing down, he had married my mother and fathered four children.

But my mother seemed content to age before she had to. I saw her turn away as several of T'Gatoi's limbs secured me closer. T'Gatoi liked our body heat, and took advantage of it whenever she could. When I was little and at home more, my mother used to try to tell me how to behave with T'Gatoi—how to be respectful and always obedient because T'Gatoi was the Tlic government official in charge of the Preserve, and thus the most important of her kind to deal directly with Terrans. It was an honor, my mother said, that such a person had chosen to come into the family. My mother was at her most formal and severe when she was lying.

I had no idea why she was lying, or even what she was lying about. It *was* an honor to have T'Gatoi in the family, but it was hardly a novelty. T'Gatoi and my mother had been friends all my mother's life, and T'Gatoi was not interested in being honored in the house she considered her second home. She simply came in, climbed onto one of her special couches and called me over to keep her warm. It was impossible to be formal with her while lying against her and hearing her complain as usual that I was too skinny.

"You're better," she said this time, probing me with six or seven of her limbs. "You're gaining weight finally. Thinness is dangerous." The probing changed subtly, became a series of caresses.

"He's still too thin," my mother said sharply.

T'Gatoi lifted her head and perhaps a meter of her body off the couch as though she were sitting up. She looked at my mother and my mother, her face lined and old-looking, turned away.

"Lien, I would like you to have what's left of Gan's egg."

"The eggs are for the children," my mother said.

"They are for the family. Please take it."

Unwillingly obedient, my mother took it from me and put it to her mouth. There were only a few drops left in the now-shrunken, elastic shell, but she squeezed them out, swallowed them, and after a few moments some of the lines of tension began to smooth from her face.

"It's good," she whispered. "Sometimes I forget how good it is."

"You should take more," T'Gatoi said. "Why are you in such a hurry to be old?"

My mother said nothing.

"I like being able to come here," T'Gatoi said. "This place is a refuge because of you, yet you won't take care of yourself."

T'Gatoi was hounded on the outside. Her people wanted more of us made available. Only she and her political faction stood between us and the hordes who did not understand why there was a Preserve—why any Terran could not be courted, paid, drafted, in some way made available to them. Or they did understand, but in their desperation, they did not care. She parceled us out to the desperate and sold us to the rich and powerful for their political support. Thus, we were necessities, status symbols, and an independent people. She oversaw the joining of families, putting an end to the final remnants of the earlier system of breaking up Terran families to suit impatient Tlic. I had lived outside with her. I had seen the desperate eagerness in the way some people looked at me. It was a little frightening to know that only she stood between us and that desperation that could so easily swallow us. My mother would look at her sometimes and say to me, "Take care of her." And I would remember that she too had been outside, had seen.

Now T'Gatoi used four of her limbs to push me away from her onto the floor. "Go on, Gan," she said. "Sit down there with your sisters and enjoy not being sober. You had most of the egg. Lien, come warm me."

My mother hesitated for no reason that I could see. One of my earliest memories is of my mother stretched alongside T'Gatoi, talking about things I could not understand, picking me up from the floor and laughing as she sat me on one of T'Gatoi's segments. She ate her share of eggs then. I wondered when she had stopped, and why.

She lay down now against T'Gatoi, and the whole left row of T'Gatoi's limbs closed around her, holding her loosely, but securely. I had always found it comfortable to lie that way but, except for my older sister, no one else in the family liked it. They said it made them feel caged.

T'Gatoi meant to cage my mother. Once she had, she moved her tail slightly, then spoke. "Not enough egg, Lien. You should have taken it when it was passed to you. You need it badly now."

T'Gatoi's tail moved once more, its whip motion so swift I wouldn't have seen it if I hadn't been watching for it. Her sting drew only a single drop of blood from my mother's bare leg.

My mother cried out—probably in surprise. Being stung doesn't hurt. Then she sighed and I could see her body relax. She moved languidly into a more comfortable position within the cage of T'Gatoi's limbs. "Why did you do that?" she asked, sounding half asleep.

"I could not watch you sitting and suffering any longer."

My mother managed to move her shoulders in a small shrug. "Tomorrow," she said.

"Yes. Tomorrow you will resume your suffering—if you must. But for now, just for now, lie here and warm me and let me ease your way a little."

"He's still mine, you know," my mother said suddenly. "Nothing can buy him from me." Sober, she would not have permitted herself to refer to such things.

"Nothing," T'Gatoi agreed, humoring her.

"Did you think I would sell him for eggs? For long life? My son?"

"Not for anything," T'Gatoi said stroking my mother's shoulders, toying with her long, graying hair.

I would like to have touched my mother, shared that moment with her. She would take my hand if I touched her now. Freed by the egg and the sting, she would smile and perhaps say things long held in. But tomorrow, she would remember all this as a humiliation. I did not want to be part of a remembered humiliation. Best just to be still and know she loved me under all the duty and pride and pain.

"Xuan Hoa, take off her shoes," T'Gatoi said. "In a little while I'll sting her again and she can sleep."

My older sister obeyed, swaying drunkenly as she stood up. When she had finished, she sat down beside me and took my hand. We had always been a unit, she and I.

My mother put the back of her head against T'Gatoi's underside and tried from that impossible angle to look up into the broad, round face. "You're going to sting me again?"

"Yes, Lien."

"I'll sleep until tomorrow noon."

"Good. You need it. When did you sleep last?"

My mother made a wordless sound of annoyance. "I should have stepped on you when you were small enough," she muttered.

It was an old joke between them. They had grown up together, sort of, though T'Gatoi had not, in my mother's lifetime, been small enough for any Terran to step on. She was nearly three times my mother's present age, yet would still be young when my mother died of age. But T'Gatoi and my mother had met as T'Gatoi was coming into a period of rapid development—a kind of Tlic adolescence. My mother was only a child, but for a while they developed at the same rate and had no better friends than each other.

T'Gatoi had even introduced my mother to the man who became my father. My parents, pleased with each other in spite of their very different ages, married as T'Gatoi was going into her family's business—politics. She and my mother saw each other less. But sometime before my older sister was born, my mother promised T'Gatoi one of her children. She would have to give one of us to someone, and she preferred T'Gatoi to some stranger.

Years passed. T'Gatoi traveled and increased her influence. The Preserve was hers by the time she came back to my mother to collect what she probably saw as her just reward for her hard work. My older sister took an instant liking to her and wanted to be chosen, but my mother was just coming to term with me and T'Gatoi liked the idea of choosing an infant and watching and taking part in all the phases of development. I'm told I was first caged within T'Gatoi's many limbs only three minutes after my birth. A few days later, I was given my first taste of egg. I tell Terrans that when they ask whether I was ever afraid of her. And I tell it to Tlic when T'Gatoi suggests a young Terran child for them and they, anxious and ignorant, demand an adolescent. Even my brother who had somehow grown up to fear and distrust the Tlic could probably have gone smoothly into one of their families if he had been adopted early enough. Sometimes, I think for his sake he should have been. I looked at him, stretched out on the floor across the room, his eyes open, but glazed as he dreamed his egg dream. No matter what he felt toward the Tlic, he always demanded his share of egg.

"Lien, can you stand up?" T'Gatoi asked suddenly.

"Stand?" my mother said. "I thought I was going to sleep."

"Later. Something sounds wrong outside." The cage was abruptly gone.

"What?"

"Up, Lien!"

My mother recognized her tone and got up just in time to avoid being dumped on the floor. T'Gatoi whipped her three meters of body off her couch, toward the door, and out at full speed. She had bones—ribs, a long spine, a skull, four sets of limbbones per segment. But when she moved that way, twisting, hurling herself into controlled falls, landing running, she seemed not only boneless, but aquatic—something swimming through the air as though it were water. I loved watching her move.

I left my sister and started to follow her out the door, though I wasn't very steady on my own feet. It would have been better to sit and dream, better yet to find a girl and share a waking dream with her. Back when the Tlic saw us as not much more than convenient big warm-blooded animals, they would pen several of us together, male and female, and feed us only eggs. That way they could be sure of getting another generation of us no matter how we tried to hold out. We were lucky that didn't go on long. A few generations of it and we would have *been* little more than convenient big animals.

"Hold the door open, Gan," T'Gatoi said. "And tell the family to stay back."

"What is it?" I asked.

"N'Tlic."

I shrank back against the door. "Here? Alone?"

"He was trying to reach a call box, I suppose." She carried the man past me, unconscious, folded like a coat over some of her limbs. He looked young—my brother's age perhaps—and he was thinner than he should have been. What T'Gatoi would have called dangerously thin.

"Gan, go to the call box," she said. She put the man on the floor and began stripping off his clothing.

I did not move.

After a moment, she looked up at me, her sudden stillness a sign of deep impatience.

"Send Qui," I told her. "I'll stay here. Maybe I can help."

She let her limbs begin to move again, lifting the man and pulling his shirt over his head. "You don't want to see this," she said. "It will be hard. I can't help this man the way his Tlic could."

"I know. But send Qui. He won't want to be of any help here. I'm at least willing to try."

She looked at my brother—older, bigger, stronger, certainly more able to help her here. He was sitting up now, braced against the wall, staring at the man on the floor with undisguised fear and revulsion. Even she could see that he would be useless.

"Qui, go!" she said.

He didn't argue. He stood up, swayed briefly, then steadied, frightened sober.

"This man's name is Bram Lomas," she told him, reading from the man's arm band. I fingered my own arm band in sympathy. "He needs T'Khotgif Teh. Do you hear?"

"Bram Lomas, T'Khotgif Teh," my brother said. "I'm going." He edged around Lomas and ran out the door.

Lomas began to regain consciousness. He only moaned at first and clutched spasmodically at a pair of T'Gatoi's limbs. My younger sister, finally awake from her egg dream, came close to look at him, until my mother pulled her back.

T'Gatoi removed the man's shoes, then his pants, all the while leaving him two of her limbs to grip. Except for the final few, all her limbs were equally dexterous. "I want no argument from you this time, Gan," she said.

I straightened. "What shall I do?"

"Go out and slaughter an animal that is at least half your size."

"Slaughter? But I've never—"

She knocked me across the room. Her tail was an efficient weapon whether she exposed the sting or not.

I got up, feeling stupid for having ignored her warning, and went into the kitchen. Maybe I could kill something with a knife or an ax. My mother raised a few Terran animals for the table and several thousand local ones for their fur. T'Gatoi would probably prefer something local. An achti, perhaps. Some of those were the right size, though they had about three times as many teeth as I did and a real love of using them. My mother, Hoa, and Qui could kill them with knives. I had never killed one at all, had never slaughtered any animal. I had spent most of my time with T'Gatoi while my brother and sisters were learning the family business. T'Gatoi had been right. I should have been the one to go to the call box. At least I could do that.

I went to the corner cabinet where my mother kept her larger house and garden tools. At the back of the cabinet there was a pipe that carried off waste water from the kitchen—except that it didn't any more. My father had rerouted the waste water before I was born. Now the pipe could be turned so that one half slid around the other and a rifle could be stored inside. This wasn't our only gun, but it was our most easily accessible one. I would have to use it to shoot one of the biggest of the achti. Then T'Gatoi would probably confiscate it. Firearms were illegal in the Preserve. There had been incidents right after the Preserve was established—Terrans shooting Tlic, shooting N'Tlic. This was before the joining of families began, before everyone had a personal stake in keeping the peace. No one had shot a Tlic in my lifetime or my mother's, but the law still stood—for our protection, we were told. There were stories of whole Terran families wiped out in reprisal back during the assassinations.

I went out to the cages and shot the biggest achti I could find. It was a handsome breeding male and my mother would not be pleased to see me bring it in. But it was the right size, and I was in a hurry.

I put the achti's long, warm body over my shoulder—glad that some of the weight I'd gained was muscle—and took it to the kitchen.

There, I put the gun back in its hiding place. If T'Gatoi noticed the achti's wounds and demanded the gun, I would give it to her. Otherwise, let it stay where my father wanted it.

I turned to take the achti to her, then hesitated. For several seconds, I stood in front of the closed door wondering why I was suddenly afraid. I knew what was going to happen. I hadn't seen it before but T'Gatoi had shown me diagrams, and drawings. She had made sure I knew the truth as soon as I was old enough to understand it.

Yet I did not want to go into that room. I wasted a little time choosing a knife from the carved, wooden box in which my mother kept them. T'Gatoi might want one, I told myself, for the tough, heavily furred hide of the achti.

"Gan!" T'Gatoi called, her voice harsh with urgency.

I swallowed. I had not imagined a simple moving of the feet could be so difficult. I realized I was trembling and that shamed me. Shame impelled me through the door.

I put the achti down near T'Gatoi and saw that Lomas was unconscious again. She, Lomas, and I were alone in the room, my mother and sisters probably sent out so they would not have to watch. I envied them.

But my mother came back into the room as T'Gatoi seized the achti. Ignoring the knife I offered her, she extended claws from several of her limbs and slit the achti from throat to anus. She looked at me, her yellow eyes intent. "Hold this man's shoulders, Gan."

I stared at Lomas in panic, realizing that I did not want to touch him, let alone hold him. This would not be like shooting an animal. Not as quick, not as merciful, and, I hoped, not as final, but there was nothing I wanted less than to be part of it.

My mother came forward. "Gan, you hold his right side," she said. "I'll hold his left." And if he came to, he would throw her off without realizing he had done it. She was a tiny woman. She often wondered aloud how she had produced, as she said, such "huge" children.

"Never mind," I told her, taking the man's shoulders. "I'll do it."

She hovered nearby.

"Don't worry," I said. "I won't shame you. You don't have to stay and watch."

She looked at me uncertainly, then touched my face in a rare caress. Finally, she went back to her bedroom.

T'Gatoi lowered her head in relief. "Thank you, Gan," she said with courtesy more Terran than Tlic. "That one . . . she is always finding new ways for me to make her suffer."

Lomas began to groan and make choked sounds. I had hoped he would stay unconscious. T'Gatoi put her face near his so that he focused on her.

"I've stung you as much as I dare for now," she told him. "When this is over, I'll sting you to sleep and you won't hurt any more."

"Please," the man begged. "Wait . . ."

"There's no more time, Bram. I'll sting you as soon as it's over. When T'Khotgif arrives she'll give you eggs to help you heal. It will be over soon."

"T'Khotgif!" the man shouted, straining against my hands.

"Soon, Bram." T'Gatoi glanced at me, then placed a claw against his abdomen slightly to the right of the middle, just below the last rib. There was movement on the right side—tiny, seemingly random pulsations moving his brown flesh, creating a concavity here, a convexity there, over and over until I could see the rhythm of it and knew where the next pulse would be.

Lomas's entire body stiffened under T'Gatoi's claw, though she merely rested it against him as she wound the rear section of her body around his legs. He might break my grip, but he would not break hers. He wept helplessly as she used his pants to tie his hands, then pushed his hands above his head so that I could kneel on the cloth between them and pin them in place. She rolled up his shirt and gave it to him to bite down on.

And she opened him.

His body convulsed with the first cut. He almost tore himself away from me. The sounds he made . . . I had never heard such sounds come from anything human. T'Gatoi seemed to pay no attention as she lengthened and deepened the cut, now and then pausing to lick away blood. His blood vessels contracted, reacting to the chemistry of her saliva, and the bleeding slowed.

I felt as though I were helping her torture him, helping her consume him. I knew I would vomit soon, didn't know why I hadn't already. I couldn't possibly last until she was finished.

She found the first grub. It was fat and deep red with his blood— both inside and out. It had already eaten its own egg case, but apparently had not yet begun to eat its host. At this stage, it would eat any flesh except its mother's. Let alone, it would have gone on excreting the poisons that had both sickened and alerted Lomas. Eventually it would have begun to eat. By the time it ate its way out of Lomas's flesh, Lomas would be dead or dying—and unable to take revenge on the thing that was killing him. There was always a grace period between the time the host sickened and the time the grubs began to eat him.

T'Gatoi picked up the writhing grub carefully, and looked at it, somehow ignoring the terrible groans of the man.

Abruptly, the man lost consciousness.

"Good." T'Gatoi looked down at him. "I wish you Terrans could do that at will." She felt nothing. And the thing she held . . .

It was limbless and boneless at this stage, perhaps fifteen centimeters long and two thick, blind and slimy with blood. It was like a large worm. T'Gatoi put it into the belly of the achti, and it began at once to burrow. It would stay there and eat as long as there was anything to eat.

Probing through Lomas's flesh, she found two more, one of them smaller and more vigorous. "A male!" she said happily. He would be dead before I would. He would be through his metamorphosis and screwing everything that would hold still before his sisters even had limbs. He was the only one to make a serious effort to bite T'Gatoi as she placed him in the achti.

Paler worms oozed to visibility in Lomas's flesh. I closed my eyes. It was worse than finding something dead, rotting, and filled with tiny animal grubs. And it was far worse than any drawing or diagram.

"Ah, there are more," T'Gatoi said, plucking out two long, thick grubs. "You may have to kill another animal, Gan. Everything lives inside you Terrans."

I had been told all my life that this was a good and necessary thing Tlic and Terran did together—a kind of birth. I had believed it until now. I knew birth was painful and bloody, no matter what. But this was something else, something worse. And I wasn't ready to see it. Maybe I never would be. Yet I couldn't *not* see it. Closing my eyes didn't help.

T'Gatoi found a grub still eating its egg case. The remains of the case were still wired into a blood vessel by their own little tube or hook or whatever. That was the way the grubs were anchored and the way they fed. They took only blood until they were ready to emerge. Then they ate their stretched, elastic egg cases. Then they ate their hosts.

T'Gatoi bit away the egg case, licked away the blood. Did she like the taste? Did childhood habits die hard—or not die at all?

The whole procedure was wrong, alien. I wouldn't have thought anything about her could seem alien to me.

"One more, I think," she said. "Perhaps two. A good family. In a host animal these days, we would be happy to find one or two alive." She glanced at me. "Go outside, Gan, and empty your stomach. Go now while the man is unconscious."

I staggered out, barely made it. Beneath the tree just beyond the front door, I vomited until there was nothing left to bring up. Finally, I stood shaking, tears streaming down my face. I did not know why I was crying, but I could not stop. I went farther from the house to avoid being seen. Every time I closed my eyes I saw red worms crawling over redder human flesh.

There was a car coming toward the house. Since Terrans were forbidden motorized vehicles except for certain farm equipment, I knew this must be Lomas's Tlic with Qui and perhaps a Terran doctor. I wiped my face on my shirt, struggled for control.

"Gan," Qui called as the car stopped. "What happened?" He crawled out of the low, round, Tlic-convenient car door. Another

Terran crawled out the other side and went into the house without speaking to me. The doctor. With his help and a few eggs, Lomas might make it.

"T'Khotgif Teh?" I said.

The Tlic driver surged out of her car, reared up half her length before me. She was paler and smaller than T'Gatoi—probably born from the body of an animal. Tlic from Terran bodies were always larger as well as more numerous.

"Six young," I told her. "Maybe seven, all alive. At least one male."

"Lomas?" she said harshly. I liked her for the question and the concern in her voice when she asked it. The last coherent thing he had said was her name.

"He's alive," I said.

She surged away to the house without another word.

"She's been sick," my brother said, watching her go. "When I called, I could hear people telling her she wasn't well enough to go out even for this."

I said nothing. I had extended courtesy to the Tlic. Now I didn't want to talk to anyone. I hoped he would go in—out of curiosity if nothing else.

"Finally found out more than you wanted to know, eh?"

I looked at him.

"Don't give me one of *her* looks," he said. "You're not her. You're just her property."

One of her looks. Had I picked up even an ability to imitate her expressions?

"What'd you do, puke?" He sniffed the air. "So now you know what you're in for."

I walked away from him. He and I had been close when we were kids. He would let me follow him around when I was home and sometimes T'Gatoi would let me bring him along when she took me into the city. But something had happened when he reached adolescence. I never knew what. He began keeping out of T'Gatoi's way. Then he began running away—until he realized there was no "away." Not in the Preserve. Certainly not outside. After that he concentrated on getting his share of every egg that came into the house, and on looking out for me in a way that made me all but hate him—a way that clearly said, as long as I was all right, he was safe from the Tlic.

"How was it, really?" he demanded, following me.

"I killed an achti. The young ate it."

"You didn't run out of the house and puke because they ate an achti."

"I had . . . never seen a person cut open before." That was true, and enough for him to know. I couldn't talk about the other. Not with him.

"Oh," he said. He glanced at me as though he wanted to say more, but he kept quiet.

We walked, not really headed anywhere. Toward the back, toward the cages, toward the fields.

"Did he say anything?" Qui asked. "Lomas, I mean."

Who else would he mean? "He said 'T'Khotgif.' "

Qui shuddered. "If she had done that to me, she'd be the last person I'd call for."

"You'd call for her. Her sting would ease your pain without killing the grubs in you."

"You think I'd care if they died?"

No. Of course he wouldn't. Would I?

"Shit!" He drew a deep breath. "I've seen what they do. You think this thing with Lomas was bad? It was nothing."

I didn't argue. He didn't know what he was talking about.

"I saw them eat a man," he said.

I turned to face him. "You're lying!"

"*I saw them eat a man.*" He paused. "It was when I was little. I had been to the Hartmund house and I was on my way home. Halfway here, I saw a man and a Tlic and the man was N'Tlic. The ground was hilly. I was able to hide from them and watch. The Tlic wouldn't open the man because she had nothing to feed the grubs. The man couldn't go any farther and there were no houses around. He was in so much pain he told her to kill him. He begged her to kill him. Finally, she did. She cut his throat.

One swipe of one claw. I saw the grubs eat their way out, then burrow in again, still eating."

His words made me see Lomas's flesh again, parasitized, crawling. "Why didn't you tell me that?" I whispered.

He looked startled, as though he'd forgotten I was listening. "I don't know."

"You started to run away not long after that, didn't you?"

"Yeah. Stupid. Running inside the Preserve. Running in a cage."

I shook my head, said what I should have said to him long ago. "She wouldn't take you, Qui. You don't have to worry."

"She would . . . if anything happened to you."

"No. She'd take Xuan Hoa. Hoa . . . wants it." She wouldn't if she had stayed to watch Lomas.

"They don't take women," he said with contempt.

"They do sometimes." I glanced at him. "Actually, they prefer women. You should be around them when they talk among themselves. They say women have more body fat to protect the grubs. But they usually take men to leave the women free to bear their own young."

"To provide the next generation of host animals," he said, switching from contempt to bitterness.

"It's more than that!" I countered. Was it?

"If it were going to happen to me, I'd want to believe it was more, too."

"It *is* more!" I felt like a kid. Stupid argument.

"Did you think so while T'Gatoi was picking worms out of that guy's guts?"

"It's not supposed to happen that way."

"Sure it is. You weren't supposed to see it, that's all. And his Tlic was supposed to do it. She could sting him unconscious and the operation wouldn't have been as painful. But she'd still open him, pick out the grubs, and if she missed even one, it would poison him and eat him from the inside out."

There was actually a time when my mother told me to show respect for Qui because he was my older brother. I walked away, hating him. In his way, he was gloating. He was safe and I wasn't.

I could have hit him, but I didn't think I would be able to stand it when he refused to hit back, when he looked at me with contempt and pity.

He wouldn't let me get away. Longer-legged, he swung ahead of me and made me feel as though I were following him.

"I'm sorry," he said.

I strode on, sick and furious.

"Look, it probably won't be that bad with you. T'Gatoi likes you. She'll be careful."

I turned back toward the house, almost running from him.

"Has she done it to you yet?" he asked, keeping up easily. "I mean, you're about the right age for implantation. Has she—"

I hit him. I didn't know I was going to do it, but I think I meant to kill him. If he hadn't been bigger and stronger, I think I would have.

He tried to hold me off, but in the end, had to defend himself. He only hit me a couple of times. That was plenty. I don't remember going down, but when I came to, he was gone. It was worth the pain to be rid of him.

I got up and walked slowly toward the house. The back was dark. No one was in the kitchen. My mother and sisters were sleeping in their bedrooms—or pretending to.

Once I was in the kitchen, I could hear voices—Tlic and Terran from the next room. I couldn't make out what they were saying— didn't want to make it out.

I sat down at my mother's table, waiting for quiet. The table was smooth and worn, heavy and well-crafted. My father had made it for her just before he died. I remembered hanging around underfoot when he built it. He didn't mind. Now I sat leaning on it, missing him. I could have talked to him. He had done it three times in his long life. Three clutches of eggs, three times being opened and sewed up. How had he done it? How did anyone do it?

I got up, took the rifle from its hiding place, and sat down again with it. It needed cleaning, oiling.

All I did was load it.

"Gan?"

She made a lot of little clicking sounds when she walked on bare floor, each limb clicking in succession as it touched down. Waves of little clicks.

She came to the table, raised the front half of her body above it, and surged onto it. Sometimes she moved so smoothly she seemed to flow like water itself. She coiled herself into a small hill in the middle of the table and looked at me.

"That was bad," she said softly. "You should not have seen it. It need not be that way."

"I know."

"T'Khotgif—Ch'Khotgif now—she will die of her disease. She will not live to raise her children. But her sister will provide for them, and for Bram Lomas." Sterile sister. One fertile female in every lot. One to keep the family going. That sister owed Lomas more than she could ever repay.

"He'll live then?"

"Yes."

"I wonder if he would do it again."

"No one would ask him to do that again."

I looked into the yellow eyes, wondering how much I saw and understood there, and how much I only imagined. "No one ever asks us," I said. "You never asked me."

She moved her head slightly. "What's the matter with your face?"

"Nothing. Nothing important." Human eyes probably wouldn't have noticed the swelling in the darkness. The only light was from one of the moons, shining through a window across the room.

"Did you use the rifle to shoot the achti?"

"Yes."

"And do you mean to use it to shoot me?"

I stared at her, outlined in moonlight—coiled, graceful body. "What does Terran blood taste like to you?"

She said nothing.

"What are you?" I whispered. "What are we to you?"

She lay still, rested her head on her topmost coil. "You know me as no other does," she said softly. "You must decide."

"That's what happened to my face," I told her.

"What?"

"Qui goaded me into deciding to do something. It didn't turn out very well." I moved the gun slightly, brought the barrel up diagonally under my own chin. "At least it was a decision I made."

"As this will be."

"Ask me, Gatoi."

"For my children's lives?"

She would say something like that. She knew how to manipulate people, Terran and Tlic. But not this time.

"I don't want to be a host animal," I said. "Not even yours."

It took her a long time to answer. "We use almost no host animals these days," she said. "You know that."

"You use us."

"We do. We wait long years for you and teach you and join our families to yours." She moved restlessly. "You know you aren't animals to us."

I stared at her, saying nothing.

"The animals we once used began killing most of our eggs after implantation long before your ancestors arrived," she said softly. "You know these things, Gan. Because your people arrived, we are relearning what it means to be a healthy, thriving people. And your ancestors, fleeing from their homeworld, from their own kind who would have killed or enslaved them—they survived because of us. We saw them as people and gave them the Preserve when they still tried to kill us as worms."

At the word "worms" I jumped. I couldn't help it, and she couldn't help noticing it.

"I see," she said quietly. "Would you really rather die than bear my young, Gan?"

I didn't answer.

"Shall I go to Xuan Hoa?"

"Yes!" Hoa wanted it. Let her have it. She hadn't had to watch Lomas. She'd be proud. . . . Not terrified.

T'Gatoi flowed off the table onto the floor, startling me almost too much.

"I'll sleep in Hoa's room tonight," she said. "And sometime tonight or in the morning, I'll tell her."

This was going too fast. My sister. Hoa had had almost as much to do with raising me as my mother. I was still close to her—not like Qui. She could want T'Gatoi and still love me.

"Wait! Gatoi!"

She looked back, then raised nearly half her length off the floor and turned it to face me. "These are adult things, Gan. This is my life, my family!"

"But she's . . . my sister."

"I have done what you demanded. I have asked you!"

"But—"

"It will be easier for Hoa. She has always expected to carry other lives inside her."

Human lives. Human young who would someday drink at her breasts, not at her veins.

I shook my head. "Don't do it to her, Gatoi." I was not Qui. It seemed I could become him, though, with no effort at all. I could make Xuan Hoa my shield. Would it be easier to know that red worms were growing in her flesh instead of mine?

"Don't do it to Hoa," I repeated.

She stared at me, utterly still.

I looked away, then back at her. "Do it to me."

I lowered the gun from my throat and she leaned forward to take it.

"No," I told her.

"It's the law," she said.

"Leave it for the family. One of them might use it to save my life someday."

She grasped the rifle barrel, but I wouldn't let go. I was pulled into a standing position over her.

"Leave it here!" I repeated. "If we're not your animals, if these are adult things, accept the risk. There is risk, Gatoi, in dealing with a partner."

It was clearly hard for her to let go of the rifle. A shudder went through her and she made a hissing sound of distress. It occurred to me that she was afraid. She was old enough to have seen what guns could do to people. Now her young and this gun would be together in the same house. She did not know about our other guns. In this dispute, they did not matter.

"I will implant the first egg tonight," she said as I put the gun away. "Do you hear, Gan?"

Why else had I been given a whole egg to eat while the rest of the family was left to share one? Why else had my mother kept looking at me as though I were going away from her, going where she could not follow? Did T'Gatoi imagine I hadn't known?

"I hear."

"Now!" I let her push me out of the kitchen, then walked ahead of her toward my bedroom. The sudden urgency in her voice sounded real. "You would have done it to Hoa tonight!" I accused.

"I must do it to someone tonight."

I stopped in spite of her urgency and stood in her way. "Don't you care who?"

She flowed around me and into my bedroom. I found her waiting on the couch we shared. There was nothing in Hoa's room that she could have used. She would have done it to Hoa on the floor. The thought of her doing it to Hoa at all disturbed me in a different way now, and I was suddenly angry.

Yet I undressed and lay down beside her. I knew what to do, what to expect. I had been told all my life. I felt the familiar sting, narcotic, mildly pleasant. Then the blind probing of her ovipositor. The puncture was painless, easy. So easy going in. She undulated slowly against me, her muscles forcing the egg from her body into mine. I held on to a pair of her limbs until I remembered Lomas holding her that way. Then I let go, moved inadvertently, and hurt her. She gave a low cry of pain and I expected to be caged at once within her limbs. When I wasn't, I held on to her again, feeling oddly ashamed.

"I'm sorry," I whispered.

She rubbed my shoulders with four of her limbs.

"Do you care?" I asked. "Do you care that it's me?"

She did not answer for some time. Finally, "You were the one making choices tonight, Gan. I made mine long ago."

"Would you have gone to Hoa?"

"Yes. How could I put my children into the care of one who hates them?"

"It wasn't . . . hate."

"I know what it was."

"I was afraid."

Silence.

"I still am." I could admit it to her here, now.

"But you came to me . . . to save Hoa."

"Yes." I leaned my forehead against her. She was cool velvet, deceptively soft. "And to keep you for myself," I said. It was so. I didn't understand it, but it was so.

She made a soft hum of contentment. "I couldn't believe I had made such a mistake with you," she said. "I chose you. I believed you had grown to choose me."

"I had, but . . ."

"Lomas."

"Yes."

"I have never known a Terran to see a birth and take it well. Qui has seen one, hasn't he?"

"Yes."

"Terrans should be protected from seeing."

I didn't like the sound of that—and I doubted that it was possible. "Not protected," I said. "Shown. Shown when we're young kids, and shown more than once. Gatoi, no Terran ever sees a birth that goes right. All we see is N'Tlic—pain and terror and maybe death."

She looked down at me. "It is a private thing. It has always been a private thing."

Her tone kept me from insisting—that and the knowledge that if she changed her mind, I might be the first public example. But I had planted the thought in her mind. Chances were it would grow, and eventually she would experiment.

"You won't see it again," she said. "I don't want you thinking any more about shooting me."

The small amount of fluid that came into me with her egg relaxed me as completely as a sterile egg would have, so that I could remember the rifle in my hands and my feelings of fear and revulsion, anger and despair. I could remember the feelings without reviving them. I could talk about them.

"I wouldn't have shot you," I said. "Not you." She had been taken from my father's flesh when he was my age.

"You could have," she insisted.

"Not you." She stood between us and her own people, protecting, interweaving.

"Would you have destroyed yourself?"

I moved carefully, uncomfortably. "I could have done that. I nearly did. That's Qui's 'away.' I wonder if he knows."

"What?"

I did not answer.

"You will live now."

"Yes." *Take care of her,* my mother used to say. Yes.

"I'm healthy and young," she said. "I won't leave you as Lomas was left—alone, N'Tlic. I'll take care of you."

The Man Who Painted
the Dragon Griaule

LUCIUS SHEPARD

Lucius Shepard's wise and humane stories have appeared in Universe, Isaac Asimov's Science Fiction Magazine, *and* The Magazine of Fantasy & Science Fiction. Green Eyes *was his first novel; a second,* Foreign Devils, *is forthcoming.*

Born in Virginia, Shepard is a traveler familiar with the Caribbean and Mediterranean areas. At one time he was a rock musician, but writing seems to have won out. He took first prize in the 1984 Clarion Awards competition, sponsored by Doubleday and Michigan State University, for his story "The Etheric Transmitter." "The Man Who Painted the Dragon Griaule" was a 1984 Nebula finalist in the novelette category. Shepard was also a finalist in the two other short fiction categories.

Dragons are reprehensible creatures, especially among literary critics, and rightly so. Too often dragons are merely themselves, not what they ought to be: protean shapes that mirror our human fears and ideals. Shepard miraculously escapes the corruption of dragons in commercial fantasy fiction and remeasures their true meanings in a story that resonates with deep feeling and strives toward the utterance of the ineffable. Edward L. Ferman, the editor who first published this story, aptly described it as "a superbly crafted tale of a man's life-long work and how that work shaped the man and defined his life."

" ... **O**ther than the Sichi Collection, Cattanay's only surviving works are to be found in the Municipal Gallery at Regensburg, a group of eight oils-on-canvas, most notable among them being *Woman With Oranges*. These paintings constitute his portion of a student exhibition hung some weeks after he had left the city of his birth and traveled south to Teocinte, there to present his proposal to the city fathers; it is unlikely he ever learned of the disposition of his work, and even more unlikely that he was aware of the general critical indifference with which it was received. Perhaps the most interesting of the group to modern scholars, the most indicative as to Cattanay's later preoccupations, is the *Self Portrait*, painted at the age of twenty-eight, a year before his departure.

"The majority of the canvas is a richly varnished black in which the vague shapes of floorboards are presented, barely visible. Two irregular slashes of gold cross the blackness, and within these we can see a section of the artist's thin features and the shoulder panel of his shirt. The perspective given is that we are looking down at the artist, perhaps through a tear in the roof, and that he is looking up at us, squinting into the light, his mouth distorted by a grimace born of intense concentration. On first viewing the painting, I was struck by the atmosphere of tension that radiated from it. It seemed I was spying upon a man imprisoned within a shadow having two golden bars, tormented by the possibilities of light beyond the walls. And though this may be the reaction of the art historian, not the less knowledgeable and therefore more trustworthy response of the gallery-goer, it also seemed that this imprisonment was self-imposed, that he could have easily escaped his confine; but that he had realized a feeling of stricture was an essential fuel to his ambition, and so had chained himself to this arduous and thoroughly unreasonable chore of perception. . . ."

—from *Meric Cattanay:
The Politics of Conception*
by Reade Holland, Ph.D.

1.

In 1853, in a country far to the south, in a world separated from this one by the thinnest margin of possibility, a dragon named Griaule dominated the region of the Carbonales Valley, a fertile area centering upon the town of Teocinte and renowned for its production of silver, mahogany, and indigo. There were other dragons in those days, most dwelling on the rocky islands west of Patagonia—tiny, irascible creatures, the largest of them no bigger than a swallow. But Griaule was one of the great Beasts who had ruled an age. Over the centuries he had grown to stand 750 feet high at the midback, and from the tip of his tail to his nose he was 6,000 feet long. (It should be noted here that the growth of dragons was due not to caloric intake, but to the absorption of energy derived from the passage of time.) Had it not been for a miscast spell, Griaule would have died millennia before. The wizard entrusted with the task of slaying him—knowing his own life would be forfeited as a result of the magical backwash—had experienced a last-second twinge of fear, and, diminished by this ounce of courage, the spell had flown a mortal inch awry. Though the wizard's whereabouts were unknown, Griaule had remained alive. His heart had stopped, his breath stilled, but his mind continued to seethe, to send forth the gloomy vibrations that enslaved all who stayed for long within range of his influence.

This dominance of Griaule's was an elusive thing. The people of the valley attributed their dour character to years of living under his mental shadow, yet there were other regional populations who maintained a harsh face to the world and had no dragon on which to blame the condition; they also attributed their frequent raids against the neighboring states to Griaule's effect, claiming to be a peaceful folk at heart—but again, was this not human nature? Perhaps the most certifiable proof of Griaule's primacy was the fact that despite a standing offer of a fortune in silver to anyone who could kill him, no one had succeeded. Hundreds of plans had been put forward, and all had failed, either through inanition or impracticality. The archives of Teocinte were filled with schematics for enormous steam-powered swords and other such improbable devices, and the architects of these plans had every one stayed too long in the valley and become part of the disgruntled populace. And so they went on with their lives, coming and going, always returning, bound to the valley, until one spring day in 1853, Meric Cattanay arrived and proposed that the dragon be painted.

He was a lanky young man with a shock of black hair and a pinched look to his cheeks; he affected the loose trousers and shirt of a peasant, and waved his arms to make a point. His eyes grew wide when listening, as if his brain were bursting with illumination, and at times he talked incoherently about "the conceptual statement of death by art." And though the city fathers could not be sure, though they allowed for the possibility that he simply had an unfortunate manner, it seemed he was mocking them. All in all, he was not the sort they were inclined to trust. But, because he had come armed with such a wealth of diagrams and charts, they were forced to give him serious consideration.

"I don't believe Griaule will be able to perceive the menace in a process as subtle as art," Meric told them. "We'll proceed as if we were going to illustrate him, grace his side with a work of true vision, and all the while we'll be poisoning him with the paint."

The city fathers voiced their incredulity, and Meric waited impatiently until they quieted. He did not enjoy dealing with these worthies. Seated at their long table, sour-faced, a huge smudge of soot on the wall above their heads like an ugly thought they were sharing, they reminded him of the Wine Merchants Association in Regensburg, the time they had rejected his group portrait.

"Paint can be deadly stuff," he said after their muttering had died down. "Take vert Veronese, for example. It's derived from oxide of chrome and barium. Just a whiff would make you keel over. But we have to go about it seriously, create a real piece of art. If we just slap paint on his side, he might see through us."

The first step in the process, he told them, would be to build a tower of scaffolding, complete with hoists and ladders, that would brace against the supraocular plates above the dragon's eye; this would provide a direct route to a seven-hundred-foot-square loading platform and base station behind the eye. He estimated it would take eighty-one thousand board feet of lumber, and a crew of ninety men should be able to finish construction within five months. Ground crews accompanied by chemists and geologists would search out limestone deposits (useful in priming the scales) and sources of pigments, whether organic or minerals such as azurite and hematite. Other teams would be set to scraping the dragon's side clean of algae, peeled skin, any decayed material, and afterward would laminate the surface with resins.

"It would be easier to bleach him with quicklime," he said. "But

that way we lose the discolorations and ridges generated by growth
and age, and I think what we'll paint will be defined by those shapes.
Anything else would look like a damn tattoo!"

There would be storage vats and mills: edge-runner mills to separate pigments from crude ores, ball mills to powder the pigments,
pug mills to mix them with oil. There would be boiling vats and
calciners—fifteen-foot-high furnaces used to produce caustic lime
for sealant solutions.

"We'll build most of them atop the dragon's head for purposes
of access," he said. "On the frontoparietal plate." He checked some
figures. "By my reckoning, the plate's about 350 feet wide. Does
that sound accurate?"

Most of the city fathers were stunned by the prospect, but one
managed a nod, and another asked, "How long will it take for him
to die?"

"Hard to say," came the answer. "Who knows how much poison
he's capable of absorbing. It might just take a few years. But in the
worst instance, within forty or fifty years, enough chemicals will
have seeped through the scales to have weakened the skeleton, and
he'll fall in like an old barn."

"Forty years!" exclaimed someone. "Preposterous!"

"Or fifty." Meric smiled. "That way we'll have time to finish the
painting." He turned and walked to the window and stood gazing
out at the white stone houses of Teocinte. This was going to be the
sticky part, but if he read them right, they would not believe in the
plan if it seemed too easy. They needed to feel they were making
a sacrifice, that they were nobly bound to a great labor. "If it does
take forty or fifty years," he went on, "the project will drain your
resources. Timber, animal life, minerals. Everything will be used
up by the work. Your lives will be totally changed. But I guarantee
you'll be rid of him."

The city fathers broke into an outraged babble.

"Do you really want to kill him?" cried Meric, stalking over to
them and planting his fists on the table. "You've been waiting
centuries for someone to come along and chop off his head or send
him up in a puff of smoke. That's not going to happen! There is

no easy solution. But there is a practical one, an elegant one. To use the stuff of the land he dominates to destroy him. It will *not* be easy, but you *will* be rid of him. And that's what you want, isn't it?"

They were silent, exchanging glances, and he saw that they now believed he could do what he proposed and were wondering if the cost was too high.

"I'll need five hundred ounces of silver to hire engineers and artisans," said Meric. "Think it over. I'll take a few days and go see this dragon of yours . . . inspect the scales and so forth. When I return, you can give me your answer."

The city fathers grumbled and scratched their heads, but at last they agreed to put the question before the body politic. They asked for a week in which to decide and appointed Jarcke, who was the mayoress of Hangtown, to guide Meric to Griaule.

The valley extended seventy miles from north to south, and was enclosed by jungled hills whose folded sides and spiny backs gave rise to the idea that beasts were sleeping beneath them. The valley floor was cultivated into fields of bananas and cane and melons, and where it was not cultivated, there were stands of thistle palms and berry thickets and the occasional giant fig brooding sentinel over the rest. Jarcke and Meric tethered their horses a half hour's ride from town and began to ascend a gentle incline that rose into the notch between two hills. Sweaty and short of breath, Meric stopped a third of the way up; but Jarcke kept plodding along, unaware he was no longer following. She was by nature as blunt as her name—a stumpy beer keg of a woman with a brown, weathered face. Though she appeared to be ten years older than Meric, she was nearly the same age. She wore a gray robe belted at the waist with a leather band that held four throwing knives, and a coil of rope was slung over her shoulder.

"How much farther?" called Meric.

She turned and frowned. "You're standin' on his tail. Rest of him's around back of the hill."

A pinprick of chill bloomed in Meric's abdomen, and he stared down at the grass, expecting it to dissolve and reveal a mass of glittering scales.

"Why don't we take the horses?" he asked.

"Horses don't like it up here." She grunted with amusement. "Neither do most people, for that matter." She trudged off.

Another twenty minutes brought them to the other side of the hill high above the valley floor. The land continued to slope upward, but more gently than before. Gnarled, stunted oaks pushed up from thickets of chokecherry, and insects sizzled in the weeds. They might have been walking on a natural shelf several hundred feet across; but ahead of them, where the ground rose abruptly, a number of thick, greenish black columns broke from the earth. Leathery folds hung between them, and these were encrusted with clumps of earth and brocaded with mold. They had the look of a collapsed palisade and the ghosted feel of ancient ruins.

"Them's the wings," said Jarcke. "Mostly they's covered, but you can catch sight of 'em off the edge, and up near Hangtown there's places where you can walk in under 'em . . . but I wouldn't advise it."

"I'd like to take a look off the edge," said Meric, unable to tear his eyes away from the wings; though the surfaces of the leaves gleamed in the strong sun, the wings seemed to absorb the light, as if their age and strangeness were proof against reflection.

Jarcke led him to a glade in which tree ferns and oaks crowded together and cast a green gloom, and where the earth sloped sharply downward. She lashed her rope to an oak and tied the other end around Meric's waist. "Give a yank when you want to stop, and another when you want to be hauled up," she said, and began paying out the rope, letting him walk backward against her pull.

Ferns tickled Meric's neck as he pushed through the brush, and the oak leaves pricked his cheeks. Suddenly he emerged into bright sunlight. On looking down, he found his feet were braced against a fold of the dragon's wing, and on looking up, he saw that the wing vanished beneath a mantle of earth and vegetation. He let Jarcke lower him a dozen feet more, yanked, and gazed off northward along the enormous swell of Griaule's side.

The swells were hexagonals thirty feet across and half that distance high; their basic color was a pale greenish gold, but some were whitish, draped with peels of dead skin, and others were overgrown by viridian moss, and the rest were scrolled with patterns of lichen and algae that resembled the characters of a serpentine alphabet. Birds had nested in the cracks, and ferns plumed from the interstices, thousands of them lifting in the breeze. It was a great hanging garden whose scope took Meric's breath away—like looking around the curve of a fossil moon. The sense of all the centuries accreted in the scales made him dizzy, and he found he could not turn his head, but could only stare at the panorama, his soul shriveling with a comprehension of the timelessness and bulk of this creature to which he clung like a fly. He lost perspective on the scene—Griaule's side was bigger than the sky, possessing its own potent gravity, and it seemed completely reasonable that he should be able to walk out along it and suffer no fall. He started to do so, and Jarcke, mistaking the strain on the rope for signal, hauled him up, dragging him across the wing, through the dirt and ferns, and back into the glade. He lay speechless and gasping at her feet.

"Big 'un, ain't he," she said, and grinned.

After Meric had gotten his legs under him, they set off toward Hangtown; but they had not gone a hundred yards, following a trail that wound through the thickets, before Jarcke whipped out a knife and hurled it at a raccoon-sized creature that leaped out in front of them.

"Skizzer," she said, kneeling beside it and pulling the knife from its neck. "Calls 'em that 'cause they hisses when they runs. They eats snakes, but they'll go after children what ain't careful."

Meric dropped down next to her. The skizzer's body was covered with short black fur, but its head was hairless, corpse-pale, the skin wrinkled as if it had been immersed too long in water. Its face was squinty-eyed, flat-nosed, with a disproportionately large jaw that hinged open to expose a nasty set of teeth.

"They's the dragon's critters," said Jarcke. "Used to live in his bunghole." She pressed one of its paws, and claws curved like hooks slid forth. "They'd hang around the lip and drop on other critters what wandered in. And if nothin' wandered in . . ." She pried out the tongue with her knife—its surface was studded with jagged points like the blade of a rasp. "Then they'd lick Griaule clean for their supper."

Back in Teocinte, the dragon had seemed to Meric a simple thing, a big lizard with a tick of life left inside, the residue of a dim sensibility; but he was beginning to suspect that this tick of life was more complex than any he had encountered.

"My gram used to say," Jarcke went on, "that the old dragons could fling themselves up to the sun in a blink and travel back to their own world, and when they come back, they'd bring the skizzers and all the rest with 'em. They was immortal, she said. Only the young ones came here 'cause later on they grew too big to fly on Earth." She made a sour face. "Don't know as I believe it."

"Then you're a fool," said Meric.

Jarcke glanced up at him, her hand twitching toward her belt.

"How can you live here and *not* believe it!" he said, surprised to hear himself so fervently defending a myth. "God! This . . ." He broke off, noticing the flicker of a smile on her face.

She clucked her tongue, apparently satisfied by something. "Come on," she said. "I want to be at the eye before sunset."

The peaks of Griaule's folded wings, completely overgrown by grass and shrubs and dwarfish trees, formed two spiny hills that cast a shadow over Hangtown and the narrow lake around which it sprawled. Jarcke said the lake was a stream flowing off the hill behind the dragon, and that it drained away through the membranes of his wing and down onto his shoulder. It was beautiful beneath the wing, she told him. Ferns and waterfalls. But it was reckoned an evil place. From a distance the town looked picturesque—rustic cabins, smoking chimneys. As they approached, however, the cabins resolved into dilapidated shanties with missing boards and broken windows; suds and garbage and offal floated in the shallows of the lake. Aside from a few men idling on the stoops, who squinted at Meric and nodded glumly at Jarcke, no one was about. The grass blades stirred in the breeze, spiders scuttled under the shanties, and there was an air of torpor and dissolution.

Jarcke seemed embarrassed by the town. She made no attempt at introductions, stopping only long enough to fetch another coil of rope from one of the shanties, and as they walked between the wings, down through the neck spines—a forest of greenish gold spikes burnished by the lowering sun—she explained how the towns-folk grubbed a livelihood from Griaule. Herbs gathered on his back were valued as medicine and charms, as were the peels of dead skin; the artifacts left by previous Hangtown generations were of some worth to various collectors.

"Then there's scale hunters," she said with disgust. "Henry Sichi from Port Chantay'll pay good money for pieces of scale, and though it's bad luck to do it, some'll have a go at chippin' off the loose 'uns." She walked a few paces in silence. "But there's others who've got better reasons for livin' here."

The frontal spike above Griaule's eyes was whorled at the base like a narwhal's horn and curved back toward the wings. Jarcke attached the ropes to eyebolts drilled into the spike, tied one about her waist, the other about Meric's; she cautioned him to wait, and rappelled off the side. In a moment she called for him to come down. Once again he grew dizzy as he descended; he glimpsed a clawed foot far below, mossy fangs jutting from an impossibly long jaw; and then he began to spin and bash against the scales. Jarcke gathered him in and helped him sit on the lip of the socket.

"Damn!" she said, stamping her foot.

A three-foot-long section of the adjoining scale shifted slowly away. Peering close, Meric saw that while in texture and hue it was indistinguishable from the scale, there was a hairline division between it and the surface. Jarcke, her face twisted in disgust, continued to harry the thing until it moved out of reach.

"Call 'em flakes," she said when he asked what it was. "Some kind of insect. Got a long tube that they pokes down between the scales and sucks the blood. See there?" She pointed off to where a flock of birds were wheeling close to Griaule's side; a chip of pale gold broke loose and went tumbling down to the valley. "Birds pry 'em off, let 'em bust open, and eats the innards." She hunkered down beside him and after a moment asked, "You really think you can do it?"

"What? You mean kill the dragon?"

She nodded.

"Certainly," he said, and then added, lying, "I've spent years devising the method."

"If all the paint's goin' to be atop his head, how're you goin' to get it to where the paintin's done?"

"That's no problem. We'll pipe it to wherever it's needed."

She nodded again. "You're a clever fellow," she said; and when Meric, pleased, made as if to thank her for the compliment, she cut in and said, "Don't mean nothin' by it. Bein' clever ain't an accomplishment. It's just somethin' you come by, like bein' tall." She turned away, ending the conversation.

Meric was weary of being awestruck, but even so he could not help marveling at the eye. By his estimate it was seventy feet long and fifty feet high, and it was shuttered by an opaque membrane that was unusually clear of algae and lichen, glistening, with vague glints of color visible behind it. As the westering sun reddened and sank between two distant hills, the membrane began to quiver and then split open down the center. With the ponderous slowness of a theater curtain opening, the halves slid apart to reveal the glowing humor. Terrified by the idea that Griaule could see him, Meric sprang to his feet, but Jarcke restrained him.

"Stay still and watch," she said.

He had no choice—the eye was mesmerizing. The pupil was slit and featureless black, but the humor . . . he had never seen such fiery blues and crimsons and golds. What had looked to be vague glints, odd refractions of the sunset, he now realized were photic reactions of some sort. Fairy rings of light developed deep within the eye, expanded into spoked shapes, flooded the humor, and faded—only to be replaced by another and another. He felt the pressure of Griaule's vision, his ancient mind, pouring through him, and as if in response to this pressure, memories bubbled up in his thoughts. Particularly sharp ones. The way a bowlful of brush water had looked after freezing over during a winter's night—a delicate, fractured flower of murky yellow. An archipelago of orange peels that his girl had left strewn across the floor of the studio. Sketching atop Jokenam Hill one sunrise, the snow-capped roofs of Regensburg below pitched at all angles like broken paving stones, and silver shafts of the sun striking down through a leaden overcast. It was as if these things were being drawn forth for his inspection. Then they were washed away by what also seemed a memory, though at the same time it was wholly unfamiliar. Essentially, it was a landscape of light, and he was plunging through it, up and up. Prisms and lattices of iridescent fire bloomed around him, and everything was a roaring fall into brightness, and finally he was clear into its white furnace heart, his own heart swelling with the joy of his strength and dominion.

It was dusk before Meric realized the eye had closed. His mouth hung open, his eyes ached from straining to see, and his tongue was glued to his palate. Jarcke sat motionless, buried in shadow.

"Th . . ." He had to swallow to clear his throat of mucus. "This is the reason you live here, isn't it?"

"Part of the reason," she said. "I can see things comin' way up here. Things to watch out for, things to study on."

She stood and walked to the lip of the socket and spat off the edge; the valley stretched out gray and unreal behind her, the folds of the hills barely visible in the gathering dusk.

"I seen you comin'," she said.

A week later, after much exploration, much talk, they went down into Teocinte. The town was a shambles—shattered windows, slogans painted on the walls, glass and torn banners and spoiled food littering the streets—as if there had been both a celebration and a battle. Which there had. The city fathers met with Meric in the town hall and informed him that his plan had been approved. They presented him a chest containing five hundred ounces of silver and said that the entire resources of the community were at his disposal. They offered a wagon and a team to transport him and the chest to Regensburg and asked if any of the preliminary work could be begun during his absence.

Meric hefted one of the silver bars. In its cold gleam he saw the object of his desire—two, perhaps three years of freedom, of doing the work he wanted and not having to accept commissions. But all that had been confused. He glanced at Jarcke; she was staring out the window, leaving it to him. He set the bar back in the chest and shut the lid.

"You'll have to send someone else," he said. And then, as the city fathers looked at each other askance, he laughed and laughed at how easily he had discarded all his dreams and expectations.

". . . It had been eleven years since I had been to the valley, twelve since work had begun on the painting, and I was appalled by the changes that had taken place. Many of the hills were scraped brown and treeless, and there was a general dearth of wildlife. Griaule, of course, was most changed. Scaffolding hung from his back; artisans, suspended by webworks of ropes, crawled over his side; and all the scales to be worked had either been painted or primed. The tower rising to his eye was swarmed by laborers, and at night the calciners and vats atop his head belched flame into the sky, making it seem there was a mill town in the heavens. At his feet was a brawling shantytown populated by prostitutes, workers, gamblers, ne'er-do-wells of every sort, and soldiers: the burdensome cost of the project had encouraged the city fathers of Teocinte to form a regular militia, which regularly plundered the adjoining states and had posted occupation forces to some areas. Herds of frightened animals milled in the slaughtering pens, waiting to be rendered into oils and pigments. Wagons filled with ores and vegetable products rattled in the streets. I myself had brought a cargo of madder roots from which a rose tint would be derived.

"It was not easy to arrange a meeting with Cattanay. While he did none of the actual painting, he was always busy in his office consulting with engineers and artisans, or involved in some other part of the logistical process. When at last I did meet with him, I found he had changed as drastically as Griaule. His hair had gone gray, deep lines scored his features, and his right shoulder had a peculiar bulge at its midpoint—the product of a fall. He was amused by the fact that I wanted to buy the painting, to collect the scales after Griaule's death, and I do not believe he took me at all seriously. But the woman Jarcke, his constant companion, informed him that I was a responsible businessman, that I had already bought the bones, the teeth, even the dirt beneath Griaule's belly (this I eventually sold as having magical properties).

" 'Well,' said Cattanay, 'I suppose someone has to own them.'

"He led me outside, and we stood looking at the painting.

" 'You'll keep them together?' he asked.

"I said, 'Yes.'

" 'If you'll put that in writing,' he said, 'then they're yours.'

"Having expected to haggle long and hard over the price, I was flabbergasted; but I was even more flabbergasted by what he said next.

" 'Do you think it's any good?' he asked.

"Cattanay did not consider the painting to be the work of *his* imagination; he felt he was simply illuminating the shapes that appeared on Griaule's side and was convinced that once the paint was applied, new shapes were produced beneath it, causing him to make constant changes. He saw himself as an artisan more than a creative artist. But to put his question into perspective, people were beginning to flock from all over the world and marvel at the painting. Some claimed they saw intimations of the future in its gleaming surface; others underwent transfiguring experiences; still others—artists themselves—attempted to capture something of the work on canvas, hopeful of establishing reputations merely by being competent copyists of Cattanay's art. The painting was nonrepresentational in character, essentially a wash of pale gold spread across the dragon's side; but buried beneath the laminated surface were a myriad tints of iridescent color that, as the sun passed through the heavens and the light bloomed and faded, solidified into innumerable forms and figures that seemed to flow back and forth. I will not try to categorize these forms, because there was no end to them; they were as varied as the conditions under which they were viewed. But I will say that on the morning I met with Cattanay, I—who was the soul of the practical man, without a visionary bone in my body—felt as though I were being whirled away into the painting, up through geometries of light, latticeworks of rainbow color that built the way the edges of a cloud build, past orbs, spirals, wheels of flame. . . ."

—from *This Business of Griaule*
by Henry Sichi

2.

There had been several women in Meric's life since he arrived in the valley; most had been attracted by his growing fame and his association with the mystery of the dragon, and most had left him for the same reasons, feeling daunted and unappreciated. But Lise was different in two respects. First, because she loved Meric truly and well; and second, because she was married—albeit unhappily— to a man named Pardiel, the foreman of the calciner crew. She did not love him as she did Meric, yet she respected him and felt obliged to consider carefully before ending the relationship. Meric had never known such an introspective soul. She was twelve years younger than he, tall and lovely, with sun-streaked hair and brown eyes that went dark and seemed to turn inward whenever she was pensive. She was in the habit of analyzing everything that affected her, drawing back from her emotions and inspecting them as if they were a clutch of strange insects she had discovered crawling on her skirt. Though her penchant for self-examination kept her from him, Meric viewed it as a kind of baffling virtue. He had the classic malady and could find no fault with her. For almost a year they were as happy as could be expected; they talked long hours and walked together, and on those occasions when Pardiel worked double shifts and was forced to bed down by his furnaces, they spent the nights making love in the cavernous spaces beneath the dragon's wing.

It was still reckoned an evil place. Something far worse than skizzers or flakes was rumored to live there, and the ravages of this creature were blamed for every disappearance, even that of the most malcontented laborer. But Meric did not give credence to the rumors. He half-believed Griaule had chosen him to be his executioner and that the dragon would never let him be harmed; and besides, it was the only place where they could be assured of privacy.

A crude stair led under the wing, handholds and steps hacked from the scales—doubtless the work of scale hunters. It was a treacherous passage, six hundred feet above the valley floor; but Lise and Meric were secured by ropes, and over the months, driven by the urgency of passion, they adapted to it. Their favorite spot lay fifty feet in (Lise would go no farther; she was afraid even if he was not), near a waterfall that trickled over the leathery folds, causing them to glisten with a mineral brilliance. It was eerily beautiful, a haunted gallery. Peels of dead skin hung down from the shadows like torn veils of ectoplasm; ferns sprouted from the vanes, which were thicker than cathedral columns; swallows curved through the black air. Sometimes, lying with her hidden by a tuck of the wing, Meric would think the beating of their hearts was what really animated the place, that the instant they left, the water ceased flowing and the swallows vanished. He had an unshakable faith in the transforming power of their affections, and one morning as they dressed, preparing to return to Hangtown, he asked her to leave with him.

"To another part of the valley?" She laughed sadly. "What good would that do? Pardiel would follow us."

"No," he said. "To another country. Anywhere far from here."

"We can't," she said, kicking at the wing. "Not until Griaule dies. Have you forgotten?"

"We haven't tried."

"Others have."

"But we'd be strong enough. I know it!"

"You're a romantic," she said gloomily, and stared out over the slope of Griaule's back at the valley. Sunrise had washed the hills to crimson, and even the tips of the wings were glowing a dull red.

"Of course I'm a romantic!" He stood, angry. "What the hell's wrong with that?"

She sighed with exasperation. "You wouldn't leave your work," she said. "And if we did leave, what work would you do? Would. . . ."

"Why must everything be a problem in advance!" he shouted. "I'll tattoo elephants! I'll paint murals on the chests of giants, I'll illuminate whales! Who else is better qualified?"

She smiled, and his anger evaporated.

"I didn't mean it that way," she said. "I just wondered if you could be satisfied with anything else."

She reached out her hand to be pulled up, and he drew her into an embrace. As he held her, inhaling the scent of vanilla water from her hair, he saw a diminutive figure silhouetted against the backdrop of the valley. It did not seem real—a black homunculus— and even when it began to come forward, growing larger and larger, it looked less a man than a magical keyhole opening in a crimson set hillside. But Meric knew from the man's rolling walk and the hulking set of his shoulders that it was Pardiel; he was carrying a long-handled hook, one of those used by artisans to maneuver along the scales.

Meric tensed, and Lise looked back to see what had alarmed him. "Oh, my God!" she said, moving out of the embrace.

Pardiel stopped a dozen feet away. He said nothing. His face was in shadow, and the hook swung lazily from his hand. Lise took a step toward him, then stepped back and stood in front of Meric as if to shield him. Seeing this, Pardiel let out an inarticulate yell and charged, slashing with the hook. Meric pushed Lise aside and ducked. He caught a brimstone whiff of the calciners as Pardiel rushed past and went sprawling, tripped by some irregularity in the scale. Deathly afraid, knowing he was no match for the foreman, Meric seized Lise's hand and ran deeper under the wing. He hoped Pardiel would be too frightened to follow, leery of the creature that was rumored to live there; but he was not. He came after them at a measured pace, tapping the hook against his leg.

Higher on Griaule's back, the wing was dimpled downward by hundreds of bulges, and this created a maze of small chambers and tunnels so low that they had to crouch to pass along them. The sound of their breathing and the scrape of their feet were amplified by the enclosed spaces, and Meric could no longer hear Pardiel. He had never been this deep before. He had thought it would be pitch-dark; but the lichen and algae adhering to the wing were luminescent and patterned every surface, even the scales beneath them, with whorls of blue and green fire that shed a sickly radiance. It was as if they were giants crawling through a universe whose starry matter had not yet congealed into galaxies and nebulas. In the wan light, Lise's face—turned back to him now and again—was teary and frantic; and then, as she straightened, passing into still another chamber, she drew in breath with a shriek.

At first Meric thought Pardiel had somehow managed to get ahead of them; but on entering he saw that the cause of her fright was a man propped in a sitting position against the far wall. He looked mummified. Wisps of brittle hair poked up from his scalp, the shapes of his bones were visible through his skin, and his eyes were empty holes. Between his legs was a scatter of dust where his genitals had been. Meric pushed Lise toward the next tunnel, but she resisted and pointed at the man.

"His eyes," she said, horror-struck.

Though the eyes were mostly a negative black, Meric now realized they were shot through by opalescent flickers. He felt compelled to kneel beside the man—it was a sudden, motiveless urge that gripped him, bent him to its will, and released him a second later. As he rested his hand on the scale, he brushed a massive ring that was lying beneath the shrunken fingers. Its stone was black, shot through by flickers identical to those within the eyes, and incised with the letter S. He found his gaze was deflected away from both the stone and the eyes, as if they contained charges repellent to the senses. He touched the man's withered arm; the flesh was rock-hard, petrified. But alive. From that brief touch he gained an impression of the man's life, of gazing for centuries at the same patch of unearthly fire, of a mind gone beyond mere madness into a perverse rapture, a meditation upon some foul principle. He snatched back his hand in revulsion.

There was a noise behind them, and Meric jumped up, pushing Lise into the next tunnel. "Go right," he whispered. "We'll circle back toward the stair." But Pardiel was too close to confuse with such tactics, and their flight became a wild chase, scrambling, falling, catching glimpses of Pardiel's smoke-stained face, until finally—as Meric came to a large chamber—he felt the hook bite into his thigh. He went down, clutching at the wound, pulling the hook loose. The next moment Pardiel was atop him; Lise appeared over his shoulder, but he knocked her away and locked his fingers in Meric's hair and smashed his head against the scale. Lise screamed, and white lights fired through Meric's skull. Again his head was smashed down. And again. Dimly, he saw Lise struggling with Pardiel, saw her shoved away, saw the hook raised high and the foreman's mouth distorted by a grimace. Then the grimace vanished. His jaw dropped open and he reached behind him as if to scratch his shoulder blade. A line of dark blood eeled from his mouth and he collapsed, smothering Meric beneath his chest. Meric heard voices. He tried to dislodge the body, and the effort drained the last of his strength. He whirled down through a blackness that seemed as negative and inexhaustible as the petrified man's eyes.

Someone had propped his head on their lap and was bathing his brow with a damp cloth. He assumed it was Lise, but when he asked what had happened, it was Jarcke who answered, saying, "Had to kill him." His head throbbed, his leg throbbed even worse, and his eyes would not focus. The peels of dead skin hanging overhead appeared to be writhing. He realized they were out near the edge of the wing.

"Where's Lise?"

"Don't worry," said Jarcke. "You'll see her again." She made it sound like an indictment.

"Where is she?"

"Sent her back to Hangtown. Won't do you two bein' seen hand in hand the same day Pardiel's missin'."

"She wouldn't have left. . . ." He blinked, trying to see her face; the lines around her mouth were etched deep and reminded him of the patterns of lichen on the dragon's scale. "What did you do?"

"Convinced her it was best," said Jarcke. "Don't you know she's just foolin' with you?"

"I've got to talk with her." He was full of remorse, and it was unthinkable that Lise should be bearing her grief alone; but when he struggled to rise, pain lanced through his leg.

"You wouldn't get ten feet," she said. "Soon as your head's clear, I'll help you with the stairs."

He closed his eyes, resolving to find Lise the instant he got back to Hangtown—together they would decide what to do. The scale beneath him was cool, and that coolness was transmitted to his skin, his flesh, as if he were merging with it, becoming one of its ridges.

"What was the wizard's name?" he asked after a while, recalling the petrified man, the ring and its incised letter. "The one who tried to kill Griaule. . . ."

"Don't know as I ever heard it," said Jarcke. "But I reckon it's him back there."

"You saw him?"

"I was chasin' a scale hunter once what stole some rope, and I found him instead. Pretty miserable sort, whoever he is."

Her fingers trailed over his shoulder—a gentle, treasuring touch. He did not understand what it signaled, being too concerned with Lise, with the terrifying potentials of all that had happened; but years later, after things had passed beyond remedy, he cursed himself for not having understood.

At length Jarcke helped him to his feet, and they climbed up to Hangtown, to bitter realizations and regrets, leaving Pardiel to the birds or the weather or worse.

". . . It seems it is considered irreligious for a woman in love to hesitate or examine the situation, to do anything other than blindly follow the impulse of her emotions. I felt the brunt of such an attitude—people judged it my fault for not having acted quickly and decisively one way or another. Perhaps I was overcautious. I do not claim to be free of blame, only innocent of sacrilege. I believe I might have eventually left Pardiel—there was not enough in the relationship to sustain happiness for either of us. But I had good reason for cautious examination. My husband was not an evil man, and there were matters of loyalty between us.

"I could not face Meric after Pardiel's death, and I moved to another part of the valley. He tried to see me on many occasions, but I always refused. Though I was greatly tempted, my guilt was greater. Four years later, after Jarcke died—crushed by a runaway wagon—one of her associates wrote and told me Jarcke had been in love with Meric, that it had been she who had informed Pardiel of the affair, and that she may well have staged the murder. The letter acted somewhat to expiate my guilt, and I weighed the possibility of seeing Meric again. But too much time had passed, and we had both assumed other lives. I decided against it. Six years later, when Griaule's influence had weakened sufficiently to allow emigration, I moved to Port Chantay. I did not hear from Meric for almost twenty years after that, and then one day I received a letter, which I will reproduce in part.

" '. . . My old friend from Regensburg, Louis Dardano, has been living here for the past few years, engaged in writing my biography. The narrative has a breezy feel, like a tale being told in a tavern, which—if you recall my telling you how this all began—is quite appropriate. But on reading it, I am amazed my life has had such a simple shape. One task, one passion. God, Lise! Seventy years old, and I still dream of you. And I still think of what happened that morning under the wing. Strange, that it has taken me all this time to realize it was not Jarcke, not you or I who were culpable, but Griaule. How obvious it seems now. I was leaving, and he needed me to complete the expression on his side, his dream of flying, of escape, to grant him the death of his desire. I am certain you will think I have leaped to this assumption, but I remind you that it has been a leap of forty years' duration. I know Griaule, know his monstrous subtlety. I can see it at work in every action that has taken place in the valley since my arrival. I was a fool not to understand that his powers were at the heart of our sad conclusion.

" 'The army now runs everything here, as no doubt you are aware. It is rumored they are planning a winter campaign against Regensburg. Can you believe it! Their fathers were ignorant, but this generation is brutally stupid. Otherwise, the work goes well and things are as usual with me. My shoulder aches, children stare at me on the street, and it is whispered I am mad. . . .' "

—from *Under Griaule's Wing*
by Lise Claverie

3.

Acne-scarred, lean, arrogant, Major Hauk was a very young major with a limp. When Meric had entered, the major had been practicing his signature—it was a thing of elegant loops and flourishes, obviously intended to have a place in posterity. As he strode back and forth during their conversation, he paused frequently to admire himself in the window glass, settling the hang of his red jacket or running his fingers along the crease of his white trousers. It was the new style of uniform, the first Meric had seen at close range, and he noted with amusement the dragons embossed on the epaulets. He wondered if Griaule was capable of such an irony, if his influence was sufficiently discreet to have planted the idea for this comic opera apparel in the brain of some general's wife.

". . . not a question of manpower," the major was saying, "but of. . . ." He broke off, and after a moment cleared his throat.

Meric, who had been studying the blotches on the backs of his hands, glanced up; the cane that had been resting against his knee slipped and clattered to the floor.

"A question of *matériel*," said the major firmly. "The price of antimony, for example. . . ."

"Hardly use it anymore," said Meric. "I'm almost done with the mineral reds."

A look of impatience crossed the major's face. "Very well," he said; he stooped to his desk and shuffled through some papers. Here's a bill for a shipment of cuttlefish from which you derive. . . ." He shuffled more papers.

"Syrian brown," said Meric gruffly. "I'm done with that, too. Golds and violets are all I need anymore. A little blue and rose." He wished the man would stop badgering him; he wanted to be at the eye before sunset.

As the major continued his accounting, Meric's gaze wandered out the window. The shantytown surrounding Griaule had swelled into a city and now sprawled across the hills. Most of the buildings were permanent, wood and stone, and the cant of the roofs, the smoke from the factories around the perimeter, put him in mind of Regensburg. All the natural beauty of the land had been drained into the painting. Blackish gray rain clouds were muscling up from the east, but the afternoon sun shone clear and shed a heavy gold radiance on Griaule's side. It looked as if the sunlight were an extension of the gleaming resins, as if the thickness of the paint were becoming infinite. He let the major's voice recede to a buzz and followed the scatter and dazzle of the images; and then, with a start, he realized the major was sounding him out about stopping the work.

The idea panicked him at first. He tried to interrupt, to raise objections; but the major talked through him, and as Meric thought it over, he grew less and less opposed. The painting would never be finished, and he was tired. Perhaps it was time to have done with it, to accept a university post somewhere and enjoy life for a while.

"We've been thinking about a temporary stoppage," said Major Hauk. "Then if the winter campaign goes well. . . ." He smiled. "If we're not visited by plague and pestilence, we'll assume things are in hand. Of course we'd like your opinion."

Meric felt a surge of anger toward this smug little monster. "In my opinion, you people are idiots," he said. "You wear Griaule's image on your shoulders, weave him on your flags, and yet you don't have the least comprehension of what that means. You think it's just a useful symbol. . . ."

"Excuse me," said the major stiffly.

"The hell I will!" Meric groped for his cane and heaved up to his feet. "You see yourselves as conquerors. Shapers of destiny. But all your rapes and slaughters are Griaule's expressions. *His* will. You're every bit as much his parasites as the skizzers."

The major sat, picked up a pen, and began to write.

"It astounds me," Meric went on, "that you can live next to a miracle, a source of mystery, and treat him as if he were an oddly shaped rock."

The major kept writing.

"What are you doing?" asked Meric.

"My recommendation," said the major without looking up.

"Which is?"

"That we initiate stoppage at once."

They exchanged hostile stares, and Meric turned to leave; but as he took hold of the doorknob, the major spoke again.

"We owe you so much," he said; he wore an expression of mingled pity and respect that further irritated Meric.

"How many men have you killed, Major?" he asked, opening the door.

"I'm not sure. I was in the artillery. We were never able to be sure."

"Well, I'm sure of my tally," said Meric. "It's taken me forty years to amass it. Fifteen hundred and ninety-three men and women. Poisoned, scalded, broken by falls, savaged by animals. Murdered. Why don't we—you and I—just call it even."

Though it was a sultry afternoon, he felt cold as he walked toward the tower—an internal cold that left him light-headed and weak. He tried to think what he would do. The idea of a university post seemed less appealing away from the major's office; he would soon grow weary of worshipful students and in-depth dissections of his work by jealous academics. A man hailed him as he turned into the market. Meric waved but did not stop, and heard another man say, *"That's* Cattanay?" (That ragged old ruin?)

The colors of the market were too bright, the smells of charcoal cookery too cloying, the crowds too thick, and he made for the side streets, hobbling past one-room stucco houses and tiny stores where they sold cooking oil by the ounce and cut cigars in half if you could not afford a whole one. Garbage, tornados of dust and flies, drunks with bloody mouths. Somebody had tied wires around a pariah dog—a bitch with slack teats; the wires had sliced into her flesh, and she lay panting in an alley mouth, gaunt ribs flecked with pink lather, gazing into nowhere. She, thought Meric, and not Griaule, should be the symbol of their flag.

As he rode the hoist up the side of the tower, he fell into his old habit of jotting down notes for the next day. *What's that cord of wood doing on level five? Slow leak of chrome yellow from pipes on level twelve.* Only when he saw a man dismantling some scaffolding did he recall Major Hauk's recommendation and understand that the order must already have been given. The loss of his work struck home to him then, and he leaned against the railing, his chest constricted and his eyes brimming. He straightened, ashamed of himself. The sun hung in a haze of iron-colored light low above the western hills, looking red and bloated and vile as a vulture's ruff. That polluted sky was his creation as much as was the painting, and it would be good to leave it behind. Once away from the valley, from all the influences of the place, he would be able to consider the future.

A young girl was sitting on the twentieth level just beneath the eye. Years before, the ritual of viewing the eye had grown to cultish proportions; there had been group chanting and praying and discussions of the experience. But these were more practical times, and no doubt the young men and women who had congregated here were now manning administrative desks somewhere in the burgeoning empire. They were the ones about whom Dardano should write; they, and all the eccentric characters who had played roles in this slow pageant. The gypsy woman who had danced every night by the eye, hoping to charm Griaule into killing her faithless lover—she had gone away satisfied. The man who had tried to extract one of the fangs—nobody knew what had become of him. The scale hunters, the artisans. A history of Hangtown would be a volume in itself.

The walk had left Meric weak and breathless; he sat down clumsily beside the girl, who smiled. He could not remember her name, but she came often to the eye. Small and dark, with an inner reserve that reminded him of Lise. He laughed inwardly—most women reminded him of Lise in some way.

"Are you all right?" she asked, her brow wrinkled with concern.

"Oh, yes," he said; he felt a need for conversation to take his mind off things, but he could think of nothing more to say. She was so young! All freshness and gleam and nerves.

"This will be my last time," she said. "At least for a while. I'll miss it." And then, before he could ask why, she added, "I'm getting married tomorrow, and we're moving away."

He offered congratulations and asked her who was the lucky fellow.

"Just a boy." She tossed her hair, as if to dismiss the boy's importance; she gazed up at the shuttered membrane. "What's it like for you when the eye opens?" she asked.

"Like everyone else," he said. "I remember . . . memories of my life. Other lives, too." He did not tell her about Griaule's memory of flight; he had never told anyone except Lise about that.

"All those bits of souls trapped in there," she said, gesturing at the eye. "What do they mean to him? Why does he show them to us?"

"I imagine he has his purposes, but I can't explain them."

"Once I remembered being with you," said the girl, peeking at him shyly through a dark curl. "We were under the wing."

He glanced at her sharply. "Tell me."

"We were . . . together," she said, blushing. "Intimate, you know. I was very afraid of the place, of the sounds and shadows. But I loved you so much, it didn't matter. We made love all night, and I was surprised because I thought that kind of passion was just in stories, something people had invented to make up for how ordinary it really was. And in the morning even that dreadful place had become beautiful, with the wing tips glowing red and the waterfall echoing . . ." She lowered her eyes. "Ever since I had that memory, I've been a little in love with you."

"Lise," he said, feeling helpless before her.

"Was that her name?"

He nodded and put a hand to his brow, trying to pinch back the emotions that flooded him.

"I'm sorry." Her lips grazed his cheek, and just that slight touch seemed to weaken him further. "I wanted to tell you how she felt in case she hadn't told you herself. She was very troubled by something, and I wasn't sure she had."

She shifted away from him, made uncomfortable by the intensity of his reaction, and they sat without speaking. Meric became lost in watching how the sun glazed the scales to reddish gold, how the light was channeled along the ridges in molten streams that paled as the day wound down. He was startled when the girl jumped to her feet and backed toward the hoist.

"He's dead," she said wonderingly.

Meric looked at her, uncomprehending.

"See?" She pointed at the sun, which showed a crimson sliver above the hill. "He's dead," she repeated, and the expression on her face flowed between fear and exultation.

The idea of Griaule's death was too large for Meric's mind to encompass, and he turned to the eye to find a counterproof—no glints of color flickered beneath the membrane. He heard the hoist creak as the girl headed down, but he continued to wait. Perhaps only the dragon's vision had failed. No. It was likely not a coincidence that work had been officially terminated today. Stunned, he sat staring at the lifeless membrane until the sun sank below the hills; then he stood and went over to the hoist. Before he could throw the switch, the cables thrummed—somebody heading up. Of course. The girl would have spread the news, and all the Major Hauks and their underlings would be hurrying to test Griaule's reflexes. He did not want to be here when they arrived, to watch them pose with their trophy like successful fishermen.

It was hard work climbing up to the frontoparietal plate. The ladder swayed, the wind buffeted him, and by the time he clambered onto the plate, he was giddy, his chest full of twinges. He hobbled forward and leaned against the rust-caked side of a boiling vat. Shadowy in the twilight, the great furnaces and vats towered around him, and it seemed this system of fiery devices reeking of cooked flesh and minerals was the actual machinery of Griaule's thought materialized above his skull. Energyless, abandoned. They had been replaced by more efficient equipment down below, and it had been—what was it?—almost five years since they were last used. Cobwebs veiled a pyramid of firewood; the stairs leading to the rims of the vats were crumbling. The plate itself was scarred and coated with sludge.

"Cattanay!"

Someone shouted from below, and the top of the ladder trembled. God, they were coming after him! Bubbling over with congratulations and plans for testimonial dinners, memorial plaques, specially struck medals. They would have him draped in bunting and bronzed and covered with pigeon shit before they were done. All these years he had been among them, both their slave and their master, yet he had never felt at home. Leaning heavily on his cane, he made his way past the frontal spike—blackened by years of oily smoke—and down between the wings to Hangtown. It was a ghost town, now. Weeds overgrowing the collapsed shanties; the lake a stinking pit, drained after some children had drowned in the summer of '91. Where Jarcke's home had stood was a huge pile of animal bones, taking a pale shine from the half-light. Wind keened through the tattered shrubs.

"Meric!" "Cattanay."

The voices were closer.

Well, there was one place where they would not follow.

The leaves of the thickets were speckled with mold and brittle, flaking away as he brushed them. He hesitated at the top of the scale hunters' stair. He had no rope. Though he had done the climb unaided many times, it had been quite a few years. The gusts of wind, the shouts, the sweep of the valley and the lights scattered across it like diamonds on gray velvet—it all seemed a single inconstant medium. He heard the brush crunch behind him, more voices. To hell with it! Gritting his teeth against a twinge of pain in his shoulder, hooking his cane over his belt, he inched onto the stair and locked his fingers in the handholds. The wind whipped his clothes and threatened to pry him loose and send him pinwheeling off. Once he slipped; once he froze, unable to move backward or forward. But at last he reached the bottom and edged upslope until he found a spot flat enough to stand.

The mystery of the place suddenly bore in upon him, and he was afraid. He half-turned to the stair, thinking he would go back to Hangtown and accept the hurly-burly. But a moment later he realized how foolish a thought that was. Waves of weakness poured through him, his heart hammered, and white dazzles flared in his vision. His chest felt heavy as iron. Rattled, he went a few steps forward, the cane pocking the silence. It was too dark to see more than outlines, but up ahead was the fold of wing where he and Lise had sheltered. He walked toward it, intent on revisiting it; then he remembered the girl beneath the eye and understood that he had already said that good-bye. And it *was* good-bye—that he understood vividly. He kept walking. Blackness looked to be welling from the wing joint, from the entrances to the maze of luminous tunnels where they had stumbled onto the petrified man. Had it really been the old wizard, doomed by magical justice to molder and live on and on? It made sense. At least it accorded with what happened to wizards who slew their dragons.

"Griaule?" he whispered to the darkness, and cocked his head, half-expecting an answer. The sound of his voice pointed up the immensity of the great gallery under the wing, the emptiness, and he recalled how vital a habitat it had once been. Flakes shifting over the surface, skizzers, peculiar insects fuming in the thickets, the glum populace of Hangtown, waterfalls. He had never been able to picture Griaule fully alive—that kind of vitality was beyond the powers of the imagination. Yet he wondered if by some miracle the dragon were alive now, flying up through his golden night to the sun's core. Or had that merely been a dream, a bit of tissue glittering deep in the cold tons of his brain? He laughed. Ask the stars for their first names, and you'd be more likely to receive a reply.

He decided not to walk any farther—it was really no decision. Pain was spreading through his shoulder, so intense he imagined it must be glowing inside. Carefully, carefully, he lowered himself and lay propped on an elbow, hanging onto the cane. Good, magical wood. Cut from a hawthorn atop Griaule's haunch. A man had once offered him a small fortune for it. Who would claim it now? Probably old Henry Sichi would snatch it for his museum, stick it in a glass case next to his boots. What a joke! He decided to lie flat on his stomach, resting his chin on an arm—the stony coolness beneath acted to muffle the pain. Amusing, how the range of one's decision dwindled. You decided to paint a dragon, to send hundreds of men searching for malachite and cochineal beetles, to love a woman, to heighten an undertone here and there, and finally to position your body a certain way. He seemed to have reached the end of the process. What next? He tried to regulate his breathing, to ease the pressure on his chest. Then, as something rustled out near the wing joint, he turned on his side. He thought he detected movement, a gleaming blackness flowing toward him . . . or else it was only the haphazard firing of his nerves playing tricks with his vision. More surprised than afraid, wanting to see, he peered into the darkness and felt his heart beating erratically against the dragon's scale.

". . . It's foolish to draw simple conclusions from complex events, but I suppose there must be both moral and truth to this life, these events. I'll leave that to the gadflies. The historians, the social scientists, the expert apologists for reality. All I know is that he had a fight with his girlfriend over money and walked out. He sent her a letter saying he had gone south and would be back in a few months with more money than she could ever spend. I had no idea what he'd done. The whole thing about Griaule had just been a bunch of us sitting around the Red Bear, drinking up my pay—I'd sold an article—and somebody said, 'Wouldn't it be great if Dardano didn't have to write articles, if we didn't have to paint pictures that color-coordinated with people's furniture or slave at getting the gooey smiles of little nieces and nephews just right?' All sorts of improbable moneymaking schemes were put forward. Robberies, kidnappings. Then the idea of swindling the city fathers of Teocinte came up, and the entire plan was fleshed out in minutes. Scribbled on napkins, scrawled on sketchpads. A group effort. I keep trying to remember if anyone got a glassy look in their eye, if I felt a cold tendril of Griaule's thought stirring my brains. But I can't. It was a half hour's sensation, nothing more. A drunken whimsy, an art-school metaphor. Shortly thereafter, we ran out of money and staggered into the streets. It was snowing—big wet flakes that melted down our collars. God, we were drunk! Laughing, balancing on the icy railing of the University Bridge. Making faces at the bundled-up burghers and their fat ladies who huffed and puffed past, spouting steam and never giving us a glance, and none of us—not even the burghers—knowing that we were living our happy ending in advance. . . ."

—from *The Man Who Painted
the Dragon Griaule*
by Louis Dardano

FOR JAMIE AND LAURA

PRESS ENTER ▮

JOHN VARLEY

John Varley won both the Nebula and Hugo awards for his novella "The Persistence of Vision." He also won the Hugo for his short story "The Pusher." His novels include Titan, Wizard, Demon *(a trilogy),* Millennium, *and* The Ophiuchi Hotline. *A short story of his, "Overdrawn at the Memory Bank," was recently adapted for television and shown on PBS's "American Playhouse."*

This story is the Nebula Award winner in the novella category (and a Hugo Award winner this year). It combines computers with the idea of an afterlife in Varley's typically vigorous way and manages also to be a mystery story with a startling resolution.

"This is a recording. Please do not hang up until—"

I slammed the phone down so hard it fell onto the floor. Then I stood there, dripping wet and shaking with anger. Eventually, the phone started to make that buzzing noise they make when a receiver is off the hook. It's twenty times as loud as any sound a phone can normally make, and I always wondered why. As though it was such a terrible disaster: "Emergency! Your telephone is off the hook!!!"

Phone answering machines are one of the small annoyances of life. Confess, do you really *like* talking to a machine? But what had just happened to me was more than a petty irritation. I had just been called by an automatic dialing machine.

They're fairly new. I'd been getting about two or three such calls a month. Most of them come from insurance companies. They give you a two-minute spiel and then a number to call if you are interested. (I called back, once, to give them a piece of my mind, and was put on hold, complete with Muzak.) They use lists. I don't know where they get them.

I went back to the bathroom, wiped water droplets from the plastic cover of the library book, and carefully lowered myself back into the water. It was too cool. I ran more hot water and was just getting my blood pressure back to normal when the phone rang again.

So I sat there through fifteen rings, trying to ignore it.

Did you ever try to read with the phone ringing?

On the sixteenth ring I got up. I dried off, put on a robe, walked slowly and deliberately into the living room. I stared at the phone for a while.

On the fiftieth ring I picked it up.

"This is a recording. Please do not hang up until the message has been completed. This call originates from the house of your next-door neighbor, Charles Kluge. It will repeat every ten minutes. Mister Kluge knows he has not been the best of neighbors, and apologizes in advance for the inconvenience. He requests that you go immediately to his house. The key is under the mat. Go inside and do what needs to be done. There will be a reward for your services. Thank you."

Click. Dial tone.

I'm not a hasty man. Ten minutes later, when the phone rang again, I was still sitting there thinking it over. I picked up the receiver and listened carefully.

It was the same message. As before, it was not Kluge's voice. It was something synthesized, with all the human warmth of a Speak'n'Spell.

I heard it out again, and cradled the receiver when it was done.

I thought about calling the police. Charles Kluge had lived next door to me for ten years. In that time I may have had a dozen conversations with him, none lasting longer than a minute. I owed him nothing.

I thought about ignoring it. I was still thinking about that when the phone rang again. I glanced at my watch. Ten minutes. I lifted the receiver and put it right back down.

I could disconnect the phone. It wouldn't change my life radically.

But in the end I got dressed and went out the front door, turned left, and walked toward Kluge's property.

My neighbor across the street, Hal Lanier, was out mowing the lawn. He waved to me, and I waved back. It was about seven in the evening of a wonderful August day. The shadows were long. There was the smell of cut grass in the air. I've always liked that smell. About time to cut my own lawn, I thought.

It was a thought Kluge had never entertained. His lawn was brown and knee-high and choked with weeds.

I rang the bell. When nobody came I knocked. Then I sighed, looked under the mat, and used the key I found there to open the door.

"Kluge?" I called out as I stuck my head in.

I went along the short hallway, tentatively, as people do when unsure of their welcome. The drapes were drawn, as always, so it was dark in there, but in what had once been the living room ten television screens gave more than enough light for me to see Kluge. He sat in a chair in front of a table, with his face pressed into a computer keyboard and the side of his head blown away.

Hal Lanier operates a computer for the L.A.P.D., so I told him what I had found and he called the police. We waited together for the first car to arrive. Hal kept asking if I'd touched anything, and I kept telling him no, except for the front door knob.

An ambulance arrived without the siren. Soon there were police all over, and neighbors standing out in their yards or talking in front of Kluge's house. Crews from some of the television stations arrived in time to get pictures of the body, wrapped in a plastic sheet, being carried out. Men and women came and went. I assumed they were doing all the standard police things, taking fingerprints, collecting evidence. I would have gone home, but had been told to stick around.

Finally I was brought in to see Detective Osborne, who was in charge of the case. I was led into Kluge's living room. All the television screens were still turned on. I shook hands with Osborne. He looked me over before he said anything. He was a short guy, balding. He seemed very tired until he looked at me. Then, though nothing really changed in his face, he didn't look tired at all.

"You're Victor Apfel?" he asked. I told him I was. He gestured at the room. "Mister Apfel, can you tell if anything has been taken from this room?"

I took another look around, approaching it as a puzzle.

There was a fireplace and there were curtains over the windows. There was a rug on the floor. Other than those items, there was nothing else you would expect to find in a living room.

All the walls were lined with tables, leaving a narrow aisle down the middle. On the tables were monitor screens, keyboards, disc drives—all the glossy bric-a-brac of the new age. They were interconnected by thick cables and cords. Beneath the tables were still more computers, and boxes full of electronic items. Above the tables were shelves that reached the ceiling and were stuffed with boxes of tapes, discs, cartridges . . . there was a word for it which I couldn't recall just then. It was software.

"There's no furniture, is there? Other than that . . ."

He was looking confused.

"You mean there was furniture here before?"

"How would I know?" Then I realized what the misunderstanding was. "Oh. You thought I'd been here before. The first time I ever set foot in this room was about an hour ago."

He frowned, and I didn't like that much.

"The medical examiner says the guy had been dead about three hours. How come you came over when you did, Victor?"

I didn't like him using my first name, but didn't see what I could do about it. And I knew I had to tell him about the phone call.

He looked dubious. But there was one easy way to check it out, and we did that. Hal and Osborne and I and several others trooped over to my house. My phone was ringing as we entered.

Osborne picked it up and listened. He got a very sour expression on his face. As the night wore on, it just got worse and worse.

We waited ten minutes for the phone to ring again. Osborne spent the time examining everything in my living room. I was glad when the phone rang again. They made a recording of the message, and we went back to Kluge's house.

Osborne went into the back yard to see Kluge's forest of antennas. He looked impressed.

"Mrs. Madison down the street thinks he was trying to contact Martians," Hal said, with a laugh. "Me, I just thought he was stealing HBO." There were three parabolic dishes. There were six tall masts, and some of those things you see on telephone company buildings for transmitting microwaves.

Osborne took me to the living room again. He asked me to describe what I had seen. I didn't know what good that would do, but I tried.

"He was sitting in that chair, which was here in front of this table. I saw the gun on the floor. His hand was hanging down toward it."

"You think it was suicide?"

"Yes, I guess I did think that." I waited for him to comment, but he didn't. "Is that what you think?"

He sighed. "There wasn't any note."

"They don't always leave notes," Hal pointed out.

"No, but they do often enough that my nose starts to twitch when they don't." He shrugged. "It's probably nothing."

"That phone call," I said. "That might be a kind of suicide note."

Osborne nodded. "Was there anything else you noticed?"

I went to the table and looked at the keyboard. It was made by Texas Instruments, model TI-99/4A. There was a large bloodstain on the right side of it, where his head had been resting.

"Just that he was sitting in front of this machine." I touched a key, and the monitor screen behind the keyboard immediately filled with words. I quickly drew my hand back, then stared at the message there.

PROGRAM NAME: GOODBYE REAL WORLD
DATE: 8/20
CONTENTS: LAST WILL AND TESTAMENT; MISC. FEATURES
PROGRAMMER: "CHARLES KLUGE"

TO RUN
PRESS ENTER ■

The black square at the end flashed on and off. Later I learned it was called a cursor.

Everyone gathered around. Hal, the computer expert, explained how many computers went blank after ten minutes of no activity, so the words wouldn't be burned into the television screen. This one had been green until I touched it, then displayed black letters on a blue background.

"Has this console been checked for prints?" Osborne asked. Nobody seemed to know, so Osborne took a pencil and used the eraser to press the ENTER key.

The screen cleared, stayed blue for a moment, then filled with little ovoid shapes that started at the top of the screen and descended like rain. There were hundreds of them in many colors.

"Those are pills," one of the cops said, in amazement. "Look, that's gotta be a Quaalude. There's a Nembutal." Other cops pointed out other pills. I recognized the distinctive red stripe around the center of a white capsule that had to be a Dilantin. I had been taking them every day for years.

Finally the pills stopped falling, and the damn thing started to play music at us. "Nearer My God To Thee," in three-part harmony.

A few people laughed. I don't think any of us thought it was funny—it was creepy as hell listening to that eerie dirge—but it sounded like it had been scored for pennywhistle, calliope, and kazoo. What could you do but laugh?

As the music played, a little figure composed entirely of squares entered from the left of the screen and jerked spastically toward the center. It was like one of those human figures from a video game, but not as detailed. You had to use your imagination to believe it was a man.

A shape appeared in the middle of the screen. The "man" stopped in front of it. He bent in the middle, and something that might have been a chair appeared under him.

"What's that supposed to be?"

"A computer. Isn't it?"

It must have been, because the little man extended his arms, which jerked up and down like Liberace at the piano. He was typing. The words appeared above him.

SOMEWHERE ALONG THE LINE I MISSED SOMETHING. I SIT HERE, NIGHT AND DAY, A SPIDER IN THE CENTER OF A COAXIAL WEB, MASTER OF ALL I SURVEY . . . AND IT IS NOT ENOUGH. THERE MUST BE MORE.

ENTER YOUR NAME HERE ■

"Jesus Christ," Hal said. "I don't believe it. An interactive suicide note."

"Come on, we've got to see the rest of this."

I was nearest the keyboard, so I leaned over and typed my name. But when I looked up, what I had typed was VICT9R.

"How do you back this up?" I asked.

"Just enter it," Osborne said. He reached around me and pressed enter.

DO YOU EVER GET THAT FEELING, VICT9R? YOU HAVE WORKED ALL YOUR LIFE TO BE THE BEST THERE IS AT WHAT YOU DO, AND ONE DAY YOU WAKE UP TO WONDER WHY YOU ARE DOING IT? THAT IS WHAT HAPPENED TO ME.

DO YOU WANT TO HEAR MORE, VICT9R? Y/N ■

The message rambled from that point. Kluge seemed to be aware of it, apologetic about it, because at the end of each forty- or fifty-word paragraph the reader was given the Y/N option.

I kept glancing from the screen to the keyboard, remembering
Kluge slumped across it. I thought about him sitting here alone,
writing this.

He said he was despondent. He didn't feel like he could go on.
He was taking too many pills (more of them rained down the screen
at this point), and he had no further goal. He had done everything
he set out to do. We didn't understand what he meant by that. He
said he no longer existed. We thought that was a figure of speech.

ARE YOU A COP, VICT9R? IF YOU ARE NOT, A COP WILL BE HERE SOON,
SO TO YOU OR THE COP: I WAS NOT SELLING NARCOTICS. THE DRUGS
IN MY BEDROOM WERE FOR MY OWN PERSONAL USE. I USED A LOT OF
THEM. AND NOW I WILL NOT NEED THEM ANYMORE.

PRESS ENTER ■

Osborne did, and a printer across the room began to chatter,
scaring the hell out of all of us. I could see the carriage zipping
back and forth, printing in both directions, when Hal pointed at
the screen and shouted.

"Look! Look at that!"

The compugraphic man was standing again. He faced us. He
had something that had to be a gun in his hand, which he now
pointed at his head.

"Don't do it!" Hal yelled.

The little man didn't listen. There was a denatured gunshot sound,
and the little man fell on his back. A line of red dripped down the
screen. Then the green background turned to blue, the printer shut
off, and there was nothing left but the little black corpse lying on its
back and the word ★★DONE★★ at the bottom of the screen.

I took a deep breath, and glanced at Osborne. It would be an
understatement to say he did not look happy.

"What's this about drugs in the bedroom?" he said.

We watched Osborne pulling out drawers in dressers and bedside
tables. He didn't find anything. He looked under the bed, and in

the closet. Like all the other rooms in the house, this one was full of computers. Holes had been knocked in walls for the thick sheaves of cables.

I had been standing near a big cardboard drum, one of several in the room. It was about thirty gallon capacity, the kind you ship things in. The lid was loose, so I lifted it. I sort of wished I hadn't.

"Osborne," I said. "You'd better look at this."

The drum was lined with a heavy-duty garbage bag. And it was two-thirds full of Quaaludes.

They pried the lids off the rest of the drums. We found drums of amphetamines, of Nembutals, of Valium. All sorts of things.

With the discovery of the drugs a lot more police returned to the scene. With them came the television camera crews.

In all the activity no one seemed concerned about me, so I slipped back to my own house and locked the door. From time to time I peeked out the curtains. I saw reporters interviewing the neighbors. Hal was there, and seemed to be having a good time. Twice crews knocked on my door, but I didn't answer. Eventually they went away.

I ran a hot bath and soaked in it for about an hour. Then I turned the heat up as high as it would go and got in bed, under the blankets.

I shivered all night.

Osborne came over about nine the next morning. I let him in. Hal followed, looking very unhappy. I realized they had been up all night. I poured coffee for them.

"You'd better read this first," Osborne said, and handed me the sheet of computer printout. I unfolded it, got out my glasses, and started to read.

It was in that awful dot-matrix printing. My policy is to throw any such trash into the fireplace, un-read, but I made an exception this time.

It was Kluge's will. Some probate court was going to have a lot of fun with it.

He stated again that he didn't exist, so he could have no relatives.

He had decided to give all his worldly property to somebody who deserved it.

But who was deserving? Kluge wondered. Well, not Mr. and Mrs. Perkins, four houses down the street. They were child abusers. He cited court records in Buffalo and Miami, and a pending case locally.

Mrs. Radnor and Mrs. Polonski, who lived across the street from each other five houses down, were gossips.

The Andersons' oldest son was a car thief.

Marian Flores cheated on her high school algebra tests.

There was a guy nearby who was diddling the city on a freeway construction project. There was one wife in the neighborhood who made out with door-to-door salesmen, and two having affairs with men other than their husbands. There was a teenage boy who got his girlfriend pregnant, dropped her, and bragged about it to his friends.

There were no fewer than nineteen couples in the immediate area who had not reported income to the IRS, or who had padded their deductions.

Kluge's neighbors in back had a dog that barked all night.

Well, I could vouch for the dog. He'd kept me awake often enough. But the rest of it was *crazy!* For one thing, where did a guy with two hundred gallons of illegal narcotics get the right to judge his neighbors so harshly? I mean, the child abusers were one thing, but was it right to tar a whole family because their son stole cars? And for another . . . how did he *know* some of this stuff?

But there was more. Specifically, four philandering husbands. One was Harold "Hal" Lanier, who for three years had been seeing a woman named Toni Jones, a co-worker at the L.A.P.D. Data Processing facility. She was pressuring him for a divorce; he was "waiting for the right time to tell his wife."

I glanced up at Hal. His red face was all the confirmation I needed.

Then it hit me. What had Kluge found out about *me?*

I hurried down the page, searching for my name. I found it in the last paragraph.

". . . for thirty years Mr. Apfel has been paying for a mistake he did not even make. I won't go so far as to nominate him for saint-hood, but by default—if for no other reason—I hereby leave all deed and title to my real property and the structure thereon to Victor Apfel."

I looked at Osborne, and those tired eyes were weighing me.

"But I don't *want* it!"

"Do you think this is the reward Kluge mentioned in the phone call?"

"It must be," I said. "What else could it be?"

Osborne sighed, and sat back in his chair. "At least he didn't try to leave you the drugs. Are you still saying you didn't know the guy?"

"Are you accusing me of something?"

He spread his hands. "Mister Apfel, I'm simply asking a question. You're never one hundred percent sure in a suicide. Maybe it was a murder. If it was, you can see that, so far, you're the only one we know of that's gained by it."

"He was almost a stranger to me."

He nodded, tapping his copy of the computer printout. I looked back at my own, wishing it would go away.

"What's this . . . mistake you didn't make?"

I was afraid that would be the next question.

"I was a prisoner of war in North Korea," I said.

Osborne chewed that over for a while.

"They brainwash you?"

"Yes." I hit the arm of my chair, and suddenly had to be up and moving. The room was getting cold. "No. I don't . . . there's been a lot of confusion about that word. Did they 'brainwash' me? Yes. Did they succeed? Did I offer a confession of my war crimes and denounce the U.S. Government? No."

Once more, I felt myself being inspected by those deceptively tired eyes.

"You still seem to have . . . strong feelings about it."

"It's not something you forget."

"Is there anything you want to say about it?"

"It's just that it was all so . . . no. No, I have nothing further to say. Not to you, not to anybody."

"I'm going to have to ask you more questions about Kluge's death."

"I think I'll have my lawyer present for those." Christ. Now I am going to have to get a lawyer. I didn't know where to begin.

Osborne just nodded again. He got up and went to the door.

"I was ready to write this one down as a suicide," he said. "The only thing that bothered me was there was no note. Now we've got a note." He gestured in the direction of Kluge's house, and started to look angry.

"This guy not only writes a note, he programs the fucking thing into his computer, complete with special effects straight out of Pac-Man.

"Now, I know people do crazy things. I've seen enough of them. But when I heard the computer playing a hymn, that's when I knew this was murder. Tell you the truth, Mr. Apfel, I don't think you did it. There must be two dozen motives for murder in that printout. Maybe he was blackmailing people around here. Maybe that's how he bought all those machines. And people with that amount of drugs usually die violently. I've got a lot of work to do on this one, and I'll find who did it." He mumbled something about not leaving town, and that he'd see me later, and left.

"Vic . . . " Hal said. I looked at him.

"About that printout," he finally said. "I'd appreciate it . . . well, they said they'd keep it confidential. If you know what I mean." He had eyes like a basset hound. I'd never noticed that before.

"Hal, if you'll just go home, you have nothing to worry about from me."

He nodded, and scuttled for the door.

"I don't think any of that will get out," he said.

It all did, of course.

It probably would have even without the letters that began arriving a few days after Kluge's death, all postmarked Trenton, New Jersey, all computer-generated from a machine no one was ever able to trace. The letters detailed the matters Kluge had mentioned in his will.

I didn't know about any of that at the time. I spent the rest of the day after Hal's departure lying in my bed, under the electric blanket. I couldn't get my feet warm. I got up only to soak in the tub or to make a sandwich.

Reporters knocked on the door but I didn't answer. On the second day I called a criminal lawyer—Martin Abrams, the first in the book—and retained him. He told me they'd probably call me down to the police station for questioning. I told him I wouldn't go, popped two Dilantin, and sprinted for the bed.

A couple of times I heard sirens in the neighborhood. Once I heard a shouted argument down the street. I resisted the temptation to look. I'll admit I was a little curious, but you know what happened to the cat.

I kept waiting for Osborne to return, but he didn't. The days turned into a week. Only two things of interest happened in that time.

The first was a knock on my door. This was two days after Kluge's death. I looked through the curtains and saw a silver Ferrari parked at the curb. I couldn't see who was on the porch, so I asked who it was.

"My names's Lisa Foo," she said. "You asked me to drop by."

"I certainly don't remember it."

"Isn't this Charles Kluge's house?"

"That's next door."

"Oh. Sorry."

I decided I ought to warn her Kluge was dead, so I opened the door. She turned around and smiled at me. It was blinding.

Where does one start in describing Lisa Foo? Remember when the newspapers used to run editorial cartoons of Hirohito and Tojo, when the *Times* used the word "Jap" without embarrassment? Little guys with faces wide as footballs, ears like jug handles, thick glasses, two big rabbity buck teeth, and pencil-thin moustaches . . .

Leaving out only the moustache, she was a dead ringer for a

cartoon Tojo. She had the glasses, and the ears, and the teeth. But her teeth had braces, like piano keys wrapped in barbed wire. And she was five-eight or five-nine and couldn't have weighed more than a hundred and ten. I'd have said a hundred, but added five pounds each for her breasts, so improbably large on her scrawny frame that all I could read of the message on her T-shirt was "POCK LIVE." It was only when she turned sideways that I saw the esses before and after.

She thrust out a slender hand.

"Looks like I'm going to be your neighbor for a while," she said. "At least until we get that dragon's lair next door straightened out." If she had an accent, it was San Fernando Valley.

"That's nice."

"Did you know him? Kluge, I mean. Or at least that's what he called himself."

"You don't think that was his name?"

"I doubt it. 'Klug' means clever in German. And it's hacker slang for being tricky. And he sure was a tricky bugger. Definitely some glitches in the wetware." She tapped the side of her head meaningfully. "Viruses and phantoms and demons jumping out every time they try to key in, software rot, bit buckets overflowing onto the floor . . ."

She babbled on in that vein for a time. It might as well have been Swahili.

"Did you say there were demons in his computers?"

"That's right."

"Sounds like they need an exorcist."

She jerked her thumb at her chest and showed me another half-acre of teeth.

"That's me. Listen, I gotta go. Drop in and see me anytime."

The second interesting event of the week happened the next day. My bank statement arrived. There were three deposits listed. The first was the regular check from the V.A., for $487.00. The second was for $392.54, interest on the money my parents had left me fifteen years ago.

The third deposit had come in on the twentieth, the day Charles Kluge died. It was for $700,083.04.

A few days later Hal Lanier dropped by.

"Boy, what a week," he said. Then he flopped down on the couch and told me all about it.

There had been a second death on the block. The letters had stirred up a lot of trouble, especially with the police going house to house questioning everyone. Some people had confessed to things when they were sure the cops were closing in on them. The woman who used to entertain salesmen while her husband was at work had admitted her infidelity, and the guy had shot her. He was in the County Jail. That was the worst incident, but there had been others, from fistfights to rocks thrown through windows. According to Hal, the IRS was thinking of setting up a branch office in the neighborhood, so many people were being audited.

I thought about the seven hundred thousand and eighty-three dollars.

And four cents.

I didn't say anything, but my feet were getting cold.

"I suppose you want to know about me and Betty," he said, at last. I didn't. I didn't want to hear *any* of this, but I tried for a sympathetic expression.

"That's all over," he said, with a satisfied sigh. "Between me and Toni, I mean. I told Betty all about it. It was real bad for a few days, but I think our marriage is stronger for it now." He was quiet for a moment, basking in the warmth of it all. I had kept a straight face under worse provocation, so I trust I did well enough then.

He wanted to tell me all they'd learned about Kluge, and he wanted to invite me over for dinner, but I begged off on both, telling him my war wounds were giving me hell. I just about had him to the door when Osborne knocked on it. There was nothing to do but let him in. Hal stuck around, too.

I offered Osborne coffee, which he gratefully accepted. He looked different. I wasn't sure what it was at first. Same old tired expression . . . no, it wasn't. Most of that weary look had been either an act

or a cop's built-in cynicism. Today it was genuine. The tiredness
had moved from his face to his shoulders, to his hands, to the way
he walked and the way he slumped in the chair. There was a sour
aura of defeat around him.

"Am I still a suspect?" I asked.

"You mean should you call your lawyer? I'd say don't bother. I
checked you out pretty good. That will ain't gonna hold up, so your
motive is pretty half-assed. Way I figure it, every coke dealer in the
Marina had a better reason to snuff Kluge than you." He sighed.
"I got a couple questions. You can answer them or not."

"Give it a try."

"You remember any unusual visitors he had? People coming and
going at night?"

"The only visitors I *ever* recall were deliveries. Post office. Federal
Express, freight companies . . . that sort of thing. I suppose the
drugs could have come in any of those shipments."

"That's what we figure, too. There's no way he was dealing nickel
and dime bags. He must have been a middle man. Ship it in, ship
it out." He brooded about that for a while, and sipped his coffee.

"So are you making any progress?" I asked.

"You want to know the truth? The case is going in the toilet.
We've got too many motives, and not a one of them that works.
As far as we can tell, nobody on the block had the slightest idea
Kluge had all that information. We've checked bank accounts and
we can't find evidence of blackmail. So the neighbors are pretty
much out of the picture. Though if he were alive, most people
around here would like to kill him *now*."

"Damn straight," Hal said.

Osborne slapped his thigh. "If the bastard was alive, *I'd* kill him,"
he said. "But I'm beginning to think he never *was* alive."

"I don't understand."

"If I hadn't seen the goddam body . . ." He sat up a little straighter.
"He said he didn't exist. Well, he practically didn't. PG&E never
heard of him. He's hooked up to their lines and a meter reader
came by every month, but they never billed him for a single kilowatt.

Same with the phone company. He had a whole exchange in that house that was *made* by the phone company, and delivered by them, and installed by them, but they have no record of him. We talked to the guy who hooked it all up. He turned in his records, and the computer swallowed them. Kluge didn't have a bank account anywhere in California, and apparently he didn't need one. We've tracked down a hundred companies that sold things to him, shipped them out, and then either marked his account paid or forgot they ever sold him anything. Some of them have check numbers and account numbers in their books, for accounts or even *banks* that don't exist."

He leaned back in his chair, simmering at the perfidy of it all.

"The only guy we've found who ever heard of him was the guy who delivered his groceries once a month. Little store down on Sepulveda. They don't have a computer, just paper receipts. He paid by check. Wells Fargo accepted them and the checks never bounced. But Wells Fargo never heard of him."

I thought it over. He seemed to expect something of me at this point, so I made a stab at it.

"He was doing all this by computers?"

"That's right. Now, the grocery store scam I understand, almost. But more often than not, Kluge got right into the basic programming of the computers and wiped himself out. The power company was never paid, by check or any other way, because as far as they were concerned, they weren't selling him anything.

"No government agency has ever heard of him. We've checked him with everybody from the post office to the CIA."

"Kluge was probably an alias, right?" I offered.

"Yeah. But the FBI doesn't have his fingerprints. We'll find out who he was, eventually. But it doesn't get us any closer to whether or not he was murdered."

He admitted there was pressure to simply close the felony part of the case, label it suicide, and forget it. But Osborne would not believe it. Naturally, the civil side would go on for some time, as they attempted to track down all Kluge's deceptions.

"It's all up to the dragon lady," Osborne said. Hal snorted.

"Fat chance," Hal said, and muttered something about boat people.

"That girl? She's still over there? Who is she?"

"She's some sort of giant brain from Cal Tech. We called out there and told them we were having problems, and she's what they sent." It was clear from Osborne's face what he thought of any help she might provide.

I finally managed to get rid of them. As they went down the walk I looked over at Kluge's house. Sure enough, Lisa Foo's silver Ferrari was sitting in his driveway.

I had no business going over there. I knew that better than anyone.

So I set about preparing my evening meal. I made a tuna casserole—which is not as bland as it sounds, the way I make it—put it in the oven and went out to the garden to pick the makings for a salad. I was slicing cherry tomatoes and thinking about chilling a bottle of white wine when it occurred to me that I had enough for two.

Since I never do anything hastily, I sat down and thought it over for a while. What finally decided me was my feet. For the first time in a week, they were warm. So I went to Kluge's house.

The front door was standing open. There was no screen. Funny how disturbing that can look, the dwelling wide open and unguarded. I stood on the porch and leaned in, but all I could see was the hallway.

"Miss Foo?" I called. There was no answer.

The last time I'd been here I had found a dead man. I hurried in.

Lisa Foo was sitting on a piano bench before a computer console. She was in profile, her back very straight, her brown legs in lotus position, her fingers poised at the keys as words sprayed rapidly onto the screen in front of her. She looked up and flashed her teeth at me.

"Somebody told me your name was Victor Apfel," she said.

"Yes. Uh, the door was open . . ."

"It's hot," she said, reasonably, pinching the fabric of her shirt

near her neck and lifting it up and down like you do when you're
sweaty. "What can I do for you?"

"Nothing, really." I came into the dimness, and stumbled on
something. It was a cardboard box, the large flat kind used for
delivering a jumbo pizza.

"I was just fixing dinner, and it looks like there's plenty for two,
so I was wondering if you . . ." I trailed off, as I had just noticed
something else. I had thought she was wearing shorts. In fact, all
she had on was the shirt and a pair of pink bikini underpants. This
did not seem to make her uneasy.

". . . would you like to join me for dinner?"

Her smile grew even broader.

"I'd love to," she said. She effortlessly unwound her legs and
bounced to her feet, then brushed past me, trailing the smells of
perspiration and sweet soap. "Be with you in a minute."

I looked around the room again but my mind kept coming back
to her. She liked Pepsi with her pizza; there were dozens of empty
cans. There was a deep scar on her knee and upper thigh. The
ashtrays were empty . . . and the long muscles of her calves bunched
strongly as she walked. Kluge must have smoked, but Lisa didn't,
and she had fine, downy hairs in the small of her back just visible
in the green computer light. I heard water running in the bathroom
sink, I looked at a yellow notepad covered with the kind of pen-
manship I hadn't seen in decades, and smelled soap and remembered tawny brown skin and an easy stride.

She appeared in the hall, wearing cut-off jeans, sandals, and a
new T-shirt. The old one had advertised BURROUGHS OFFICE
SYSTEMS. This one featured Mickey Mouse and Snow White's
Castle and smelled of fresh bleached cotton. Mickey's ears were laid
back on the upper slopes of her incongruous breasts.

I followed her out the door. Tinkerbell twinkled in pixie dust
from the back of her shirt.

"I like this kitchen," she said.

You don't really look at a place until someone says something
like that.

The kitchen was a time capsule. It could have been lifted bodily from an issue of *Life* in the early fifties. There was the hump-shouldered Frigidaire, of a vintage when that word had been a generic term, like kleenex or coke. The counter tops were yellow tile, the sort that's only found in bathrooms these days. There wasn't an ounce of Formica in the place. Instead of a dishwasher I had a wire rack and a double sink. There was no electric can opener, Cuisinart, trash compacter, or microwave oven. The newest thing in the whole room was a fifteen-year-old blender.

I'm good with my hands. I like to repair things.

"This bread is terrific," she said.

I had baked it myself. I watched her mop her plate with a crust, and she asked if she might have seconds.

I understand cleaning one's plate with bread is bad manners. Not that I cared; I do it myself. And other than that, her manners were impeccable. She polished off three helpings of my casserole and when she was done the plate hardly needed washing. I had a sense of ravenous appetite barely held in check.

She settled back in her chair and I re-filled her glass with white wine.

"Are you sure you wouldn't like some more peas?"

"I'd bust." She patted her stomach contentedly. "Thank you so much, Mister Apfel. I haven't had a home-cooked meal in ages."

"You can call me Victor."

"I just love American food."

"I didn't know there was such a thing. I mean, not like Chinese or . . . you *are* American, aren't you?" She just smiled. "What I mean—"

"I know what you meant, Victor. I'm a citizen, but not native-born. Would you excuse me for a moment? I know it's impolite to jump right up, but with these braces I find I have to brush *instantly* after eating."

I could hear her as I cleared the table. I ran water in the sink and started doing the dishes. Before long she joined me, grabbed a dish towel, and began drying the things in the rack, over my protests.

"You live alone here?" she asked.

"Yes. Have ever since my parents died."

"Ever married? If it's none of my business, just say so."

"That's all right. No, I never married."

"You do pretty good for not having a woman around."

"I've had a lot of practice. Can I ask you a question?"

"Shoot."

"Where are you from? Taiwan?"

"I have a knack for languages. Back home, I spoke pidgin American, but when I got here I cleaned up my act. I also speak rotten French, illiterate Chinese in four or five varieties, gutter Vietnamese, and enough Thai to holler, 'Me wanna see American Consul, pretty-damn-quick, you!' "

I laughed. When she said it, her accent was thick.

"I been here eight years now. You figured out where home is?"

"Vietnam?" I ventured.

"The sidewalks of Saigon, fer shure. Or Ho Chi Minh's Shitty, as the pajama-heads re-named it, may their dinks rot off and their butts be filled with jagged punjee-sticks. Pardon my French."

She ducked her head in embarrassment. What had started out light had turned hot very quickly. I sensed a hurt at least as deep as my own, and we both backed off from it.

"I took you for a Japanese," I said.

"Yeah, ain't it a pisser? I'll tell you about it some day. Victor, is that a laundry room through that door there? With an electric washer?"

"That's right."

"Would it be too much trouble if I did a load?"

It was no trouble at all. She had seven pairs of faded jeans, some with the legs cut away, and about two dozen T-shirts. It could have been a load of boy's clothing except for the frilly underwear.

We went into the backyard to sit in the last rays of the setting sun, then she had to see my garden. I'm quite proud of it. When I'm well, I spend four or five hours a day working out there, year-round, usually in the morning hours. You can do that in southern California. I have a small greenhouse I built myself.

She loved it, though it was not in its best shape. I had spent most of the week in bed or in the tub. As a result, weeds were sprouting here and there.

"We had a garden when I was little," she said. "And I spent two years in a rice paddy."

"That must be a lot different than this."

"Damn straight. Put me off rice for *years.*"

She discovered an infestation of aphids, so we squatted down to pick them off. She had that double-jointed Asian peasant's way of sitting that I remembered so well and could never imitate. Her fingers were long and narrow, and soon the tips of them were green from squashed bugs.

We talked about this and that. I don't remember quite how it came up, but I told her I had fought in Korea. I learned she was twenty-five. It turned out we had the same birthday, so some months back I had been exactly twice her age.

The only time Kluge's name came up was when she mentioned how she liked to cook. She hadn't been able to at Kluge's house.

"He has a freezer in the garage full of frozen dinners," she said. "He had one plate, one fork, one spoon, and one glass. He's got the best microwave oven on the market. And that's *it,* man. Ain't nothing else in his kitchen at *all.*" She shook her head, and executed an aphid. "He was one weird dude."

When her laundry was done it was late evening, almost dark. She loaded it into my wicker basket and we took it out to the clothesline. It got to be a game. I would shake out a T-shirt and study the picture or message there. Sometimes I got it, and sometimes I didn't. There were pictures of rock groups, a map of Los Angeles, Star Trek tie-ins . . . a little of everything.

"What's the L5 Society?" I asked her.

"Guys that want to build these great big farms in space. I asked 'em if they were gonna grow rice, and they said they didn't think it was the best crop for zero gee, so I bought the shirt."

"How many of these things do you have?"

"Wow, it's gotta be four or five hundred. I usually wear 'em two or three times and then put them away."

I picked up another shirt, and a bra fell out. It wasn't the kind of bra girls wore when I was growing up. It was very sheer, though somehow functional at the same time.

"You like, Yank?" Her accent was very thick. "You oughtta see my sister!"

I glanced at her, and her face fell.

"I'm sorry, Victor," she said. "You don't have to blush." She took the bra from me and clipped it to the line.

She must have mis-read my face. True, I had been embarrassed, but I was also pleased in some strange way. It had been a long time since anybody had called me anything but Victor or Mr. Apfel.

The next day's mail brought a letter from a law firm in Chicago. It was about the seven hundred thousand dollars. The money had come from a Delaware holding company which had been set up in 1933 to provide for me in my old age. My mother and father were listed as the founders. Certain long-term investments had matured, resulting in my recent windfall. The amount in my bank was *after* taxes.

It was ridiculous on the face of it. My parents had never had that kind of money. I didn't want it. I would have given it back if I could find out who Kluge had stolen it from.

I decided that, if I wasn't in jail this time next year, I'd give it all to some charity. Save the Whales, maybe, or the L5 Society.

I spent the morning in the garden. Later I walked to the market and bought some fresh ground beef and pork. I was feeling good as I pulled my purchases home in my fold-up wire basket. When I passed the silver Ferrari I smiled.

She hadn't come to get her laundry. I took it off the line and folded it, then knocked on Kluge's door.

"It's me. Victor."

"Come on in, Yank."

She was where she had been before, but decently dressed this time. She smiled at me, then hit her forehead when she saw the laundry basket. She hurried to take it from me.

"I'm sorry, Victor. I meant to get this—"

"Don't worry about it," I said. "It was no trouble. And it gives me the chance to ask if you'd like to dine with me again."

Something happened to her face which she covered quickly. Perhaps she didn't like "American" food as much as she professed to. Or maybe it was the cook.

"Sure, Victor, I'd love to. Let me take care of this. And why don't you open those drapes? It's like a tomb in here."

She hurried away. I glanced at the screen she had been using. It was blank, but for one word: intercourse-p. I assumed it was a typo.

I pulled the drapes open in time to see Osborne's car park at the curb. Then Lisa was back, wearing a new T-shirt. This one said A CHANGE OF HOBBIT, and had a picture of a squat, hairy-footed creature. She glanced out the window and saw Osborne coming up the walk.

"I say, Watson," she said. "It's Lestrade of the Yard. Do show him in."

That wasn't nice of her. He gave me a suspicious glance as he entered. I burst out laughing. Lisa sat on the piano bench, poker-faced. She slumped indolently, one arm resting near the keyboard.

"Well, Apfel," Osborne started. "We've finally found out who Kluge really was."

"Patrick William Gavin," Lisa said.

Quite a time went by before Osborne was able to close his mouth. Then he opened it right up again.

"How the hell did you find that out?"

She lazily caressed the keyboard beside her.

"Well, of course I got it when it came into your office this morning. There's a little stoolie program tucked away in your computer that whispers in my ear every time the name Kluge is mentioned. But I didn't need that. I figured it out five days ago."

"Then why the . . . why didn't you tell me?"

"You didn't ask me."

They glared at each other for a while. I had no idea what events had led up to this moment, but it was quite clear they didn't like each other even a little bit. Lisa was on top just now, and seemed to be enjoying it. Then she glanced at her screen, looked surprised, and quickly tapped a key. The word that had been there vanished. She gave me an inscrutable glance, then faced Osborne again.

"If you recall, you brought me in because all your own guys were getting was a lot of crashes. This system was brain-damaged when I got here, practically catatonic. Most of it was down and your guys couldn't get it up." She had to grin at that.

"You decided I couldn't do any worse than your guys were doing. So you asked me to try and break Kluge's codes without frying the system. Well, I did it. All you had to do was come by and interface and I would have downloaded N tons of wallpaper right in your lap."

Osborne listened quietly. Maybe he even knew he had made a mistake.

"What did you get? Can I see it now?"

She nodded, and pressed a few keys. Words started to fill her screen, and one close to Osborne. I got up and read Lisa's terminal.

It was a brief bio of Kluge/Gavin. He was about my age, but while I was getting shot at in a foreign land, he was cutting a swath through the infant computer industry. He had been there from the ground up, working at many of the top research facilities. It surprised me that it had taken over a week to identify him.

"I compiled this anecdotally," Lisa said, as we read. "The first thing you have to realize about Gavin is that he exists nowhere in any computerized information system. So I called people all over the country—interesting phone system he's got, by the way; it generates a new number for each call, and you can't call back or trace it—and started asking who the top people were in the fifties and sixties. I got a lot of names. After that, it was a matter of finding out who no longer existed in the files. He faked his death in 1967. I located one account of it in a newspaper file. Everybody I talked to who had known him knew of his death. There is a paper birth certificate in Florida. That's the only other evidence I found of him. He was the only guy so many people in the field knew who left no mark on the world. That seemed conclusive to me."

Osborne finished reading, then looked up.

"All right, Ms. Foo. What else have you found out?"

"I've broken some of his codes. I had a piece of luck, getting into a basic rape-and-plunder program he'd written to attack *other* people's programs, and I've managed to use it against a few of his own. I've unlocked a file of passwords with notes on where they came from. And I've learned a few of his tricks. But it's the tip of the iceberg."

She waved a hand at the silent metal brains in the room.

"What I haven't gotten across to anyone is just what this *is*. This is the most devious electronic weapon ever devised. It's armored like a battleship. It has to be; there's a lot of very slick programs out there that grab an invader and hang on like a terrier. If they ever got this far Kluge could deflect them. But usually they never even knew they'd been burgled. Kluge'd come in like a cruise missile, low and fast and twisty. And he'd route his attack through a dozen cut-offs.

"He had a lot of advantages. Big systems these days are heavily protected. People use passwords and very sophisticated codes. But Kluge helped *invent* most of them. You need a damn good lock to keep out a locksmith. He helped *install* a lot of the major systems. He left informants behind, hidden in the software. If the codes were changed, the computer *itself* would send the information to a safe system that Kluge could tap later. It's like you buy the biggest, meanest, best-trained watchdog you can. And that night, the guy who *trained* the dog comes in, pats him on the head, and robs you blind."

There was a lot more in that vein. I'm afraid that when Lisa began talking about computers, ninety percent of my head shut off.

"I'd like to know something, Osborne," Lisa said.

"What would that be?"

"What is my status here? Am I supposed to be solving your crime for you, or just trying to get this system back to where a competent user can deal with it?"

Osborne thought it over.

"What worries me," she added, "is that I'm poking around in a lot of restricted data banks. I'm worried about somebody knocking on the door and handcuffing me. *You* ought to be worried, too. Some of these agencies wouldn't like a homicide cop looking into their affairs."

Osborne bridled at that. Maybe that's what she intended.

"What do I have to do?" he snarled. "Beg you to stay?"

"No. I just want your authorization. You don't have to put it in writing. Just say you're behind me."

"Look. As far as L.A. County and the State of California are concerned, this house doesn't exist. There is no lot here. It doesn't appear in the assessor's records. This place is in a legal limbo. If anybody can authorize you to use this stuff, it's me, because I believe a murder was committed in it. So you just keep doing what you've been doing."

"That's not much of a commitment," she mused.

"It's all you're going to get. Now, what else have you got?"

She turned to her keyboard and typed for a while. Pretty soon a printer started, and Lisa leaned back. I glanced at her screen. It said: osculate posterior-p. I remembered that osculate meant kiss. Well, these people have their own language. Lisa looked up at me and grinned.

"Not you," she said, quietly. *"Him."*

I hadn't the faintest notion of what she was talking about.

Osborne got his printout and was ready to leave. Again, he couldn't resist turning at the door for final orders.

"If you find anything to indicate he didn't commit suicide, let me know."

"Okay. He didn't commit suicide."

Osborne didn't understand for a moment.

"I want proof."

"Well, I have it, but you probably can't use it. He didn't write that ridiculous suicide note."

"How do you know that?"

"I knew that my first day here. I had the computer list the program. Then I compared it to Kluge's style. No *way* he could have written it. It's tighter'n a bug's ass. Not a spare line in it. Kluge didn't pick his alias for nothing. You know what it means?"

"Clever," I said.

"Literally. But it means . . . a Rube Goldberg device. Something overly complex. Something that works, but for the wrong reason. You 'kluge around' bugs in a program. It's the hacker's vaseline."

"So?" Osborne wanted to know.

"So Kluge's programs were really crocked. They were full of bells and whistles he never bothered to clean out. He was a genius, and his programs worked, but you wonder why they did. Routines so bletcherous they'd make your skin crawl. Real crufty bagbiters. But good programming's so rare, even his diddles were better than most people's super-moby hacks."

I suspect Osborne understood about as much of that as I did.

"So you base your opinion on his programming style."

"Yeah. Unfortunately, it's gonna be ten years or so before that's admissable in court, like graphology or fingerprints. But if you know anything about programming you can look at it and see it. Somebody else wrote that suicide note—somebody damn good, by the way. That program called up his last will and testament as a sub-routine. And he definitely *did* write that. It's got his fingerprints all over it. He spent the last five years spying on the neighbors as a hobby. He tapped into military records, school records, work records, tax files, and bank accounts. And he turned every telephone for three blocks into a listening device. He was one hell of a snoop."

"Did he mention anywhere why he did that?" Osborne asked.

"I think he was more than half crazy. Possibly he was suicidal. He sure wasn't doing himself any good with all those pills he took. But he was preparing himself for death, and Victor was the only one he found worthy of leaving it all to. I'd have *believed* he committed suicide if not for that note. But he didn't write it. I'll swear to that."

We eventually got rid of him, and I went home to fix the dinner. Lisa joined me when it was ready. Once more she had a huge appetite.

I fixed lemonade and we sat on my small patio and watched evening gather around us.

I woke up in the middle of the night, sweating. I sat up, thinking it out, and I didn't like my conclusions. So I put on my robe and slippers and went over to Kluge's.

The front door was open again. I knocked anyway. Lisa stuck her head around the corner.

"Victor? Is something wrong?"

"I'm not sure," I said. "May I come in?"

She gestured, and I followed her into the living room. An open can of Pepsi sat beside her console. Her eyes were red as she sat on her bench.

"What's up?" she said, and yawned.

"You should be asleep, for one thing," I said.

She shrugged, and nodded.

"Yeah. I can't seem to get in the right phase. Just now I'm in day mode. But Victor, I'm used to working odd hours, and long hours, and you didn't come over here to lecture me about that, did you?"

"No. You say Kluge was murdered."

"He didn't write his suicide note. That seems to leave murder."

"I was wondering why someone would kill him. He never left the house, so it was for something he did here with his computers. And now you're . . . well, I don't know *what* you're doing, frankly, but you seem to be poking into the same things. Isn't there a danger the same people will come after you?"

"People?" She raised an eyebrow.

I felt helpless. My fears were not well-formed enough to make sense.

"I don't know . . . you mentioned agencies . . ."

"You notice how impressed Osborne was with that? You think there's some kind of conspiracy Kluge tumbled to, or you think the CIA killed him because he found out too much about something, or—"

"I don't know, Lisa. But I'm worried the same thing could happen to you."

Surprisingly, she smiled at me.

"Thank you so much, Victor. I wasn't going to admit it to Osborne, but I've been worried about that, too."

"Well, what are you going to do?"

"I want to stay here and keep working. So I gave some thought to what I could do to protect myself. I decided there wasn't anything."

"Surely there's something."

"Well, I got a gun, if that's what you mean. But think about it. Kluge was offed in the middle of the day. Nobody saw anybody enter or leave the house. So I asked myself, who can walk into a house in broad daylight, shoot Kluge, program that suicide note, and walk away, leaving no traces he'd ever been there?"

"Somebody very good."

"Goddam good. So good there's not much chance one little gook's gonna be able to stop him if he decides to waste her."

She shocked me, both by her words and by her apparent lack of concern for her own fate. But she had said she was worried.

"Then you have to stop this. Get out of here."

"I won't be pushed around that way," she said. There was a tone of finality to it. I thought of things I might say, and rejected them all.

"You could at least . . . lock your front door," I concluded, lamely.

She laughed, and kissed my cheek.

"I'll do that, Yank. And I appreciate your concern. I really do."

I watched her close the door behind me, listened to her lock it, then trudged through the moonlight toward my house. Halfway there I stopped. I could suggest she stay in my spare bedroom. I could offer to stay with her at Kluge's.

No, I decided. She would probably take that the wrong way.

I was back in bed before I realized, with a touch of chagrin and more than a little disgust at myself, that she had every reason to take it the wrong way.

And me exactly twice her age.

I spent the morning in the garden, planning the evening's menu. I have always liked to cook, but dinner with Lisa had rapidly become the high point of my day. Not only that, I was already taking it for granted. So it hit me hard, around noon, when I looked out the front and saw her car gone.

I hurried to Kluge's front door. It was standing open. I made a quick search of the house. I found nothing until the master bedroom, where her clothes were stacked neatly on the floor.

Shivering, I pounded on the Laniers' front door. Betty answered, and immediately saw my agitation.

"The girl at Kluge's house," I said. "I'm afraid something's wrong. Maybe we'd better call the police."

"What happened?" Betty asked, looking over my shoulder. "Did she call you? I see she's not back yet."

"Back?"

"I saw her drive away about an hour ago. That's quite a car she has."

Feeling like a fool, I tried to make nothing of it, but I caught a look in Betty's eye. I think she'd have liked to pat me on the head. It made me furious.

But she'd left her clothes, so surely she was coming back.

I kept telling myself that, then went to run a bath, as hot as I could stand it.

When I answered the door she was standing there with a grocery bag in each arm and her usual blinding smile on her face.

"I wanted to do this yesterday but I forgot until you came over, and I know I should have asked first, but then I wanted to surprise you, so I just went to get one or two items you didn't have in your garden and a couple of things that weren't in your spice rack . . ."

She kept talking as we unloaded the bags in the kitchen. I said nothing. She was wearing a new T-shirt. There was a big V, and under it a picture of a screw, followed by a hyphen and a small case "p." I thought it over as she babbled on. V, screw-p. I was determined not to ask what it meant.

"Do you like Vietnamese cooking?"

I looked at her, and finally realized she was very nervous.

"I don't know," I said. "I've never had it. But I like Chinese, and Japanese, and Indian. I like to try new things." The last part was a lie, but not as bad as it might have been. I do try new recipes, and my tastes in food are catholic. I didn't expect to have much trouble with southeast Asian cuisine.

"Well, when I get through you *still* won't know," she laughed. "My momma was half-Chinese. So what you're gonna get here is a mongrel meal." She glanced up, saw my face, and laughed.

"I forgot. You've been to Asia. No, Yank, I ain't gonna serve any dog meat."

There was only one intolerable thing, and that was the chopsticks. I used them for as long as I could, then put them aside and got a fork.

"I'm sorry," I said. "Chopsticks happen to be a problem for me."

"You use them very well."

"I had plenty of time to learn how."

It was very good, and I told her so. Each dish was a revelation, not quite like anything I had ever had. Toward the end, I broke down halfway.

"Does the V stand for victory?" I asked.

"Maybe."

"Beethoven? Churchill? World War Two?"

She just smiled.

"Think of it as a challenge, Yank."

"Do I frighten you, Victor?"

"You did at first."

"It's my face, isn't it?"

"It's a generalized phobia of Orientals. I suppose I'm a racist. Not because I want to be."

She nodded slowly, there in the dark. We were on the patio again, but the sun had gone down a long time ago. I can't recall what we had talked about for all those hours. It had kept us busy, anyway.

"I have the same problem," she said.

"Fear of Orientals?" I had meant it as a joke.

"Of Cambodians." She let me take that in for a while, then went on. "When Saigon fell, I fled to Cambodia. It took me two years with stops when the Khmer Rouge put me in labor camps. I'm lucky to be alive, really."

"I thought they called it Kampuchea now."

She spat. I'm not even sure she was aware she had done it.

"It's the People's Republic of Syphilitic Dogs. The North Koreans treated you very badly, didn't they, Victor?"

"That's right."

"Koreans are pus suckers." I must have looked surprised, because she chuckled.

"You Americans feel so guilty about racism. As if you had invented it and nobody else—except maybe the South Africans and the Nazis—had ever practiced it as heinously as you. And you can't tell one yellow face from another, so you think of the yellow races as one homogeneous block. When in fact orientals are among the most racist peoples on the earth. The Vietnamese have hated the Cambodians for a thousand years. The Chinese hate the Japanese. The Koreans hate everybody. And *everybody* hates the 'ethnic Chinese.' The Chinese are the Jews of the East."

"I've heard that."

She nodded, lost in her own thoughts.

"And I hate all Cambodians," she said, at last. "Like you, I don't wish to. Most of the people who suffered in the camps were Cambodians. It was the genocidal leaders, the Pol Pot scum, who I should hate." She looked at me. "But sometimes we don't get a lot of choice about things like that, do we, Yank?"

The next day I visited her at noon. It had cooled down, but was still warm in her dark den. She had not changed her shirt.

She told me a few things about computers. When she let me try some things on the keyboard I quickly got lost. We decided I needn't plan on a career as a computer programmer.

One of the things she showed me was called a telephone modem, whereby she could reach other computers all over the world. She "interfaced" with someone at Stanford who she had never met, and who she knew only as "Bubble Sorter." They typed things back and forth at each other.

At the end, Bubble Sorter wrote "bye-p." Lisa typed T.

"What's T?" I asked.

"True. Means yes, but yes would be too straightforward for a hacker."

"You told me what a byte is. What's a byep?"

She looked up at me seriously.

"It's a question. Add p to a word, and make it a question. So bye-p means Bubble Sorter was asking if I wanted to log out. Sign off."

I thought that over.

"So how would you translate 'osculate posterior-p'?"

" 'You wanna kiss my ass?' But remember, that was for Osborne."

I looked at her T-shirt again, then up to her eyes, which were quite serious and serene. She waited, hands folded in her lap.

Intercourse-p.

"Yes," I said. "I would."

She put her glasses on the table and pulled her shirt over her head.

We made love in Kluge's big waterbed.

I had a certain amount of performance anxiety—it had been a long, *long* time. After that, I was so caught up in the touch and smell and taste of her that I went a little crazy. She didn't seem to mind.

At last we were done, and bathed in sweat. She rolled over, stood, and went to the window. She opened it, and a breath of air blew over me. Then she put one knee on the bed, leaned over me, and got a pack of cigarettes from the bedside table. She lit one.

"I hope you're not allergic to smoke," she said.

"No. My father smoked. But I didn't know you did."

"Only afterwards," she said, with a quick smile. She took a deep drag. "Everybody in Saigon smoked, I think." She stretched out on her back beside me and we lay like that, soaking wet, holding hands.

She opened her legs so one of her bare feet touched mine. It seemed enough contact. I watched the smoke rise from her right hand.

"I haven't felt warm in thirty years," I said. "I've been hot, but I've never been warm. I feel warm now."

"Tell me about it," she said.

So I did, as much as I could, wondering if it would work this time. At thirty years remove, my story does not sound so horrible. We've seen so much in that time. There were people in jails at that very moment, enduring conditions as bad as any I encountered. The paraphernalia of oppression is still pretty much the same. Nothing physical happened to me that would account for thirty years lived as a recluse.

"I *was* badly injured," I told her. "My skull was fractured. I still have . . . problems from that. Korea can get very cold, and I was never warm enough. But it was the other stuff. What they call brainwashing now.

"We didn't know what it was. We couldn't understand that even after a man had told them all he knew they'd keep on at us. Keeping us awake. Disorienting us. Some guys signed confessions, made up all sorts of stuff, but even that wasn't enough. They'd just keep on at you.

"I never did figure it out. I guess I couldn't understand an evil that big. But when they were sending us back and some of the prisoners wouldn't go . . . they really didn't *want* to go, they really believed . . ."

I had to pause there. Lisa sat up, moved quietly to the end of the bed, and began massaging my feet.

"We got a taste of what the Vietnam guys got, later. Only for us it was reversed. The G.I.'s were heroes, and the prisoners were . . ."

"You didn't break," she said. It wasn't a question.

"No, I didn't."

"That would be worse."

I looked at her. She had my foot pressed against her flat belly, holding me by the heel while her other hand massaged my toes.

"The country was shocked," I said. "They didn't understand what brainwashing was. I tried telling people how it was. I thought they were looking at me funny. After a while, I stopped talking about it. And I didn't have anything else to talk about.

"A few years back the Army changed its policy. Now they don't expect you to withstand psychological conditioning. It's understood you can say anything or sign anything."

She just looked at me, kept massaging my foot, and nodded slowly. Finally she spoke.

"Cambodia was hot," she said. "I kept telling myself when I finally got to the U.S. I'd live in Maine or someplace, where it snowed. And I did go to Cambridge, but I found out I didn't like snow."

She told me about it. The last I heard, a million people had died over there. It was a whole country frothing at the mouth and snapping at anything that moved. Or like one of those sharks you read about that, when its guts are ripped out, bends in a circle and starts devouring itself.

She told me about being forced to build a pyramid of severed heads. Twenty of them working all day in the hot sun finally got it ten feet high before it collapsed. If any of them stopped working, their own heads were added to the pile.

"It didn't mean anything to me. It was just another job. I was pretty crazy by then. I didn't start to come out of it until I got across the Thai border."

That she had survived it at all seemed a miracle. She had gone through more horror than I could imagine. And she had come through it in much better shape. It made me feel small. When I was her age, I was well on my way to building the prison I have lived in ever since. I told her that.

"Part of it is preparation," she said, wryly. "What you expect out of life, what your life has been so far. You said it yourself. Korea was new to you. I'm not saying I was ready for Cambodia, but my life up to that point hadn't been what you'd call sheltered. I hope you haven't been thinking I made a living in the streets by selling apples."

She kept rubbing my feet, staring off into scenes I could not see.

"How old were you when your mother died?"

"She was killed during Tet, 1968. I was ten."

"By the Viet Cong?"

"Who knows? Lot of bullets flying, lot of grenades being thrown."

She sighed, dropped my foot, and sat there, a scrawny Buddha without a robe.

"You ready to do it again, Yank?"

"I don't think I can, Lisa. I'm an old man."

She moved over me and lowered herself with her chin just below my sternum, settling her breasts in the most delicious place possible.

"We'll see," she said, and giggled. "There's an alternative sex act I'm pretty good at, and I'm pretty sure it would make you a young man again. But I haven't been able to do it for about a year on account of these." She tapped her braces. "It'd be sort of like sticking it in a buzz saw. So now I do this instead. I call it 'touring the silicone valley.' " She started moving her body up and down, just a few inches at a time. She blinked innocently a couple times, then laughed.

"At last, I can see you," she said. "I'm awfully myopic."

I let her do that for a while, then lifted my head.

"Did you say silicone?"

"Uh-huh. You didn't think they were real, did you?"

I confessed that I had.

"I don't think I've ever been so happy with anything I ever bought. Not even the car."

"Why did you?"

"Does it bother you?"

It didn't, and I told her so. But I couldn't conceal my curiosity.

"Because it was safe to. In Saigon I was always angry that I never developed. I could have made a good living as a prostitute, but I was always too tall, too skinny, and too ugly. Then in Cambodia I was lucky. I managed to pass for a boy some of the time. If not for that I'd have been raped a lot more than I was. And in Thailand I knew I'd get to the West one way or another, and when I got there, I'd get the best car there was, eat anything I wanted any time I wanted to, and purchase the best tits money could buy. You can't imagine what the West looks like from the camps. A place where you can buy tits!"

She looked down between them, then back at my face.

"Looks like it was a good investment," she said.

"They do seem to work okay," I had to admit.

We agreed that she would spend the nights at my house. There were certain things she had to do at Kluge's, involving equipment that had to be physically loaded, but many things she could do with a remote terminal and an armload of software. So we selected one of Kluge's best computers and about a dozen peripherals and installed her at a cafeteria table in my bedroom.

I guess we both knew it wasn't much protection if the people who got Kluge decided to get her. But I know I felt better about it, and I think she did, too.

The second day she was there a delivery van pulled up outside, and two guys started unloading a king-size waterbed. She laughed and laughed when she saw my face.

"Listen, you're not using Kluge's computers to—"

"Relax, Yank. How'd you think I could afford a Ferrari?"

"I've been curious."

"If you're really good at writing software you can make a lot of money. I own my own company. But every hacker picks up tricks here and there. I used to run a few Kluge scams, myself."

"But not anymore?"

She shrugged. "Once a thief, always a thief, Victor. I told you I couldn't make ends meet selling my bod."

Lisa didn't need much sleep.

We got up at seven, and I made breakfast every morning. Then we would spend an hour or two working in the garden. She would go to Kluge's and I'd bring her a sandwich at noon, then drop in on her several times during the day. That was for my own peace of mind; I never stayed more than a minute. Sometime during the afternoon I would shop or do household chores, then at seven one of us would cook dinner. We alternated. I taught her "American" cooking, and she taught me a little of everything. She complained about the lack of vital ingredients in American markets. No dogs, of course, but she claimed to know great ways of preparing monkey, snake, and rat. I never knew how hard she was pulling my leg, and didn't ask.

After dinner she stayed at my house. We would talk, make love, bathe.

She loved my tub. It is about the only alteration I have made in the house, and my only real luxury. I put it in—having to expand the bathroom to do so—in 1975, and never regretted it. We would soak for twenty minutes or an hour, turning the jets and bubblers on and off, washing each other, giggling like kids. Once we used bubble bath and made a mountain of suds four feet high, then destroyed it, splashing water all over the place. Most nights she let me wash her long black hair.

She didn't have any bad habits—or at least none that clashed with mine. She was neat and clean, changing her clothes twice a day and never so much as leaving a dirty glass on the sink. She never left a mess in the bathroom. Two glasses of wine was her limit.

I felt like Lazarus.

Osborne came by three times in the next two weeks. Lisa met him at Kluge's and gave him what she had learned. It was getting to be quite a list.

"Kluge once had an account in a New York bank with nine *trillion* dollars in it," she told me after one of Osborne's visits. "I think he did it just to see if he could. He left it in for one day, took the interest and fed it to a bank in the Bahamas, then destroyed the principal. Which never existed anyway."

In return, Osborne told her what was new on the murder investigation—which was nothing—and on the status of Kluge's property, which was chaotic. Various agencies had sent people out to look the place over. Some FBI men came, wanting to take over the investigation. Lisa, when talking about computers, had the power to cloud men's minds. She did it first by explaining exactly what she was doing, in terms so abstruse that no one could understand her. Sometimes that was enough. If it wasn't, if they started to get tough, she just moved out of the driver's seat and let them try to handle Kluge's contraption. She let them watch in horror as dragons leaped out of nowhere and ate up all the data on a disc, then printed "You Stupid Putz!" on the screen.

"I'm cheating them," she confessed to me. "I'm giving them stuff I *know* they're gonna step in, because I already stepped in it myself. I've lost about forty percent of the data Kluge had stored away. But the others lose a hundred percent. You ought to see their faces when Kluge drops a logic bomb into their work. That second guy threw a three thousand dollar printer clear across the room. Then tried to bribe me to be quiet about it."

When some federal agency sent out an expert from Stanford, and he seemed perfectly content to destroy everything in sight in the firm belief that he was *bound* to get it right sooner or later, Lisa showed him how Kluge entered the IRS main computer in Washington and neglected to mention how Kluge had gotten out. The guy tangled with some watchdog program. During his struggles, it seemed he had erased all the tax records from the letter S down into the W's. Lisa let him think that for half an hour.

"I thought he was having a heart attack," she told me. "All the blood drained out of his face and he couldn't talk. So I showed him where I had—with my usual foresight—arranged for that data to be recorded, told him how to put it back where he found it, and how to pacify the watchdog. He couldn't get out of that house fast enough. Pretty soon he's gonna realize you *can't* destroy that much information with anything short of dynamite because of the backups and the limits of how much can be running at any one time. But I don't think he'll be back."

"It sounds like a very fancy video game," I said.

"It is, in a way. But it's more like Dungeons and Dragons. It's an endless series of closed rooms with dangers on the other side. You don't dare take it a step at a time. You take it a *hundredth* of a step at a time. Your questions are like, 'Now this isn't a question, but if it entered my mind to *ask* this question—which I'm not about

to do—concerning what might happen if I looked at this door here—
and I'm not touching it, I'm not even in the next room—what do
you suppose you might do?' And the program crunches on that,
decides if you fulfilled the conditions for getting a great big cream
pie in the face, then either throws it or allows as how it *might* just
move from step A to step A Prime. Then you say, 'Well, maybe I
am looking at that door.' And sometimes the program says 'You
looked, you looked, you dirty crook!' And the fireworks start."

Silly as all that sounds, it was very close to the best explanation
she was ever able to give me about what she was doing.

"Are you telling everything, Lisa?" I asked her.

"Well not, *every*thing. I didn't mention the four cents."

Four cents? Oh my god.

"Lisa, I didn't want that, I didn't ask for it, I wish he'd
never—"

"Calm down, Yank. It's going to be all right."

"He kept records of all that, didn't he?"

"That's what I spend most of my time doing. Decoding his records."

"How long have you known?"

"About the seven hundred thousand dollars? It was in the first
disc I cracked."

"I just want to give it back."

She thought that over, and shook her head.

"Victor, it'd be more dangerous to get rid of it now than it would
be to keep it. It was imaginary money at first. But now it's got a
history. The IRS thinks it knows where it came from. The taxes are
paid on it. The State of Delaware is convinced that a legally char-
tered corporation disbursed it. An Illinois law firm has been paid
for handling it. Your bank has been paying you interest on it. I'm
not saying it would be impossible to go back and wipe all that
out, but I wouldn't like to try. I'm good, but I don't have Kluge's
touch."

"How could he *do* all that? You say it was imaginary money.
That's not the way I thought money worked. He could just pull it
out of thin air?"

Lisa patted the top of her computer console, and smiled at me. "This is money, Yank," she said, and her eyes glittered.

At night she worked by candlelight so she wouldn't disturb me. That turned out to be my downfall. She typed by touch, and needed the candle only to locate software.

So that's how I'd go to sleep every night, looking at her slender body bathed in the glow of the candle. I was always reminded of melting butter dripping down a roasted ear of corn. Golden light on golden skin.

Ugly, she had called herself. Skinny. It was true she was thin. I could see her ribs when she sat with her back impossibly straight, her tummy sucked in, her chin up. She worked in the nude these days, sitting in lotus position. For long periods she would not move, her hands lying on her thighs, then she would poise, as if to pound the keys. But her touch was light, almost silent. It looked more like yoga than programming. She said she went into a meditative state for her best work.

I had expected a bony angularity, all sharp elbows and knees. She wasn't like that. I had guessed her weight ten pounds too low, and still didn't know where she put it. But she was soft and rounded, and strong beneath.

No one was ever going to call her face glamorous. Few would even go so far as to call her pretty. The braces did that, I think. They caught the eye and held it, drawing attention to that unsightly jumble.

But her skin was wonderful. She had scars. Not as many as I had expected. She seemed to heal quickly, and well.

I thought she was beautiful.

I had just completed my nightly survey when my eye was caught by the candle. I looked at it, then tried to look away.

Candles do that sometimes. I don't know why. In still air, with the flame perfectly vertical, they begin to flicker. The flame leaps up then squats down, up and down, up and down, brighter and brighter in regular rhythm, two or three beats to the second—

—and I tried to call out to her, wishing the candle would stop its regular flickering, but already I couldn't speak—

—I could only gasp, and I tried once more, as hard as I could, to yell, to scream, to tell her not to worry, and felt the nausea building . . .

I tasted blood. I took an experimental breath, did not find the smells of vomit, urine, feces. The overhead lights were on.

Lisa was on her hands and knees leaning over me, her face very close. A tear dropped on my forehead. I was on the carpet, on my back.

"Victor, can you hear me?"

I nodded. There was a spoon in my mouth. I spit it out.

"What happened? Are you going to be all right?"

I nodded again, and struggled to speak.

"You just lie there. The ambulance is on its way."

"No. Don't need it."

"Well, it's on its way. You just take it easy and—"

"Help me up."

"Not yet. You're not ready."

She was right. I tried to sit up, and fell back quickly. I took deep breaths for a while. Then the doorbell rang.

She stood up and started to the door. I just managed to get my hand around her ankle. Then she was leaning over me again, her eyes as wide as they would go.

"What is it? What's wrong now?"

"Get some clothes on," I told her. She looked down at herself, surprised.

"Oh. Right."

She got rid of the ambulance crew. Lisa was a lot calmer after she made coffee and we were sitting at the kitchen table. It was one o'clock, and I was still pretty rocky. But it hadn't been a bad one.

I went to the bathroom and got the bottle of Dilantin I'd hidden when she moved in. I let her see me take one.

"I forgot to do this today," I told her.

"It's because you hid them. That was stupid."

"I know." There must have been something else I could have said. It didn't please me to see her look hurt. But she was hurt because I wasn't defending myself against her attack, and that was a bit too complicated for me to dope out just after a grand mal.

"You can move out if you want to," I said. I was in rare form. So was she. She reached across the table and shook me by the shoulders. She glared at me.

"I won't take a lot more of that kind of shit," she said, and I nodded, and began to cry.

She let me do it. I think that was probably best. She could have babied me, but I do a pretty good job of that myself.

"How long has this been going on?" she finally said. "Is that why you've stayed in your house for thirty years?"

I shrugged. "I guess it's part of it. When I got back they operated, but it just made it worse."

"Okay. I'm mad at you because you didn't tell me about it, so I didn't know what to do. I want to stay, but you'll have to tell me how. Then I won't be mad anymore."

I could have blown the whole thing right there. I'm amazed I didn't. Through the years I'd developed very good methods for doing things like that. But I pulled through when I saw her face. She really did want to stay. I didn't know why, but it was enough.

"The spoon was a mistake," I said. "If there's time, and if you can do it without risking your fingers, you could jam a piece of cloth in there. Part of a sheet, or something. But nothing hard." I explored my mouth with a finger. "I think I broke a tooth."

"Serves you right," she said. I looked at her, and smiled, then we were both laughing. She came around the table and kissed me, then sat on my knee.

"The biggest danger is drowning. During the first part of the seizure, all my muscles go rigid. That doesn't last long. Then they all start contracting and relaxing at random. It's *very* strong."

"I know. I watched, and I tried to hold you."

"Don't do that. Get me on my side. Stay behind me, and watch out for flailing arms. Get a pillow under my head if you can. Keep me away from things I could injure myself on." I looked her square in the eye. "I want to emphasize this. Just *try* to do all those things. If I'm getting too violent, it's better you stand off to the side. Better for both of us. If I knock you out, you won't be able to help me if I start strangling on vomit."

I kept looking at her eyes. She must have read my mind, because she smiled slightly.

"Sorry, Yank. I am not freaked out. I mean, like, it's totally gross, you know, and it barfs me out to the max, you could—"

"—gag me with a spoon, I know. Okay, right, I know I was dumb. And that's about it. I might bite my tongue or the inside of my cheek. Don't worry about it. There is one more thing."

She waited, and I wondered how much to tell her. There wasn't a lot she could do, but if I died on her I didn't want her to feel it was her fault.

"Sometimes I have to go to the hospital. Sometimes one seizure will follow another. If that keeps up for too long, I won't breathe, and my brain will die of oxygen starvation."

"That only takes about five minutes," she said, alarmed.

"I know. It's only a problem if I start having them frequently, so we could plan for it if I do. But if I don't come out of one, start having another right on the heels of the first, or if you can't detect any breathing for three or four minutes, you'd better call an ambulance."

"Three or four minutes? You'd be dead before they got here."

"It's that or live in a hospital. I don't like hospitals."

"Neither do I."

The next day she took me for a ride in her Ferrari. I was nervous about it, wondering if she was going to do crazy things. If anything, she was too slow. People behind her kept honking. I could tell she hadn't been driving long from the exaggerated attention she put into every movement.

"A Ferrari is wasted on me, I'm afraid," she confessed at one point. "I never drive it faster than fifty-five."

We went to an interior decorator in Beverly Hills and she bought a low-watt gooseneck lamp at an outrageous price.

I had a hard time getting to sleep that night. I suppose I was afraid of having another seizure, though Lisa's new lamp wasn't going to set it off.

Funny about seizures. When I first started having them, everyone called them fits. Then, gradually, it was seizures, until fits began to sound dirty.

I guess it's a sign of growing old, when the language changes on you.

There were rafts of new words. A lot of them were for things that didn't even exist when I was growing up. Like software. I always visualized a limp wrench.

"What got you interested in computers, Lisa?" I asked her.

She didn't move. Her concentration when sitting at the machine was pretty damn good. I rolled onto my back and tried to sleep.

"It's where the power is, Yank." I looked up. She had turned to face me.

"Did you pick it all up since you got to America?"

"I had a head start. I didn't tell you about my Captain, did I?"

"I don't think you did."

"He was strange. I knew that. I was about fourteen. He was an American, and he took an interest in me. He got me a nice apartment in Saigon. And he put me in school."

She was studying me, looking for a reaction. I didn't give her one.

"He was surely a pedophile, and probably had homosexual tendencies, since I looked so much like a skinny little boy."

Again the wait. This time she smiled.

"He was good to me. I learned to read well. From there on, anything is possible."

"I didn't actually ask you about your Captain. I asked why you got interested in computers."

"That's right. You did."

"Is it just a living?"

"It started that way. It's the future, Victor."

"God knows I've read that enough times."

"It's true. It's already here. It's power, if you know how to use it. You've seen what Kluge was able to do. You can make money with one of these things. I don't mean earn it, I mean *make* it, like if you had a printing press. Remember Osborne mentioned that Kluge's house didn't exist? Did you think what that means?"

"That he wiped it out of the memory banks."

"That was the first step. But the lot exists in the county plat books, wouldn't you think? I mean, this country hasn't *entirely* given up paper."

"So the county really does have a record of that house."

"No. That page was torn out of the records."

"I don't get it. Kluge never left the house."

"Oldest way in the world, friend. Kluge looked through the L.A.P.D. files until he found a guy known as Sammy. He sent him a cashier's check for a thousand dollars, along with a letter saying he could earn twice that if he'd go to the hall of records and do something. Sammy didn't bite, and neither did McGee, or Molly Unger. But Little Billy Phipps did, and he got a check just like the letter said, and he and Kluge had a wonderful business relationship for many years. Little Billy drives a new Cadillac now, and hasn't the faintest notion who Kluge was or where he lived. It didn't matter to Kluge how much he spent. He just pulled it out of thin air."

I thought that over for a while. I guess it's true that with enough money you can do just about anything, and Kluge had all the money in the world.

"Did you tell Osborne about Little Billy?"

"I erased that disc, just like I erased your seven hundred thousand. You never know when you might need somebody like Little Billy."

"You're not afraid of getting into trouble over it?"

"Life is risk, Victor. I'm keeping the best stuff for myself. Not because I intend to use it, but because if I ever needed it badly and didn't have it, I'd feel like such a fool."

She cocked her head and narrowed her eyes, which made them practically disappear.

"Tell me something, Yank. Kluge picked you out of all your neighbors because you'd been a Boy Scout for thirty years. How do you react to what I'm doing?"

"You're cheerfully amoral, and you're a survivor, and you're basically decent. And I pity anybody who gets in your way."

She grinned, stretched, and stood up.

" 'Cheerfully amoral.' I like that." She sat beside me, making a great sloshing in the bed. "You want to be amoral again?"

"In a little bit." She started rubbing my chest. "So you got into computers because they were the wave of the future. Don't you ever worry about them . . . I don't know, I guess it sounds corny . . . do you think they'll take over?"

"Everybody thinks that until they start to use them," she said. "You've got to realize just how stupid they are. Without programming they are good for nothing, literally. Now, what I do believe is that the people who *run* the computers will take over. They already have. That's why I study them."

"I guess that's not what I meant. Maybe I can't say it right."

She frowned. "Kluge was looking into something. He'd been eavesdropping in artificial intelligence labs, and reading a lot of neurological research. I think he was trying to find a common thread."

"Between human brains and computers?"

"Not quite. He was thinking of computers and neurons. Brain cells." She pointed to her computer. "That thing, or any other computer, is light-years away from being a human brain. It can't generalize, or infer, or categorize, or invent. With good programming it can appear to do some of those things, but it's an illusion.

"There's an old speculation about what would happen if we finally built a computer with as many transistors as the human brain has neurons. Would there be a self-awareness? I think that's baloney. A transistor isn't a neuron, and a quintillion of them aren't any better than a dozen.

"So Kluge—who seems to have felt the same way—started looking into the possible similarities between a neuron and an 8-bit computer. That's why he had all that consumer junk sitting around his house, those Trash-80's and Atari's and TI's and Sinclair's, for chrissake. He was used to *much* more powerful instruments. He ate up the home units like candy."

"What did he find out?"

"Nothing, it looks like. An 8-bit unit is more complex than a neuron, and no computer is in the same galaxy as an organic brain. But see, the words get tricky. I said an Atari is more complex than a neuron, but it's hard to really compare them. It's like comparing a direction with a distance, or a color with a mass. The units are different. Except for one similarity."

"What's that?"

"The connections. Again, it's different, but the concept of networking is the same. A neuron is connected to a lot of others. There are trillions of them, and the way messages pulse through them determines what we are and what we think and what we remember. And with that computer I can reach a million others. It's bigger than the human brain, really, because the information in that network is more than all humanity could cope with in a million years. It reaches from Pioneer Ten, out beyond the orbit of Pluto, right into every living room that has a telephone in it. With that computer you can tap tons of data that has been collected but nobody's even had the time to look at.

"That's what Kluge was interested in. The old 'critical mass computer' idea, the computer that becomes aware, but with a new angle. Maybe it wouldn't be the size of the computer, but the *number* of computers. There used to be thousands of them. Now there's millions. They're putting them in cars. In wristwatches. Every home has several, from the simple timer on a microwave oven up to a video game or home terminal. Kluge was trying to find out if critical mass could be reached that way."

"What did he think?"

"I don't know. He was just getting started." She glanced down at me. "But you know what, Yank? I think you've reached critical mass while I wasn't looking."

"I think you're right." I reached for her.

———

Lisa liked to cuddle. I didn't, at first, after fifty years of sleeping alone. But I got to like it pretty quickly.

That's what we were doing when we resumed the conversation we had been having. We just lay in each other's arms and talked about things. Nobody had mentioned love yet, but I knew I loved her. I didn't know what to do about it, but I would think of something.

"Critical mass," I said. She nuzzled my neck, and yawned.

"What about it?"

"What would it be like? It seems like it would be such a vast intelligence. So quick, so omniscient. God-like."

"Could be."

"Wouldn't it . . . run our lives? I guess I'm asking the same questions I started off with. Would it take over?"

She thought about it for a long time.

"I wonder if there would be anything to take over. I mean, why should it care? How could we figure what its concerns would be? Would it want to be worshipped, for instance? I doubt it. Would it want to 'rationalize all human behavior, to eliminate all emotion,' as I'm sure some sci-fi film computer must have told some damsel in distress in the 'fifties.

"You can use a word like awareness, but what does it mean? An amoeba must be aware. Plants probably are. There may be a level of awareness in a neuron. Even in an integrated circuit chip. We don't even know what our own awareness really is. We've never been able to shine a light on it, dissect it, figure out where it comes from or where it goes when we're dead. To apply human values to a thing like this hypothetical computer-net consciousness would be pretty stupid. But I don't see how it could interact with human awareness at all. It might not even notice us, any more than we notice cells in our bodies, or neutrinos passing through us, or the vibrations of the atoms in the air around us."

So she had to explain what a neutrino was. One thing I always provided her with was an ignorant audience. And after that, I pretty much forgot about our mythical hyper-computer.

———

"What about your Captain?" I asked, much later.

"Do you really want to know, Yank?" she mumbled, sleepily.

"I'm not afraid to know."

She sat up and reached for her cigarettes. I had come to know she sometimes smoked them in times of stress. She had told me she smoked after making love, but that first time had been the only time. The lighter flared in the dark. I heard her exhale.

"My Major, actually. He got a promotion. Do you want to know his name?"

"Lisa, I don't want to know any of it if you don't want to tell me. But if you do, what I want to know is did he stand by you."

"He didn't marry me, if that's what you mean. When he knew he had to go, he said he would, but I talked him out of it. Maybe it was the most noble thing I ever did. Maybe it was the most stupid.

"It's no accident I look Japanese. My grandmother was raped in '42 by a Jap soldier of the occupation. She was Chinese, living in Hanoi. My mother was born there. They went south after Dien Bien Phu. My grandmother died. My mother had it hard. Being Chinese was tough enough, but being half Chinese and half Japanese was worse. My father was half French and half Annamese. Another bad combination. I never knew him. But I'm sort of a capsule history of Vietnam."

The end of her cigarette glowed brighter once more.

"I've got one grandfather's face and the other grandfather's height. With tits by Goodyear. About all I missed was some American genes, but I was working on that for my children.

"When Saigon was falling I tried to get to the American Embassy. Didn't make it. You know the rest, until I got to Thailand, and when I finally got Americans to notice me, it turned out my Major was still looking for me. He sponsored me over here, and I made it in time to watch him die of cancer. Two months I had with him, all of it in the hospital."

"My god." I had a horrible thought. "That wasn't the war, too, was it? I mean, the story of your life—"

"—is the rape of Asia. No, Victor. Not that war, anyway. But he was one of those guys who got to see atom bombs up close, out

in Nevada. He was too Regular Army to complain about it, but I
think he knew that's what killed him."
"Did you love him?"
"What do you want me to say? He got me out of hell."
Again the cigarette flared, and I saw her stub it out.
"No," she said. "I didn't love him. He knew that. I've never
loved anybody. He was very dear, very special to me. I would have
done almost anything for him. He was fatherly to me." I felt her
looking at me in the dark. "Aren't you going to ask how old he
was?"
"Fiftyish," I said.
"On the nose. Can I ask you something?"
"I guess it's your turn."
"How many girls have you had since you got back from Korea?"
I held up my hand and pretended to count on my fingers.
"One," I said, at last.
"How many before you went?"
"One. We broke up before I left for the war."
"How many in Korea?"
"Nine. All at Madame Park's jolly whorehouse in Pusan."
"So you've made love to one white and ten Asians. I bet none
of the others were as tall as me."
"Korean girls have fatter cheeks, too. But they all had your eyes."
She nuzzled against my chest, took a deep breath, and sighed.
"We're a hell of a pair, aren't we?"
I hugged her, and her breath came again, hot on my chest. I
wondered how I'd lived so long without such a simple miracle as
that.
"Yes. I think we really are."

Osborne came by again about a week later. He seemed subdued.
He listened to the things Lisa had decided to give him without much
interest. He took the printout she handed him, and promised to
turn it over to the departments that handled those things. But he
didn't get up to leave.

"I thought I ought to tell you, Apfel," he said, at last. "The Gavin case has been closed."

I had to think a moment to remember Kluge's real name had been Gavin.

"The coroner ruled suicide a long time ago. I was able to keep the case open quite a while on the strength of my suspicions." He nodded toward Lisa. "And on what she said about the suicide note. But there was just no evidence at all."

"It probably happened quickly," Lisa said. "Somebody caught him, tracked him back—it can be done; Kluge was lucky for a long time—and did him the same day."

"You don't think it was suicide?" I asked Osborne.

"No. But whoever did it is home free unless something new turns up."

"I'll tell you if it does," Lisa said.

"That's something else," Osborne said. "I can't authorize you to work over there any more. The county's taken possession of house and contents."

"Don't worry about it," Lisa said, softly.

There was a short silence as she leaned over to shake a cigarette from the pack on the coffee table. She lit it, exhaled, and leaned back beside me, giving Osborne her most inscrutable look. He sighed.

"I'd hate to play poker with you, lady," he said. "What do you mean, 'Don't worry about it'?"

"I bought the house four days ago. And its contents. If anything turns up that would help you re-open the murder investigation, I will let you know."

Osborne was too defeated to get angry. He studied her quietly for a while.

"I'd like to know how you swung that."

"I did nothing illegal. You're free to check it out. I paid good cash money for it. The house came onto the market. I got a good price at the Sheriff's sale."

"How'd you like it if I put my best men on the transaction? See

if they can dig up some funny money? Maybe fraud. How about I
get the FBI in to look it all over?"

She gave him a cool look.

"You're welcome to. Frankly, Detective Osborne, I could have
stolen that house, Griffith Park, and the Harbor Freeway and I don't
think you could have caught me."

"So where does that leave me?"

"Just where you were. With a closed case, and a promise from
me."

"I don't like you having all that stuff, if it can do the things you
say it can do."

"I didn't expect you would. But that's not your department, is it?
The county owned it for a while, through simple confiscation. They
didn't know what they had, and they let it go."

"Maybe I can get the Fraud detail out here to confiscate your
software. There's criminal evidence on it."

"You could try that," she agreed.

They stared at each other for a while. Lisa won. Osborne rubbed
his eyes and nodded. Then he heaved himself to his feet and slumped
to the door.

Lisa stubbed out her cigarette. We listened to him going down
the walk.

"I'm surprised he gave up so easy," I said. "Or did he? Do you
think he'll try a raid?"

"It's not likely. He knows the score."

"Maybe you could tell it to me."

"For one thing, it's not his department, and he knows it."

"Why did you buy the house?"

"You ought to ask *how*."

I looked at her closely. There was a gleam of amusement behind
the poker face.

"Lisa. What did you do?"

"That's what Osborne asked himself. He got the right answer,
because he understands Kluge's machines. And he knows how things
get done. It was no accident that house going on the market, and

no accident I was the only bidder. I used one of Kluge's pet councilmen."

"You bribed him?"

She laughed, and kissed me.

"I think I finally managed to shock you, Yank. That's gotta be the biggest difference between me and a native-born American. Average citizens don't spend much on bribes over here. In Saigon, everybody bribes."

"Did you bribe him?"

"Nothing so indelicate. One has to go in the back door over here. Several entirely legal campaign contributions appeared in the accounts of a State Senator, who mentioned a certain situation to someone, who happened to be in the position to do legally what I happened to want done." She looked at me askance. "Of *course* I bribed him, Victor. You'd be amazed to know how cheaply. Does that bother you?"

"Yes," I admitted. "I don't like bribery."

"I'm indifferent to it. It happens, like gravity. It may not be admirable, but it gets things done."

"I assume you covered yourself."

"Reasonably well. You're never entirely covered with a bribe, because of the human element. The councilman might geek if they got him in front of a grand jury. But they won't, because Osborne won't pursue it. That's the second reason he walked out of here without a fight. *He* knows how the world wobbles, he knows what kind of force I now possess, and he knows he can't fight it."

There was a long silence after that. I had a lot to think about, and I didn't feel good about most of it. At one point Lisa reached for the pack of cigarettes, then changed her mind. She waited for me to work it out.

"It is a terrific force, isn't it," I finally said.

"It's frightening," she agreed. "Don't think it doesn't scare me. Don't think I haven't had fantasies of being superwoman. Power is an awful temptation, and it's not easy to reject. There's so much I could do."

"Will you?"

"I'm not talking about stealing things, or getting rich."

"I didn't think you were."

"This is political power. But I don't know how to wield it . . . it sounds corny, but to use it for good. I've seen so much evil come from good intentions. I don't think I'm wise enough to do any good. And the chances of getting torn up like Kluge did are large. But I'm not wise enough to walk away from it. I'm still a street urchin from Saigon, Yank. I'm smart enough not to use it unless I have to. But I can't give it away, and I can't destroy it. Is that stupid?"

I didn't have a good answer for that one. But I had a bad feeling.

My doubts had another week to work on me. I didn't come to any great moral conclusions. Lisa knew of some crimes, and she wasn't reporting them to the authorities. That didn't bother me much. She had at her fingertips the means to commit more crimes, and that bothered me a lot. Yet I really didn't think she planned to do anything. She was smart enough to use the things she had only in a defensive way—but with Lisa that could cover a lot of ground.

When she didn't show up for dinner one evening, I went over to Kluge's and found her busy in the living room. A nine-foot section of shelving had been cleared. The dics and tapes were stacked on a table. She had a big plastic garbage can and a magnet the size of a softball. I watched her wave a tape near the magnet, then toss it in the garbage can, which was almost full. She glanced up, did the same operation with a handful of discs, then took off her glasses and wiped her eyes.

"Feel any better now, Victor?" she asked.

"What do you mean? I feel fine."

"No you don't. And I haven't felt right, either. It hurts me to do it, but I have to. You want to go get the other trash can?"

I did, and helped her pull more software from the shelves.

"You're not going to wipe it all, are you?"

"No. I'm wiping records, and . . . something else."

"Are you going to tell me what?"

"There are things it's better not to know," she said, darkly.

I finally managed to convince her to talk over dinner. She had said little just eating and shaking her head. But she gave in.

"Rather dreary, actually," she said. "I've been probing around some delicate places the last couple days. These are places Kluge visited at will, but they scare the hell out of me. Dirty places. Places where they know things I thought I'd like to find out."

She shivered, and seemed reluctant to go on.

"Are you talking about military computers? The CIA?"

"The CIA is where it starts. It's the easiest. I've looked around at NORAD—that's the guys who get to fight the next war. It makes me shiver to see how easy Kluge got in there. He cobbled up a way to start World War Three, just as an exercise. That's one of the things we just erased. The last two days I was nibbling around the edges of the big boys. The Defense Intelligence Agency and the National Security . . . something. DIA and NSA. Each of them is bigger than the CIA. Something knew I was there. Some watchdog program. As soon as I realized that I got out quick, and I've spent the last five hours being sure it didn't follow me. And now I'm sure, and I've destroyed all that, too."

"You think they're the ones who killed Kluge?"

"They're surely the best candidates. He had tons of their stuff. I know he helped design the biggest installations at NSA, and he'd been poking around in there for years. One false step is all it would take."

"Did you get it all? I mean, are you sure?"

"I'm sure they didn't track me. I'm not sure I've destroyed all the records. I'm going back now to take a last look."

"I'll go with you."

We worked until well after midnight. Lisa would review a tape or a disc, and if she was in any doubt, toss it to me for the magnetic treatment. At one point, simply because she was unsure, she took the magnet and passed it in front of an entire shelf of software.

It was amazing to think about it. With that one wipe she had randomized billions of bits of information. Some of it might not exist anywhere else in the world. I found myself confronted by even harder questions. Did she have the right to do it? Didn't knowledge exist for everyone? But I confess I had little trouble quelling my protests. Mostly I was happy to see it go. The old reactionary in me found it easier to believe There Are Things We Are Not Meant To Know.

We were almost through when her monitor screen began to malfunction. It actually gave off a few hisses and pops, so Lisa stood back from it for a moment, then the screen started to flicker. I stared at it for a while. It seemed to me there was an image trying to form in the screen. Something three-dimensional. Just as I was starting to get a picture of it I happened to glance at Lisa, and she was looking at me. Her face was flickering. She came to me and put her hands over my eyes.

"Victor, you shouldn't look at that."

"It's okay," I told her. And when I said it, it was, but as soon as I had the words out I knew it wasn't. And that is the last thing I remembered for a long time.

I'm told it was a very bad two weeks. I remember very little of it. I was kept under high dosage of drugs, and my few lucid periods were always followed by a fresh seizure.

The first thing I recall clearly was looking up at Doctor Stuart's face. I was in a hospital bed. I later learned it was in Cedars-Sinai, not the Veterans' Hospital. Lisa had paid for a private room.

Stuart put me through the usual questions. I was able to answer them, though I was very tired. When he was satisfied as to my conditon he finally began to answer some of my questions. I learned how long I had been there, and how it had happened.

"You went into consecutive seizures," he confirmed. "I don't know why, frankly. You haven't been prone to them for a decade. I was thinking you were well under control. But nothing is ever really stable, I guess."

"So Lisa got me here in time."

"She did more than that. She didn't want to level with me at first. It seems that after the first seizure she witnessed she read everything she could find. From that day, she had a syringe and a solution of Valium handy. When she saw you couldn't breathe she injected you with 100 milligrams, and there's no doubt it saved your life."

Stuart and I had known each other a long time. He knew I had no prescription for Valium, though we had talked about it the last time I was hospitalized. Since I lived alone, there would be no one to inject me if I got in trouble.

He was more interested in results than anything else, and what Lisa did had the desired result. I was still alive.

He wouldn't let me have any visitors that day. I protested, but soon was asleep. The next day she came. She wore a new T-shirt. This one had a picture of a robot wearing a gown and mortarboard, and said "Class of 11111000000." It turns out that was 1984 in binary notation.

She had a big smile and said "Hi, Yank!" and as she sat on the bed I started to shake. She looked alarmed and asked if she should call the doctor.

"It's not that," I managed to say. "I'd like it if you just held me."

She took off her shoes and got under the covers with me. She held me tightly. At some point a nurse came in and tried to shoo her out. Lisa gave her profanities in Vietnamese, Chinese, and a few startling ones in English, and the nurse left. I saw Doctor Stuart glance in later.

I felt much better when I finally stopped crying. Lisa's eyes were wet, too.

"I've been here every day," she said. "You look awful, Victor."

"I feel a lot better."

"Well, you look better than you did. But your doctor says you'd better stick around another couple of days, just to make sure."

"I think he's right."

"I'm planning a big dinner for when you get back. You think we should invite the neighbors?"

I didn't say anything for a while. There were so many things we hadn't faced. Just how long could it go on between us? How long before I got sour about being so useless? How long before she got tired of being with an old man? I don't know just when I had started to think of Lisa as a permanent part of my life. And I wondered how I could have thought that.

"Do you want to spend more years waiting in hospitals for a man to die?"

"What do you want, Victor? I'll marry you if you want me to. Or I'll live with you in sin. I prefer sin, myself, but if it'll make you happy—"

"I don't know why you want to saddle yourself with an epileptic old fart."

"Because I love you."

It was the first time she had said it. I could have gone on questioning—bringing up her Major again, for instance—but I had no urge. I'm very glad I didn't. So I changed the subject.

"Did you get the job finished?"

She knew which job I was talking about. She lowered her voice and put her mouth close to my ear.

"Let's don't be specific about it here, Victor. I don't trust any place I haven't swept for bugs. But, to put your mind at ease, I did finish, and it's been a quiet couple of weeks. No one is any wiser, and I'll never meddle in things like that again."

I felt a lot better. I was also exhausted. I tried to conceal my yawns, but she sensed it was time to go. She gave me one more kiss, promising many more to come, and left me.

It was the last time I ever saw her.

At about ten 'clock that evening Lisa went into Kluge's kitchen with a screwdriver and some other tools and got to work on the microwave oven.

The manufacturers of those appliances are very careful to insure they can't be turned on with the door open, as they emit lethal radiation. But with simple tools and a good brain it is possible to circumvent the safety interlocks. Lisa had no trouble with them. About ten minutes after she entered the kitchen she put her head in the oven and turned it on.

It is impossible to say how long she held her head in there. It was long enough to turn her eyeballs to the consistency of boiled eggs. At some point she lost voluntary muscle control and fell to the floor, pulling the microwave down with her. It shorted out, and a fire started.

The fire set off the sophisticated burglar alarm she had installed a month before. Betty Lanier saw the flames and called the fire department as Hal ran across the street and into the burning kitchen. He dragged what was left of Lisa out onto the grass. When he saw what the fire had done to her upper body, and in particular her breasts, he threw up.

She was rushed to the hospital. The doctors there amputated one arm and cut away the frightful masses of vulcanized silicone, pulled all her teeth, and didn't know what to do about the eyes. They put her on a respirator.

It was an orderly who first noticed the blackened and bloody T-shirt they had cut from her. Some of the message was unreadable, but it began, "I can't go on this way anymore . . ."

There is no other way I could have told all that. I discovered it piecemeal, starting with the disturbed look on Doctor Stuart's face when Lisa didn't show up the next day. He wouldn't tell me anything, and I had another seizure shortly after.

The next week is a blur. I remember being released from the hospital, but I don't remember the trip home. Betty was very good to me. They gave me a tranquilizer called Tranxene, and it was even better. I ate them like candy. I wandered in a drugged haze, eating only when Betty insisted, sleeping sitting up in my chair, coming awake not knowing where or who I was. I returned to the prison camp many times. Once I recall helping Lisa stack severed heads.

When I saw myself in the mirror, there was a vague smile on

my face. It was Tranxene, caressing my frontal lobes. I knew that if I was to live much longer, me and Tranxene would have to become very good friends.

I eventually became capable of something that passed for rational thought. I was helped along somewhat by a visit from Osborne. I was trying, at that time, to find reasons to live, and wondered if he had any.

"I'm very sorry," he started off. I said nothing. "This is on my own time," he went on. "The department doesn't know I'm here."

"Was it suicide?" I asked him.

"I brought along a copy of the . . . the note. She ordered it from a shirt company in Westwood, three days before the . . . accident."

He handed it to me, and I read it. I was mentioned, though not by name. I was "the man I love." She said she couldn't cope with my problems. It was a short note. You can't get too much on a T-shirt. I read it through five times, then handed it back to him.

"She told you Kluge didn't write his note. I tell you she didn't write this."

He nodded reluctantly. I felt a vast calm, with a howling nightmare just below it. Praise Tranxene.

"Can you back that up?"

"She saw me in the hospital shortly before the . . . accident. She was full of life and hope. You say she ordered the shirt three days before. I would have felt that. And that note is pathetic. Lisa was never pathetic."

He nodded again.

"Some things I want to tell you. There were no signs of a struggle. Mrs. Lanier is sure no one came in the front. The crime lab went over the whole place and we're sure no one was in there with her. I'd stake my life on the fact that no one entered or left that house. Now, I don't believe it was suicide, either, but do you have any suggestions?"

"The NSA," I said.

I explained about the last things she had done while I was still there. I told him of her fear of the government spy agencies. That was all I had.

"Well, I guess they're the ones who could do a thing like that, if anyone could. But I'll tell you, I have a hard time swallowing it. I don't know why, for one thing. Maybe you believe those people kill like you and I'd swat a fly." His look made it into a question.

"I don't know what I believe."

"I'm not saying they wouldn't kill for national security, or some such shit. But they'd have taken the computers, too. They wouldn't have left her alone, they wouldn't even have let her *near* that stuff after they killed Kluge."

"What you're saying makes sense."

He muttered on about it for quite some time. Eventually I offered him some wine. He accepted thankfully. I considered joining him—it would be a quick way to die—but did not. He drank the whole bottle, and was comfortably drunk when he suggested we go next door and look it over one more time. I was planning on visiting Lisa the next day, and knew I had to start somewhere building myself up for that, so I agreed to go with him.

We inspected the kitchen. The fire had blackened the counters and melted some linoleum, but not much else. Water had made a mess of the place. There was a brown stain on the floor which I was able to look at with no emotion.

So we went back to the living room, and one of the computers was turned on. There was a short message on the screen.

IF YOU WISH TO KNOW MORE
PRESS ENTER ■

"Don't do it," I told him. But he did. He stood, blinking solemnly, as the words wiped themselves out and a new message appeared.

YOU LOOKED

The screen started to flicker and I was in my car, in darkness, with a pill in my mouth and another in my hand. I spit out the pill, and sat for a moment, listening to the old engine ticking over. In my other hand was the plastic pill bottle. I felt very tired, but opened the car door and shut off the engine. I felt my way to the garage door and opened it. The air outside was fresh and sweet. I looked down at the pill bottle and hurried into the bathroom.

When I got through what had to be done there were a dozen pills floating in the toilet that hadn't even dissolved. There were the wasted shells of many more, and a lot of other stuff I won't bother to describe. I counted the pills in the bottle, remembered how many there had been, and wondered if I would make it.

I went over to Kluge's house and could not find Osborne. I was getting tired, but I made it back to my house and stretched out on the couch to see if I would live or die.

The next day I found the story in the paper. Osborne had gone home and blown out the back of his head with his revolver. It was not a big story. It happens to cops all the time. He didn't leave a note.

I got on the bus and rode out to the hospital and spent three hours trying to get in to see Lisa. I wasn't able to do it. I was not a relative and the doctors were quite firm about her having no visitors. When I got angry they were as gentle as possible. It was then I learned the extent of her injuries. Hal had kept the worst from me. None of it would have mattered, but the doctors swore there was nothing left in her head. So I went home.

She died two days later.

She had left a will, to my surprise. I got the house and contents. I picked up the phone as soon as I learned of it, and called a garbage company. While they were on the way I went for the last time into Kluge's house.

The same computer was still on, and it gave the same message.

PRESS ENTER ■

I cautiously located the power switch, and turned it off. I had the garbage people strip the place to the bare walls.

I went over my own house very carefully, looking for anything that was even the first cousin to a computer. I threw out the radio. I sold the car, and refrigerator, and the stove, and the blender, and the electric clock. I drained the waterbed and threw out the heater.

Then I bought the best propane stove on the market, and hunted a long time before I found an old icebox. I had the garage stacked to the ceiling with firewood. I had the chimney cleaned. It would be getting cold soon.

One day I took the bus to Pasadena and established the Lisa Foo Memorial Scholarship fund for Vietnamese refugees and their children. I endowed it with seven hundred thousand eighty-three dollars and four cents. I told them it could be used for any field of study except computer science. I could tell they thought me eccentric.

And I really thought I was safe, until the phone rang.

I thought it over for a long time before answering it. In the end, I knew it would just keep on going until I did. So I picked it up.

For a few seconds there was a dial tone, but I was not fooled. I kept holding it to my ear, and finally the tone turned off. There was just silence. I listened intently. I heard some of those far-off musical tones that live in phone wires. Echoes of conversations taking place a thousand miles away. And something infinitely more distant and cool.

I do not know what they have incubated out there at the NSA. I don't know if they did it on purpose, or if it just happened, or if it even has anything to do with them, in the end. But I know it's out there, because I heard its soul breathing on the wires. I spoke very carefully.

"I do not wish to know any more," I said. "I won't tell anyone anything. Kluge, Lisa, and Osborne all committed suicide. I am just a lonely man, and I won't cause you any trouble."

There was a click, and a dial tone.

Getting the phone taken out was easy. Getting them to remove all the wires was a little harder, since once a place is wired they expect it to be wired forever. They grumbled, but when I started pulling them out myself, they relented, though they warned me it was going to cost.

PG&E was harder. They actually seemed to believe there was a regulation requiring each house to be hooked up to the grid. They were willing to shut off my power—though hardly pleased about it—but they just weren't going to take the wires away from my house. I went up on the roof with an axe and demolished four feet of eaves as they gaped at me. Then they coiled up their wires and went home.

I threw out of all my lamps, all things electrical. Wih hammer, chisel, and handsaw I went to work on the drywall just above the baseboards.

As I stripped the house of wiring I wondered many times why I was doing it. Why was it worth it? I couldn't have very many more years before a final seizure finished me off. Those years were not going to be a lot of fun.

Lisa had been a survivor. She would have known why I was doing this. She had once said I was a survivor, too. I survived the camp. I survived the death of my mother and father and managed to fashion a solitary life. Lisa survived the death of just about everything. No survivor expects to live through it all. But while she was alive, she would have worked to stay alive.

And that's what I did. I got all the wires out of the walls, went over the house with a magnet to see if I had missed any metal, then spent a week cleaning up, fixing the holes I had knocked in the walls, ceiling, and attic. I was amused trying to picture the real-estate agent selling this place after I was gone.

It's a great little house, folks. No electricity . . .

Now I live quietly, as before.

I work in my garden during most of the daylight hours. I've expanded it considerably, and even have things growing in the front yard now.

I live by candlelight, and kerosene lamp. I grow most of what I eat.

It took a long time to taper off the Tranxene and the Dilantin, but I did it, and now take the seizures as they come. I've usually got bruises to show for it.

In the middle of a vast city I have cut myself off. I am not part of the network growing faster than I can conceive. I don't even know if it's dangerous, to ordinary people. It noticed me, and Kluge, and Osborne. And Lisa. It brushed against our minds like I would brush away a mosquito, never noticing I had crushed it. Only I survived.

But I wonder.

It would be very hard . . .

Lisa told me how it can get in through the wiring. There's something called a carrier wave that can move over wires carrying household current. That's why the electricity had to go.

I need water for my garden. There's just not enough rain here in southern California, and I don't know how else I could get the water.

Do you think it could come through the pipes?

New Rose Hotel

WILLIAM GIBSON

William Gibson is this year's Nebula Award winner in the novel category. Neuromancer *is also his first novel and a paperback original. For it to win out over the other very notable nominees is exceptional. A first novel and paperback original had not won since Alexei Panshin's* Rite of Passage *in 1968.* Neuromancer *also won the Philip K. Dick Award, the Australian Ditmar Award, and the Hugo Award.*

Gibson was born in Conway, South Carolina, in 1948 and spent his childhood in southwest Virginia. A U.S. citizen, he has been a resident of Canda since 1970. His first story was published in 1977; later stories have appeared in Universe *and* Omni. *"Burning Chrome," a previous Nebula nominee, is being produced in London as a feature film. His newest novel is* Count Zero.

"New Rose Hotel" is set in the same future as Neuromancer. *Told with a jazzy economy, the story's charged poetic imagery presents a personal view of high-tech corporate espionage in the early decades of the twenty-first century.*

Seven rented nights in this coffin, Sandii. New Rose Hotel. How I want you now. Sometimes I hit you. Replay it so slow and sweet and mean, I can almost feel it. Sometimes I take your little automatic out of my bag, run my thumb down smooth, cheap chrome. Chinese .22, its bore no wider than the dilated pupils of your vanished eyes.

Fox is dead now, Sandii.

Fox told me to forget you.

I remember Fox leaning against the padded bar in the dark lounge of some Singapore hotel, Bencoolen Street, his hands describing different spheres of influence, internal rivalries, the arc of a particular career, a point of weakness he had discovered in the armor of some think tank. Fox was point man in the skull wars, a middleman for corporate crossovers. He was a soldier in the secret skirmishes of the zaibatsus, the multinational corporations that control entire economies.

I see Fox grinning, talking fast, dismissing my ventures into intercorporate espionage with a shake of his head. The Edge, he said, have to find that Edge. He made you hear the capital *E*. The Edge was Fox's grail, that essential fraction of sheer human talent, nontransferable, locked in the skulls of the world's hottest research scientists.

You can't put Edge down on paper, Fox said, can't punch Edge into a diskette.

The money was in corporate defectors.

Fox was smooth, the severity of his dark, French suits offset by a boyish forelock that wouldn't stay in place. I never liked the way the effect was ruined when he stepped back from the bar, his left shoulder skewed at an angle no Paris tailor could conceal. Someone had run him over with a taxi in Berne, and nobody quite knew how to put him together again.

I guess I went with him because he said he was after that Edge.

And somewhere out there, on our way to find the Edge, I found you, Sandii.

The New Rose Hotel is a coffin rack on the ragged fringes of Narita International. Plastic capsules a meter high and three long, stacked like surplus Godzilla teeth in a concrete lot off the main road to the airport. Each capsule has a television mounted flush with the ceiling. I spend whole days watching Japanese game shows and old movies. Sometimes I have your gun in my hand.

Sometimes I can hear the jets, laced into holding patterns over Narita. I close my eyes and imagine the sharp, white contrails fading, losing definition.

You walked into a bar in Yokohama, the first time I saw you. Eurasian, half gaijin, long-hipped and fluid in a Chinese knockoff of some Tokyo designer's original. Dark European eyes, Asian cheekbones. I remember you dumping your purse out on the bed, later, in some hotel room, pawing through your makeup. A crumpled wad of New Yen, dilapidated address book held together with rubber bands, a Mitsubishi bank chip, Japanese passport with a gold chrysanthemum stamped on the cover, and the Chinese .22.

You told me your story. Your father had been an executive in Tokyo, but now he was disgraced, disowned, cast down by Hosaka, the biggest zaibatsu of all. That night your mother was Dutch, and I listened as you spun out those summers in Amsterdam for me, the pigeons in Dam Square like a soft, brown carpet.

I never asked what your father might have done to earn his disgrace. I watched you dress; watched the swing of your dark, straight hair, how it cut the air.

Now Hosaka hunts me.

The coffins of New Rose are racked in recycled scaffolding, steel pipes under bright enamel. Paint flakes away when I climb the ladder, falls with each step as I follow the catwalk. My left hand counts off the coffin hatches, their multilingual decals warning of fines levied for the loss of a key.

I look up as the jets rise out of Narita, passage home, distant now as any moon.

Fox was quick to see how we could use you, but not sharp enough to credit you with ambition. But then he never lay all night with you on the beach at Kamakura, never listened to your nightmares, never heard an entire imagined childhood shift under those stars, shift and roll over, your child's mouth opening to reveal some fresh past, and always the one, you swore, that was really and finally the truth.

I didn't care, holding your hips while the sand cooled against your skin.

Once you left me, ran back to that beach saying you'd forgotten our key. I found it in the door and went after you, to find you ankle deep in surf, your smooth back rigid, trembling; your eyes far away. You couldn't talk. Shivering. Gone. Shaking for different futures and better pasts.

Sandii, you left me here.

You left me all your things.

This gun. Your makeup, all the shadows and blushes capped in plastic. Your Cray microcomputer, a gift from Fox, with a shopping list you entered. Sometimes I play that back, watching each item cross the little silver screen.

A freezer. A fermenter. An incubator. An electrophoresis system with integrated agarose cell and transilluminator. A tissue embedder. A high-performance liquid chromatograph. A flow cytometer. A spectrophotometer. Four gross of borosilicate scintillation vials. A microcentrifuge. And one DNA synthesizer, with in-built computer. Plus software.

Expensive, Sandii, but then Hosaka was footing our bills. Later you made them pay even more, but you were already gone.

Hiroshi drew up that list for you. In bed, probably. Hiroshi Yomiuri. Maas Biolabs GmbH had him. Hosaka wanted him.

He was hot. Edge and lots of it. Fox followed genetic engineers the way a fan follows players in a favorite game. Fox wanted Hiroshi so bad he could taste it.

He'd sent me up to Frankfurt three times before you turned up, just to have a look-see at Hiroshi. Not to make a pass or even to give him a wink and a nod. Just to watch.

Hiroshi showed all the signs of having settled in. He'd found a German girl with a taste for conservative loden and riding boots polished the shade of a fresh chestnut. He'd bought a renovated townhouse on just the right square. He'd taken up fencing and given up kendo.

And everywhere the Maas security teams, smooth and heavy, a rich, clear syrup of surveillance. I came back and told Fox we'd never touch him.

You touched him for us, Sandii. You touched him just right.

Our Hosaka contacts were like specialized cells protecting the parent organism. We were mutagens, Fox and I, dubious agents adrift on the dark side of the intercorporate sea.

When we had you in place in Vienna, we offered them Hiroshi. They didn't even blink. Dead calm in an L.A. hotel room. They said they had to think about it.

Fox spoke the name of Hosaka's primary competitor in the gene game, let it fall out naked, broke the protocol forbidding the use of proper names.

They had to think about it, they said.

Fox gave them three days.

I took you to Barcelona a week before I took you to Vienna. I remember you with your hair tucked back into a gray beret, your high Mongol cheekbones reflected in the windows of ancient shops. Strolling down the Ramblas to the Phoenician harbor, past the glass-roofed Mercado selling oranges out of Africa.

The old Ritz, warm in our room, dark, with all the soft weight of Europe pulled over us like a quilt. I could enter you in your sleep. You were always ready. Seeing your lips in a soft, round O of surprise, your face about to sink into the thick, white pillow—archaic linen of the Ritz. Inside you I imagined all that neon, the crowds surging around Shinjuku Station, wired electric night. You moved that way, rhythm of a new age, dreamy and far from any nation's soil.

When we flew to Vienna, I installed you in Hiroshi's wife's favorite hotel. Quiet, solid, the lobby tiled like a marble chessboard, with brass elevators smelling of lemon oil and small cigars. It was easy to imagine her there, the highlights on her riding boots reflected in polished marble, but we knew she wouldn't be coming along, not this trip.

She was off to some Rhineland spa, and Hiroshi was in Vienna for a conference. When Maas security flowed in to scan the hotel, you were out of sight.

Hiroshi arrived an hour later, alone.

Imagine an alien, Fox once said, who's come here to identify the planet's dominant form of intelligence. The alien has a look, then chooses. What do you think he picks? I probably shrugged.

The zaibatsus, Fox said, the multinationals. The blood of a zaibatsu is information, not people. The structure is independent of the individual lives that comprise it. Corporation as life form.

Not the Edge lecture again, I said.

Maas isn't like that, he said, ignoring me.

Maas was small, fast, ruthless. An atavism. Maas was all Edge.
I remember Fox talking about the nature of Hiroshi's Edge. Ra-
dioactive nucleases, monoclonal antibodies, something to do with
the linkage of proteins, nucleotides . . . Hot, Fox called them, hot
proteins. High-speed links. He said Hiroshi was a freak, the kind
who shatters paradigms, inverts a whole field of science, brings on
the violent revision of an entire body of knowledge. Basic patents,
he said, his throat tight with the sheer wealth of it, with the high,
thin smell of tax-free millions that clung to those two words.

Hosaka wanted Hiroshi, but his Edge was radical enough to worry
them. They wanted him to work in isolation.

I went to Marrakech, to the old city, the Medina. I found a
heroin lab that had been converted to the extraction of pheromones.
I bought it, with Hosaka's money.

I walked the marketplace at Djemaa-el-Fna with a sweating Portuguese businessman, discussing fluorescent lighting and the in-
stallation of ventilated specimen cages. Beyond the city walls, the
high Atlas. Djemaa-el-Fna was thick with jugglers, dancers, story-
tellers, small boys turning lathes with their feet, legless beggars with
wooden bowls under animated holograms advertising French software.

We strolled past bales of raw wool and plastic tubs of Chinese
microchips. I hinted that my employers planned to manufacture
synthetic beta-endorphin. Always try to give them something they
understand.

Sandii, I remember you in Harajuku, sometimes. Close my eyes
in this coffin and I can see you there—all the glitter, crystal maze
of the boutiques, the smell of new clothes. I see your cheekbones
ride past chrome racks of Paris leathers. Sometimes I hold your
hand.

We thought we'd found you. Sandii, but really you'd found us.
Now I know you were looking for us or for someone like us. Fox
was delighted, grinning over our find: such a pretty new tool, bright
as any scalpel. Just the thing to help us sever a stubborn Edge, like
Hiroshi's, from the jealous parent-body of Maas Biolabs.

You must have been searching a long time, looking for a way

out, all those nights down Shinjuku. Nights you carefully cut from
the scattered deck of your past.

My own past had gone down years before, lost with all hands,
no trace. I understood Fox's late-night habit of emptying his wallet,
shuffling through his identification. He'd lay the pieces out in different patterns, rearrange them, wait for a picture to form. I knew
what he was looking for. You did the same thing with your child-
hoods.

In New Rose, tonight, I choose from your deck of pasts.

I choose the original version, the famous Yokohama hotel-room
text, recited to me that first night in bed. I choose the disgraced
father, Hosaka executive. Hosaka. How perfect. And the Dutch
mother, the summers in Amsterdam, the soft blanket of pigeons in
the Dam Square afternoon.

I came in out of the heat of Marrakech into Hilton air conditioning. Wet shirt clinging cold to the small of my back while I
read the message you'd relayed through Fox. You were in all the
way; Hiroshi would leave his wife. It wasn't difficult for you to
communicate with us, even through the clear, tight film of Maas
security; you'd shown Hiroshi the perfect little place for coffee and
kipferl. Your favorite waiter was white haired, kindly, walked with
a limp, and worked for us. You left your messages under the linen
napkin.

All day today I watched a small helicopter cut a tight grid above
this country of mine, the land of my exile, the New Rose Hotel.
Watched from my hatch as its patient shadow crossed the grease-
stained concrete. Close. Very close.

I left Marrakech for Berlin. I met with a Welshman in a bar and
began to arrange for Hiroshi's disappearance.

It would be a complicated business, intricate as the brass gears
and sliding mirrors of Victorian stage magic, but the desired effect
was simple enough. Hiroshi would step behind a hydrogen-cell
Mercedes and vanish. The dozen Maas agents who followed him
constantly would swarm around the van like ants; the Maas security
apparatus would harden around his point of departure like epoxy.

They know how to do business promptly in Berlin. I was even

able to arrange a last night with you. I kept it secret from Fox; he might not have approved. Now I've forgotten the town's name. I knew it for an hour on the autobahn, under a gray Rhenish sky, and forgot it in your arms.

The rain began, sometime toward morning. Our room had a single window, high and narrow, where I stood and watched the rain fur the river with silver needles. Sound of your breathing. The river flowed beneath low, stone arches. The street was empty. Europe was a dead museum.

I'd already booked your flight to Marrakech, out of Orly, under your newest name. You'd be on your way when I pulled the final string and dropped Hiroshi out of sight.

You'd left your purse on the dark, old bureau. While you slept I went through your things, removing anything that might clash with the new cover I'd bought for you in Berlin. I took the Chinese .22, your microcomputer, and your bank chip. I took a new passport, Dutch, from my bag, a Swiss bank chip in the same name, and tucked them into your purse.

My hand brushed something flat. I drew it out, held the thing, a diskette. No labels.

It lay there in the palm of my hand, all that death. Latent, coded, waiting.

I stood there and watched you breathe, watched your breasts rise and fall. Saw your lips slightly parted, and in the jut and fullness of your lower lip, the faintest suggestion of bruising.

I put the diskette back into your purse. When I lay down beside you, you rolled against me, waking, on your breath all the electric night of a new Asia, the future rising in you like a bright fluid, washing me of everything but the moment. That was your magic, that you lived outside of history, all now.

And you knew how to take me there.

For the very last time, you took me.

While I was shaving, I heard you empty your makeup into my bag. I'm Dutch now, you said, I'll want a new look.

Dr. Hiroshi Yomiuri went missing in Vienna, in a quiet street off Singerstrasse, two blocks from his wife's favorite hotel. On a clear afternoon in October, in the presence of a dozen expert witnesses, Dr. Yomiuri vanished.

He stepped through a looking glass. Somewhere, offstage, the oiled play of Victorian clockwork.

I sat in a hotel room in Geneva and took the Welshman's call. It was done, Hiroshi down my rabbit hole and headed for Marrakech. I poured myself a drink and thought about your legs.

Fox and I met in Narita a day later, in a sushi bar in the JAL terminal. He'd just stepped off an Air Maroc jet, exhausted and triumphant.

Loves it there, he said, meaning Hiroshi. Loves her, he said, meaning you.

I smiled. You'd promised to meet me in Shinjuku in a month.

Your cheap, little gun in the New Rose Hotel. The chrome is starting to peel. The machining is clumsy, blurry Chinese stamped into rough steel. The grips are red plastic, molded with a dragon on either side. Like a child's toy.

Fox ate sushi in the JAL terminal, high on what we'd done. The shoulder had been giving him trouble, but he said he didn't care. Money now for better doctors. Money now for everything.

Somehow it didn't seem very important to me, the money we'd gotten from Hosaka. Not that I doubted our new wealth, but that last night with you had left me convinced that it all came to us naturally, in the new order of things, as a function of who and what we were.

Poor Fox. With his blue oxford shirts crisper than ever, his Paris suits darker and richer. Sitting there in JAL, dabbing sushi into a little rectangular tray of green horseradish, he had less than a week to live.

Dark now, and the coffin racks of New Rose are lit all night by floodlights, high on painted metal masts. Nothing here seems to serve its original purpose. Everything is surplus, recycled, even the coffins. Forty years ago these plastic capsules were stacked in Tokyo or Yokohama, a modern convenience for traveling businessmen. Maybe your father slept in one. When the scaffolding was new, it rose around the shell of some mirrored tower on the Ginza, swarmed over by crews of builders.

The breeze tonight brings the rattle of a pachinko parlor, the smell of stewed vegetables from the pushcarts across the road.

I spread crab-flavored krill paste on orange rice crackers. I can hear the planes.

Those last few days in Tokyo, Fox and I had adjoining suites on the fifty-third floor of the Hyatt. No contact with Hosaka. They paid us, then erased us from official corporate memory.

But Fox couldn't let go. Hiroshi was his baby, his pet project. He'd developed a proprietary, almost fatherly, interest in Hiroshi. He loved him for his Edge. So Fox had me keep in touch with my Portuguese businessman in the Medina, who was willing to keep a very partial eye on Hiroshi's lab for us.

When he phoned, he'd phone from a stall in Djemaa-el-Fna, with a background of wailing vendors and Atlas panpipes. Someone was moving security into Marrakech, he told us. Fox nodded. Hosaka.

After less than a dozen calls, I saw the change in Fox, a tension, a look of abstraction. I'd find him at the window, staring down fifty-three floors into the Imperial gardens, lost in something he wouldn't talk about.

Ask him for a more detailed description, he said, after one particular call. He thought a man our contact had seen entering Hiroshi's lab might be Moenner, Hosaka's leading gene man.

That was Moenner, he said, after the next call. Another call and he thought he'd identified Chedanne, who headed Hosaka's protein team. Neither had been seen outside the corporate arcology in over two years.

By then it was obvious that Hosaka's leading researchers were pooling quietly in the Medina, the black executive Lears whispering into the Marrakech airport on carbon-fiber wings. Fox shook his head. He was a professional, a specialist, and he saw the sudden accumulation of all that prime Hosaka Edge in the Medina as a drastic failure in the zaibatsu's tradecraft.

Christ, he said, pouring himself a Black Label, they've got their whole bio section in there right now. One bomb. He shook his head. One granade in the right place at the right time . . .

I reminded him of the saturation techniques Hosaka security was obviously employing. Hosaka had lines to the heart of the Diet, and their massive infiltration of agents into Marrakech could only be taking place with the knowledge and cooperation of the Moroccan government.

Hang it up, I said. It's over. You've sold them Hiroshi. Now forget him.

I know what it is, he said. I know. I saw it once before.

He said that there was a certain wild factor in lab work. The edge of Edge, he called it. When a researcher develops a breakthrough, others sometimes find it impossible to duplicate the first researcher's results. This was even more likely with Hiroshi, whose work went against the conceptual grain of his field. The answer, often, was to fly the breakthrough boy from lab to corporate lab for a ritual laying on of hands. A few pointless adjustments in the equipment, and the process would work. Crazy thing, he said, nobody knows why it works that way, but it does. He grinned.

But they're taking a chance, he said. Bastards told us they wanted to isolate Hiroshi, keep him away from their central research thrust. Balls. Bet your ass there's some kind of power struggle going on in Hosaka research. Somebody big's flying his favorites in and rubbing them all over Hiroshi for luck. When Hiroshi shoots the legs out from under genetic engineering, the Medina crowd's going to be ready.

He drank his scotch and shrugged.

Go to bed, he said. You're right, it's over.

I did go to bed, but the phone woke me. Marrakech again, the white static of a satellite link, a rush of frightened Portuguese.

Hosaka didn't freeze our credit, they caused it to evaporate. Fairy gold. One minute we were millionaires in the world's hardest currency, and the next we were paupers. I woke Fox.

Sandii, he said. She sold out. Maas security turned her in Vienna. Sweet Jesus.

I watched him slit his battered suitcase apart with a Swiss army knife. He had three gold bars glued in there with contact cement. Soft plates, each one proofed and stamped by the treasury of some extinct African government.

I should've seen it, he said, his voice flat.

I said no. I think I said your name.

Forget her, he said. Hosaka wants us dead. They'll assume we crossed them. Get on the phone and check our credit.

Our credit was gone. They denied that either of us had ever had an account.

Haul ass, Fox said.

We ran. Out a service door, into Tokyo traffic, and down into Shinjuku. That was when I understood for the first time the real extent of Hosaka's reach.

Every door was closed. People we'd done business with for two years saw us coming, and I'd see steel shutters slam behind their eyes. We'd get out before they had a chance to reach for the phone. The surface tension of the underworld had been tripled, and everywhere we'd meet that same taut membrane and be thrown back. No chance to sink, to get out of sight.

Hosaka let us run for most of that first day. Then they sent someone to break Fox's back a second time.

I didn't see them do it, but I saw him fall. We were in a Ginza department store an hour before closing, and I saw his arc off that polished mezzanine, down into all the wares of the new Asia.

They missed me somehow, and I just kept running. Fox took the gold with him, but I had a hundred New Yen in my pocket. I ran. All the way to the New Rose Hotel.

Now it's time.

Come with me, Sandii. Hear the neon humming on the road to Narita International. A few late moths trace stop-motion circles around the floodlights that shine on New Rose.

And the funny thing, Sandii, is how sometimes you just don't seem real to me. Fox once said you were ectoplasm, a ghost called up by the extremes of economics. Ghost of the new century, congealing on a thousand beds in the world's Hyatts, the world's Hiltons.

Now I've got your gun in my hand, jacket pocket, and my hand seems so far away. Disconnected.

I remember my Portuguese business friend forgetting his English, trying to get it across in four languages I barely understood, and I thought he was telling me that the Medina was burning. Not the Medina. The brains of Hosaka's best research people. Plague, he was whispering, my businessman, plague and fever and death.

Smart Fox, he put it together on the run. I didn't even have to mention finding the diskette in your bag in Germany.

Someone had reprogrammed the DNA synthesizer, he said. The thing was there for the overnight construction of just the right macromolecule. With its built-in computer and its custom software. Expensive, Sandii. But not as expensive as you turned out to be for Hosaka.

I hope you got a good price from Maas.

The diskette in my hand. Rain on the river. I knew, but I couldn't face it. I put the code for that meningeal virus back into your purse and lay down beside you.

So Moenner died, along with other Hosaka researchers. Including Hiroshi. Chedanne suffered permanent brain damage.

Hiroshi hadn't worried about contamination. The proteins he punched for were harmless. So the synthesizer hummed to itself all night long, building a virus to the specifications of Maas Biolabs GmbH.

Maas. Small, fast, ruthless. All Edge.

The airport road is a long, straight shot. Keep to the shadows.

And I was shouting at that Portuguese voice, I made him tell me what happened to the girl, to Hiroshi's woman. Vanished, he said. The whir of Victorian clockwork.

So Fox had to fall, fall with his three pathetic plates of gold, and snap his spine for the last time. On the floor of a Ginza department store, every shopper staring in the instant before they screamed.

I just can't hate you, baby.

And Hosaka's helicopter is back, no lights at all, hunting on infrared, feeling for body heat. A muffled whine as it turns, a kilometer away, swinging back toward us, toward New Rose. Too fast a shadow, against the glow of Narita.

It's alright, baby. Only please come here. Hold my hand.

The Greening
of Bed-Stuy

FREDERIK POHL

Frederik Pohl has been just about everything a science fiction writer can be: novelist and story writer, magazine and book editor, lecturer, consultant, futurist, and a president of SFWA. He is the complete science fiction professional. He received Nebula awards for the novels Gateway *and* Man Plus *and has also won the American Book Award, the Hugo, and the John W. Campbell Memorial Award. Pohl's many books include* Jem, The Cool War, Black Star Rising, The Years of the City, *and the classic* The Space Merchants, *written with C. M. Kornbluth.*

"The Greening of Bed-Stuy" is a near-future, sociological extrapolation seen from inside pointedly drawn characters. It was a Nebula Award finalist for 1984 and one of the stories in The Years of the City, *for which Pohl received his second John W. Campbell Award. He is the only author to receive this honor twice.*

1.

Marcus Garvey de Harcourt's last class of the day was H.E., meaning "Health Education," meaning climbing up ropes in the smelly, bare gymnasium of P.S. 388. It was a matter of honor with him to avoid that when he could. Today he could. He had a note from his father that would get him out of school—and besides, it was a raid day. The police were in the school. It was a drug bust, or possibly a weapons search; or maybe some fragile old American History teacher had passed the terror point at the uproar in his class and called for help. Whatever. The police were in school, and the door monitors were knotted at the stairwells, listening to the sounds of scuffling upstairs. It was a break he didn't really need, because

at the best of times the door monitors at P.S. 388 were instructed
not to try too hard to keep the students in—else they simply wouldn't
show up at all.

Once across the street, Marcus ducked behind the tall mound of
garbage bags to see which of his schoolmates—or teachers!—would
come out in handcuffs, but that was a disappointment because the
cops came out alone. This time, at least, the cops had found nothing
worth an arrest—meaning, no doubt, that the problem was over,
and the teacher involved wouldn't, or didn't dare to, identify the
culprits.

One forty, and his father had ordered him to be ready to leave
for the prison by two o'clock. No problem. He threaded his way
past the CONSTRUCTION—ALL TRAFFIC DETOUR signs on
Nostrand Avenue; climbed one of the great soil heaps; gazed long-
ingly at the rows of earthmoving machines, silenced by some sort
of work stoppage; and rummaged in the dirt for something to throw
at them. There was plenty. There were pieces of bulldozed homes
in that dump—Art Deco storefronts from the 1920s, bay-window
frames from the 1900s, sweat-equity cinder blocks from the 1980s—
all crushed together. Marcus found a china doorknob, just right.
When it struck the nearest parked backhoe, the doorknob splintered
with a crash.

They said Bedford-Stuyvesant was a jungle, and maybe it was. It
was a jungle that young Marcus de Harcourt had lived all his life
in. He didn't fear it—was wary of parts of it, sure, but it was all
familiar. And it was filled with interesting creatures, mostly known
to Marcus, Marcus known to a few of them—like the young men
in clerical collars outside the Franciscan mission. They waved to
him from across the road. Bloody Bess at the corner didn't wave.
As he passed her she was having a perfectly reasonable, if agitated,
conversation: "She having an *abor*tion. She having an in*flatable*
abortion. He having intercourse with her ten *times*, so she having
it." The only odd part was that she was talking to a fire hydrant.
The bearded man in a doorway, head pillowed on a sack of garbage,
didn't wave either, but that was because he was asleep. Marcus
considered stealing his shoes and hiding them, but you never knew

about these doorway dudes. Sometimes they were cops. Besides, when he looked closer at the shoes, he didn't want to touch them.

One forty-five by the clock on the top of the Williamsburgh Bank Building, and time to move along. He trotted and swaggered along the open cut of the Long Island Rail Road yards. Down below were the concrete railguides with their silent, silent seams of metal. Marcus kicked hubcaps until he found a loose one. He pried it off, one eye open for cops, and then scaled it down onto the tracks. Its momentum carried it down to crash against the concrete guide strip, but the magnetic levitation had it already. It was beginning to move sidewise before it struck. It picked up speed, wobbling up and down in the field, showering sparks as it struck against the rail, until the maglev steadied it. It was out of sight into the Atlantic Avenue tunnel in a moment, and Marcus, pleased, looked up again at the bank clock. One fifty-five; he was already late, but not late enough for a taste of the cat if he hurried. So he hurried.

Marcus Garvey de Harcourt's neighborhood did not look bleak to him. It looked like the place where he had always lived, although of course all the big construction machines were new. Marcus understood that the project was going to change the neighborhood drastically, they said for the better. He had seen the model of the way Bedford-Stuyvesant was going to look, had listened to politicians brag about it on television, had been told about it over and over in school. It would be really nice, he accepted, but it wasn't nice yet. Between the burned-out tenements and the vacant lots of the year before, and the current bare excavations and half-finished structures, there was not much to choose—except that now the rats had been disturbed in their dwellings and were more often seen creeping across the sidewalks and digging into the trash heaps. Marcus ran the last six blocks to his father's candy store, past the big breeder power plant that fed a quarter of Brooklyn with electricity, cutting across the scarred open spaces, ducking through the barbed wire, and trotting between rows of tall towers that one day would be windmills. He paused at the corner to survey the situation. The big black car wasn't there, which was good. His mother wasn't waiting for him outside the store, either; but as he reached the door, panting a little harder than necessary to show how fast he'd been running, she opened it for him. His father was there, too, with his coat on already. He didn't speak, but looked up at the clock behind the soda fountain. "Damn, Marcus," his mother said crossly, "you know your daddy don't like to be kept waiting; what's the matter with you?"

"Wouldn't let me out no sooner, Nillie."

His father glanced at him, then at the storeroom door. Behind it, Marcus knew, the cat-o'-nine-tails was hanging. Marcus's mother said, "You want trouble, Marcus, you know damn well he's gone give it to you."

"No trouble, Nillie. Couldn't help it, could I?" There wasn't any sense in arguing the question, because the old man either would get the cat out or wouldn't. Most likely he wouldn't, because this thing at the prison was important to him and he wouldn't want to waste any more time, but either way it was out of Marcus's hands.

The old man jerked his head at Marcus and limped out of the store. He didn't speak. He never did talk much, because it hurt him to try. At the curb he lifted an imperious hand. A cruising gypsy cab pulled up, surprising Marcus. His father did not walk very well on the kneecaps that had once been methodically crushed, but the place they were going was only a dozen blocks away. You had to sell a lot of Sunday newspapers to make the price of a cab fare. Marcus didn't comment. He spoke to his father almost as seldom as his father spoke to him. He hopped in, scrunched himself against the opposite side of the seat, and gazed out of the window as his father ordered, "Nathanael Greene Institute, fast."

Because the Nathanael Greene Institute for Men was built underground, the approach to it looked like the entrance to a park. Nathanael Greene wasn't a park. It had forty-eight hundred residents and a staff of fifty-three hundred to attend them. Each resident had a nearly private room with a television set, toilet facilities, and air conditioning; and its construction cost, more than eighty-five thousand dollars per room, slightly exceeded the cost of building a first-class hotel. Nathanael Greene was not a hotel, either, and most of its luxuries were also utilitarian: the air-conditioning ducts were partly so that tear gas or sternutants could be administered to any part of the structure; the limit of two persons per cell was to prevent rioting. Nathanael Greene was a place to work, with a production line of microelectronic components; a place to learn, with optional classes in everything from remedial English to table tennis; a place to improve oneself, with nonoptional programs designed to correct even the most severe character flaws. Such as murder, robbery, and rape. Nathanael Greene had very little turnover among its occupants. The average resident remained there eleven years, eight months, and some days. If he left earlier, he usually found himself in a far less attractive place—an Alaskan stockade, for example, or a gas chamber. Nathanael Greene was not a place where just anyone could go. You had to earn it, with at least four felonies of average grade, or one or two really good ones, murder two and up. Major General Nathanael Greene of Potowomut, Rhode Island, the Quaker commander whose only experience of penology had been to preside over the court-martial of John André, might not have approved the use of his name for New York City's maximal of maximum-security prisons. But as he had been dead for more than two centuries, his opinion was not registered.

Of course there was a line of prison visitors, nearly a hundred people waiting to reach the kiosk that looked like a movie theater's box office. Most were poorly dressed, more than half black, all of them surly at being kept waiting. Marcus's father nudged him toward the Bed-Stuy model as he limped to take his place in the queue. The boy did what was expected of him. He skipped over to study the model. It was a huger, more detailed copy of the one in the public library. Marcus tried to locate the place where his father's candy store was, but would not be any longer once the project was completed. He circled it carefully, according to orders, but when he had done that, he had run out of orders, and his father was still far down the waiting line.

Marcus took a chance and let himself drift along the graveled path, farther and farther away from the line of visitors. What the top of Nathanael Greene looked like was a rather eccentric farm; you had no feeling, strolling between the railings that fenced off soybeans on one side and tomato vines on the other, that you were walking over the heads of ten thousand convicts and guards. It looked as much like Marcus's concept of the South African plains as anything else, and he imagined himself a black warrior infiltrating from one of the black republics toward Cape Town—except that the concrete igloos really were machine-gun posts, not termite nests, and the guard who yelled at him to go back carried a real rifle. A group of convicts, he saw, were busy hand-setting pine-tree seedlings into plowed rows. Christmas trees for sale in a year or two, probably. They would not be allowed to grow very tall, because nothing on this parklike roof of the prison was allowed to grow high enough to interfere with the guards' field of fire. A squint at the bank clock told him that if he didn't get inside the prison pretty soon, he was going to be late for his after-hours job with old Mr. Feigerman and his whee-clickety-beep machinery; a glance at his father told him it was time to hurry back into line.

But his father hadn't noticed. His father was staring straight ahead, and when they moved up a few steps, his limp was very bad. Marcus felt a warning stab of worry, and turned just in time to see a long black car disappear around the corner and out of sight.

There were a lot of long black cars in the world, but not very many that could make his father limp more painfully. For Marcus there was no doubt that the car was the one that the scar-faced man used, the one who came around to the candy store now and then to make sure the numbers and the handbook that kept them eating were being attended to; the one who always gave him candy, and always made his father's limp worse and his gravelly voice harder to understand; and it was not good news at all for Marcus to know that that man had interested himself in Marcus's visit to the prison.

When they got to the head of the line, the woman gave them an argument. She wore old-fashioned tinted glasses, concealing her eyes. Her voice was shrill, and made worse by the speaker system that let them talk through the bulletproof glass. "You any relative of the inmate?" she demanded, the glasses disagreeably aimed toward Marcus's father.

"No, ma'am." The voice was hoarse and gravelly, but under-standable—Nillie had told the boy that his father was lucky to be able to talk at all, after what they did to his throat: "Not *relative*, exactly. But kind of family," he explained, his expression apologetic, his tone deferential, " 'cause little Marcus here's his kid, and my wife's sister's his mother. But no, ma'am, no *blood* relation."

"Then you can't see him," she said positively, glasses flashing. "The only visitors permitted are immediate family, no exceptions."

Marcus's father was very good at wheedling, and very good at knowing when other tactics were better. "*See* him?" he cried in his gravelly voice, expression outraged. "What would I want to see the sonbitch for? Why, he ruined my wife's sister's life! But the man's got a right to see his own kid, don't he?"

The woman pursed her lips, and the glasses shone first on Marcus's father, then on the boy. "You'll have to get permission from the chief duty officer," she declared. "Window Eight."

The chief duty officer was young, black, bald, and male, and he opened the door of his tiny cubicle and allowed them in, studying Marcus carefully. "Who is it you want to see here, Marc?"

"My father," the boy said promptly, according to script. "I ain't seen him since I was little. Name's Marcus, not Marc," he added.

"Marcus, then." The officer touched buttons on his console, and the file photograph of Inmate Booking Number 838–10647 sprang up. Harvey, John T., sentenced to three consecutive terms of twelve to twenty years each for murder one, all three homicides committed during the commission of a major felony—in this case, the robbery of a liquor store. There was not much resemblance between the inmate and the boy. The inmate was stout, middle-aged, bearded—and white. The boy was none of those things. Still, his skin color was light enough to permit one white parent. "This is your daddy, Marcus?"

"Yes, sir, that's him," said Marcus, peering at the stranger on the screen.

"Do you know what he's here for?"

"Yes, sir. He here because he broke the law. But he still my daddy."

"That's right, Marcus," sighed the duty officer, and stamped the pass. He handed it to Marcus's father. "This is for the boy, not you. You can escort the boy as far as the visiting section, but you can't go in. You'll be able to see through the windows, though," he added, but did not add that so would everyone else, most especially the guards.

The pass let them into the elevator, and the elevator took them down and down, eight floors below the surface of the ground, with an obligatory stop at the fourth level while an armed guard checked the passes again. Nathanael Greene Institute did not call itself escape-proof, because there is no such thing, but it had designed in a great many safeguards to make escape unlikely. Every prisoner wore a magnetically coded ankle band, so his location was known to the central computers at every minute of the day; visitors like Marcus and his father were given, and obliged to wear, badges with a quite different magnetic imprint; the visiting area was nowhere near the doors to the outside world, and in fact even the elevators that served it were isolated from the main body of the prison. And as Marcus left his father in a sealed waiting room, two guards surrounded Marcus and led him away to a private room. A rather friendly, but thorough, matron helped undress him and went through everything he possessed, looking for a message, an illicit gift, anything. Then he was conducted to the bare room with the wooden chairs and the steel screen dividing them.

Marcus had been well rehearsed in what to say and do, and he had no trouble picking out Inmate 838–10647 from his photograph. "Hello, Da," he said, with just enough quaver in his voice to be plausible for the watching guards.

"Hello, Marcus," said his putative father, leaning toward the steel screen as a father might on seeing his long-lost son. The lines for the interview had also been well rehearsed, and Marcus was prepared to be asked how his mother was, how he was doing in school, whether he had a job to help his ma out. None of that was any trouble to respond to, and Marcus was able to study this heavyset, stern-looking white man who was playing the part of his father as he told him about Nillie's arthritis and her part-time job as companion to old Mr. Feigerman's dying wife; about how well he had done on the test on William Shakespeare's *Julius Caesar*, and his B + grade in history; about his own job that his ma had got him with Mr. Feigerman himself, the blind man with the funny machinery that let him see, sort of, and even work as a consulting engineer on the Bed-Stuy project . . . all the same, he was glad when it was over, and he could get out of that place. Toward the end he got to thinking about the eighty feet of rock and steel and convicts and guards over his head, and it had seemed to be closing in on him. The guards at Nathanael Greene had an average of ten years on the job, and they had experience before of kids running errands that adults could not do, so they searched him again on the way out. Marcus submitted peacefully. They didn't find anything, of course, because there hadn't been anything to find. On that visit.

2.

Marcus's after-school job was waiting impatiently for him. The name of the job was Rintelen Feigerman, and he was a very old man as well as quite a strange-looking one. Mr. Feigerman was in a wheelchair. This was not so much because his legs were worn out—they were not, quite—as because of the amount of machinery he had to carry with him. He wore a spangled sweatband around his thin, long hair, supporting a lacy metallic structure. His eyes were closed. Closed permanently. There were no eyeballs in the sockets anymore, just plastic marbles that kept them from looking sunken, and behind where the eyeballs had been there was a surgical wasteland where his entire visual system had been cut out and thrown away. The operation saved his life when it was done, but it removed Feigerman permanently from the class of people who could ever hope to see again. Transplants worked for some. The only transplant that could change things for Feigerman was a whole new head.

And yet, as Marcus came up the hill, the white old head turned toward him and Feigerman called him by name. "You're late, Marcus," he complained in his shrill old-man's voice.

"I'm sorry, Mr. Feigerman. They made me stay after school."

"Who's that 'they' you keep talking about, Marcus? Never mind. I was thinking of some falafel. What do you say to that?"

Actually, Marcus had been thinking of a Big Mac for himself, but that would mean making two stops, in different directions. "Falafel sounds good enough to me, Mr. Feigerman," he said, and took the bills the old man expertly shuffled out of his wallet, the singles unfolded, the fives creased at one corner for identification, the tens at two. "I'll tell Julius I'm here," he promised, and started down the long hill toward the limousine that waited on Myrtle Avenue.

The old man touched the buttons that swung his chair around. He could not really see down the hill, toward where the project was being born. The machinery that replaced his eyes was not too bad at short range, but beyond the edge of the paved area atop Fort Greene Park, it was of no use at all. But he didn't need eyes to know what was going on—to know that not much was. Half the project was silent. By turning up his hearing aid and switching to the parabolic microscope, he could could hear the distant scream of the turbines at the breeder reactor and the chomp and roar of the power shovels where excavation was still happening, underlain with the fainter sounds of intervening traffic. But the bulldozers weren't moving. Their crews were spending the week at home, waiting to be told when payroll money would be available again. Bad. Worse than it seemed, because if they didn't get the word soon, the best of them would be drifting off to other jobs where the funds were already in the bank, not waiting for a bunch of politicians to get their shit together and pass the bill—If, indeed, the politicians were going to. That was the worst of all; because Feigerman admitted to himself that that part was not sure at all. It was a nice, sunny day in Fort Greene Park, but there were too many worries in it for it to be enjoyed—including the one special troubling thing, in a quite different area, that Feigerman was trying not to think about.

While they ate their late lunch, or early dinner, or whatever the

meal was that they had formed the habit of sharing after Marcus's
school got out, the boy did his job. "They've got one wall of the
pumphouse poured," he reported, squinting out over the distant,
scarred landscape that had once been a normal, scarred Brooklyn
neighborhood. Silently, the old man handed him the field glasses,
and Marcus confirmed what he had said. "Yeah, the pumphouse
is coming along, and—and—they're digging for the shit pit, all
right. But no bulldozers. Just sitting there, Mr. Feigerman; I guess
they didn't turn loose your money yet. I don't see why they want
to do that, anyway."

"Do what?"

"Make another hill there. They got this one right here already."

"This one's the wrong shape," Feigerman said, not impatiently—
he liked the boy, welcomed his questions, wished sometimes that
he had had a real son of his own, since the semireal stepson that
he did have had no detectable love for his adopted father. "Besides,
this one is historic, so they don't want to build windmills on top of
it. George Washington held the British off right here—read the
inscription on the monument sometime." He licked some of the
falafel juice off his lips, and Marcus, unbidden, unfolded a paper
napkin and dabbed the missed spatters off the old man's bristly chin.
Feigerman clicked in his long-range optical scanner in place of the
sonar and gazed out over the city, but of course he could see only
vague shapes without detail. "It's a big thing," he said—as much
to the unheeding city as to Marcus.

"I know it is, Mr. Feigerman. Gonna make things real nice for
Bed-Stuy."

"I hope so." But it was more than a hope. In Feigerman's mind
it was certain: the energy-sufficient, self-contained urban area that
he had lobbied for for more than twenty years. It was wonderful
that it was going in in Brooklyn, so close to his home. Of course,
that was just luck—and a few influential friends. The project could
have been built anywhere—which is to say, in any thoroughly
blighted urban neighborhood, where landlords were walking away
from their tenements. And those were the good landlords; the bad
ones were torching their buildings for the insurance. South Bronx

wanted it. So did three neighborhoods in Chicago, three in Detroit, almost all of Newark, half of Philadelphia—yes, it could have been almost anywhere. Brooklyn won the prize for two reasons. One was the clout of the influential political friends. The other was its soft alluvial soil. What Brooklyn was made of, basically, was the rubble the glaciers had pushed ahead of them in the last Ice Age, filled in with silt from the rivers. It cut like cheese.

When Bed-Stuy was done, it would not have to import one kilowatt-hour of energy from anywhere else—not from Ontario Hydro, not from Appalachia, not from the chancy and riot-torn oil fields of the Arab states. Not from anywhere. Winter heating would come from the thermal aquifer storage, in the natural brine reservoirs under the city, nine hundred feet down. Summer cooling would help to warm the aquifers up again, topped off with extra chill from the ice ponds. By using ice and water to store heat and cold, the summer air-conditioning and winter heating peaks wouldn't happen, which meant that maximum capacity could be less. Low enough to be well within the design parameters of the windmills, the methane generators from the shit pit, and all the other renewable-resource sources; and the ghetto would bloom. Bedford-Stuyvesant was a demonstration project. If it worked, there would be more, all over the country—and Watts and Libertyville and the Ironbound and the Northside would get their chances—and it would work!

But it was not, of course, likely that Rintelen Feigerman would be around to see those second-generation heavens.

Reminded of mortality, Feigerman raised his wrist to his ear and his watch beeped the time. "I have to get going now," he said. "My wife's going to die this evening."

"She made up her mind to do it, Mr. Feigerman?"

"It looks that way. I'm sorry about that; I guess your mother will be out of a job. Has she got any plans, outside of helping out in the store?"

"Friend of my daddy's, he says he can get her work as a bag lady."

Feigerman sighed; but it was not, after all, his problem. "Take us on down the hill, Marcus," he said. "The car ought to be back by now."

"All right, Mr. Feigerman." Marcus disengaged the electric motor and turned the wheelchair toward the steep path. "Seems funny, though."

"What seems funny, Marcus?"

"Picking the time you're going to die."

"I suppose it is," Feigerman said thoughtfully, listening to the chatter of teenagers on a park bench, and the distant grumble of traffic. Marcus was a careful wheelchair handler, but Feigerman kept his hand near the brake anyway. "The time to die," he said, "is the day when you've put off root-canal work as long as possible, and you're running out of clean clothes, and you're beginning to need a haircut." And he was getting close enough to that time, he thought, as he heard his driver, Julius, call a greeting.

There was a confusion at Mercy General Hospital, because they seemed to have misplaced his wife. Feigerman waited in his wheelchair, watching the orderlies steer the gurneys from room to room, the nurses punching in data and queries to their monitors as they walked the halls, the paramedics making their rounds with pharmaceuticals and enema tubes, while Marcus raced off to find out what had happened. He came back, puffing. "They moved her," he reported. "Fifth floor. Room 583."

Jocelyn Feigerman had been taken out of the intensive-care section, because the care she needed now was too intensive for that. In fact, in any significant sense of the word, her body was dead itself, with its myriad factories for processing materials and its machines for keeping itself going, there was left only a shell. External machines pumped her blood and filtered it, and moved what was left of her lungs. None of that was new, and not even particularly serious. Fatal, yes. Sooner or later the system would fail. But that time could be put off for days, weeks, months. There were people in hospices all around the country who had been maintained for actual years—as long as the bills were paid; as long as they or their relatives did not call a halt. Jocelyn Feigerman's case was worse than theirs. It could be tolerated that she could never leave the bed, could remain awake only for an hour or so at a time, could eat only through IVs and could talk only through a machine; but when she could no longer *think*, there was no more reason to live. And that time was approaching. The minute trace materials like acetylcholine and noradrenaline that governed the functioning of the brain cells themselves were dwindling within her, as tiny groups of cells in places buried deep in the brain, places with names like the locus coeruleus and the nucleus basalis of Meynert, began to die. Memory was weakening. Habits of thought and behavior were deserting her. The missing chemicals could be restored, for a time, from pharmaceuticals; but that postponement was sharply limited by side effects as bad as the disease.

It was time for her to die.

So the hospital had moved her to a sunny, large room in a corner, gaily painted, filled with flowers, with chairs for visitors and 3-D landscape photographs on the walls, all surrounding the engineering marvel that was the bed she lay in. The room was terribly expensive—an unimportant fact, because it was never occupied except by the most terminal of cases, and rarely for more than a few hours.

As Feigerman rolled in, the room was filled with people—half a dozen of them not counting Marcus or himself. Or the still figure on the bed, almost hidden in its life-support systems. There was his daughter-in-law, Gloria, tiny and fast-talking, engaged in an argument with a solid, bearded, dark-skinned man Feigerman recognized as the borough president of Brooklyn. There was his stepson, now an elderly man, smoking a cigarette by the window and gazing contemplatively at the shrouded form of his mother. There was a doctor, stethoscope around his neck, tube looped through his lapel, all the emblems of his office visibly ready, though there was not in fact much for him to do but listen to the argument between Gloria and Borough President Haisal—a nurse—a notary public, with his computer terminal already out and ready on a desk by the wall. It was a noisy room. You could not hear the hiss of Jocelyn Feigerman's artificial lung or the purr of her dialysis machine under the

conversation, and she was not speaking. Asleep, Feigerman thought—
or hoped so. Everybody had to die, but to set one's own time for
it seemed horribly cold-blooded. . . . He raised his chin and addressed the room at large: "What are we waiting for?"

His stepson, David, stabbed his cigarette out in a fern pot and
answered. "Mother wanted Nillie here for some reason."

"She's got a right," Gloria flashed, interrupting her argument
with Haisal to start one with her semisibling. Haisal was of Arab
stock, from the Palestinian neighborhoods along Atlantic Avenue;
Gloria was Vietnamese, brought to the United States when she was
a scared and sick three-year-old; it was queer to hear the New York–
American voices come out of the exotic faces. "Father! Haisal says
they're going to go to referendum."

Feigerman felt a sudden surge of anger. He wheeled his chair
closer toward the arguing couple. "What the hell, Haisal? You've
got the votes in Albany!"

"Now, Rinty," the Arab protested. "You know how these things
work. There's a lot of pressure—"

"You've got plenty of pressure yourself!"

"Please, Rinty," he boomed. "You know what Bed-Stuy means
to me; don't you think I'm doing everything I can?"

"I do not."

Haisal made a hissing sound of annoyance. "What is this, Rinty?
Gloria asked me to come here because you need a magistrate for
your wife's testamentation, not to fight about money for the project!
This is a deathbed gathering. Where's your respect?"

"Where's your sense of honor?" Gloria demanded. "You promised, Haisal!"

"I do what I can," the borough president growled. "It's going to
have to go to referendum, and that's all there is to it—now let's get
going on this goddamn testamentation, can we?"

"We have to wait for Vanilla de Harcourt," Feigerman snapped,
"and anyway, Haisal—what is it?"

From the doorway, the nurse said, "She's here, Mr. Feigerman.
Just came in."

"Then we go ahead," said Haisal irritably. "Quiet down, everybody. Sam, you ready to take all this down? Doctor, can you wake her up?"

The room became still as the notary public turned on his monitor, and the doctor and nurse gave Jocelyn Feigerman the gentle electric nudge that would rouse her. Then the borough president spoke:

"Mrs. Feigerman, this is Agbal Haisal. Do you hear me?"

On the CRT over her bed there was a quick pulsing of alpha waves, and a tinny voice said, "Yes." It wasn't Jocelyn's voice, of course, since she had none. It was synthesized speech, generated electronically, controlled not by the nerves that led to the paralyzed vocal cords but by practical manipulation of the brain's alpha rhythms, and its vocabulary was very small.

"I will ask the doctor to explain your medical situation to you, as we discussed," said Haisal formally, "and if you have any questions simply say 'No.' Go ahead, doctor."

The young resident cleared his throat, frowning over his notes. He wanted to get this exactly right; it was his first case of this kind. "Mrs. Feigerman," he began, "in addition to the gross physical problems you are aware of, you have been diagnosed as being in the early stages of Alzheimer's syndrome, sometimes called senile dementia. The laboratory has demonstrated fibrous protein deposits in your brain, which are increasing in size and number. This condition is progressive and at present irreversible; and the prognosis is loss of memory, loss of control of behavior, psychotic episodes, and death. I have discussed this with you earlier, and repeat it now so that you may answer this question. Do you understand your condition?"

Pause. Flicker of lines in the CRT. "Yes."

"Thank you, doctor," rumbled the borough president. "In that case, Mrs. Feigerman—Joss—I have a series of questions to ask you, and they may sound repetitive, but they're what the law says a magistrate has to ask. First, do you know why we are here?"

"Yes."

"Are you aware that you are suffering from physical conditions that will bring about irreversible brain damage and death within an estimated time of less than thirty days?"

"Yes."

"Then, Mrs. Feigerman," he said solemnly, "your options are as follows. One. You may continue as you are, in which case you will continue on the life-support systems until brain-scan and induction tests indicate you are brain-dead, with no further medical procedures available. Two. You may elect to terminate life-support systems at this time, or at any later time you choose, as a voluntary matter, without further medical procedures. Three. You may elect to terminate life-support and enter voluntary cryonic suspension. In this case you should be informed that the prognosis is uncertain but that the necessary financial and physical arrangements have been made for your storage and to attempt to cure and revive you when and if such procedures become available.

"I will now ask you if you accept one of these alternatives."

The pause was quite long this time, and Feigerman was suddenly aware that he was very tired. Perhaps it was more than fatigue; it might have been even bereavement, for although he had no desire to shriek or rend his clothes, he felt the dismal certainty that a part of his life was being taken away from him. It had not always been a happy part. It was many years since it had been a sensually obsessive part . . . but it had been his. He tried to make out the vague images before him to see if his wife's eyes were open, at least, but the detail was far inadequate. . . . "Yes," said the tinny voice at last, without emotion, or emphasis. Or life. It was, almost literally, a voice from the grave; and it was hard to remember how very alive that wasted body had once been.

"In that case, Mrs. Feigerman, is it Alternative No. 1, continuing as you are?"

"No."

"Is it Alternative No. 2, terminating life-support without further procedures?"

"No."

"Is it Alternative No. 3, terminating life-support and entering cryonic suspension?"

"Yes." A long sigh from everyone in the room; none of them could help himself. The borough president went on:

"Thank you, Mrs. Feigerman. I must now ask you to make a choice. You may elect to enter neurocryonic suspension, which is, to say, the freezing of your head and brain only. Or you may elect whole-body suspension. Your doctor has explained to you that the damage suffered by your body has been so extensive that any revival and repair is quite unlikely in the next years or even decades. On the other hand, suspension of the head and brain entails only the necessity for providing an entire body for you at some future day— through cloning, through grafting of a whole new donor body to your head and brain, or through some procedure at present unknown. No such procedures exist at present. This decision is entirely yours to make, Mrs. Feigerman; your next of kin have been consulted and agree to implement whatever choice you make. Have you understood all this, Mrs. Feigerman?"

"Yes."

Haisal sighed heavily. "Very well, Joss, I will now ask you which alternative you prefer. Do you accept Alternative No. 1, the cryonic suspension of head and brain only?"

"No."

"Do you accept whole-body suspension, then?"

"Yes."

"So be it," rumbled the borough president heavily, and signed to the notary public. The man slipped the hard-copy transparency out of his monitor, pressed his thumb in one corner, and passed the transparency around to the witnesses to do the same. "Now," said the borough president, "I think we'll leave the family to say their good-byes." He gathered up the notary, the nurse, and Marcus's mother with his eyes; and to the doctor he signaled, his lips forming the words: *Then pull the plug.*

3.

On the first morning of Van Rintelen Feigerman's new life as a widower, he awoke with a shock, and then a terrible sense of loss.

The loss was not the loss of his wife; even in his dreams he had accepted that Jocelyn was dead, or if not exactly dead, certainly both legally and practically no longer alive in the sense that he was. The shock was that he had not dreamed that he was blind. In Rinty's dreams he could always see. That was a given: everyone could see. Humans beings saw, just as they breathed and ate and shit. So in his dreams he experienced, without particularly remarking, the glowing red and green headlamps of the IRT subway train coming into the Clark Street station, and the silent fall of great white snowflakes over the East River, and the yellow heat of summer sun on a beach, and women's blue eyes, and stars, and clouds. It was only when he woke up that it was always darkness.

Rosalyn, his big old Weimaraner, growled softly from beside the bed as Feigerman sat up. There was no significance to the growl, except that it was her way of letting Feigerman know where she was. He reached down and touched her smooth head, finding it just where it ought to be, right under his descending hand. He didn't really need the morning growl anymore. He could pretty nearly locate her by the smell, because Rosalyn was becoming quite an old dog. "Lie," he said, and heard her whuffle obediently as she lay down again beside his bed. He was aware of a need to go to the bathroom, but there was a need before that. He picked up the handset from the bedside table, listened to the beeps that told him the time, pressed the code that connected him to his office. "Rinty here," he said. "Situation report, please."

"Good morning, Mr. Feigerman," said the night duty officer. He knew her voice, a pretty young woman, or one whose face felt smooth and regular under his fingers and whose hair was short and soft. Janice something. "Today's weather, no problems. Overnight maintenance on schedule; no major outages. Shift supervisors are reporting in now, and we anticipate full crews. We've been getting, though," she added, a note of concern creeping into her voice, "a lot of queries from the furloughed crews. They want to know when they're going to go back to work."

"I wish I could tell them, Janice. Talk to you later." He hung up, sighed, and got ready for the memorized trip to the toilet, the shower, the coffee pot—he could already feel the heat from it as it automatically began to brew his first morning cup—and all the other blind man's chores. He had to face them every morning, and the most difficult was summoning up the resolution to get through one more day.

Rinty Feigerman had lived in this apartment for more than thirty years. As soon as Jocelyn's son, David, was out of the house, they had bought this condo in Brooklyn Heights. It was big and luxurious, high up in what had once been a fashionable Brooklyn hotel, when Brooklyn had still considered itself remote enough from The City to want its own hotels. Fashionable people stopped staying there in the thirties and forties. In the fifties and sixties, it had become a welfare hotel, where the city's poor huddled up in rooms that, every year, grew shabbier and smelled worse, as the big dining restaurant, the swimming pool, the health club, the saunas, the meeting rooms, the rooftop nightclub withered and died. Then a developer turned it into apartments. It was Rinty Feigerman who picked the place, studying the views and the builders' plans while he still had eyes that worked. But Jocelyn had furnished it. She had put in end tables and planters, thick rugs on slippery floors, a kitchen like a machine shop, with blenders and food processors and every automatic machine in the catalog. When Feigerman lost his eyes, every one of those things became a booby trap.

For the first couple of years, Jocelyn grimly replaced candy dishes and lamps as they crashed. She had not quite accepted the fact that the problem was not going to get better. After the damage toll began to be substantial—the week a whole tray of porcelain figures smashed to the floor and and a coffeemaker burned itself out until the electrical reek woke her up—Jocelyn, sullen but thorough, attacked the job of blindproofing their home. The living spaces she kept ornate. Rinty stayed out of them, except on the well-established routes from door to door. They wound up with three separate establishments. One was for company. One was Jocelyn's own space, formerly dainty but in the past two years more like a hospital suite. And the rest was Feigerman's own: a bedroom, a bath, a guest room converted into a study, a guest bath rebuilt into a bare-bones kitchen, all crafted for someone who preferred using only his sense of touch. And the terrace.

For a blind man with a seeing-eye dog, that was maybe the best thing of all. It had started out flagstoned, with two tiny evergreens in wooden pots. Jocelyn's son had had a better idea, so he filled it from wall to wall with twenty cubic yards of topsoil. It grew grass, though nothing much else, and so became a perfect dog's toilet. No one had to walk Rosalyn in the morning. Rinty opened the thermal french windows, Rosalyn paced gravely out; when she had done what she had to do, she scratched to come back in, and then lay attentively near her master until he called her to put on her harness. Feigerman always accoutred Rosalyn before he did himself. He wondered if she disliked it as much as he did, but of course he had no way to know. Rosalyn never complained. Not even when he was so busy working that he forgot to feed her for hours past her time; she would take food from no one else, and he supposed that if he continued to forget, she would simply starve. Not even now, when she was so slow and tired so quickly that he left her home on almost every day, except when guilt made him take her—and a human being like the boy Marcus, for insurance—for a walk in a park. He stood in the open doorway, letting the morning sun warm his face, trying to believe that he could see at least a reddening of the darkness under his eyelids, until Rosalyn came back and whined softly as she put her cold nose in his hand.

Someone was in the apartment. Feigerman hadn't put his hearing aid on because, as he told himself, he wasn't really *deaf*, just a little hard of hearing; but he had not heard the door. He opened the door to his own room and called, "Is that you, Gloria?"

"No, Mr. Feigerman, it's me. Nillie. Want me to fix you a cup of coffee?"

"I've got some in here. Wait a minute." He reached for the robe at the foot of his bed, slid into it, tied it over his skinny belly—how could he be so thin and yet so flabby?—and invited her in. When she had poured herself a cup out of his own supply and was sitting in the armchair by the terrace window, he said, "I'll be sorry to be losing you, Nillie. Have you got something else lined up?"

"Yes, I do, Mr. Feigerman. There's a job in the recycling plant, just the right hours, too, so don't worry about me."

"Of course, I'd like Marcus to keep on guiding me, if that's all right."

"Surely, Mr. Feigerman." Pause. "I'm really sorry about Mrs. Feigerman."

"Yes." He had not really figured out how to approach that particular subject. If your wife was dead, that was one thing; if she was sick, but there was some hope of recovery, that was another. A wife now resting at a temperature about a dozen degrees above absolute zero was something else. Not to mention the five or six years as her aging body had begun to deteriorate—or the years before that when their aging marriage was doing the same. Jocelyn's life was political and dedicated. His was no less dedicated, but his social objectives were carried out in bricks, steel, and mortar instead of laws. The two life-styles did not well match—"I beg your pardon?"

"I said I'm going to clear my stuff out of Mrs. Feigerman's room now, Mr. Feigerman."

"Oh, sure. Go ahead, Nillie." He realized he had been sitting silent, his coffee cooling, while his mind circled around the difficulties and problems in his world. And he realized, too, if a bit tardily, that Vanilla Fudge de Harcourt's voice had sounded strained. Particularly when she mentioned her son. Small puzzle. Sighing, Feigerman fumbled his way to the sink, poured the cold coffee away, and set himself to the job of dressing.

"Dressing," for Rinty Feigerman, was not just a matter of clothes. He also had to put on the artificial vision system which he disliked, and postponed as long as he could every day. It wasn't any good for reading, little better for getting around his rooms. Information Feigerman took in through Braille and through audio tapes, the voices of the readers electronically chopped to speed them up to triple speed, without raising the frequency to chipmunk chirps. Nearly everything he chose to do in his rooms he could do without the vision system. He could speak on the phone. He could listen to the radio. He could dictate, he could typewrite; he could even work his computer console, with its audio and tactile readouts, at least for word processing and mathematics, though the graphics functions were of no use at all to him anymore. Feigerman was never able to see the grand designs he helped to create, except in the form of models. There were plenty of those, made in the shops of the consulting firm he owned with his stepson; but it was not the same as being able to look down on, say, the future Bed-Stuy in the God's-eye view of every sighted person. At the computer he was quite deft, as artificial speech synthesizers read him the numbers he punched into the keyboard and the results that flashed on the CRT, now usually turned off. Of course, he did not really need to see—or even to feel a model of—Bed-Stuy. The whole plan was stored in his mind. . . . He was stalling again, he realized.

No help for it. He patted Rosalyn and sat down on the foot of his bed, reaching out for the gear.

The first step was to strap the tickler to his chest. Between the nipples, in a rectangular field seven inches across and five deep, a stiff brush of electrical contacts touched his skin. Feigerman had never been a hairy man, but even so, once a week or so, he had to shave what few sparse hairs grew there to make sure the contacts worked. Then the shirt went on, and the pants, and the jacket with the heavy-duty pockets that held most of the electronics and the flat, dense battery. Then he would reach down under the bed to where he had left the battery itself recharging all night long, pull it gingerly from the charger, clip it to the gadget's leads, and slip it into the pocket. Then came the crown. Feigerman had never seen the crown, but it felt like the sort of tiara dowagers used to wear to be presented to the queen. It wasn't heavy. The straps that held the crown made it possible to wear it over a wool cap in winter, or attached to a simple yarmulke in warm weather. It beeped at a frequency most people couldn't hear, though young children's ears could sometimes pick it up—Marcus claimed to hear it, and there was no doubt that Rosalyn did. When he first got the improved model, the dog whined all the time it was on—perhaps, Feigerman thought, because she knew it was taking her job away from her.

When he turned the unit on now, she didn't whine, but he could feel her move restlessly against his leg as he sat and let the impressions reach his brain. It had taken a lot of practice. The returning echo of the beeps was picked up, analyzed, and converted into a mosaic that the ticklers drew across his chest with a pattern of tiny electric shocks. Even now it was not easy to read, and after a long day there was more pain than information in it; but it served. For a long time the patterns had meant nothing at all to Feigerman, except as a sort of demented practical joke someone was playing on him with tiny cattle prods. But the teacher promised he would learn to read it in time. And he did. Distance and size were hard to estimate from the prickling little shocks until he came to realize that the sonar's image of a parked car covering a certain area of his chest had to represent a real vehicle ten feet away. When he became accustomed to the sonar, he didn't really need Rosalyn very much, and she was already beginning to limp on long walks. But he kept her. He had grown to like the dog, and did not want to see her among the technologically unemployed. . . . Then the coat; then the shoes; then Feigerman was ready to summon his driver and be taken to the offices in the Williamsburgh Bank Building for one more day of dealing with the world.

It was ever so much better, Feigerman's teacher had said, than the way things had been for the sightless even a few years earlier. Better than being dead, anyway, in Feigerman's estimation. Marginally so.

By the time Feigerman was at his office in the Williamsburgh Bank Building, he was almost cheerful, mostly because his driver was in a good mood. Julius was a suspended cop; he had been a moonlighting cop, working for Feigerman only in his off-duty hours, until his suspension. The suspension was because he had been caught in a surprise blood test with marginal levels of tetrahydrocannabinal breakdown products in his system. Julius claimed he was innocent. Feigerman thought it didn't matter, since everybody was doing it, cops and all; and what made Julius's mood high was that his rabbi had phoned to say the charges were going to be dropped. So he joked and laughed all the way to the office, and left Feigerman still smiling as he got out of the elevator and beeped his way to his desk, answering the good-mornings of the staff all the way.

The first thing to do was to get out of the heaviest part of the harness again, which he did with one hand while he was reaching for his stepson's intercom button with the other. "David?" he called, lifting off the headpiece. "I'm in and, listen, I'm going to need another driver next week. Julius is getting reinstated."

"That's good," said the voice of his stepson, although that voice hardly ever sounded as though it found anything good. "I need you for a conference in half an hour, Dad."

Dad. Feigerman paused in the act of rubbing the imprinted red lines on his forehead, scowling. "Dad" was something new for David. Was it because his mother's death had reminded him that they were a family? David didn't seem to show any other effect. If he had shed one tear, it had not been in Feigerman's presence. That wasn't surprising, maybe, because David's mother had devoted far more of her attention to her political causes than to her son. Or to her daughter-in-law. Or, for that matter, to her husband. . . . "What kind of conference?" Feigerman asked.

There was a definite note of strain in David's voice, part wheedling, part defiant. "It's a man from S.G. and H."

"And who are S.G. and H. when they're home?"

"They're investment bankers. They're also the people who own all the legislators from Buffalo to Rochester, and the ones who can get the Bed-Stuy money out of committee."

Feigerman leaned back, the scowl deepening. There was enough tension in David's voice to make him wish he could see David's face. But that was doubly impossible—"The man from S.G. and H. wouldn't be named Gambiage, would he?"

"That's the one."

"He's a goddamned gangster!"

"He's never been convicted, but, yes, I would agree with you, Dad." The truculence was suppressed, but the wheedling was almost naked now. "All you have to do is listen to him, you know. His people have been buying utility stock options, and naturally he has an interest in Bed-Stuy—"

"I know what that interest is! He wants to own it!"

"He wants a piece of it, probably. Dad? I know how you feel—but don't you want to get it built?"

Feigerman breathed out slowly. "I'll see him when he comes in," he said, and snapped the connection.

If he had only thirty minutes before a very unpleasant task, he needed to get ready for it. He reached to the gadget beside his chair and switched it on. It was his third set of eyes, the only ones that were any good at all over a distance exceeding a few yards. They had another advantage. Feigerman called them his daydreaming eyes, because they were the ones that allowed him to see what wasn't there—yet.

Feigerman had designed the gadget himself, and the machine on and around his desk had cost more than three hundred thousand dollars—less than half recouped when he licensed it for manufacture. It was not a mass-market item. Even the production models cost more than a hundred thousand, and there were no models that were in any sense portable. The size constraints could not be removed by engineering brilliance; they were built into the limitations of the human finger.

The heart of the device was a photon-multiplier video camera that captured whatever was before it, located the areas of contrast, expressed them digitally, canceled out features too small to be displayed within its limits of resolution, and did it all twice, electronically splitting the images to produce stereo. Then it drove a pinboard matrix of 200 × 200 elements, each one a rounded plastic cylinder thinner than a toothpick—forty thousand pixels all told, each one thrust out of the matrix board a distance ranging anywhere from not at all to just over a quarter of an inch.

What came out of it all was a bas-relief that Feigerman could run his fingers over, as he might gently touch the face of a friend.

Feigerman could, in fact, recognize faces from it, and so could nearly a hundred other blind people well connected enough to be given or rich enough to buy the device. He could even read expressions—sometimes. He could even take a "snapshot"—freeze the relief at any point, to study in motionless form as long as he liked.

What was astonishing was that even sighted persons could recognize faces, too; and it was not just faces. Feigerman had no use for paintings on the walls, but if he wanted to "behold" the Sierra Nevada or the surface of the moon, his device had their stereotactile images stored in digital form, and a simple command let him trace with his fingers the Donner Pass or walk along the slopes of Tycho.

What he chose to do this morning, waiting for the gangster to show up and ruin his day—maybe even ruin his project!—was to "look out the window."

For that the electronic camera mounted behind his chair was not good enough. The electronic "pupillary distance" was too small for a stereoscopic image. But he had mounted a pair of cameras high up on the wall of the observation deck of the building, and when he switched over to them, all of Bedford-Stuyvesant rippled under his fingers.

What Feigerman felt with his fingers was not really much unlike the surface of the moon. There were the craters of excavation, for the underground apartment dwellings that would house two hundred thousand human beings and for the garment workshops, the electronic assembly plants, and all the other clean, undegrading industries that would give the two hundred thousand people work to do. There were the existing structures—the tenements not yet torn down, the guardhouses atop Nathanael Greene, the derelict factories, the containment shell over the breeder reactor, the Long Island Rail Road lines—a late shoppers' express came hissing in on its maglev suspension, and the ripple of its passage tickled his fingers. There were the projects begun and the projects now going up—he recognized the slow, steady turn of a crane as it hoisted preformed concrete slabs onto the thermal water basin.

And there were the silent rows of dumpsters and diggers, backhoes and augers that were not moving at all because of the lack of funds.

Rintelen Feigerman didn't count up his years anymore. Now that his wife was a rimy corpsicle somewhere under Inwood, no one alive knew the total; but everyone knew that it was a lot of years. There could not be very many more. Feigerman was used to delays.

You did not make a career of major construction in the most complicated city in the world without accepting longtime overruns. But this one time in all his life, he was not patient, for every minute wasted was a minute taken off what had to be a slender reserve.

And this was his masterpiece. East River East was just one more big damn housing development. The Inwood Freezer complex was only a cold-storage plant. Nathanael Greene was just another jail. But Bed-Stuy—

Bed-Stuy was the closest human beings could come to heaven on earth. The original idea wasn't his; he had ferreted it out from old publications and dusty data chips; somebody named Charles Engelke had described a way of making a small suburban community self-sufficient for energy as far back as the 1970s—but who was interested in suburbs after that? Somebody else had pointed out that the blighted areas of American cities, the South Bronxes and the Detroits, could be rebuilt in new, human ways. But it was Rintelen Feigerman who put it all together, and had the muscle, the *auteur* prestige, the political connections, the access to capital— had all the things that could make the dreams come true. Solar energy. Solar energy used in a thousand different ways: to heat water in the summer and pump it down into rechargeable lenses of fossil water far under the surface; the new hot water squeezes out the old cool, and the cool water that comes up drives summer air conditioning. In winter the pumps go the other way, and the hot summer water warms the homes. Solar energy as wind, also for generating electricty, more typically for pumping water in and out of the thermal aquifers. Solar energy, most of all, for the thing it was best equipped to do, domestic heating. Feigerman made an adjustment, and under his fingers the vista of Bed-Stuy grew from what it was to what it would be, as his data store fed in the picture of the completed project.

Even forty thousand pixels could not give much detail in a plan that encompassed something about the size of a truck; a pedestrian, a fire hydrant, even a parked car was simply too tiny to be seen.

But what a glorious view! Feigerman's fingers rested lovingly on the huge, aerodynamically formed hill that would enclose the surface-level water store and support the wind engines that would do the pumping. The smaller dome for the ice pond, where freezing winter temperatures would provide low-temperature reserves for summer cooling, even for food processing. The milder slope that hid the great methane digesters—perhaps he loved the methane digesters best of all, for what could be more elegant than to take the most obnoxious of human by-products—shit!—and turn it into the most valuable of human resources—fuel? All the sewage of the homes and offices and factories would come here, to join with the lesser, but considerable wastes from the men's prison next to it. The shit would stew itself into sludge and methane; the heat of the process would kill off all the bacteria; the sludge would feed the farms, the methane would burn for process heat. Industries like glassmaking, needing the precise heating that gas could produce better than anything else, would find cheap and reliable supplies—meaning jobs—meaning more self-sufficiency—meaning—

Feigerman sighed and brought himself back to reality. At command, the future Utopia melted away under his fingers and he was touching the pattern of Bed-Stuy as it was. The methane generator was still only an ugly hole in the ground next to the prison. The great wind hill was no more than a ragged Stonehenge circle of concrete, open at the top. The idle construction machinery was still ranked along a roadway—

"I didn't want to disturb you, so I just let myself in, O.K.?"

The blind man started, twisted in his chair, banged his head against the support for the camera behind him. He was trying to do two things at once, to reach for the sonar crown that would let him see this intruder, to switch the tactile matrix back to the inside cameras so he could feel him. The man said gently, amusedly, "You don't need that gadget, Feigerman. It's me, Mr. Gambiage. We've got business to talk."

Feigerman abandoned his search for the coronet; the camera behind his head had caught the image of his visitor, and Feigerman could feel it under his fingers. "Sit down, Mr. Gambiage," he said—pointedly, because the man was already sitting down. He moved

silently enough! "You're holding up my money," Feigerman said.
"Is that what you want to talk about?"

The image rippled under his fingers as Gambiage made an impatient gesture. "We're not going to crap around," he informed
Feigerman. "I can get your money loose from Albany, no problem,
or I can hold it up forever, and that's no problem, too. On the
other hand, you could cost me a lot of money, so I'm offering you
a deal."

Feigerman let him talk. The tactile impression of Gambiage did
not tell much about the man. Feigerman knew, because the news
reports said so, that Gambiage was about fifty years old. He could
feel that the man was short and heavyset, but that his features were
sharp and strong. Classic nose. Heavy brows. Stubborn broad chin.
But were his eyes mean or warm? Was his expression smile or leer
or grimace? Gambiage's voice was soft and, queerly, his accent was
educated under the street-talk grammar. It could even be Ivy League
—after all, there was nothing to say that the sons of the godfathers
couldn't go to college. And Feigerman had to admit that the man
smelled good, smelled of washed hair and expensive leather shoes
and the best of after-shave lotion. He could hear the faint sound of
movement as Gambiage made himself comfortable as he went on
talking: could smell, could hear, could feel . . . could be frightened.
For this man represented a kind of power that could not be ignored.

Feigerman had dealt with the mob before—you could not be
involved in large construction in America without finding you had
them for partners in a thousand ways. The unions; the suppliers;
the politicians—the city planners, the building inspectors, the code
writers—wherever a thousand-dollar bribe could get a million-dollar
vote or approval or license, there the mob was. It did not always
control. But it could not be set aside. The ways of dealing with the
mob were only two: you went along or you fought. Feigerman had
done both.

But this time he could do neither. He couldn't fight, because he
didn't have time in his life for a prolonged battle. And he couldn't
go along with what came to nothing less than the perversion of the
dream.

"It's the co-generation thing," Gambiage explained. "You make your own power, you cost the utilities a fortune. I've got stock options. They're not going to be worth shit if the price doesn't go up—and you're the one that's keeping the price from going up."

"Mr. Gambiage, the whole point of the Bed-Stuy project is to be self-sufficient in energy so that—"

"I said we're not going to crap around," Gambiage reminded him. "Now we're going to talk deal. You're going to change your recommendations. You'll agree to selling all the power-generating facilities to the utilities. Then I'll recommend to my friends in Albany that they release your funds, and everything goes smoothly from there on. And I'll make it more attractive to you. I'll sell you my stock options for fifty thousand shares for what I paid for them. Thirty cents a share, for purchase at ninety-one and a quarter."

Feigerman didn't respond at once. He turned to his data processor and punched out the commands for a stock quotation. As he held the little earpiece to his ear, the sexless synthesized-speech voice said: "Consolidated Metropolitan Utilities current sale, eighty-five."

"Eighty-five!" Feigerman repeated.

"Right," said Gambiage, and his voice was smiling. "That's what you cost me so far, Feigerman. Now get a projection with us owning the co-generation facilities and see what you get. We make it a hundred and ten, anyway."

Feigerman didn't bother to check that; there would be no point in lying about it. He simply punched out a simple problem in arithmetic: $110—(91.25 + .30)$—say, 1% for brokers' fees, $\times$ 50,000. And the voice whispered, "Nine hundred thirteen thousand two hundred seventy-five dollars."

He was being offered a bribe of nearly a million dollars.

A million dollars. It had been a legacy of less than a tenth of that that had put him through school and given him the capital to start his career in the first place. It was a magic number. Never mind that his assets were already considerably more than that. Never mind that money was not of much use to a man who was already too old to spend what he had. A million dollars! And simply for

making a decision that could be well argued as being the right thing
to do in any case.

It was very easy to see how Mr. Gambiage exercised his power.
But out loud Feigerman said, his voice cracking, "How many shares
have you got left? A million or two?"

"My associates and I have quite a few, yes."

"Do you know we could all go to jail for that?"

"Feigerman," said Gambiage wearily, "that's what you pay lawyers for. The whole transaction can be handled offshore anyway,
in any name you like. No U.S. laws violated. Grand Cayman is
where the options are registered right now."

"What happens if I say no?"

With his fingers on the bas-relief, Feigerman could feel the ripple
of motion as Gambiage shrugged. "Then Albany doesn't release the
funds, the project dies, and the stock bounces back to where it
belongs. Maybe a hundred."

"And the reason you come to me," Feigerman said, clarifying
the point, "is that you think I come cheaper than a couple of dozen
legislators."

"Somewhat cheaper, yes. But the bottom line comes out good
for me and my associates anyway." The needles tickled Feigerman's
palm as the man stood up; irritably, Feigerman froze the image.
"I'll be in touch," Gambiage promised, and left.

It would be, Feigerman calculated, not more than three minutes
before his stepson would be on the intercom.

He wasn't ready for that. He slapped the privacy switch, cutting
off calls, locking the door.

The important thing, now, was to decide what was the important thing forever. To get the project built? Or to get it built in
a fashion in which he could take smug and virtuous personal
pride?

Feigerman knew what he wanted—he wanted that sense of triumph
and virtue that would carry him through that not-long-to-be-delayed
deathbed scene, for which he found himself rehearsing almost every
day. His task now was to reconcile himself to second best—or to
find a way to achieve the best. He could fight, of course. The major

battles had been long won. The general outlines of the project had been approved, the land acquired, the blueprints drawn, the construction begun. Whatever Gambiage might now deploy in the way of bribed legislators or court injunctions—or whatever other strategies he could command, of which there were thousands—in the long run the game would go to Feigerman.

Except that Feigerman might well not be alive to see his victory.

He sighed and released the hold button; and of course his stepson's voice sounded at once, angry: "Don't cut me off like that, Dad. Why did you cut me off? What did he say?"

"He wants to be our partner, David."

"Dad! Dad, he already *is* our partner. Are you going to change the recommendation?"

"What I'm going to do is think about it for a while." He paused, then added on impulse, "David? Have you been picking up any stock options lately?"

Silence for a moment. Then: "Your seeing-eye kid is here," said David, and hung up.

When Marcus came in to help Mr. Feigerman get ready, he was prepared for a bad time. The other guy, Mr. Tisdale, was all in a sweat and grumbling to himself about trouble; the trouble centered around old Feigerman, so maybe the day's walk was off, maybe he'd be in a bad mood—at his age, maybe he'd be having a stroke or something.

But actually he was none of those things. He was struggling to put his camera thing on his head by himself, but spoke quite cheerfully: "Hello, Marcus. You ready for a little walk?"

"Sure thing, Mr. Feigerman." Marcus came around behind Feigerman to snap the straps for him and his glance fell on that pinboard thing the old man used in order to see.

"What's the matter?" Feigerman said sharply.

"Aw, nothing," said Marcus, but it was a lie. He had no trouble recognizing the face on the pinboard. It was not a face he would forget. He had seen it many times before, arriving at his father's candy store in the black limousine.

4.

Inmate 838–10647 HARVEY John T. did not merely have one of the best jobs in Nathanael Greene Institute for Men, he had two of them. In the afternoons he had yard detail, up on the surface. That was partly because of his towering seniority in the prison, mostly because he had been able to produce medical records to show that he needed sunshine and open air every day. Inmate Harvey had no trouble producing just about any medical records he liked. In the mornings he worked in the library. That was partly seniority, too, but even more because of his special skills with data processors. Inmate Harvey's library work generally involved fixing the data-retrieval system when it broke down, once in a while checking out books for other inmates. This morning he was busy at something else. It was like putting together a jigsaw puzzle. Under the eyes of two angry guards and the worried head librarian, Harvey was painfully assembling the shards of broken glass that had once been a 10- × 26-inch window in the locked bookshelves. When it was whole it had kept a shelf of "restricted" books safe—books that most of the inmates were not permitted to have because they were politically dangerous. Now that it was a clutter of razor-sharp fragments, it was something that inmates were even less permitted to have, because they were dangerous, period. On the edge of Harvey's desk, watched by a third guard, sat the two other inmates whose scuffling had broken the glass. One had a bleeding nose. The other had a bleeding hand. Their names were Esposito and La Croy, and neither of them looked particularly worried—either by their injuries or by the forty-eight-hour loss of privileges that was the inevitable penalty for fighting.

Those were small prices to pay for the chance to escape.

Hardly anyone ever escaped from Nathanael Greene. Of course, a lot of inmates tried. Every inmate knew that there were exactly three ways to do it, and that two of them were obvious and the other one impossible.

The obvious ways, obviously, were the ways through which people normally exited the prison—the "visitors' gate," which was also where supplies came in and manufactured products and waste went out; and the high-security "prisoner-transfer gate." Trusties lucky enough to be working on the surface, farming or cutting grass, could pretty nearly walk right out of the visitors' gate. Sometimes they made the try; but electronic surveillance caught them every time. The prisoner-transfer facility had been a little easier—three times there had been a successful escape that way, usually with fake transfer orders. But after the third time the system was changed, and that way looked to be closed permanently.

Scratch the two obvious ways. The only way left was the impossible one. To wit, leaving the prison through some other exit.

What made that impossible was that there wasn't any. Nathanael Greene was underground. You could try to dig a tunnel if you wanted to, but there wasn't anywhere to tunnel to nearer than a hundred yards—mostly straight up—and besides, there were the geophones. The same echo-sounding devices that located oil domes and seismic faults could locate a tunnel—usually in the first three yards—assuming any prisoner could escape the twenty-four-hour electronic surveillance long enough to start digging in the first place.

That was why it was impossible, for almost everyone, almost all the time. But inmates still hoped—as Esposito and La Croy hoped. And even took chances, as Esposito and La Croy were willing to do; because there never was a perfect system, and if there was anyone who could find a way through the safeguards of Nathanael Greene, it was Inmate 838–10647 HARVEY John T.

He never did get the jigsaw put back together to suit the guards, but after two hours of trying, after he had crunched some of the pieces twice with his foot and it was obvious that no one was ever going to reconstruct the pane properly anymore, the guards settled for picking up all the pieces they could find and marching Esposito and La Croy away. They had no reason to hassle Inmate Harvey. That didn't stop them from threatening, of course. But when the lunch-break signal sounded, they let him go.

The trip from the library to his cell took three flights of stairs and six long corridors, and Harvey did it all on his own. So did every other prisoner, because no matter where they were or what they were doing, the master locator file tagged them in and out every time they came to a checkpoint. You lifted your leg to present the ID on your ankle to the optical scanner. The scanner made sure you were you by voiceprints or pattern recognition of face or form, sometimes even by smell. It queried the master file to find out if you were supposed to be going where you were going, and if all was in order, you simply walked right through. The whole process took no longer than opening an ordinary door, and you didn't screw around if you could help it because you were under continuous closed-circuit surveillance all the time. Inmate Harvey, carrying his book and his clean librarian's shirt, nodding to acquaintances hurrying along the same corridors and exchanging comments about the methane stink that was beginning to pervade the entire prison, reached his cell in less than five minutes.

His cellmate was a man named Albert Muzzi, and he was waiting for Harvey. "Gimme," said Moots, extending his hand for the copy of *God-Emperor of Dune.*

Harvey entered the cell warily—you watched yourself with Muzzi. "You're fucking up the whole plan," he pointed out. "You don't need this." But he handed the volume over just the same, and watched Muzzi open it to the page where the shard of glass lay.

"It's too fucking short, asshole," Muzzi growled. He wasn't particularly angry. He always talked that way. He ripped a couple of pages out of the book, folded them over, and wrapped them around the thick end of the glass sliver. When he held it as though for stabbing, about three inches of razor-edged stiletto protruded from his fist—sharp, deadly, and invisible to the prison's metal detectors. "Too fucking short," he repeated fiercely, but his eyes were gleaming with what passed in Muzzi for pleasure.

"It's the best I could do." Harvey didn't bother to tell him how long he had sat with the fragments, pretending to try to reconstruct a complete pane; Muzzi wouldn't be interested. But he offered, "The screws were going to give me a twenty-four." Muzzi would be interested in that.

And he was. "Shithead! Did you fuck up your meet with the

kid?" This time the voice was dangerous, and Harvey was quick in defense.

"No, it's cool, Moots, that's not till Thursday. I was just telling you why that was the best I could do."

"You told me. Now shut up." Harvey didn't wait to see where Muzzi would conceal the weapon. He didn't want to know. Fortunately, he and Muzzi didn't eat on the same shift, so Harvey left without looking back.

The thing was, Muzzi didn't need the shiv. It would be useless in the first stages. When it stopped being useless, it would be unnecessary. But you didn't argue with Muzzi. Not when he told you to steal him a glass blade. Not when he added more people to the plan and made two of them break the glass to get it. Not ever. It wasn't just that Muzzi's connections made the whole project possible, it was the man himself. "Man" was the wrong word. Muzzi was a rabid animal.

Tuesday lunch was always the same, sloppy joe sandwiches, salad from the surface farm or the hothouse, milk. What they called "milk," anyway; it had never seen a cow, being made of vegetable fats and whitener. What made it worse than usual was the methane stink from where the digging of the new sewer pits had seeped through the soil into the cellblocks themselves. Harvey didn't join in the catcalls or complaints, didn't let sticky soup from the sloppy joes spill on the floor or accidently drop a meatball into the Jell-O. He didn't do any of the things the other inmates did to indicate their displeasure, because the last thing Harvey wanted was to get even a slap-on-the-wrist twenty-four-hour loss of privileges just now. All the same, he suffered with every bite. Inmate Harvey was used to better things.

Inmate 838–10647 HARVEY John T. had a record that went back thirty years, to when he was a bright and skinny kid. He hadn't intended to get into violence. He started out as a PhonePhreak, rival of the semilegendary Captain Crunch. When Ma Bell got mad enough to put the captain in jail, young Johnny Harvey got the message. Making free phone calls to the pope on his blue box just wasn't worth it, so he looked for less painful ways to have fun. He found them in proprietary computer programs. Johnny Harvey could wreck anybody's security. No matter how many traps Apple built into its software, Johnny Harvey could bypass them in a week, and make copies and be passing them out, like popcorn, to all his friends before the company knew they'd been screwed. Apple even got desperate enough to offer him a job—don't crack our security programs, design them—but that got boring. So did program swiping. For a while Harvey worked for the city, mostly on the programs for electronic voting and the Universal Town Meeting, but that was kind of boring, too, in the long run, and then somebody came along with more larceny in his heart than Harvey had ever owned, and saw what treasures the young man could unlock.

He unlocked six big ones. Two were major payoffs from insurance companies of life policies that had never existed, on assureds who had never been born. Three were sales of stock Harvey had never owned, except in the tampered data store of a brokerage house's computers. One was a cash transfer from branch to branch of a bank that thought its codes could never be compromised.

When the bank found out how wrong it was, it set a trap. The next time Harvey tried to collect a quarter of a million dollars that didn't belong to him, the teller scratched her nose in just the right way and two plainclothes bank security officers took Johnny Harvey away.

Since it was a white-collar crime and nobody loves a bank anyway, the prosecutor didn't dare go for a jury trial. He let Harvey go for a plea-bargained reduced charge. No one was really mad. They just put him away for eighteen months. But they put him in Attica, world's finest training school for street crime and buggery. After that Harvey couldn't get a job, and the codes had got a lot tougher, and, by and large, the easiest way he could find to support the habit he had picked up in stir was with a gun.

And when that went wrong, and they put him away again, and he got out once more, the situation hadn't improved. He tried the same project. This time things went very wrong, and when he finished trying to shoot his way out of a stakeout, there were three people dead. One of the victims was a cop. One was a pregnant shopper. The third was her three-year-old kid. Well, the forgiving State of New York could make a deal on a homicide or two, but this time they were calling him "Mad Dog" on the six o'clock news, and he was convicted in public opinion before the first juror was called. He was looking at three consecutive twenty-five-to-life sentences. If he was the most model of prisoners, he could hope to get out two months past his one hundred and ninth birthday.

That wasn't good enough.

So Johnny Harvey summoned up his resources. He still had his winning ways with a computer, and Nathanael Greene was a computer-controlled prison. The central file always knew where every inmate was and whether he had a right to be there, because at every door, every stair, every cell there was a checkpoint. Each inmate's anklet ID checked him in and out for all the hours of his sentence, everywhere.

That wasn't good enough, either, but then two more events filled out the pattern. The first was when his first cellmate, No Meat, stuck his hand in the microwave oven. It was Harvey's fault, in a way. He had told No Meat how to bypass the oven's safety interlocks. But he hadn't really thought No Meat would carry his protest against prison diet that far, until he didn't show up at evening lockup, and the screw told him No Meat was now well on his way to a different kind of institution, and the next day Harvey got a new companion. His name was Muzzi, and he looked a lot like bad news. He was short and scowling. He came into the cell as though he were returning to a summer home and unsatisfied with the way the caretakers had kept it up, and Harvey was cast in the role of the caretaker. Muzzi's first words to Harvey were: "You're too fucking old. I don't screw anybody over twenty-two." What struck Harvey most strongly, even more than the violence and the paranoid brutality in the man, was his smell: a sort of catbox rankness, overlaid with expensive men's cologne. What struck Harvey later on, when Muzzi finished explaining to him who he was and how Harvey was going to behave, was that here was a man who was well connected. Not just connected, but holding. Muzzi was serving his sentence without the

clemency he could have had in a minute for a little testimony.
Muzzi chose instead to serve his time. So he was owed; and by
somebody big.

The other event was that excavation started, no more than ten
yards from the retaining walls of the prison, for the Bed-Stuy methane generating pit.

On Thursday morning Inmate 838-10647 HARVEY returned to
his cell after breakfast, along with all the other inmates in his
cellblock, for morning showdown. Bedding stripped. Mattress on
the floor. Personal-effects locker open. Inmates standing by the
door. As always, the guards strolled past in teams of three. Usually
there was just a quick glance into each cell. Sometimes, a random
dash and a shakedown: body search, sometimes going over the
mattress with hand-held metal detectors, sometimes even taking it
away to the lab and replacing it with a new one, or rather, an even
older, worse-stained, fouler smelling one off the pallet the trusty
pulled behind them. Harvey and Muzzi stood impassively as they
went by. This time the screws didn't bother them; but from the end
of the cellblock Harvey could hear cursing and whining. Somebody,
possibly the black kid who had just come in, had been caught with
contraband.

Then, for some minutes, nothing, until the speaker grilles rattled
and said, "All inmates, proceed to your duty stations."

Muzzi's work in the bakery was one way, Harvey's library job the
other. They didn't say good-bye to each other. They didn't speak
at all.

Harvey was not surprised when, toward the end of his morning
shift, the speaker in the library defied the QUIET! signs and blared,
"Six Four Seven Harvey! Report to Visitors' Center!"

The well-connected Muzzi had used his connections well. He
had procured them a reception party to be waiting once they were
outside the prison. He had procured a couple of assistants to manufacture the plastic explosive and help with the digging—and, of
course, to get him his personal shiv as well. He had also procured
for Harvey a "son" to serve as a courier, and not a bad son at that.

The kid even reminded Harvey a little of himself at that age—not counting color, anyway. Not counting their family backgrounds, either, which were Short Hills vs. Bed-Stuy, and certainly not counting parentage—in Harvey's case a pair of college teachers, in Marcus's a retired hooker and her pimp. It was hard to see any resemblance at all, to be truthful, except that the young Johnny Harvey and the young Marcus de Harcourt shared the lively, bursting curiosity about the world and everything that made it go. So when Marcus came in, he was right in character to be bubbling, "I seen the model of Bed-Stuy, Dad! Boy! There's some neat stuff there—they got windmills that're gonna pump hot and cold water, they got a place to turn sewage into gas, they got solar panels and an ice pond—"

"Which did you like best?" Harvey asked, and promptly the answer came back:

"The windmills!"

And that was the heart of the visit, the rest was just window dressing.

Because Harvey had an artist's urge for perfection, he took pleasure in spinning out the talk to its full half hour. He asked Marcus all about his school, and about his mom, and about his cousin Will and his aunt Flo and half a dozen other made-up relatives. The boy was quick at making up answers, because he, too, obviously enjoyed playing the game. When it was time to go, Harvey reached around the desk and hugged him, and of course the guard reacted. "Oh, hell, Harvey," she sighed—not unpleasantly, because she didn't believe in shaming a man before his kid. "You know better than that. Now we got to frisk you both."

"That's all right," said Harvey generously. It was. He wasn't carrying anything that he wasn't supposed to, of course, and neither was the boy. Anymore.

An excuse to clean up around the model on his afternoon shift, a pretext to return to library after dinner—Harvey's glib tongue was good enough for both, though not without some sweat. He was carrying, now; if he happened to hit a routine stop-and-search with

the contraband in his possession . . . but he didn't. Before bedcheck
that night, Harvey's part was done. The chip was in place in the
library computer.

The chip Marcus had smuggled in wasn't exactly a chip. It was
a planar-doped barrier, a layer cake with gallium arsenide for the
cake and fillings of silicon and beryllium. Once Harvey had retrieved
it from the niche under the model windmills and slipped it into
place in the library terminal, it took only a few simple commands—
"Just checking," he grinned at the night duty officer in the library—
and the chip had redefined for the master computer a whole series
of its instructions.

So, back in his cell, Harvey stretched out and grinned happily
at the ceiling. Even Muzzi was smiling, or as close to smiling as
he ever got. They were ready. Esposito had already stolen the Vaseline and the other chemicals to make plastic. La Croy had the
hammers, the shovels, and the spike to make a hole in the wall for
the plastic charge.

And the chip was in place.

It functioned perfectly, as Harvey had designed it to do, which
meant that at that moment it did nothing at all. As each inmate
passed a checkpoint, his ankle ID registered his presence and was
checked against the master file of what inmates were permitted to
be in what locations at which times. In the seven and half hours
after Harvey did his job, about a dozen inmates come up wrong on
the computer. Their sector doors locked hard until a human guard
ambled by to check it out. Three of the inmates were stoned. One
was simply an incorrigible troublemaker who had no business being
in a nice place like Nathanael Greene. The others all had good
excuses. None of them was Inmate HARVEY John T. 838-10647.
Neither he nor any of his three confederates had tripped any alert,
and they never would again. The computer registered their various
presences readily enough. When it consulted the file of any one of
them, the computer was redirected to a special instruction table,
which informed it that Inmates Harvey, Muzzi, Esposito, and La
Croy were permitted to be anyplace they chose to be at any time.
When it sought for any one of them in his cell and registered an

absence, the same redirection told the computer that this particular indication of absence was to be treated as registering "present." The computer did not question any of that. Neither did the guards. The function of the guards was not really to guard anything, only to enforce the commands of the computer—and now and then, to be sure, to see that none of the inmates dumbly or deliberately jammed the optical scanners by kicking their IDs in backward, thus locking everybody in everywhere. The guards didn't ask questions, since they were as sure as any bank or brokerage firm that the computer would not fail.

And were about to learn the same lesson from Johnny Harvey.

So at five o'clock the next morning, all four of them had strolled to a cell in the east wing of Nathanael Greene, part of the block that had been evacuated while the outside digging for the Bed-Stuy shit pit was going on. "Do it, fuckheads," Muzzi ordered, licking his lips, as Esposito held the spike and La Croy got ready to strike the first blow. "I'll be back in ten minutes."

He was fondling the paper-wrapped shiv, and Harvey had a dismal feeling. "We all really ought to stay right here, Moots," he offered; and Muzzi said, without malice:

"I got business with a guard." And he was gone.

"Oh, shit," sighed Harvey, and nodded to La Croy to swing the hammer.

Since no one else was in that wing, no one heard. Or no one but the geophones, who relayed the information to the central computer, where the same chip informed it that the digging noises were part of the excavation for the shit pit. The geophone heard the sound of the plastic going off in the drillhole five minutes later, too, and reported it, and got the same response; and they were through the wall. All that remained was furious digging for about a dozen yards. When they were well begun, Muzzi came staggering back, holding his face, his jaw at an unusual angle. "Fuckin' cock-thucker thapped me," he groaned. "Get the fuckin' hole dug!" And dig they did, frantic shoveling, now and then noisy and nerve-racking sledgehammering as they hit a rock, and all the time Muzzi

ranting and complaining as he held his fractured jaw: the shiv had
been too short, it had broken off, the fuckin' guard fought back,
Muzzi had had to strangle the fucker to teach him a fuckin' lesson
for giving him a fuckin' hard time—Harvey began to panic, to fear;
the grand plan was going all to pieces because this raving maniac
was part of it—

And then they made it through the dirt and broke out into open
space, into the excavation. Out onto a narrow plank walk over four
stories of open steelwork. To a ladder and up it, five stories up, all
the way to the surface; seeing buildings, seeing city streets, seeing
the lightening predawn sky—and it was working; it was all working,
after all!

They even saw the black car that was waiting where it was supposed to wait, with its clothes and guns and money—

And then it all went wrong again—Jesus, Harvey moaned, how
terribly wrong—as a construction-site security guard, who did not
have a computer to tell him what to do, observed four men clam-
bering out of the excavation, and tried to stop them.

It was too bad for him. But the shots gave the alarm, and the
noise and the commotion was too much for the person in the black
car, and the car rolled away and around the corner, and there they
were: Esposito dead, Muzzi with a bullet in his ass, out of prison,
free—but also alone in a world that hated them.

5.

Marcus was early at Mr. Feigerman's office, not just the early that
he wanted to be because the errand he had to run couldn't wait,
but too early for Mr. Feigerman to stand for it. He couldn't help
himself. All the way from the candy store, his feet kept hurrying
him, although his head told him to slow down. His feet knew what
they were doing. They were scared.

So was the rest of Marcus Garvey de Harcourt. It was bad to be
summoned out of school because his father had been hurt. It was
worse that when he got to the candy store, his father was in a

stretcher, a paramedic hovering by, while two cops questioned him angrily and dangerously. The store had been robbed, Marcus gathered. The robbers were not just robbers, they were escaped prisoners from Nathanael Greene; and they had held up the store, beaten up his father, stolen all the money, and ridden off in a commandeered panel truck with Jersey plates. None of that really scared Marcus. It was only the normal perils of the jungle, surprising only because his father was known to be under the protection of someone big. It did not occur to Marcus that the story was a whole, huge lie until his father waved the cops away so he could whisper to his son. What he whispered was: "Around the corner. Mr. Gambiage. Do what he say." It was serious—so serious that Dandy de Harcourt didn't bother to threaten Marcus with the cat, because he knew the boy would understand that any punishment for failure would be a lot worse. That was when Marcus began to be scared; and what finished the job was when Mr. Gambiage snatched him into the black car and told him what he had to do.

So he took the knapsack and the orders and went trotting off, and if the boy warrior did not wet his pants with fear, it was only because he was too scared to pee. He had been told that a diversion had been organized. The diversion was beginning to take shape all around him, people in threes and fours hurrying toward the heart of the Bed-Stuy project, some carrying banners, some huddled on the sidewalks as they lettered new ones. It made slow going, but not slow enough; he got to the Williamsburgh Bank Building more than ninety minutes before he was expected, and that was too early. The best thing to do was to pee himself a break in the twenty-ninth-floor men's room to collect his thoughts and calm himself down, but a security guard followed him in and stood behind him at the urinal. "What's in the backpack, kid?" the guard asked, not very aggressively.

Marcus took his time answering. It was a good thing he'd finally managed to get tall enough for the man-sized urinals, because there weren't any kid-sized ones here. He urinated at a comfortable pace, and when he was quite finished and his fly glitched shut, he turned and said, "I'm Mr. Rintelen Feigerman's personal assistant, and these are things for Mr. Feigerman." The guard was a small man. He was lighter-skinned than Marcus, but for a minute there he looked a lot like Dandy getting ready to reach for the cat. Then he relaxed and grinned. "Aw, hell, sure. Mr. Feigerman's seeing-eye kid, that right?" He didn't wait for an answer, but reached under his web belt and pulled out a pack of cigarettes. "If you see anybody coming in, kid, you give a real loud cough, you hear?" he ordered, just like Dandy, and disappeared into a stall. In a moment Marcus smelled weed. Cheap chickenshit, he said, but not out loud, because he knew there was no hope that a guard working for Mr. Feigerman would offer a hit to Feigerman's young protégé, no matter how much the protégé needed to steady his nerves.

In the waiting room of Feigerman and Tisdale Engineering Associates, Marcus dusted off his best society manners before he approached the receptionist. It was, "Mr. Feigerman's expecting me, sir," and, "I know I'm too early, sir," and "I'll just sit over here out of the way, so please don't disturb Mr. Feigerman, sir." So of course the receptionist relayed it all to Feigerman practically at once, and Marcus was ushered into the old man's presence nearly an hour before his time. But not into the big office with the useless huge windows. Feigerman was down where he liked to be, in his model room, and he turned toward the boy at once, his head set wheeping and clicking away. "I heard about your dad, Marcus," he said anxiously. "I hope he's all right."

"Just beaten up pretty bad, Mr. Feigerman. They're taking him to the hospital, but they say he'll be O.K."

"Terrible, terrible. Those animals. I hope the police catch them."

"Yes, sir," said Marcus, not bothering to tell Mr. Feigerman that it was not likely to have been the escaped convicts that had done the beating as much as one of Mr. Gambiage's associates, just to make the story look good.

"Terrible," Feigerman repeated. "And there's some kind of demonstration going on against the Bed-Stuy project, did you see it? I swear, Marcus," he said, not waiting for an answer, "I don't know how Gambiage gets these people out! They must know what he is. And they have to know, too, that the project is for their own good, don't they?"

"Sure they do," said Marcus, again refraining from the obvious: the project could do them good, but not nearly as much good, or bad, as Gambiage could do them. "We going to go take a look at it?"

"Oh, yes," said Feigerman, but not with enthusiasm; it was a bad day for the old man, Marcus could see, and if it hadn't been for the nagging terror in his own mind, he would have felt sympathy. Feigerman reached out to fondle a sixteenth-scale model of one of the wind rotors and brightened. "You haven't been down there lately, Marcus. Would you like me to show you around?"

If Marcus had been able to afford the truth, he would surely have said yes, because almost the best part of working for Mr. Feigerman was seeing the working models of the windmills, the thermal aquifer storage with oil substituting for the water, the really-truly working photovoltaics, which registered a current when you turned a light on them—all of them, actually. And there was something new, an Erector-set construction of glass tubing with something like Freon turning itself into vapor at the bottom and bubbling up through a column of water and pulling the water along, then the water passing through another tube and a turbine on the way down to generate more power.

Feigerman's sonar eyes could not tell him what someone was thinking, but he could see where Marcus was looking. "That's what we call the woperator," he said proudly. "It can use warm underground water to circulate that fluid all winter long, boiling another fluid at the bottom and condensing it again at the top—what's the matter?" he added anxiously, seeing that Marcus was shaking his head.

"It's Dandy," Marcus explained. "Before they took him away, he told me I had to deliver some cigarettes for him—they're good customers, over by the power plant—"

Feigerman was disappointed, then annoyed. "Oh, hell, boy, what are you telling me? Cigarettes don't come in tin cans."

Fuck the old bastard! Sometimes you forgot that he saw things in a different way, and that metal would give off a conspicuous echo even inside a canvas backpack. "Sure, Mr. Feigerman," Marcus improvised, "but there's two containers of coffee there, too. And Dandy said he'd get the cat out if it got there cold."

"Oh, hell." Since Feigerman wasn't much good at reading other people's expressions, perhaps in compensation his own face showed few. But it was clear this time that he was disappointed. He said in resignation, "I don't want to get you in trouble with your dad, Marcus, especially after those thugs beat him up. Sam!" he called to the modelmaker chief, standing silent across the room. "Call down for my car, will you?" But all the way down in the elevator, he was silent and obviously depressed. No more than Marcus, who was not only depressed but scared; not only scared but despairing, because he was beginning to understand that sooner or later somebody was going to connect his visits to the prison with the fact that the escaped prisoners had just happened to stop at his father's candy store . . . and so, very likely, this was the last time he would spend with Mr. Feigerman.

Julius was waiting for them with the car, illegally parked right in front of the main entrance because it had begun to rain. Mr. Feigerman's machine was doing its whee-clickety-beep thing, and he turned his head restlessly about, but the sonar did not work through the windows of the limousine. "There's a lot of people out there," said Marcus, trying to help without upsetting the old man.

"I can hear that, damn it! What are they doing?"

What they were doing was shouting and chanting, and there were a lot more of them than Marcus had expected. Old Man Feigerman was not satisfied. Blind he might be, but his otoliths were in fine shape; he could feel the pattern of acceleration and deceleration, and knew that the driver, Julius, was having a hard time getting through the crowds. "Is it that maniac Gambiage's demonstration?" he demanded.

Marcus said apologetically, "I guess that's it, Mr. Feigerman. There's a lot of them carrying signs."

"Read me the signs, damn it!"

Obediently, Marcus rattled off the nearest few. There was a "Give Bed-Stuy Freedom of Choice!" and a "*Salvemos nostras casas!*" and "Jobs, not Theories!" and two or three that made specific reference to Mr. Feigerman himself, which Marcus did not read aloud. Or have to. As they inched along, block by block, the yelling got louder and more personal. "Listen, Feigerman," bawled one man, leaning over the hood of the car, "Bed-Stuy's our home—love it or leave it!" And Old Man Feigerman, looking even older than usual, sank back on the seat, gnawing his thumb.

The rain did not seem to slow anybody down—not anybody, of all the dozens of different kinds of anybodies thronging the streets. There were dozens, even hundreds, of the neighborhood characters—five or six tottering winos, fat old Bloody Bess the moocher, even two young brothers from the Franciscan rescue mission, swinging their rain-soaked signs and shouting. Marcus could make out neither the slogans nor the signs, because they seemed to be in Latin. There were solid clumps of blue-collars, some of them construction workers, some from the truckers and the airline drivers; there were people who looked like bank clerks and people who looked like store salespersons—put them all together and it was a tremendous testimonial to Mr. Gambiage's ability to whip a spontaneous riot on a moment's notice. And they were not all pacific. Ahead there was a whine of sirens and a plop of tear-gas shells from where the construction equipment stood idle.

"They're getting rough," bawled Julius over his shoulder, and he looked worried. "Looks like they're smashing the backhoes!"

Mr. Feigerman nodded without answering, but his face looked terribly drawn. Marcus, looking at him, began to worry that the old man was not up to this sort of ordeal—if, indeed Marcus himself was. He craned his neck to peer at the clock on the Williamsburgh Bank Building and gritted his teeth. They were running very late, and it was not the kind of errand where an excuse would get off. It didn't get faster. A block along, a police trike whined up beside them, scattering a gaggle of high school girls shouting, "Soak the rich, help the poor; make Bed-Stuy an open door!" The cop ran down his window and yelled across at Julius, then recognized him as a fellow policeman and peered into the back to see Mr. Feigerman.

"You sure you want to go in here?" he demanded. There was a tone of outrage in his voice—a beat cop who had spent the first hour of his shift expecting to find desperate escaped convicts, received the welcome word that they were probably across the Hudson River, and then been confronted with a quick, dirty, and huge burgeoning riot.

Julius referred the question to higher authority. "What do you say, Mr. Feigerman?" he called over his shoulder. "Any minute now some of these thugs are going to start thinking about turning cars over."

Feigerman shook his head. "I want to see what they're doing," he said, his voice shrill and unhappy. "But maybe not you, Marcus. Maybe you ought to get out and go back."

The boy stiffened. "Aw, no, please, Mr. Feigerman!" he begged. "I got to deliver this, uh, coffee—and anyway," he improvised, "I'd be scared to be alone in that bunch! I'm a lot better off with you and Julius!" It was a doubtful thesis at best, but the cop in the trike was too busy to argue, and Mr. Feigerman too full of woe. Only Julius was shaking his head as he wormed the big car through the ever-narrower spaces between the yelling, chanting groups. But as they crossed the Long Island Rail Road tracks, the crowds thinned. "Down there," Marcus ordered. "Over between the power plant and the shit pit, the stuff's for the guards at the excavation—"

Julius paused to crane his neck around and stare at Marcus, but when Feigerman didn't protest, he obediently turned the car down a rutted, chewed-up street. Feigerman gasped, as the car jolted over potholes, "Damn that Gambiage! I thought he was still planning to buy me off—why does he do this now?"

Marcus did not answer, but he could have guessed that it had something to do with the stuff in his backpack. "Right by the guard shack," he directed, and Julius turned into an entrance with a wire-mesh gate. A man in uniform came strolling out. "Got the stuff for us, kid?" he asked, chewing on a straw, his hand resting on the butt of a gun.

"Yes, sir!" cried Marcus, shucking the pack and rolling down the window, delighted to get his errand run so peacefully.

But it didn't stay peaceful long. Julius was staring at the man in the guard's uniform and, with increasing concern, at the quiet excavation and the absence of anyone else. Before Marcus could get the pack off, Julius shouted, "Son of a bitch, it's Jack La Croy—get down, Mr. Feigerman!"

But not fast enough. La Croy had the guard's gun, and he had not taken his hand off it. The shot went into Julius's throat, right between the Adam's apple and the chin, and spatters of blood flew back to strike Marcus's face like hot little raindrops. Two other men boiled out of the guard shack, one limping and swearing, the other Marcus's pretend-father, his face scared and dangerous. As La Croy pushed Julius out of the way and shoved himself behind the wheel, the other two jumped into the back of the car, fat, fearsome Muzzi reaching for the backpack of weapons and money with an expression of savage joy. . . .

And from behind them, a sudden roar of an engine and the quick zap of a siren.

Everybody was shouting at once. Marcus, crushed under the weight of the killer Muzzi, could not see what was happening, but he could feel the car surge forward, stop, spin, and make a dash in another direction. There was a sudden lurch and crash as they broke through something, and then it stopped and the men were out of the car, firing at something behind them. Julius would never get back on the force, Marcus thought, struggling to wipe the blood off his face—and whether he himself would live through the next hour was at best an open question.

For Johnny Harvey everything had begun going terribly wrong before they broke through the wall, and gone downhill ever since. It was just luck they'd been able to kill the security guard and get his gun, just luck that they'd been able to hide in a place where there was a telephone, long enough for Muzzi to make his phone call on the secret number and beg, or threaten, the big man to get them out. The arrangements were complicated—a delivery of guns and money, a faked holdup to send the cops in the wrong direction, a whomped-up riot to keep the cops busy—but they'd been working pretty well, and that was luck, too, lots of luck, more than they had a right to expect—

But the luck had run out.

When the boy came with the guns, it was bad luck that the driver was an off-duty cop who recognized La Croy, worse luck still that there was a police car right behind them. La Croy did the only thing he could do. There was no way out of the street they were in except back past the cops, and that was impossible. So he'd slammed the car through the gate of the power plant. And there they were, inside the power plant, with four terrified engineers lying face down on the floor of the control room, and forty thousand New York City cops gathering outside. The boy was scared shitless; the old man, his vision gear crushed, was lying hopeless and paralyzed beside the guards. "At least we've got hostages," said La Croy, fondling his gun, and Muzzi, staring around the control room of the nuclear plant, said:

"Asshole! We've got the whole fucking *city* for a hostage!"

6.

The job as companion and bedpan-changer to old Mrs. Feigerman paid well, worked easy, and was generally too good to last. When it ended, Nillie de Harcourt didn't complain. She turned to the next chapter in her life: bag lady. That meant eight hours a day sitting before a screening table in her pale green smock, chatting with the bag ladies on either side of her, while magnets pulled out the ferrous metals: glass went one way, to be separated by color; organics went another. The biggest part of the job was to isolate organics so they would not poison the sludge-making garbage. The work was easy enough, and not particularly unpleasant once you got past the smell. But that was too good to last, too, because anything good was always going to be too good for Gwenna Marie Anderson Vanilla Fudge de Harcourt. So when she saw The Man moving purposefully toward her through the clinking, clattering, smelly aisles, she was not surprised. "Downstairs, Nillie," he said, flashing the potsie. "We need you." She didn't ask why. She just looked toward her supervisor, who shrugged and nodded; and took off the green smock regretfully, and folded it away, and did as she was told. He didn't tell her what it was about. He didn't have to. Trouble was what it was about, because that was always what it was about. She followed him into the waiting police car without comment. The driver in the front started away at once, siren screaming. In the back, the cop turned on a tape recorder, cleared his throat, and said, "This interview is being conducted by Sergeant Marvin Wasserman. Is your name Gwenna Anderson?"

"That was my name before I married de Harcourt."

"According to records, Mrs. de Harcourt, you have fourteen arrests and six convictions for prostitution; five arrests, no convictions for shoplifting; two arrests, one conviction for possession of a controlled substance; and one arrest, no conviction for open lewdness."

Nillie shrugged. "You're talking about fifteen years ago, man."

Wasserman looked at her with annoyance, but also, Nillie noted, a lot more tension than anything he had said so far would justify. "Right," he said sarcastically, "so now you're a success story. You married the boss and went into business for yourself. Dope business, numbers business, bookmaking business."

"If I was all those things, would I have to get work as a bag lady?"

"I ask the questions," he reminded her, but it was a fair question and he knew it. He didn't know the answer, but then hardly anybody did but Nillie herself—and most people wouldn't have believed it if told. "You have a son named Marcus Garvey de Harcourt?" he went on.

Suddenly Nillie sat bolt upright. "Mister, did something happen to Marcus?"

The sergeant was human, after all; he hesitated, and then said,

"I'm not supposed to tell you anything, just make sure I've got the right person. But your son's in good health last I heard."

"*Mister!*"

"I have to ask you these questions! Now, did you ever work for Henry Gambiage?"

"Not exactly. Sort of; all the girls did, at least he was getting a cut on everything. But that was before his name was Gambiage. What about Marcus?"

"And do you and your husband work for him now?"

"Not me!"

"But your husband?" he insisted.

"Take the Fifth," she said shortly. "Anyway, you ain't read me my rights."

"You're not under arrest," he told her, and then clicked off the tape recorder. "That's all I can say, Ms. de Harcourt," he finished, "so please don't ask me any more questions." And she didn't, but she was moving rapidly from worry to terror. Mentioning her son was bad enough; mentioning Gambiage was a lot worse. But when a cop called her "Ms." and used the word "please"—then it was time to get scared.

It was all but physically impossible for Nillie to plead with a policeman, but she came as close to it in the rest of this ride as ever since the first afternoon she'd been picked up for soliciting a plainclothes on the corner of Eighth Avenue and Forty-fifth Street, fifteen years ago, turned out on the turf just two days before, and still thinking that someday, maybe, she'd get back to the Smokies of eastern Tennessee. She gazed out at the dirty, rainy streets as they whizzed by at fifty miles an hour through rapidly moving traffic, and wished she could be sick. Marcus! If anything happened to him—

Her view of the dingy streets was suddenly streaked with tears, and Nillie began to pray.

When Nillie prayed she did not address any god. What religion she had she picked up in the Women's House of Detention, the last time she was there—the last time she ever would be there, she had vowed. It was just after the big riots in New York, and the first night in her cell she dropped off to sleep and found herself being touched by a big, strong woman with a hard, huge face. Nillie automatically assumed she was bull-dyke. She was wrong. The woman was a missionary. She got herself arrested simply so she could preach to the inmates. Her religion was called "Temple I"— I am a temple, I myself, I am holy. It didn't matter in her church what god you worshipped. You could worship any, or none at all; but you had to worship in, for, and to yourself. You should not drug, whore, or steal; above all, no matter what wickedness went on around you, you should not let them make you an accomplice . . . and so when Nillie got out, she went to seek her pimp to tell him that she was through. . . .

And found Dandy in far worse shape than she. No more girls to run. No money left. And both kneecaps shattered, because he had made the mistake of getting in the middle of a power struggle in the mob. So she nursed him; and when she found out she was pregnant by him, she kept it to herself until he was able to hobble around, and by then it was too late to think about a quick and easy abortion. It was a surprise to her that he married her. Dandy wasn't really a bad man—for a pimp—though even for a pimp he damn sure wasn't an especially good one; but he wanted a son, and it was joy for both of them when it turned out she was giving him one. Uneasy joy, sometimes—the boy was born small, caught every bug that was going around, missed half of every school year until he was eight. But that wasn't a bad thing; in the hospitals were Gray Ladies and nurses to teach him to read and give him the habit; he was smarter than either of his parents right now, Nillie thought—

If he was alive.

She straightened up and rubbed the last dampness from the corners of her eyes. She recognized the streets fleeting by—they were in her own neighborhood now, only blocks from the candy store. But what had happened? The streets were littered with rain-smeared placards, and the smell of tear gas was strong. Distant bullhorns blared something about evacuation and *warning* and nuclear accident—

The police car nosed across the LIRR tracks, with a commuter special flashing away along the maglev lines as though it were running from something. As Nillie saw that the car was approaching the power plant, she thought that it was probably time to run, all right, if there was anywhere to run to.

They parked at the end of the cul-de-sac, with barricades and police cars blocking off the road, and ran, dazzled by the spinning blue and white and red emergency lights, along one side of the street, across the utility's chain link fence, into a storefront. And there were cops by the dozen, and not just cops. There was supercop, the Commissioner Himself, giving orders to half a dozen gray-haired police with gold braid on their caps; and there was a hospital stretcher, and out of a turban of white bandages looked eyes that Nillie instinctively recognized as her husband's; and there was Mrs. Feigerman's sullen elderly son, David Tisdale, looking both frightened and furious—

And there, his scar pale and his lips compressed, staring at her with the cold consideration of a butcher about to put the mercy killer to the skull of a steer, was Henry Gambiage.

The situation wasn't only bad, it was worse than Nillie had dreamed possible. If Marc was alive—and he had been, at least, a few minutes earlier on the telephone—he was also a hostage. Not just any hostage. Captive of one of the maddest, meanest murderers in the New York prison system, Albert Muzzi. And not just at the mercy of the mad dog's weapons, but right at Ground Zero for what the convicts threatened would be the damnedest biggest explosion the much-bombed city had ever seen. The argument that was going on when Nillie came in had nothing to do with the hostages. It was among three people—two engineers from Con Ed and a professor from Brooklyn College's physics department—and what they were arguing was whether it lay within the capacities of the escaped convicts merely to poison all of Bedford-Stuyvesant, or if they could take out the whole city and most of Long Island and the North Jersey coast. The commissioner was having none of that. "Clear them out," he ordered tersely. "The mayor's going to be here in half an hour, and I want this settled before then." But Nillie wasn't listening.

She was thinking about Marcus Garvey de Harcourt, age ten, in the middle of a nuclear explosion of any kind. Nothing else made much impression. She heard two of the police wrangling with each other over whether they had done the right thing by following Marcus with his bag of weapons to see where the escapees were, instead of simply preventing him from delivering them as soon as they realized the story of the candy-store holdup was a lie. She heard the commissioner roaring at Gambiage, and Gambiage stolidly, repetitiously, demanding to see his lawyer. She heard her husband whisper—even harder to understand than usual, because his lips were swollen like a Ubangi maiden's—that Muzzi had made him get the boy to try to deliver weapons, had made him lie about the fake holdup, and then had beaten him senseless to make the story more realistic. She gathered, vaguely, that the reason she and Dandy were there was to force Gambiage to get his criminals away from the power plant by threatening to testify against him—David Tisdale the same—and none of it made any impression on her. She sat silent by the window, peering at the chain link fence and the low, sullen building that lay behind it. "Listen, shithead," the commissioner was roaring, "your lawyer wouldn't come if I let him, because if you don't get Muzzi out of that control room, the whole city might go up!"

And Gambiage spread his hands. "You think I don't care about the city? Jesus. I *own* half of it. But there's nothing I can do with Muzzi." And then he went flying, looking more surprised than angered, as Nillie pushed past him. "There's something *I* can do," she cried. "I can talk to my little boy! Where's that phone?"

Marcus H. Garvey de Harcourt, King of the jungle, strong and fearless—Marcus who faced up every day to the threat of Dandy's cat-o'nine-tails, and the menace of bigger kids willing to beat him bloody for the dimes in the pocket, and the peril of pederasts who carried switchblade knives to convince their victims, and stray dogs, and mean-hearted cops, and raunchy winos—that dauntless Marcus was scared out of his tree. Dead people, sure. You couldn't live a decade in Bed-Stuy without coming across an occasional stiff. Not often stiffs you had known. Not often seeing them die. Julius had not been any friend of his—at best, a piece of the furniture of Marcus's life—but seeing him sob and bubble his life away had been terrifying. It was all terrifying. There was old Mr. Feigerman, his seeing gear crushed and broken; the blind man was really blind now, and it seemed to cost him his speech and hearing as well, for he just lay against a wall of the power station control center, unmoving. There was his *soi-disant* father, Johnny Harvey, not jovial now, not even paying attention to him; he was standing by the window with a stitch-gun in his hand, and Marcus feared for the life of anyone who showed in Harvey's field of fire. There were the power station engineers, bound and gagged, not to mention beaten up, lying in the doorway so if anyone started shooting from outside, they would be the first to get it. There was that loopy little guy with the crazy eyes, La Croy, screaming rage and obscenities, shrieking as though he were being skinned alive, although he didn't have a mark on him. And there was—

There was Muzzi. Marcus swallowed and looked away, for Muzzi had looked at him a time or two in a fashion that scared him most of all. Marcus was profoundly grateful that Muzzi was more interested in the telephone to the outside world than in himself. There he was, looking like Pancho Villa with his holstered guns and the twin bandoliers crossed over his steel-ribbed flak jacket, yelling at the unseen, but not unheard, Mr. Gambiage. "Out!" he roared. "What we want ith fuckin' out, and fuckin' damn thoon!"

"Now, Moots," soothed the voice over the speakerphone.

"Now *thit!* We had a fuckin' deal! I keep my fuckin mouth thut about MacReady, and you get me out of the fuckin' joint!"

"I didn't kill MacReady—"

"You wath fuckin' right there watching when I gave him the fuckin' ithe pick, tho get fuckin' movin'!"

Gambiage's self-control was considerable, but there was an edge to his voice as he said, placatingly. "I'm doing what I can, Moots. The mayor's on his way, and he's agreed to be a hostage while you get on the plane—"

"Not jutht the mayor. I want the fuckin' governor and the fuckin' govern'th fuckin' kid! All three of them, and right away, or I blow up the whole fuckin' thity!"

Just to hear the words made icy little mice run up and down Marcus's spine. Blow up the city! It was one thing to listen to Mrs. Spiegal tell about it in the third grade, and a whole other, far worse thing to imagine it really happening. Could it happen? Marcus shrank back into his corner, looking at the men around him. Muzzi certainly wouldn't have the brains to make it happen; neither would La Croy. The engineers and Mr. Feigerman might know how, but Marcus couldn't imagine anything the convicts could do that would make them do it.

That left Johnny Harvey.

Ah, shit, Marcus thought to himself, sure. Johnny Harvey could figure out how to do it if anybody could. *Would* he?

The more Marcus thought about it, the more he thought that Harvey just might. What little Marcus had seen of Nathanael Greene made him think that living there must be pretty lousy, lousy enough so that even dying in a mushroom cloud might be better than spending the rest of your life in a place like that. Or a worse one. . . . But it wouldn't be better for Marcus. Marcus didn't want to die. And the only thing he could think of that might keep him from it, if Muzzi blew his stack terminally and Harvey carried out the bluff, would be for him to kill Harvey first—"Hey, kid!"

Marcus stiffened and saw that Muzzi was glowering at him, holding the phone in his hand. "Wh-what?" he got out.

Muzzi studied him carefully, and the scowl became what Muzzi might have thought was an ingratiating grin. "It'th your mom, thweetie. Wantth to talk to you."

The question of how it had all gone to hell no longer interested Johnny Harvey; the question of what, if anything, there was left to hope for was taking up all his attention. He sat before the winking signal lights and dials of the power controls, wolfing down his third hamburger and carton of cold coffee, wondering what Marcus had been wondering. Would he do it? Was there a point in blowing up a city out of rage and revenge? Or was there a point in not doing

it, if that meant going back to Nathanael Greene?—or some
worse place. He reached for another hamburger, and then
pushed the cardboard tray away in disgust. Trust Muzzi to
demand food that a decent palate couldn't stand! But those
two words, "trust" and "Muzzi," didn't belong in the same
sentence.

Trusting Muzzi had got him this far. It wasn't far enough. There
was Muzzi, stroking the nigger kid's arm as the boy talked to his
mother, on the ragged edge of hysteria; Muzzi with his jaw broken
and one hand just about ruined, and still filled with enough rage
and enough lust for a dozen ordinary human beings. You could
forget about Feigerman and the engineers; they were just about out
of it. There was Muzzi and that asshole La Croy, and the boy and
himself, and how were they going to get out of here? Assume the
governor gave in. Assume there really was a jet waiting for them at
Kennedy. The first thing they had to do was get out of this place
and into a car—not here in this street, where there could be a
thousand booby traps that would wreck any plan, but out in the
open, say on the other side of the avenue toward the airport. It was
almost like one of those cannibals-and-missionaries puzzles of his
boyhood. Johnny Harvey had been really good at those puzzles.
Was there a way to solve this one? Let the first missionary take the
first cannibal across the river in the boat—only this time it was
across the railroad tracks—then come back by himself to where the
other missionaries and cannibals were waiting—

Only this time he was one of the cannibals, and the game was
for keeps.

The boy was still on the phone, weeping now, and Muzzi had
evidently got some kind of crazed idea in his head, because he had
moved over to the corner where Feigerman was lying. Callously,
he wrenched the remains of the harness off Feigerman's unpro-
testing body. The old man wasn't dead, but he made no sound as
Muzzi began straightening out the bent metal and twisted crown.
Then he got up and walked toward Johnny Harvey.

Who got up and moved cautiously away; you never knew what
Muzzi was going to do.

And then he saw that Muzzi, glowering over the power station controls, was reaching his hand out toward them; and then Johnny Harvey was really scared.

When Nillie got off the phone she just sat. She didn't weep. Nillie de Harcourt had had much practice restraining tears in her life. They were a luxury she couldn't afford, not now, not while Marcus was in that place with those men—with that one particular man, for she had known Muzzi by reputation and gossip and by personal pain, and she knew what particular perils her son was in. So she sat dry-eyed and alert, and watched and waited. When she heard Johnny Harvey on the phone, warning that Muzzi was getting ready to explode, demanding better food than the crap they'd been given, she looked thoughtful for a moment. But she didn't say anything, even when the mayor and Mr. Gambiage retreated to another room for a while. Whatever they were cooking up, it satisfied neither of them. When they came out, the mayor was scowling and Mr. Gambiage was shaking his head. "Do not underestimate Moots," he warned. "He's an animal, but he knows a trap when he sees one."

"Shut up," said the mayor, for once careless of a major campaign contributor. The mayor was looking truly scared. He listened irritably to some distant sound, then turned to Gambiage. "They're still shouting out there. I thought you said you'd call off the demonstration."

"It is called off," said Gambiage heavily. "It takes time. It is easier to start things than to stop them." And Nillie was listening alertly, one hand in the hand of her husband. Only when two policemen came in with a room-service rolling hotel tray of food did she let go and move forward.

"It's all ready," one of them said, and the mayor nodded, and Nillie de Harcourt put her hand on the cart.

"I'm taking it over there," she said.

The mayor looked actually startled—maybe even frightened for reasons Nillie did not try to guess. "No chance, Mrs. de Harcourt. You don't know what kind of men they are."

"I do know," Nillie said steadily. "Who better? And I'm taking this food over so I can be with my son."

The mayor opened his mouth angrily, but Mr. Gambiage put a hand on his shoulder. "Why not?" he said softly.

"Why not? Don't be an idiot, Gambiage—" And then the mayor had second thoughts. He paused, irresolute, then shrugged. "If you insist in front of witnesses," he said, "I do not feel I have the right to stop you."

Nillie was moving toward the door with the cart before he could change his mind. A train flashed underneath the bridge, but she didn't even look at it. She was absolutely certain that something was going on that she didn't understand, something very wrong—something that would make the mayor of the city and the city's boss of all boss criminals whisper together in front of witnesses; but what it was she did not know, and did not consider that it mattered. She went steadily across the tracks and did not falter even when she saw crazy La Croy shouting out the window to her, with his gun pointed at her head. She didn't speak, and she didn't stop. She pushed right in through the door, kicking the power plant engineers out of the way.

There they were, crazy Muzzi and crazy La Croy, both swearing at her, and sane but treacherous Johnny Harvey with his hand on a gun, moving uncertainly toward the food; and there was old Mr. Feigerman looking like death days past—

And there was Marcus, looking scared but almost unharmed. "Honey, honey!" she cried, and abandoned the food and ran to take him in her arms.

"Leave him alone, bitch!" shouted La Croy, and Muzzi thundered behind him:

"Fuckin' handth up, you! Who knowth what you've got there—"

She turned to face them calmly. "I've got nothing but me," she said, and waited for them to do whatever they were going to do.

But what they did was nothing. Johnny Harvey, not very interested in her or in his companions, was moving on the cart of food, the big dish with the silver dome; he lifted the dome—

Bright bursts of light flared from under it, thunder roared, and something picked Nillie de Harcourt up and threw her against the wall.

A shard of metal had caught La Croy in the back of the head; he probably had never felt it. What there was left of Johnny Harvey was almost nothing at all. Muzzi struggled to his feet, the terrible pain in his jaw worse than ever, and stared furiously around the battered room. He could hardly see. It had not just been a bomb— they wouldn't have risked a bomb big enough to do the job, in that place; there was something like tear gas in with it, and Muzzi was choking and gasping. But, blurredly, he could see young Marcus trying to help his half-conscious mother out of the door, and he bawled, "Thtop or I blow your fuckin' headth off!" And the kid turned at him, and his face was a hundred years older than his age, and for a moment, even Muzzi felt an unaccustomed tingle of fright. If that kid had had a gun—

But he didn't. "Move your fuckin' atheth back in here!" roared Muzzi, and slowly, hopelessly, they came back into the choking air.

But not for long.

Two minutes later they were going out again, but there had been a change. Nillie de Harcourt stumbled ahead, barely conscious. Marcus Garvey de Harcourt pushed the wheelchair, and the occupant of the wheelchair, muffled in a turned-up jacket . . . was Muzzi.

And Marcus was the most frightened he had ever been in his life, because he could not see a way to live to the other side of the bridge. He could see the governor coming toward them, with a flanking line of police, all their guns drawn; and he knew what was in Muzzi's mind. The man had gone ape. If he couldn't get away and couldn't blow up the city, the next best thing was to kill the governor.

Halfway across the bridge, the governor made his move; but Marcus also made his.

It wasn't that he cared about the governor, but between the governor and Muzzi's gun was someone he cared about a lot. He took a deep breath, aimed the wheelchair toward a place where the rail was down and only wooden sawhorses were between the sidewalk and the maglev strips below . . .and shoved.

Muzzi was quick, but not quick enough. He was not quite out of the wheelchair when it passed the point of no return.

Marcus ran to the rail and stared down, and there was Muzzi in his bandoliers and steel-ribbed jacket, plummeting toward the maglev strips, beginning to move even before he hit, bouncing up, hitting again, and all the time moving with gathering speed until he flashed out of sight, no longer alive, no longer a threat to anyone.

The Lucky Strike

KIM STANLEY ROBINSON

Kim Stanley Robinson's short fiction has appeared in Orbit, The
Magazine of Fantasy & Science Fiction, *and* Universe. *His work
has been nominated for Hugo and Nebula awards, and he won a
World Fantasy Award in 1984 for his novella "Black Air." His first
novel,* The Wild Shore, *was a Nebula finalist this year, as was the
story that follows. A second novel,* Icehenge, *was also published in
1984. Robinson teaches at the University of California, Davis.*

*"The Lucky Strike" is a story set in our alternative history, depicting
events that might have happened in the past. It's a story many writers
have thought about writing at one time or another, done with sensitivity and grace. It also points up a feature of much recent science
fiction, including the works in this book: there is a lot of reality in
these stories, both emotional and intellectual, and these realities are
brought forward in ways not possible in a purely contemporary approach. This, of course, is a defining characteristic of successful science
fiction.*

War breeds strange pastimes. In July of 1945 on Tinian
Island in the North Pacific, Captain Frank January had taken to
piling pebble cairns on the crown of Mount Lasso—one pebble for
each B-29 takeoff, one cairn for each mission. It was a mindless
pastime, but so was poker. The men of the 509th had played a
million hands of poker, sitting in the shade of a palm around an
upturned crate, sweating in their skivvies, swearing and betting all
their pay and cigarettes, playing hand after hand, until the cards
got so soft and dog-eared you could have used them for toilet paper.
Captain January had gotten sick of it, and after he lit out for the
hilltop a few times some of his crew mates started trailing him.
When their pilot, Jim Fitch, joined them it became an official
pastime, like throwing flares into the compound or going hunting

for stray Japs. What Captain January thought of the development
he didn't say. The others grouped near Captain Fitch, who passed
around his battered flask. "Hey, January," Fitch called. "Come
have a shot."

January wandered over and took the flask. Fitch laughed at his
pebble. "Practicing your bombing up here, eh, Professor?"

"Yeah," January said sullenly. Anyone who read more than the
funnies was Professor to Fitch. Thirstily January knocked back some
rum. He passed the flask on to Lieutenant Matthews, their navigator.

"That's why he's the best," Matthews joked. "Always practicing."

Fitch laughed. "He's best because I make him be best, right,
Professor?"

January frowned. Fitch was a bulky youth, thick-featured, pig-
eyed—a thug, in January's opinion. The rest of the crew were all
in their mid-twenties, like Fitch, and they liked the captain's bossy
roughhouse style. January, who was thirty-seven, didn't go for it.
He wandered away, back to the cairn he had been building. From
Mount Lasso they had an overview of the whole island, from the
harbor at Wall Street to the north field in Harlem. January had
observed hundreds of B-29s roar off the four parallel runways of the
north field and head for Japan. The last quartet of this particular
mission buzzed across the width of the island, and January dropped
four more pebbles, aiming for crevices in the pile. One of them
stuck nicely.

"There they are!" said Matthews. "They're on the taxiing strip."

January located the 509th's first plane. Today, the first of August,
there was something more interesting to watch than the usual
Superfortress parade. Word was out that General LeMay wanted to
take the 509th's mission away from it. Their commander, Colonel
Tibbets, had gone and bitched to LeMay in person, and the general
had agreed the mission was theirs, but on one condition—one of
the general's men was to make a test flight with the 509th to make
sure they were fit for combat over Japan. The general's man had
arrived, and now he was down there in the strike plane with Tibbets
and the whole first team. January sidled back to his mates to view
the takeoff with them.

"Why don't the strike plane have a name, though?" Haddock was saying.

Fitch said, "Lewis won't give it a name because it's not his plane, and he knows it." The others laughed. Lewis and his crew were naturally unpopular, being Tibbets's favorites.

"What do you think he'll do to the general's man?" Matthews asked.

The others laughed at the very idea. "He'll kill an engine at takeoff, I bet you anything," Fitch said. He pointed at the wrecked B-29s that marked the end of every runway. "He'll want to show that he wouldn't go down if it happened to him."

"Course he wouldn't!" Matthews said.

"You hope," January said under his breath.

"They let those Wrights out too soon," Haddock said seriously. "They keep busting under the takeoff load."

"Won't matter to the old bull," Matthews said. Then they all started in about Tibbets's flying ability, even Fitch. They all thought Tibbets was the greatest. January, on the other hand, liked Tibbets even less than he liked Fitch. That had started right after he was assigned to the 509th. He had been told he was part of the most important group in the war and then given a leave. In Vicksburg a couple of fliers just back from England had bought him a lot of whiskeys, and since January had spent several months stationed near London they had talked for a good long time and gotten pretty drunk. The two were really curious about what January was up to now, but he had stayed vague on it and kept returning the talk to the blitz. He had seen an English nurse, for instance, whose flat had been bombed, family killed . . . But they had really wanted to know. So he had told them he was onto something special, and they had flipped out their badges and told him they were Army Intelligence, and that if he ever broke security like that again he'd be transferred to Alaska. It was a dirty trick. January had gone back to Wendover and told Tibbets so to his face, and Tibbets had turned red and threatened him some more. January despised him for that. During their year's training he had bombed better than ever, as a way of showing the old bull he was wrong. Every time their eyes had met it was clear what was going on. But Tibbets never backed off no matter how precise January's bombing got. Just thinking about it was enough to cause January to line up a pebble over an ant and drop it.

"Will you cut that out?" Fitch complained.

January pointed. "They're going."

Tibbets's plane had taxied to runway Baker. Fitch passed the flask around again. The tropical sun beat on them, and the ocean surrounding the island blazed white. January put up a sweaty hand to aid the bill of his baseball cap.

The four props cut in hard, and the sleek Superfortress quickly trundled up to speed and roared down Baker. Three quarters of the way down the strip the outside right prop feathered.

"Yow!" Fitch crowed. "I told you he'd do it!"

The plane nosed off the ground and slewed right, then pulled back on course to cheers from the four young men around January. January pointed again. "He's cut number three, too."

The inside right prop feathered, and now the plane was pulled up by the left wing only, while the two right props windmilled uselessly. "Holy smoke!" Haddock cried. "Ain't the old bull something?"

They whooped to see the plane's power and Tibbets's nervy arrogance.

"By God, LeMay's man will remember this flight," Fitch hooted. "Why, look at that! He's banking!"

Apparently taking off on two engines wasn't enough for Tibbets; he banked the plane right until it was standing on its dead wing, and it curved back toward Tinian.

Then the inside left engine feathered.

War tears at the imagination. For three years Frank January had kept his imagination trapped, refusing to give it any play whatsoever. The dangers threatening him, the effects of the bombs, the fate of the other participants in the war—he had refused to think about any of it. But the war tore at his control. That English nurse's flat. The missions over the Ruhr. The bomber just below him blown apart by flak. And then there had been a year in Utah, and the viselike grip that he had once kept on his imagination had slipped away.

So when he saw the number two prop feather, his heart gave a little jump against his sternum, and helplessly he was up there with Ferebee, the first-team bombardier. He would be looking over the pilots' shoulders . . .

"Only one engine?" Fitch said.

"That one's for real," January said harshly. Despite himself he *saw* the panic in the cockpit, the frantic rush to power the two right engines. The plane was dropping fast and Tibbets leveled it off, leaving them on a course back toward the island. The two right props spun, blurred to a shimmer. January held his breath. They needed more lift; Tibbets was trying to pull it over the island. Maybe he was trying for the short runway on the south half of the island.

But Tinian was too tall, the plane too heavy. It roared right into the jungle above the beach, where Forty-second Street met their East River. It exploded in a bloom of fire. By the time the sound of it struck them they knew no one in the plane had survived.

Black smoke towered into white sky. In the shocked silence on Mount Lasso, insects buzzed and creaked. The air left January's lungs with a gulp. He had been with Ferebee, he had heard the desperate shouts, seen the last green rush, been stunned by the dentist-drill-all-over pain of the impact.

"Oh my God," Fitch was saying. "Oh my God." Matthews was sitting. January picked up the flask, tossed it at Fitch.

"C-come on," he stuttered. He hadn't stuttered since he was sixteen. He led the others in a rush down the hill. When they got to Broadway a jeep careened toward them and skidded to a halt. It was Colonel Scholes, the old bull's exec. "What happened?"

Fitch told him.

"Those damned Wrights," Scholes said as the men piled in. This time one had failed at just the wrong moment; some welder in the States had kept flame to metal a second less than usual—or something equally minor, equally trivial—and that had made all the difference.

They left the jeep at Forty-second and Broadway and hiked east over a narrow track to the shore. A fairly large circle of trees was burning. The fire trucks were already there.

Scholes stood beside January, his expression bleak. "That was the whole first team," he said.

"I know," said January. He was still in shock, his imagination crushed, incinerated, destroyed. Once as a kid he had tied sheets to his arms and waist, jumped off the roof, and landed right on his chest; this felt like that had. He had no way of knowing what would come of this crash, but he had a suspicion that he had indeed smacked into something hard.

Scholes shook his head. A half hour had passed, the fire was nearly out. January's four mates were over chattering with the Seabees. "He was going to name the plane after his mother," Scholes said to the ground. "He told me that just this morning. He was going to call it *Enola Gay.*"

At night the jungle breathed, and its hot wet breath washed over the 509th's compound. January stood in the doorway of his Quonset barracks hoping for a real breeze. No poker tonight. Noises were hushed, faces solemn. Some of the men had helped box up the dead crew's gear. Now most lay on their bunks. January gave up on the breeze, climbed onto his top bunk to stare at the ceiling.

He observed the corrugated arch over him. Cricket song sawed through his thoughts. Below him a rapid conversation was being carried on in guilty undertones, Fitch at its center. "January is the best bombardier left," he said. "And I'm as good as Lewis was."

"But so is Sweeney," Matthews said. "And he's in with Scholes."

They were figuring out who would take over the strike. January scowled. Tibbets and the rest were less than twelve hours dead, and they were squabbling over who would replace them.

January grabbed a shirt, rolled off his bunk, put the shirt on.

"Hey, Professor," Fitch said, "where you going?"

"Out."

Though midnight was near, it was still sweltering. Crickets shut up as he walked by, started again behind him. He lit a cigarette. In the dark the MPs patrolling their compound were like pairs of walking armbands. Forcefully January expelled smoke, as if he could expel his disgust with it. They were only kids, he told himself. Their minds had been shaped in the war, by the war, and for the war. They knew you couldn't mourn the dead for long; carry around a load like that and your own engines might fail. That was all right with January. It was an attitude that Tibbets had helped to form, so it was what he deserved. Tibbets would *want* to be forgotten in favor of the mission; all he had lived for was to drop the gimmick on the Japs, and he was oblivious to anything else—men, wife, family, anything.

So it wasn't the lack of feeling in his mates that bothered January. And it was natural of them to want to fly the strike they had been training a year for. Natural, that is, if you were a kid with a mind shaped by fanatics like Tibbets, shaped to take orders and never imagine consequences. But January was not a kid, and he wasn't going to let men like Tibbets do a thing to his mind. And the gimmick . . . the gimmick was not natural. A chemical bomb of some sort, he guessed. Against the Geneva convention. He stubbed his cigarette against the sole of his sneaker, tossed the butt over the fence. The tropical night breathed over him. He had a headache.

For months now he had been sure he would never fly a strike. The dislike Tibbets and he had exchanged in their looks (January was acutely aware of looks) had been real and strong. Tibbets had understood that January's record of pinpoint accuracy in the runs over the Salton Sea had been a way of showing contempt. The record had forced him to keep January on one of the four second-string teams, but with the fuss they were making over the gimmick January had figured that would be far enough down the ladder to keep him out of things.

Now he wasn't so sure. Tibbets was dead. He lit another cigarette, found his hand shaking. The Camel tasted bitter. He threw it over the fence at a receding armband and regretted it instantly. A waste. He went back inside.

Before climbing onto his bunk he got a paperback out of his footlocker. "Hey, Professor, what you reading now?" Fitch said, grinning.

January showed him the blue cover. *Winter's Tales*, by an Isak Dinesen. Fitch examined the little wartime edition. "Pretty racy, eh?"

"You bet," January said heavily. "This guy puts sex on every page." He climbed onto his bunk, opened the book. The stories were strange, hard to follow. The voices below bothered him. He concentrated harder.

As a boy on the farm in Arkansas, January had read everything he could lay his hands on. On Saturday afternoons he would race his father down the muddy lane to the mailbox (his father was a reader too), grab *The Saturday Evening Post*, and run off to devour every word of it. That meant he had another week with nothing new to read, but he couldn't help it. It was a way off the farm, a way into the world. He had become a man who could slip between the covers of a book whenever he chose.

But not on this night.

The next day the chaplain gave a memorial service, and on the morning after that Colonel Scholes looked in the door of their hut right after mess. "Briefing at eleven," he announced. His face was haggard. "Be there early." He looked at Fitch with bloodshot eyes, crooked a finger. "Fitch, January, Matthews—come with me."

January put on his shoes. The rest of the men sat on their bunks and watched them wordlessly. January followed Fitch and Matthews out of the hut.

"I've spent most of the night on the radio with General LeMay," Scholes said. He looked them each in the eye. "We've decided you're to be the first crew to make a strike."

Fitch was nodding, as if he had expected it.

"Think you can do it?" Scholes said.

"Of course," Fitch replied. Watching him, January understood why they had chosen him to replace Tibbets. Fitch was like the old bull, he had that same ruthlessness. The young bull.

"Yes sir," Matthews said.

Scholes was looking at him. "Sure," January said, not wanting to think about it. "Sure." His heart was pounding directly on his sternum. But Fitch and Matthews looked serious as owls, so he wasn't going to stick out by looking odd. It was big news, after all; anyone would be taken aback by it. Nevertheless, January made an effort to nod.

"Okay," Scholes said. "McDonald will be flying with you as copilot." Fitch frowned. "I've got to go tell those British officers that LeMay doesn't want them on the strike with you. See you at the briefing."

"Yes sir."

As soon as Scholes was around the corner Fitch swung a fist at the sky. "Yow!" Matthews cried. He and Fitch shook hands. "We did it!" Matthews took January's hand and wrung it, his face plastered with a goofy grin. "We did it!"

"Somebody did it, anyway," January said.

"Ah, Frank," Matthews said. "Show some spunk. You're always so cool."

"Old Professor Stoneface," Fitch said, glancing at January with a trace of amused contempt. "Come on, let's get to the briefing."

The briefing hut, one of the longer Quonsets, was completely surrounded by MPs holding carbines. "Gosh," Matthews said, subdued by the sight. Inside, it was already smoky. The walls were covered by the usual maps of Japan. Two blackboards at the front were draped with sheets. Captain Shepard, the naval officer who worked with the scientists on the gimmick, was in back with his assistant Lieutenant Stone, winding a reel of film onto a projector. Dr. Nelson, the group psychiatrist, was already seated on a front bench near the wall. Tibbets had recently sicced the psychiatrist on the group—another one of his great ideas, like the spies in the bar. The man's questions had struck January as stupid. He hadn't even been able to figure out that Easterly was a flake, something that was clear to anybody who flew with him or even played him in a single round of poker. January slid onto a bench beside his mates.

The two Brits entered, looking furious in their stiff-upper-lip way. They sat on the bench behind January. Sweeney's and Easterly's crews filed in, followed by the other men, and soon the room was full. Fitch and the rest pulled out Lucky Strikes and lit up; since they had named the plane only January had stuck with Camels.

Scholes came in with several men January didn't recognize and went to the front. The chatter died, and all the smoke plumes ribboned steadily into the air.

Scholes nodded, and two intelligence officers took the sheets off the blackboards, revealing aerial reconnaissance photos.

"Men," Scholes said, "these are the target cities."

Someone cleared his throat.

"In order of priority they are Hiroshima, Kokura, and Nagasaki. There will be three weather scouts—*Straight Flush* to Hiroshima, *Strange Cargo* to Kokura, and *Full House* to Nagasaki. *The Great Artiste* and *Number 91* will be accompanying the mission to take photos. And *Lucky Strike* will fly the bomb."

There were rustles, coughs. Men turned to look at January and his mates, and they all sat up straight. Sweeney stretched back to shake Fitch's hand, and there were some quick laughs. Fitch grinned.

"Now listen up," Scholes went on. "The weapon we are going to deliver was successfully tested stateside a couple weeks ago. And now we've got orders to drop it on the enemy." He paused to let that sink in. "I'll let Captain Shepard tell you more."

Shepard walked to the blackboard slowly, savoring his entrance. His forehead was shiny with sweat, and January realized he was excited or nervous. He wondered what the psychiatrist would make of that.

"I'm going to come right to the point," Shepard said. "The bomb you are going to drop is something new in history. We think it will knock out everything within four miles."

Now the room was completely still. January noticed that he could see a great deal of his nose, eyebrows, and cheeks; it was as if he were receding back into his body, like a fox into its hole. He kept his gaze rigidly on Shepard, steadfastly ignoring the feeling. Shepard pulled a sheet back over a blackboard while someone else turned down the lights.

"This is a film of the only test we have made," Shepard said. The film started, caught, started again. A wavery cone of bright cigarette smoke speared the length of the room, and on the sheet sprang a dead gray landscape—a lot of sky, a smooth desert floor, hills in the distance. The projector went *click-click-click-click, click-click-click-click.* "The bomb is on top of the tower," Shepard said, and January focused on the pinlike object sticking out of the desert floor, off against the hills. It was between eight and ten miles from the camera, he judged; he had gotten good at calculating distances. He was still distracted by his face.

Click-click-click-click, click—then the screen went white for a second, filling even their room with light. When the picture returned the desert floor was filled with a white bloom of fire. The fireball coalesced, and then quite suddenly it leaped off the earth all the way into the *stratosphere,* by God, like a tracer bullet leaving a machine gun, trailing a whitish pillar of smoke behind it. The pillar gushed up, and a growing ball of smoke billowed outward, capping the pillar. January calculated the size of the cloud but was sure he got it wrong. There it stood. The picture flickered, and then the screen went white again, as if the camera had melted or that part of the world had come apart. But the flapping from the projector told them it was the end of the film.

January felt the air suck in and out of his open mouth. The lights came on in the smoky room, and for a second he panicked. He struggled to shove his features into an accepted pattern—the psychiatrist would be looking around at them all—and then he glanced around and realized he needn't have worried, that he wasn't alone. Faces were bloodless, eyes were blinky or bugged out with shock, mouths hung open or were clamped whitely shut. For a few moments they all had to acknowledge what they were doing. January, scaring himself, felt an urge to say, "Play it again, will you?" Fitch was pulling his curled black hair off his thug's forehead uneasily. Beyond him January saw that one of the Limeys had already reconsidered how mad he was about missing the flight. Now he looked sick. Someone let out a long *whew,* another whistled. January looked to the front again, where Dr. Nelson watched them, undisturbed.

Shepard said, "It's big, all right. And no one knows what will

happen when it's dropped from the air. But the mushroom cloud
you saw will go to at least thirty thousand feet, probably sixty. And
the flash you saw at the beginning was hotter than the sun."

Hotter than the sun. More licked lips, hard swallows, readjusted
baseball caps. One of the intelligence officers passed out tinted
goggles like welder's glasses. January took his and twiddled the opac-
ity dial.

Scholes said, "You're the hottest thing in the armed forces, now.
So no talking, even among yourselves." He took a deep breath.
"Let's do it the way Colonel Tibbets would have wanted us to. He
picked every one of you because you were the best, and now's the
time to show he was right. So—so let's make the old man proud."

The briefing was over. Men filed out into the sudden sunlight.
Into the heat and glare. Captain Shepard approached Fitch. "Stone
and I will be flying with you to take care of the bomb," he said.

Fitch nodded. "Do you know how many strikes we'll fly?"

"As many as it takes to make them quit." Shepard stared hard at
all of them. "But it will only take one."

War breeds strange dreams. That night, January writhed over his
sheets in the hot, wet, vegetable night, in that frightening half sleep
when you sometimes know you are dreaming but can do nothing
about it, and he dreamed he was walking . . .

. . . *walking through the streets when suddenly the sun swoops
down, the sun touches down and everything is instantly darkness
and smoke and silence, a deaf roaring. Walls of fire. His head hurts
and in the middle of his vision is a blue-white blur as if God's camera
went off in his face. Ah—the sun fell, he thinks. His arm is burned.
Blinking is painful. People stumbling by, mouths open, horribly
burned—*

*He is a priest, he can feel the clerical collar, and the wounded ask
him for help. He points to his ears, tries to touch them but can't.
Pall of black smoke over everything, the city has fallen into the streets.
Ah, it's the end of the world. In a park he finds shade and cleared
ground. People crouch under bushes like animals. Where the park*

meets the river, red and black figures crowd into steaming water. A figure gestures from a copse of bamboo. He enters it, finds five or six faceless soldiers huddling. Their eyes have melted, their mouths are holes. Deafness spares him their words. The sighted soldier mimes drinking. The soldiers are thirsty. He nods and goes to the river in search of a container. Bodies float downstream.

Hours pass as he hunts fruitlessly for a bucket. He pulls people from the rubble. He hears a bird screeching, and he realizes that his deafness is the roar of the city burning, a roar like the blood in his ears, but he is not deaf, he only thought he was because there are no human cries. The people are suffering in silence. Through the dusky night he stumbles back to the river, pain crashing through his head. In a field, men are pulling potatoes out of the ground that have been baked well enough to eat. He shares one with them. At the river everyone is dead—

—and he struggled out of the nightmare drenched in rank sweat, the taste of dirt in his mouth, his stomach knotted with horror. He sat up, and the wet, rough sheet clung to his skin. His heart felt crushed between lungs desperate for air. The flowery rotting-jungle smell filled him, and images from the dream flashed before him so vividly that in the dim hut he saw nothing else. He grabbed his cigarettes and jumped off the bunk, hurried out into the compound. Trembling, he lit up, started pacing around. For a moment he worried that the idiot psychiatrist might see him, but then he dismissed the idea. Nelson would be asleep. They were all asleep. He shook his head, looked down at his right arm, and almost dropped his cigarette—but it was just his stove scar, an old scar. He'd had it most of his life, since the day he'd pulled the frypan off the stove and onto his arm, burning it with oil. He could still remember the round O of fear that his mother's mouth had made as she rushed in to see what was wrong. Just an old burn scar, he thought, let's not go overboard here. He pulled his sleeve down.

For the rest of the night he tried to walk it off, cigarette after cigarette. The dome of the sky lightened until all the compound and the jungle beyond it was visible. He was forced by the light of day to walk back into his hut and lie down as if nothing had happened.

Two days later Scholes ordered them to take one of LeMay's men over Rota for a test run. This new lieutenant colonel ordered Fitch not to play with the engines on takeoff. They flew a perfect run, January put the dummy gimmick right on the aiming point, and Fitch powered the plane down into the violent bank that started their 150-degree turn and flight for safety. Back on Tinian the lieutenant colonel congratulated them and shook each of their hands. January smiled with the rest, palms cool, heart steady. It was as if his body were a shell, something he could manipulate from without, like a bombsight. He ate well, he chatted as much as he ever had, and when the psychiatrist ran him to earth for some questions, he was friendly and seemed open.

"Hello, Doc."

"How do you feel about all this, Frank?"

"Just like I always have, sir. Fine."

"Eating well?"

"Better than ever."

"Sleeping well?"

"As well as I can in this humidity. I got used to Utah, I'm afraid."

Dr. Nelson laughed. Actually January had hardly slept since his dream. He was afraid of sleep. Couldn't the man see that?

"And how do you feel about being part of the crew chosen to make the first strike?"

"Well, it was the right choice, I reckon. We're the b—— the best crew left."

"Do you feel sorry about Tibbets's crew's accident?"

"Yes sir, I do." You better believe it.

After the jokes that ended the interview, January walked out into the blaze of the tropical noon and lit a cigarette. He allowed himself to feel how much he despised the psychiatrist and his blind profession at the same time he was waving good-bye to the man. Ounce brain. Why couldn't he have seen? Whatever happened it would be his fault . . . With a rush of smoke out of him January realized how painfully easy it was to fool someone if you wanted to. All action was no more than a mask that could be perfectly manipulated from somewhere else. And all the while in that somewhere else, January lived in a *click-click-click* of film, in the silent roaring of a dream, struggling against images he couldn't dispel. The heat of the tropical sun—ninety-three million miles away, wasn't it?—pulsed painfully on the back of his neck.

As he watched the psychiatrist collar their tail gunner, Kochenski, he thought of walking up to the man and saying *I quit.* I don't want to do this. In imagination he saw the look that would form in the man's eye, in Fitch's eye, in Tibbets's eye, and his mind recoiled from the idea. He felt too much contempt for them. He wouldn't for anything give them a means to despise him, a reason to call him coward. Stubbornly he banished the whole complex of thought. Easier to go along with it.

And so a couple of disjointed days later, just after midnight of August 9, he found himself preparing for the strike. Around him Fitch and Matthews and Haddock were doing the same. How odd were the everyday motions of getting dressed when you were off to demolish a city! January found himself examining his hands, his boots, the cracks in the linoleum. He put on his survival vest, checked the pockets abstractedly for fishhooks, water kit, first-aid package, emergency rations. Then the parachute harness, and his coveralls over it all. Tying his bootlaces took minutes; he couldn't do it when watching his fingers so closely.

"Come on, Professor!" Fitch's voice was tight. "The big day is here."

He followed the others into the night. A cool wind was blowing. The chaplain said a prayer for them. They took jeeps down Broadway to runway Able. *Lucky Strike* stood in a circle of spotlights and men, half of them with cameras, the rest with reporters' pads. They surrounded the crew; it reminded January of a Hollywood premiere. Eventually he escaped up the hatch and into the plane. Others followed. Half an hour passed before Fitch joined them, grinning like a movie star. They started the engines, and January was thankful for their vibrating, thought-smothering roar. They taxied away from

the Hollywood scene, and January felt relief for a moment, until
he remembered where they were going. On runway Able the engines
pitched up to their twenty-three-hundred-RPM whine, and looking
out the clear windscreen, he saw the runway paint marks move by
ever faster. Fitch kept them on the runway till Tinian had run out
from under them, then quickly pulled up. They were on their way.

When they got to altitude, January climbed past Fitch and Mc-
Donald to the bombardier's seat and placed his parachute on it. He
leaned back. The roar of the four engines packed around him like
cotton batting. He was on the flight, nothing to be done about it
now. The heavy vibration was a comfort, he liked the feel of it there
in the nose of the plane. A drowsy, sad acceptance hummed through
him.

Against his closed eyelids flashed a black eyeless face, and he
jerked awake, heart racing. He was on the flight, no way out. Now
he realized how easy it would have been to get out of it. He could
have just said he didn't want to. The simplicity of it appalled him.
Who gave a damn what the shrink or Tibbets or anyone else thought,
compared to this? Now there was no way out. It was a comfort, in
a way. Now he could stop worrying, stop thinking he had any choice.

Sitting there with his knees bracketing the bombsight, January
dozed, and as he dozed he daydreamed his way out. He could climb
the step to Fitch and McDonald and declare he had been secretly
promoted to major and ordered to redirect the mission. They were
to go to Tokyo and drop the bomb in the bay. The Jap War Cabinet
had been told to watch this demonstration of the new weapon, and
when they saw that fireball boil the bay and bounce into heaven
they'd run and sign surrender papers as fast as they could write,
kamikazes or not. They weren't crazy, after all. No need to murder
a whole city. It was such a good plan that the generals were no
doubt changing the mission at this very minute, desperately radioing
their instructions to Tinian, only to find out it was too late . . . so
that when they returned to Tinian, January would become a hero
for guessing what the generals really wanted and for risking all to

do it. It would be like one of the Hornblower stories he had read in *The Saturday Evening Post*.

Once again January jerked awake. The drowsy pleasure of the fantasy was replaced with desperate scorn. There wasn't a chance in hell that he could convince Fitch and the rest that he had secret orders superseding theirs. And he couldn't go up there and wave his pistol around and *order* them to drop the bomb in Tokyo Bay, because he was the one who had to actually drop it, and he couldn't be down in front dropping the bomb and up ordering the others around at the same time. Pipe dreams.

Time swept on, slow as a second hand. January's thoughts, however, matched the spin of the props; desperately they cast about, now this way now that, like an animal caught by the leg in a trap. The crew was silent. The clouds below were a white scree on the black ocean. January's knee vibrated abainst the bombsight. He was the one who had to drop the bomb. No matter where his thoughts lunged, they were brought up short by that. He was the one, not Fitch or the crew, not LeMay, not the generals and scientists back home, not Truman and his advisors. Truman—suddenly January hated him. Roosevelt would have done it differently. If only Roosevelt had lived! The grief that had filled January when he learned of Roosevelt's death reverberated through him more strongly than ever. It was unfair to have worked so hard and then not see the war's end. And FDR would have ended it differently. Back at the start of it all he had declared that civilian centers were never to be bombed, and if he had lived, if, if, if. But he hadn't. And now it was smiling bastard Harry Truman, ordering *him*, Frank January, to drop the sun on two hundred thousand women and children. Once his father had taken him to see the Browns play before twenty thousand, a giant crowd—"I never voted for you," January whispered viciously and jerked to realize he had spoken aloud. Luckily his microphone was off. And Roosevelt would have done it differently, he *would have*.

The bombsight rose before him, spearing the black sky and blocking some of the hundreds of little cruciform stars. *Lucky Strike* ground on toward Iwo Jima, minute by minute flying four miles closer to their target. January leaned forward and put his face in the cool headrest of the bombsight, hoping that its grasp might hold his thoughts as well as his forehead. It worked surprisingly well.

His earphones crackled and he sat up. "Captain January." It was Shepard. "We're going to arm the bomb now, want to watch?"

"Sure thing." He shook his head, surprised at his own duplicity. Stepping up between the pilots, he moved stiffly to the roomy cabin behind the cockpit. Matthews was at his desk taking a navigational fix on the radio signals from Iwo Jima and Okinawa, and Haddock stood beside him. At the back of the compartment was a small circular hatch, below the larger tunnel leading to the rear of the plane. January opened it, sat down, and swung himself feet first through the hole.

The bomb bay was unheated, and the cold air felt good. He stood facing the bomb. Stone was sitting on the floor of the bay; Shepard was laid out under the bomb, reaching into it. On a rubber pad next to Stone were tools, plates, several cylindrical blocks. Shepard pulled back, sat up, sucked a scraped knuckle. He shook his head ruefully. "I don't dare wear gloves with this one."

"I'd be just as happy myself if you didn't let something slip," January joked nervously. The two men laughed.

"Nothing can blow till I change those wires," Stone said.

"Give me the wrench," Shepard said. Stone handed it to him, and he stretched under the bomb again. After some awkward wrenching inside it he lifted out a cylindrical plug. "Breech plug," he said, and set it on the mat.

January found his skin goose-pimpling in the cold air. Stone handed Shepard one of the blocks. Shepard extended under the bomb again. Watching them, January was reminded of auto mechanics on the oily floor of a garage, working under a car. He had spent a few years doing that himself, after his family moved to Vicksburg. Hiroshima was a river town. One time a flatbed truck carrying bags of cement powder down Fourth Street hill had lost its brakes and careened into the intersection with River Road, where, despite the driver's efforts to turn, it smashed into a passing car.

Frank had been out in the yard playing and heard the crash and saw the cement dust rising. He had been one of the first there. The woman and child in the passenger seat of the Model T had been killed. The woman driving was okay. They were from Chicago. A group of folks subdued the driver of the truck, who kept trying to help at the Model T, though he had a bad cut on his head and was covered with white dust.

"Okay, let's tighten the breech plug." Stone gave Shepard the wrench. "Sixteen turns exactly," Shepard said. He was sweating even in the bay's chill, and he paused to wipe his forehead. "Let's hope we don't get hit by lightning." He put the wrench down, shifted onto his knees, and picked up a circular plate. Hubcap, January thought. Stone connected wires, then helped Shepard install two more plates. Good old American know-how, January thought, goose pimples rippling across his skin like cat's-paws over water. There was Shepard, a scientist, putting together a bomb like he was an auto mechanic changing oil. January felt a tight rush of rage at the scientists who had designed the bomb. They had worked on it for over a year. Had none of them in all that time ever stopped to think what they were doing?

But none of them had to drop it. January turned to hide his face from Shepard, stepped down the bay. The bomb looked like a big long trash can, with fins at one end and little antennae at the other. Just a bomb, he thought, damn it, it's just another bomb.

Shepard stood and patted the bomb gently. "We've got a live one now." Never a thought about what it would do. January hurried by the man, afraid that hatred would crack his shell and give him away. The pistol strapped to his belt caught on the hatchway, and he imagined shooting Shepard—shooting Fitch and McDonald and plunging the controls forward so that *Lucky Strike* tilted and spun down into the sea like a spent tracer bullet, like a plane broken by flak, following the arc of all human ambition. Nobody would ever know what had happened to them, and their trash can would be dumped to the bottom of the Pacific. He could even shoot everyone, parachute out, and perhaps be rescued by one of the Superdumbos following them . . .

The thought passed, and remembering it January squinted with disgust. But another part of him agreed that it was a possibility. It could be done. It would solve his problem.

"Want some coffee?" Matthews asked.

"Sure," January said, and took a cup. He sipped—hot. He watched Matthews and Benton tune the loran equipment. As the beeps came in, Matthews took a straightedge and drew lines from Okinawa and Iwo Jima. He tapped a finger on the intersection. "They've taken the art out of navigation," he said to January. "They might as well stop making the navigator's dome," thumbing up at the little Plexiglas bubble over them.

"Good old American know-how," January said.

Matthews nodded. With two fingers he measured the distance between their position and Iwo Jima. Benton measured with a ruler.

"Rendezvous at five thirty-five, eh?" Matthews said. They were to rendezvous with the two trailing planes over Iwo.

Benton disagreed. "I'd say five-fifty."

"What? Check again, guy, we're not in no tugboat here."

"The wind—"

"Yeah, the wind. Frank, you want to add a bet to the pool?"

"Five thirty-six," January said promptly.

They laughed. "See, he's got more confidence in me," Matthews said with a dopey grin.

January recalled his plan to shoot the crew and tip the plane into the sea, and he pursed his lips, repelled. Not for anything would he be able to shoot these men, who, if not friends, were at least companions. They passed for friends. They meant no harm.

Shepard and Stone climbed into the cabin. Matthews offered them coffee. "The gimmick's ready to kick their ass, eh?" Shepard nodded and drank.

January moved forward, past Haddock's console. Another plan that wouldn't work. What to do? All the flight engineer's dials and gauges showed conditions were normal. Maybe he could sabotage something? Cut a line somewhere?

Fitch looked back at him and said, "When are we due over Iwo?"

"Five forty, Matthews says."

"He better be right."

A thug. In peacetime Fitch would be hanging around a pool table giving the cops trouble. He was perfect for war. Tibbets had chosen his men well—most of them, anyway. Moving back past Haddock, January stopped to stare at the group of men in the navigation cabin. They joked, drank coffee. They were all a bit like Fitch—young toughs, capable and thoughtless. They were having a good time, an adventure. That was January's dominant impression of his companions in the 509th; despite all the bitching and the occasional moments of overmastering fear, they were having a good time. His mind spun forward, and he saw what these young men would grow up to be like as clearly as if they stood before him in businessmen's suits, prosperous and balding. They would be tough and capable and thoughtless, and as the years passed and the great war receded in time they would look back on it with ever-increasing nostalgia, for they would be the survivors and not the dead. Every year of this war would feel like ten in their memories, so that the war would always remain the central experience of their lives—a time when history lay palpable in their hands, when each of their daily acts affected it, when moral issues were simple, and others told them what to do—so that as more years passed and the survivors aged, bodies falling apart, lives in one rut or another, they would unconsciously push harder and harder to thrust the world into war again, thinking somewhere inside themselves that if they could only return to world war then they would magically be again as they were in the last one—young and free and happy. And by that time they would hold the positions of power, they would be capable of doing it.

So there would be more wars, January saw. He heard it in Matthews's laughter, saw it in their excited eyes. "There's Iwo, and it's five thirty-one. Pay up! I win!" And in future wars they'd have more bombs like the gimmick, hundreds of them no doubt. He saw more planes, more young crews like this one, flying to Moscow, no doubt, or to wherever, fireballs in every capital. Why not? And to what end? To what end? So that the old men could hope to become magically young again. Nothing more sane than that. It made January sick.

They were over Iwo Jima. Three more hours to Japan. Voices from *The Great Artiste* and *Number 91* crackled on the radio. Rendezvous accomplished, the three planes flew northwest, toward Shikoku, the first Japanese island in their path. January maneuvered down into the nose. "Good shooting," Matthews called after him.

Forward it seemed quieter. January got settled, put his headphones on, and leaned forward to look out the ribbed Plexiglas.

Dawn had turned the whole vault of the sky pink. Slowly the radiant shade shifted through lavender to blue, pulse by pulse a different color. The ocean below was a glittering blue plane, marbled by a pattern of puffy pink cloud. The sky above was a vast dome, darker above than on the horizon. January had always thought that dawn was the time when you could see most clearly how big the earth was and how high above it they flew. It seemed they flew at the very upper edge of the atmosphere, and January saw how thin it was, how it was just a skin of air really, so that even if you flew up to its top the earth still extended away infinitely in every direction. The coffee had warmed January, he was sweating. Sunlight blinked off the Plexiglas. His watch said six. Plane and hemisphere of blue were split down the middle by the bombsight. His earphones crackled, and he listened in to the reports from the lead planes flying over the target cities. Kokura, Nagasaki, Hiroshima, all of them had six-tenths cloud cover. Maybe they would have to cancel the whole mission because of weather. "We'll look at Hiroshima first," Fitch said. January peered down at the fields of miniature clouds with renewed interest. His parachute slipped under him. Readjusting it, he imagined putting it on, sneaking back to the central escape hatch under the navigator's cabin, opening the hatch . . . He could be out of the plane and gone before anyone noticed. They could bomb or not but it wouldn't be January's doing. He could float down onto the world like a puff of dandelion, feel cool air rush around him, watch the silk canopy dome hang over him like a miniature sky, a private world.

An eyeless black face. January shuddered; it was as though the nightmare could return any time. If he jumped nothing would change, the bomb would still fall—would he feel any better, floating on his Inland Sea? Sure, one part of him shouted; maybe, another conceded; the rest of him saw that face . . .

Earphones crackled. Shepard said, "Lieutenant Stone has now armed the bomb, and I can now tell you all what we are carrying. Aboard with us is the world's first atomic bomb."

Not exactly, January thought. Whistles squeaked in his earphones. The first one went off in New Mexico. Splitting atoms. January had heard the term before. Tremendous energy in every atom, Einstein had said. Break one, and—he had seen the result on film. Shepard was talking about radiation, which brought back more to January. Energy released in the form of X rays. Killed by X rays! It would be against the Geneva convention if they had thought of it.

Fitch cut in. "When the bomb is dropped Lieutenant Benton will record our reaction to what we see. This recording is being made for history, so watch your language." Watch your language! January choked back a laugh. Don't curse or blaspheme God at the sight of the first atomic bomb incinerating a city with X rays!

Six-twenty. January found his hands clenched together on the headrest of the bombsight. He felt as if he had a fever. In the harsh wash of morning light the skin on the backs of his hands appeared slightly translucent. The whorls in the skin looked like the delicate patterning of waves on the sea's surface. His hands were made of atoms. Atoms were the smallest building blocks of matter. It took billions of them to make those tense, trembling hands. Split one atom and you had the fireball. That meant that the energy contained in even one hand . . . He turned up a palm to look at the lines and the mottled flesh under the transparent skin. A person was a bomb that could blow up the world. January felt that latent power stir in him, pulsing with every hard heart knock. What beings they were, and in what a blue expanse of a world! And here they spun on to drop a bomb and kill a hundred thousand of these astonishing beings.

When a fox or raccoon is caught by the leg in a trap, it lunges until the leg is frayed, twisted, perhaps broken, and only then does the animal's pain and exhaustion force it to quit. Now in the same way January wanted to quit. His mind hurt. His plans to escape were so much crap—stupid, useless. Better to quit. He tried to stop thinking, but it was hopeless. How could he stop? As long as he was conscious he would be thinking. The mind struggles longer than any fox.

Lucky Strike tilted up and began the long climb to bombing altitude. On the horizon the clouds lay over a green island. Japan. Surely it had gotten hotter. The heater must be broken, he thought. Don't think. Every few minutes Matthews gave Fitch small course adjustments. "Two seventy-five, now. That's it." To escape the moment, January recalled his childhood. Following a mule and plow. Moving to Vicksburg (rivers). For a while there in Vicksburg, since his stutter made it hard to gain friends, he had played a game with himself. He had passed the time by imagining that everything he did was vitally important and determined the fate of the world. If he crossed a road in front of a certain car, for instance, then the car wouldn't make it through the next intersection before a truck hit it, and so the man driving would be killed and wouldn't be able to invent the flying boat that would save President Wilson from kidnappers, so he had to wait for that car, oh damn it, he thought, damn it, think of something *different*. The last Hornblower story he had read—how would *he* get out of this? The round O of his mother's face as she ran in and saw his arm—The Mississippi, mud-brown behind its levees—Abruptly he shook his head, face twisted in frustration and despair, aware at last that no possible avenue of memory would serve as an escape for him now; for now there was no part of his life that did not apply to the situation he was in, and no matter where he cast his mind it was going to shore up against the hour facing him.

Less than an hour. They were at thirty thousand feet, bombing altitude. Fitch gave him altimeter readings to dial into the bomb-sight. Matthews gave him wind speeds. Sweat got in his eye and he blinked furiously. The sun rose behind them like an atomic bomb, glinting off every corner and edge of the Plexiglas, illuminating his bubble compartment with a fierce glare. Broken plans jumbled together in his mind, his breath was short, his throat dry. Uselessly and repeatedly he damned the scientists, damned Truman. Damned the Japanese for causing the whole mess in the first place, damned yellow killers, they had brought this on themselves. Remember Pearl. American men had died under bombs when no war had been declared; they had started it and now it was coming back to them with a vengeance. And they deserved it. And an invasion of Japan would take years, cost millions of lives. End it now, end it, they deserved it, they deserved it, steaming river full of charcoal people silently dying, damned stubborn race of maniacs!

"There's Honshu," Fitch said, and January returned to the world of the plane. They were over the Inland Sea. Soon they would pass the secondary target, Kokura, a bit to the south. Seven-thirty. The island was draped more heavily than the sea by clouds, and again January's heart leaped with the idea that weather would cancel the mission. But they did deserve it. It was a mission like any other mission. He had dropped bombs on Africa, Sicily, Italy, all Germany . . . He leaned forward to take a look through the sight. Under the X of the cross hairs was the sea, but at the lead edge of the sight was land. Honshu. At two hundred and thirty miles an hour that gave them about a half hour to Hiroshima. Maybe less. He wondered if his heart could beat so hard for that long.

Fitch said, "Matthews, I'm giving over guidance to you. Just tell us what to do."

"Bear south two degrees," was all Matthews said. At last their voices had taken on a touch of awareness.

"January, are you ready?" Fitch asked.

"I'm just waiting," January said. He sat up so Fitch could see the back of his head. The bombsight stood between his legs. A switch on its side would start the bombing sequence—the bomb would not leave the plane immediately upon the flick of the switch but would drop after a fifteen-second radio tone warned the following planes. The sight was adjusted accordingly.

"Adjust to a heading of two sixty-five," Matthews said. "We're

coming in directly upwind." This was to make any side-drift adjustments for the bomb unnecessary. "January, dial it down to two
hundred and thirty-one miles per hour."

"Two thirty-one."

Fitch said, "Everyone but January and Matthews, get your goggles
on."

January took the darkened goggles from the floor. One needed
to protect one's eyes or they might melt. He put them on, put his
forehead on the headrest. They were in the way. He took them off.
When he looked through the sight again there was land under the
cross hairs. He checked his watch. Eight o'clock. Up and reading
the papers, drinking tea.

"Ten minutes to AP," Matthews said. The aiming point was Aioi
Bridge, a T-shaped bridge in the middle of the delta-straddling city.
Easy to recognize.

"There's a lot of cloud down there," Fitch noted. "Are you going
to be able to see?"

"I won't be sure until we try it," January said.

"We can make another pass and use radar if we need to," Matthews said.

Fitch said, "Don't drop it unless you're sure, January."

"Yes sir."

Through the sight a grouping of rooftops and gray roads was just
visible between broken clouds. Around it green forest. "All right,"
Matthews exclaimed, "here we go! Keep it right on this heading,
Captain! January, we'll stay at two thirty-one."

"And same heading," Fitch said. "January, she's all yours. Everyone be ready for the turn."

January's world contracted to the view through the bombsight. A
stippled field of cloud and forest. Over a small range of hills and
into Hiroshima's watershed. The broad river was mud brown, the
land pale hazy green, the growing network of roads flat gray. Now
the tiny rectangular shapes of buildings covered almost all the land,
and swimming into the sight came the city proper, narrow islands
thrusting into a dark blue bay. Under the cross hairs the city moved

island by island, cloud by cloud. January had stopped breathing.
His fingers were rigid as stone on the switch. And there was Aioi
Bridge. It slid right under the cross hairs, a tiny T right in a gap in
the clouds. January's fingers crushed the switch. Deliberately he
took a breath, held it. Clouds swam under the cross hairs, then the
next island. "Almost there," he said calmly into his microphone.
"Steady." Now that he was committed his heart was humming like
the Wrights. He counted to ten. Now flowing under the cross hairs
were clouds alternating with green forest, leaden roads. "I've turned
the switch, but I'm not getting a tone!" he croaked into the mike.
His right hand held the switch firmly in place. Behind him Fitch
was shouting something; Matthews's voice cracked across it. "Flip-
ping it b-back and forth," January shouted, shielding the bombsight with his body from the eyes of the pilots. "But *still*—wait a
second—"

He pushed the switch down. A low hum filled his ears. "That's
it! It started!"

"But where will it land?" Matthews cried.

"Hold steady!" January shouted.

Lucky Strike shuddered and lofted up ten or twenty feet. January
twisted to look down, and there was the bomb, flying just below
the plane. Then with a wobble it fell away.

The plane banked right and dove so hard that the centrifugal
force threw January against the Plexiglas. Several thousand feet
lower, Fitch leveled it out and they hurtled north.

"Do you see anything?" Fitch cried.

From the tail gun Kochenski gasped, "Nothing." January struggled upright. He reached for the welder's goggles, but they were no
longer on his head. He couldn't find them. "How long has it been?"
he said.

"Thirty seconds," Matthews replied.

January shut his eyes.

The blood in his eyelids lit up red, then white.

On the earphones a clutter of voices—"Oh my God. Oh my
God." The plane bounced and tumbled, metallically shrieking.

January pressed himself off the Plexiglas. " 'Nother shock wave!" Kochenski yelled. The plane rocked again. This is it, January thought, end of the world, I guess that solves my problem.

He opened his eyes and found he could still see. The engines still roared, the props spun. "Those were the shock waves from the bomb," Fitch called. "We're okay now. Look at that! Will you look at that son of a bitch go!"

January looked. The cloud layer below had burst apart, and a black column of smoke billowed up from a core of red fire. Already the top of the column was at their height. Exclamations of shock hurt January's ears. He stared at the fiery base of the cloud, at the scores of fires feeding into it. Suddenly he could see past the cloud, and his fingernails cut into his palms. Through a gap in the clouds he saw it clearly, the delta, the six rivers, there off to the left of the tower of smoke—the city of Hiroshima, untouched.

"We missed!" Kochenski yelled. "We missed it!"

January turned to hide his face from the pilots; on it was a grin like a rictus. He sat back in his seat and let the relief fill him.

Then it was back to it. "Goddamn it!" Fitch shouted down at him. McDonald was trying to restrain him. "January, get up here!"

"Yes sir." Now there was a new set of problems.

January stood and turned, legs weak. His right fingertips throbbed painfully. The men were crowded forward to look out the Plexiglas. January looked with them.

The mushroom cloud was forming. It roiled out as if it might continue to extend forever, fed by the inferno and the black stalk below it. It looked about two-miles wide and half-a-mile tall, and it extended well above the height they flew at, dwarfing their plane entirely. "Do you think we'll all be sterile?" Matthews said.

"I can taste the radiation," McDonald declared. "Can you? It tastes like lead."

Bursts of flame shot up into the cloud from below, giving a purplish tint to the stalk. There it stood—lifelike, malignant, sixty-thousand-feet tall. One bomb. January shoved past the pilots into the navigation cabin, overwhelmed.

"Should I start recording everyone's reactions, Captain?" asked Benton.

"To hell with that," Fitch said, following January back. But Shepard got there first, descending quickly from the navigation dome. He rushed across the cabin, caught January on the shoulder. "You bastard!" he screamed as January stumbled back. "You lost your nerve, coward!"

January went for Shepard, happy to have a target at last, but Fitch cut in and grabbed him by the collar, pulled him around until they were face to face.

"Is that right?" Fitch cried, as angry as Shepard. "Did you screw up on purpose?"

"No," January grunted, and knocked Fitch's hands away from his neck. He swung and smacked Fitch on the mouth, caught him solid. Fitch staggered back, recovered, and no doubt would have beaten January up, but Matthews and Benton and Stone leaped in and held him back, shouting for order. "Shut up! Shut up!" McDonald screamed from the cockpit, and for a moment it was bedlam. But Fitch let himself be restrained, and soon only McDonald's shouts for quiet were heard. January retreated to between the pilot seats, right hand on his pistol holster.

"The city was in the cross hairs when I flipped the switch," he said. "But the first couple of times I flipped it nothing happened—"

"That's a lie!" Shepard shouted. "There was nothing wrong with the switch, I checked it myself. Besides the bomb exploded *miles* beyond Hiroshima, look for yourself! That's *minutes*." He wiped spit from his chin and pointed at January. "You did it."

"You don't know that," January said. But he could see the men had been convinced by Shepard, and he took a step back. "You just get me to a board of inquiry, quick. And leave me alone till then. If you touch me again," glaring venomously at Fitch and then Shepard, "I'll shoot you." He turned and hopped down to his seat, feeling exposed and vulnerable, like a treed raccoon.

"They'll shoot *you* for this," Shepard screamed after him. "Disobeying orders—treason—" Matthews and Stone were shutting him up.

"Let's get out of here," he heard McDonald say. "I can taste the lead, can't you?"

January looked out the Plexiglas. The giant cloud still burned and roiled. One atom . . . Well, they had really done it to that forest. He almost laughed but stopped himself, afraid of hysteria. Through a break in the clouds he got a clear view of Hiroshima for the first time. It lay spread over its islands like a map, unharmed. Well, that was that. The inferno at the base of the mushroom cloud was eight or ten miles around the shore of the bay and a mile or two inland. A certain patch of forest would be gone, destroyed— utterly blasted from the face of the earth. The Japs would be able to go out and investigate the damage. And if they were told it was a demonstration, a warning—and if they acted fast—well, they had their chance. Maybe it would work.

The release of tension made January feel sick. Then he recalled Shepard's words, and he knew that whether his plan worked or not he was still in trouble. In trouble! It was worse than that. Bitterly he cursed the Japanese. He even wished for a moment that he *had* dropped it on them. Wearily he let his despair empty him.

A long while later he sat up straight. Once again he was a trapped animal. He began lunging for escape, casting about for plans. One alternative after another. All during the long, grim flight home he considered it, mind spinning at the speed of the props and beyond. And when they came down on Tinian he had a plan. It was a long shot, he reckoned, but it was the best he could do.

The briefing hut was surrounded by MPs again. January stumbled from the truck with the rest and walked inside. He was more than ever aware of the looks given him, and they were hard, accusatory. He was too tired to care. He hadn't slept in more than thirty-six hours and had slept very little since the last time he had been in the hut, a week before. Now the room quivered with the lack of engine vibration to stabilize it, and the silence roared. It was all he could do to hold on to his plan. The glares of Fitch and Shepard, the hurt incomprehension of Matthews, they had to be thrust out of his focus. Thankfully he lit a cigarette.

In a clamor of question and argument the others described the strike. Then the haggard Scholes and an intelligence officer led them through the bombing run. January's plan made it necessary to hold to his story. ". . . and when the AP was under the cross hairs I pushed down the switch, but got no signal. I flipped it up and down repeatedly until the tone kicked in. At that point there was still fifteen seconds to the release."

"Was there anything that may have caused the tone to start when it did?"

"Not that I noticed immediately, but—"

"It's impossible," Shepard interrupted, face red. "I checked the switch before we flew and there was nothing wrong with it. Besides, the drop occurred over a minute—"

"Captain Shepard," Scholes said. "We'll hear from you presently."

"But he's obviously lying—"

"Captain Shepard! It's not at all obvious. Don't speak unless questioned."

"Anyway," January said, hoping to shift the questions away from the issue of the long delay, "I noticed something about the bomb when it was falling that could explain why it stuck. I need to discuss it with one of the scientists familiar with the bomb's design."

"What was that?" Scholes asked suspiciously.

January hesitated. "There's going to be an inquiry, right?"

Scholes frowned. "This is the inquiry, Captain January. Tell us what you saw."

"But there will be some proceeding beyond this one?"

"It looks like there's going to be a court-martial, yes, Captain."

"That's what I thought. I don't want to talk to anyone but my counsel, and some scientist familiar with the bomb."

"*I'm* a scientist familiar with the bomb," Shepard burst out. "You could tell me if you really had anything, you—"

"I said I need a scientist!" January exclaimed, rising to face the scarlet Shepard across the table. "Not a g-goddamned mechanic." Shepard started to shout, others joined in, and the room rang with argument. While Scholes restored order January sat down, and he refused to be drawn out again.

"I'll see you're assigned counsel and initiate the court-martial," Scholes said, clearly at a loss. "Meanwhile you are under arrest, on suspicion of disobeying orders in combat." January nodded, and Scholes gave him over to MPs.

"One last thing," January said, fighting exhaustion. "Tell General LeMay that if the Japs are told this drop was a warning, it might have the same effect as—"

"I told you!" Shepard shouted, "I told you he did it on purpose!" Men around Shepard restrained him. But he had convinced most of them, and even Matthews stared at him with surprised anger.

January shook his head wearily. He had the dull feeling that his plan, while it had succeeded so far, was ultimately not a good one. "Just trying to make the best of it." It took all of his remaining will to force his legs to carry him in a dignified manner out of the hut.

His cell was an empty NCO's office. MPs brought his meals. For the first couple of days he did little but sleep. On the third day he glanced out the office's barred window and saw a tractor pulling a tarpaulin-draped trolley out of the compound, followed by jeeps filled with MPs. It looked like a military funeral. January rushed to the door and banged on it until one of the young MPs came.

"What's that they're doing out there?" January demanded.

Eyes cold and mouth twisted, the MP said, "They're making another strike. They're going to do it right this time."

"No!" January cried, "No!" He rushed the MP, who knocked him back and locked the door. "No!" He beat the door until his hands hurt, cursing wildly. "You don't *need* to do it, it isn't *necessary*." Shell shattered at last, he collapsed on the bed and wept. Now everything he had done would be rendered meaningless. He had sacrificed himself for nothing.

A day or two after that the MPs led in a colonel, an iron-haired man who stood stiffly and crushed January's hand when he shook it. His eyes were a pale icy blue.

"I am Colonel Dray," he said. "I have been ordered to defend you in court-martial." January could feel the dislike pouring from the man. "To do that I'm going to need every fact you have, so let's get started."

"I'm not talking to anybody until I've seen an atomic scientist."

"I am your *defense* counsel—"

"I don't care who you are," January said. "Your defense of me depends on you getting one of the scientists *here*. The higher up he is, the better. And I want to speak to him alone."

"I will have to be present."

So he would do it. But now January's counsel, too, was an enemy.

"Naturally," January said. "You're my counsel. But no one else. Our atomic secrecy may depend on it."

"You saw evidence of sabotage?"

"Not one word more until that scientist is here."

Angrily the colonel nodded and left.

Late the next day the colonel returned with another man. "This is Dr. Forest."

"I helped develop the bomb," Forest said. He had a crew cut and was dressed in fatigues, and to January he looked more Army than the colonel. Suspiciously he stared back and forth at the two men.

"You'll vouch for this man's identity on your word as an officer?" he asked Dray.

"Of course," the colonel said stiffly, offended.

"So," Dr. Forest said. "You had some trouble getting it off when you wanted to. Tell me what you saw."

"I saw nothing," January said harshly. He took a deep breath; it was time to commit himself. "I want you to take a message back to the scientists. You folks have been working on this thing for years, and you must have had time to consider how the bomb should have been used. You know we could have convinced the Japs to surrender by showing them a demonstration—"

"Wait a minute," Forest said. "You're saying you didn't see anything? There wasn't a malfunction?"

"That's right," January said, and cleared his throat. "It wasn't *necessary*, do you understand?"

Forest was looking at Colonel Dray. Dray gave him a disgusted shrug. "He told me he saw evidence of sabotage."

"I want you to go back and ask the scientists to intercede for me," January said, raising his voice to get the man's attention. "I haven't got a chance in that court-martial. But if the scientists defend me then maybe they'll let me live, see? I don't want to get shot for doing something every one of you scientists would have done."

Dr. Forest had backed away. Color rising, he said, "What makes you think that's what we would have done? Don't you think we considered it? Don't you think men better qualified than you made the decision?" He waved a hand. "Goddamn it—what made you think you were competent to decide something as important as that!"

January was appalled at the man's reaction; in his plan it had gone differently. Angrily he jabbed a finger at Forest. "Because *I* was the man doing it, *Doctor* Forest. You take even one step back from that and suddenly you can pretend it's not your doing. Fine for you, but *I was there.*"

At every word the man's color was rising. It looked like he might pop a vein in his neck. January tried once more. "Have you ever tried to imagine what one of your bombs would do to a city full of people?"

"I've had enough!" the man exploded. He turned to Dray. "I'm under no obligation to keep what I've heard here confidential. You can be sure it will be used as evidence in Captain January's court-martial." He turned and gave January a look of such blazing hatred that January understood it. For these men to admit he was right would mean admitting that they were wrong—that every one of them was responsible for his part in the construction of the weapon January had refused to use. Understanding that, January knew he was doomed.

The bang of Dr. Forest's departure still shook the little office. January sat on his cot, got out a smoke. Under Colonel Dray's cold gaze he lit one shakily, took a drag. He looked up at the colonel, shrugged. "It was my best chance," he explained. That did something—for the first and only time the cold disdain in the colonel's eyes shifted, to a little, hard, lawyerly gleam of respect.

The court-martial lasted two days. The verdict was guilty of disobeying orders in combat and of giving aid and comfort to the enemy. The sentence was death by firing squad.

For most of his remaining days January rarely spoke, drawing ever further behind the mask that had hidden him for so long. A clergyman came to see him, but it was the 509th's chaplain, the one who had said the prayer blessing the *Lucky Strike*'s mission before they took off. Angrily January sent him packing.

Later, however, a young Catholic priest dropped by. His name was Patrick Getty. He was a little pudgy man, bespectacled and, it seemed, somewhat afraid of January. January let the man talk to him. When he returned the next day January talked back a bit, and on the day after that he talked some more. It became a habit.

Usually January talked about his childhood. He talked of plowing mucky black bottomland behind a mule. Of running down the lane to the mailbox. Of reading books by the light of the moon after he had been ordered to sleep. And of being beaten by his mother for it with a high-heeled shoe. He told the priest the story of the time his arm had been burned, and about the car crash at the bottom of Fourth Street. "It's the truck driver's face I remember, do you see, Father?"

"Yes," the young priest said. "Yes."

And he told him about the game he had played in which every action he took tipped the balance of world affairs. "When I remembered that game I thought it was dumb. Step on a sidewalk crack and cause an earthquake—you know, it's stupid. Kids are like that." The priest nodded. "But now I've been thinking that if everybody were to live their whole lives like that, thinking that every move they made really was important, then . . . it might make a difference." He waved a hand vaguely, expelled cigarette smoke. "You're accountable for what you do."

"Yes," the priest said. "Yes, you are."

"And if you're given orders to do something wrong, you're still accountable, right? The orders don't change it."

"That's right."

"Hmph." January smoked a while. "So they say, anyway. But look what happens." He waved at the office. "I'm like the guy in a story I read—he thought everything in books was true, and after reading a bunch of westerns he tried to rob a train. They tossed him in jail." He laughed shortly. "Books are full of crap."

"Not all of them," the priest said. "Besides, you weren't trying to rob a train."

They laughed at the notion. "Did you read that story?"

"No."

"It was the strangest book—there were two stories in it, and they alternated chapter by chapter, but they didn't have a thing to do with each other! I didn't get it."

"Maybe the writer was trying to say that everything connects to everything else."

"Maybe. But it's a funny way to say it."

"I like it."

And so they passed the time, talking.

So it was the priest who was the one to come by and tell January that his request for a presidential pardon had been refused. Getty said awkwardly, "It seems the President approves the sentence."

"That bastard," January said weakly. He sat on his cot.

Time passed. It was another hot, humid day.

"Well, the priest said. "Let me give you some better news. Given your situation I don't think telling you matters, though I've been told not to. The second mission—you know there was a second strike?"

"Yes."

"Well, they missed too."

"What?" January cried, and bounced to his feet. "You're kidding!"

"No. They flew to Kokura but found it covered by clouds. It was the same over Nagasaki and Hiroshima, so they flew back to Kokura and tried to drop the bomb using radar to guide it, but apparently there was a . . . a genuine equipment failure this time, and the bomb fell on an island."

January was hopping up and down, mouth hanging open, "So we n-never—"

"We never dropped an atom bomb on a Japanese city. That's right." Getty grinned. "And get this—I heard this from my superior—they sent a message to the Japanese Government telling them that the two explosions were warnings, and that if they didn't surrender by September 1 we would drop bombs on Kyoto and Tokyo, and then wherever else we had to. Word is that the Emperor went to Hiroshima to survey the damage, and when he saw it he ordered the Cabinet to surrender. So . . ."

"So it worked," January said. He hopped around. "It worked, it worked!"

"Yes."

"Just like I said it would!" he cried, and hopping in front of the priest he laughed.

Getty was jumping around a little too, and the sight of the priest bouncing was too much for January. He sat on his cot and laughed till the tears ran down his cheeks.

"So—" He sobered quickly. "So Truman's going to shoot me anyway, eh?"

"Yes," the priest said unhappily. "I guess that's right."

This time January's laugh was bitter. "He's a bastard, all right. And proud of being a bastard, which makes it worse." He shook his head. "If Roosevelt had lived . . ."

"It would have been different," Getty finished. "Yes. Maybe so. But he didn't." He sat beside January. "Cigarette?" He held out a pack, and January noticed the green wrapper, the round bull's-eye. He frowned.

"You haven't got a Camel?"

"Oh. Sorry."

"Oh well. That's all right." January took one of the Lucky Strikes, lit up. "That's awfully good news." He breathed out. "I never believed Truman would pardon me anyway, so mostly you've brought good news. Ha. They *missed*. You have no idea how much better that makes me feel."

"I think I do."

January smoked the cigarette.

"So I'm a good American after all. I *am* a good American," he insisted, "no matter what Truman says."

"Yes," Getty replied, and coughed. "You're better than Truman any day."

"Better watch what you say, Father." He looked into the eyes behind the glasses, and the expression he saw there gave him pause. Since the drop every look directed at him had been filled with contempt. He'd seen it so often during the court-martial that he'd learned to stop looking; and now he had to teach himself to see again. The priest looked at him as if he were . . . as if he were some kind of hero. That wasn't exactly right. But seeing it . . .

January would not live to see the years that followed, so he would never know what came of his action. He had given up casting his mind forward and imagining possibilities, because there was no point to it. His planning was ended. In any case he would not have been able to imagine the course of the post-war years. That the world would quickly become an armed camp pitched on the edge of atomic war, he might have predicted. But he never would have guessed that so many people would join a January Society. He would never know of the effect the Society had on Dewey during the Korean crisis, never know of the Society's successful campaign for the test-ban treaty, and never learn that, thanks in part to the Society and its allies, a treaty would be signed by the great powers that would reduce the number of atomic bombs year by year, until there were none left.

Frank January would never know any of that. But in that moment on his cot looking into the eyes of young Patrick Getty, he guessed an inkling of it—he felt, just for an instant, the impact on history.

And with that he relaxed. In his last week everyone who met him carried away the same impression—that of a calm, quiet man, angry at Truman and others, but in a withdrawn, matter-of-fact way. Patrick Getty, a strong force in the January Society ever after, said

January was talkative for some time after he learned of the missed attack on Kokura. Then he got quieter, as the day approached. On the morning that they woke him at dawn to march him out to a hastily constructed execution shed, his MPs shook his hand. The priest was with him as he smoked a final cigarette, and they prepared to put the hood over his head. January looked at him calmly. "They load one of the guns with a blank cartridge, right?"

"Yes," Getty said.

"So each man in the squad can imagine he may not have shot me?"

"Yes. That's right."

A tight, unhumorous smile was January's last expression. He threw down the cigarette, ground it out, poked the priest in the arm. "But I *know*." Then the mask slipped back into place for good, making the hood redundant, and with a firm step January went to the wall. One might have said he was at peace.

Morning Child

GARDNER DOZOIS

Gardner Dozois's short stories have been appearing since 1966. He has published a novel, Strangers, *and his short fiction has been collected in* The Visible Man. *He is also the editor of many anthologies, including a best-of-the-year series. "The Peacemaker," a short story, received a Nebula Award last year. His winning short story this year presents—against a subtly drawn, tragic backdrop—a human predicament that is at once grotesque and sensitively observed.*

The old house had been hit by something sometime during the war and mashed nearly flat. The front was caved in as though crushed by a giant fist: wood pulped and splintered, beams protruding at odd angles like broken fingers, the second floor collapsed onto the remnants of the first. The rubble of a chimney covered everything with a red mortar blanket. On the right a gaping hole cross-sectioned the ruins, laying bare all the strata of fused stone and plaster and charred wood—everything curling back on itself like the lips of a gangrenous wound. Weeds had swarmed up the low hillside from the road and swept over the house, wrapping the ruins in wildflowers and grapevines, softening the edges of destruction with green.

Williams brought John here almost every day. They had lived here once, in this house, many years ago, and although John's memory of that time was dim, the place seemed to have pleasant associations for him, in spite of its ruined condition. John was at his happiest here and would play contentedly with sticks and pebbles on the shattered stone steps, or go whooping through the tangled weeds that had turned the lawn into a jungle, or play-stalk in ominous circles around Williams while Williams worked at filling his bags with blueberries, daylilies, Indian potatoes, dandelions, and other edible plants and roots.

Even Williams took a bittersweet pleasure in visiting the ruins, although coming here stirred memories that he would rather have left undisturbed. There was a pleasant melancholy to the spot and something oddly soothing about the mixture of mossy old stone and tender new green, a reminder of the inevitability of cycles—life-in-death, death-in-life.

John erupted out of the tall weeds and ran laughing to where Williams stood with the foraging bags. "I been fighting dinosaurs!" John said. "Great *big* ones!" Williams smiled crookedly and said, "That's good." He reached down and rumpled John's hair. They stood there for a second, John panting like a dog from all the running he'd been doing, his eyes bright, Williams letting his touch linger on the small, tousled head. At this time of the morning, John seemed always in motion, motion so continuous that it gave nearly the illusion of rest, like a stream of water that looks solid until something makes it momentarily sputter and stop.

This early in the day, John rarely stopped. When he did, as now, he seemed to freeze solid, his face startled and intent, as though he were listening to sounds that no one else could hear. At such times Williams would study him with painful intensity, trying to see himself in him, sometimes succeeding, sometimes failing, and wondering which hurt more, and why.

Sighing, Williams took his hand away. The sun was getting high, and they'd better be heading back to camp if they wanted to be there at the right time for the heavier chores. Slowly, Williams bent over and picked up the foraging bags, grunting a little at their weight as he settled them across his shoulder—they had done very well for themselves this morning.

"Come on now, John," Williams said, "time to go," and started off, limping a bit more than usual under the extra weight. John, trotting alongside, his short legs pumping, seemed to notice. "Can I help you carry the bags?" John said eagerly. "Can I? I'm big enough!" Williams smiled at him and shook his head. "Not yet, John," he said. "A little bit later, maybe."

They passed out of the cool shadow of the ruined house and began to hike back to camp along the deserted highway.

The sun was baking down now from out of a cloudless sky, and heat-bugs began to chirrup somewhere, producing a harsh and me- tallic stridulation that sounded amazingly like a buzz saw. There were no other sounds besides the soughing of wind through tall grass and wild wheat, the tossing and whispering of trees, and the shrill piping of John's voice. Weeds had thrust up through the macadam—tiny, green fingers that had cracked and buckled the road's surface, chopped it up into lopsided blocks. Another few years and there would be no road here, only a faint track in the undergrowth—and then not even that. Time would erase every- thing, burying it beneath new trees, gradually building new hills, laying down a fresh landscape to cover the old. Already grass and vetch had nibbled away the corners of the sharper curves, and the wind had drifted topsoil onto the road. There were saplings now in some places, growing green and shivering in the middle of the highway, negating the faded signs that pointed to distances and towns.

John ran ahead, found a rock to throw, ran back, circling around Williams as though on an invisible tether. They walked in the middle of the road, John pretending that the faded white line was a tightrope, waving his arms for balance, shouting warnings to himself about the abyss creatures who would gobble him up if he should misstep and fall.

Williams maintained a steady pace, not hurrying: the epitome of the ramrod-straight old man, his snow-white hair gleaming in the sunlight, a bush knife at his belt, an old Winchester 30.30 slung across his back—although he no longer believed that they'd need it. They weren't the only people left in the world, he knew—however much it felt like it sometimes—but this region had been emptied of its population years ago, and since he and John had returned this way on their long journey up from the south, they had seen no one else at all. No one would find them here.

There were traces of buildings along the way now, all that was left of a small country town: the burnt-out spine of a roof ridge meshed with weeds; gaping stone foundations like battlements for dwarfs; a ruined water faucet clogged with spider-webs; a shattered gas pump inhabited by birds and rodents. They turned off onto a gravel secondary road, past the burnt-out shell of another filling station and a dilapidated roadside stand full of windblown trash. Overhead a rusty traffic light swayed on a sagging wire. Someone had tied a big orange-and-black hex sign to one side of the light, and on the other side, the side facing away from town and out into the hostile world, was the evil eye, painted against a white background in vivid, shocking red. Things had gotten very strange during the Last Days.

Williams was having trouble now keeping up with John's ever-lengthening stride, and he decided that it was time to let him carry the bags. John hefted the bags easily, flashing his strong white teeth at Williams in a grin, and set off up the last long slope to camp, his long legs carrying him up the hill at a pace Williams couldn't hope to match. Williams swore good-naturedly, and John laughed and stopped to wait for him at the top of the rise.

Their camp was set well back from the road, on top of a bluff, just above a small river. There had been a restaurant here once, and a corner of the building still stood, two walls and part of the roof, needing only the tarpaulin stretched across the open end to make it into a reasonably snug shelter. They'd have to find something better by winter, of course, but this was good enough for July, reasonably well hidden and close to a supply of water.

Rolling, wooded hills were around them to the north and east.

To the south, across the river, the hills dwindled away into flatland, and the world opened up into a vista that stretched to the horizon.

They grabbed a quick lunch and then set to work, chopping wood, hauling in the nets that Williams had set across the river to catch fish, carrying water, for cooking, up the steep slope to camp. Williams let John do most of the heavy work. John sang and whistled happily while he worked, and once, on his way back from carrying some firewood to the shelter, he laughed, grabbed Williams under the arms, boosted him into the air, and danced him around in a little circle before setting him back down on his feet again.

"Feeling your oats, eh?" Williams said with mock severity, looking up into the sweaty face that smiled down at him.

"*Somebody* has to do the work around here," John said cheerfully, and they both laughed. "I can't wait to get back to my outfit," John said eagerly. "I feel much better now. I feel *terrific*. Are we going to stay out here much longer?" His eyes pleaded with Williams. "We can go back soon, can't we?"

"Yeah," Williams lied, "we can go back real soon."

But already John was tiring. By dusk his footsteps were beginning to drag, and his breathing was becoming heavy and labored. He paused in the middle of what he was doing, put down the wood-chopping ax, and stood silently for a moment, staring blankly at nothing.

His face was suddenly intent and withdrawn, and his eyes were dull. He swayed unsteadily and wiped the back of his hand across his forehead. Williams got him to sit down on a stump near the improvised fireplace. He sat there silently, staring at the ground in abstraction while Williams bustled around, lighting a fire, cleaning and filleting the fish, cutting up dandelion roots and chicory crowns, boiling water. The sun was down now, and fireflies began to float above the river, winking like fairy lanterns through the velvet darkness.

Williams did his best to interest John in supper, hoping that he'd eat something while he still had some of his teeth, but John would eat little. After a few moments he put his tin plate down and sat staring dully to the south, out over the darkened lands beyond the river, just barely visible in the dim light of a crescent moon. His face was preoccupied and glum and beginning to get jowly. His hairline had retreated in a wide arc from his forehead, creating a large bald spot. He worked his mouth indecisively several times and at last said, "Have I been . . . ill?"

"Yes, John," Williams said gently. "You have been ill."

"I can't . . . I can't *remember*," John complained. His voice was cracked and husky, querulous. "Everything's so confused. I can't keep things *straight*."

Somewhere on the invisible horizon, perhaps a hundred miles away, a pillar of fire leapt up from the edge of the world.

As they watched, startled, it climbed higher and higher, towering miles into the air, until it was a slender column of brilliant flame that divided the sullen, black sky in two from ground to stratosphere. The pillar of fire blazed steadily on the horizon for a minute or two, and then it began to coruscate, burning green and blue and silver and orange, the colors flaring and flickering fitfully as they merged into one another. Slowly, with a kind of stately and awful symmetry, the pillar broadened out to become a flattened diamond shape of blue-white fire. The diamond began to rotate slowly on its axis, and as it rotated it grew eye-searingly bright. Gargantuan, unseen shapes floated around the blazing diamond, like moths beating around a candle flame, throwing huge, tangled shadows across the world.

Something with a huge, melancholy voice hooted, and hooted again, a forlorn and terrible sound that beat back and forth between the hills until it rumbled slowly away into silence.

The blazing diamond winked out. Hot white stars danced where it had been. The stars faded to sullenly glowing orange dots that flickered away down the spectrum and were gone.

It was dark again.

The night had been shocked silent. For a while that silence was complete, and then slowly, tentatively, one by one, the crickets and tree frogs began to make their night sounds again.

"The war—" John whispered. His voice was reedy and thin and weary now, and there was pain in it. "It still goes on?"

"The war got . . . strange," Williams said quietly. "The longer it lasted, the stranger it got. New allies, new weapons—" He stared off into the darkness in the direction where the fire had danced: there was still an uneasy shimmer to the night air on the horizon, not quite a glow. "You were hurt by such a weapon, I guess. Something like *that*, maybe." He nodded toward the horizon, and his face hardened. "I don't know. I don't even know what *that* was. I don't understand much that happens in the world anymore. . . . Maybe it wasn't even a weapon that hurt you. Maybe they were experimenting on you biologically before you got away. Who knows why? Maybe it was done deliberately—as a punishment or a reward. Who knows how they think? Maybe it was a side effect of some device designed to do something else entirely. Maybe it was an accident; maybe you just got too close to something like *that* when it was doing whatever it is it does." Williams was silent for a moment, and then he sighed. "Whatever happened, you got to me afterward somehow, and I took care of you. We've been hiding out ever since, moving from place to place."

They had both been nearly blind while their eyes readjusted to the night, but now, squinting in the dim glow of the low-burning cooking fire, Williams could see John again. John was now totally bald, his cheeks had caved in, and his dulled and yellowing eyes were sunken deeply into his ravaged face. He struggled to get to his feet, then sank back down onto the stump again. "I can't—" he whispered. Weak tears began to run down his cheeks. He started to shiver.

Sighing, Williams got up and threw a double handful of pine needles into boiling water to make white-pine-needle tea. He helped John limp over to his pallet, supporting most of his weight, almost carrying him—it was easy; John had become shrunken and frail and amazingly light, as if he were now made out of cloth and cotton and dry sticks instead of flesh and bone. He got John to lie down, tucked a blanket around him in spite of the heat of the evening, and concentrated on getting some of the tea into him.

He drank two full cups before his fingers became too weak to hold the cup, before even the effort of holding up his head became too great for him. John's eyes had become blank and shiny and unseeing, and his face was like a skull, earth-brown and blotched, with the skin drawn tightly over the bones.

His hands plucked aimlessly at the blanket; they looked mummified now, the skin as translucent as parchment, the blue veins showing through beneath.

As the evening wore on, John began to fret and whine incoherently, turning his face blindly back and forth, muttering random fragments of words and sentences, sometimes raising his voice in a strangled, gurgling shout that had no words at all in it, only bewilderment and outrage and pain. Williams sat patiently beside him, stroking his shriveled hands, wiping sweat from his hot forehead.

"Sleep now," Williams said soothingly. John moaned and whined in the back of his throat. "Sleep. Tomorrow we'll go to the house again. You'll like that, won't you? But sleep now, sleep—"

At last John quieted, his eyes slowly closed, and his breathing grew deeper and more regular.

Williams sat patiently by his side, keeping a calming hand on his shoulder. Already John's hair was beginning to grow back, and the lines were smoothing out of his face as he melted toward childhood.

When Williams was sure that John was asleep, he tucked the blanket closer around him and said, "Sleep well, Father," and then slowly, passionately, soundlessly, he started to weep.

The Aliens Who Knew, I Mean, Everything

GEORGE ALEC EFFINGER

George Alec Effinger's many novels include The Wolves of Memory, Death in Florence, Relatives, *and* What Entropy Means to Me. Felicia, *a contemporary novel, was favorably compared in the* New York Times *to the work of William Faulkner. His countless stories have appeared in nearly all the science fiction and fantasy publications, as well as in* The Twilight Zone Magazine, New Dimensions, *and* Light Years and Dark. *Collections of his stories include* Dirty Tricks, Mixed Feelings, *and* Irrational Numbers.

The following short story was a runner-up for the 1984 Nebula Award. It is typically outrageous and has been known to start arguments.

I was sitting at my desk, reading a report on the brown pelican situation, when the secretary of state burst in. "Mr. President," he said, his eyes wide, "the aliens are here!" Just like that. "The aliens are here!" As if I had any idea what to do about them.

"I see," I said. I learned early in my first term that "I see" was one of the safest and most useful comments I could possibly make in any situation. When I said, "I see," it indicated that I had digested the news and was waiting intelligently and calmly for further data. That knocked the ball back into my advisers' court. I looked at the secretary of state expectantly. I was all prepared with my next utterance, in the event that he had nothing further to add. My next utterance would be, "Well?" That would indicate that I was on top of the problem, but that I couldn't be expected to make an executive decision without sufficient information, and that he should have known better than to burst into the Oval Office unless he had that information. That's why we had protocol; that's why we had proper channels; that's why I had advisers. The voters out there didn't want me to make decisions without sufficient information. If the secretary didn't have anything more to tell me, he shouldn't have burst in in the first place. I looked at him a while longer. "Well?" I asked at last.

"That's about all we have at the moment," he said uncomfortably. I looked at him sternly for a few seconds, scoring a couple of points while he stood there all flustered. I turned back to the pelican report, dismissing him. I certainly wasn't going to get all flustered. I could think of only one president in recent memory who was ever flustered in office, and we all know what happened to him. As the secretary of state closed the door to my office behind him, I smiled. The aliens were probably going to be a bitch of a problem eventually, but it wasn't my problem yet. I had a little time.

But I found that I couldn't really keep my mind on the pelican question. Even the president of the United States has *some* imagination, and if the secretary of state was correct, I was going to have to confront these aliens pretty damn soon. I'd read stories about aliens when I was a kid, I'd seen all sorts of aliens in movies and television, but these were the first aliens who'd actually stopped by for a chat. Well, I wasn't going to be the first American president to make a fool of himself in front of visitors from another world. I was going to be briefed. I telephoned the secretary of defense. "We must have some contingency plans drawn up for this," I told him. "We have plans for every other possible situation." This was true; the Defense Department has scenarios for such bizarre events as the rise of an imperialist fascist regime in Liechtenstein or the spontaneous depletion of all the world's selenium.

"Just a second, Mr. President," said the secretary. I could hear him muttering to someone else. I held the phone and stared out the window. There were crowds of people running around hysterically out there. Probably because of the aliens. "Mr. President?" came the voice of the secretary of defense. "I have one of the aliens here, and he suggests that we use the same plan that President Eisenhower used."

I closed my eyes and sighed. I hated it when they said stuff like that. I wanted information, and they told me these things knowing that I would have to ask four or five more questions just to understand the answer to the first one. "You have an alien with you?" I said in a pleasant enough voice.

"Yes, sir. They prefer not to be called 'aliens.' He tells me he's a 'nup.' "

"Thank you, Luis. Tell me, why do you have an al— Why do you have a nup and I don't?"

Luis muttered the question to his nup. "He says it's because they wanted to go through proper channels. They learned about all that from President Eisenhower."

"Very good, Luis." This was going to take all day, I could see that; and I had a photo session with Mick Jagger's granddaughter. "My second question, Luis, is what the hell does he mean by 'the same plan that President Eisenhower used'?"

Another muffled consultation. "He says that this isn't the first time that the nuhp have landed on Earth. A scout ship with two nuhp aboard landed at Edwards Air Force Base in 1954. The two nuhp met with President Eisenhower. It was apparently a very cordial occasion, and President Eisenhower impressed the nuhp as a warm and sincere old gentleman. They've been planning to return to Earth ever since, but they've been very busy, what with one thing and another. President Eisenhower requested that the nuhp not reveal themselves to the people of Earth in general, until our government decided how to control the inevitable hysteria. My guess is that the government never got around to that, and when the nuhp departed, the matter was studied and then shelved. As the years passed, few people were even aware that the first meeting ever occurred. The nuhp have returned now in great numbers, expecting that we'd have prepared the populace by now. It's not their fault that we haven't. They just sort of took it for granted that they'd be welcome."

"Uh-huh," I said. That was my usual utterance when I didn't

know what the hell else to say. "Assure them that they are, indeed, welcome. I don't suppose the study they did during the Eisenhower administration was ever completed. I don't suppose there really is a plan to break the news to the public."

"Unfortunately, Mr. President, that seems to be the case."

"Uh-huh." That's Republicans for you, I thought. "Ask your nup something for me, Luis. Ask him if he knows what they told Eisenhower. They must be full of outer-space wisdom. Maybe they have some ideas about how we should deal with this."

There was yet another pause. "Mr. President, he says all they discussed with Mr. Eisenhower was his golf game. They helped to correct his putting stroke. But they are definitely full of wisdom. They know all sorts of things. My nup—that is, his name is Hurv—anyway, he says that they'd be happy to give you some advice."

"Tell him that I'm grateful, Luis. Can they have someone meet with me in, say, half an hour?"

"There are three nuhp on their way to the Oval Office at this moment. One of them is the leader of their expedition, and one of the others is the commander of their mother ship."

"Mother ship?" I asked.

"You haven't seen it? It's tethered on the Mall. They're real sorry about what they did to the Washington Monument. They say they can take care of it tomorrow."

I just shuddered and hung up the phone. I called my secretary. "There are going to be three—"

"They're here now, Mr. President."

I sighed. "Send them in." And that's how I met the nuhp. Just as President Eisenhower had.

They were handsome people. Likable, too. They smiled and shook hands and suggested that photographs be taken of the historic moment, so we called in the media; and then I had to sort of wing the most important diplomatic meeting of my entire political career. I welcomed the nuhp to Earth. "Welcome to Earth," I said, "and welcome to the United States."

"Thank you," said the nup I would come to know as Pleen. "We're glad to be here."

"How long do you plan to be with us?" I hated myself when I said that, in front of the Associated Press and UPI and all the network news people. I sounded like a room clerk at a Holiday Inn.

"We don't know, exactly," said Pleen. "We don't have to be back to work until a week from Monday."

"Uh-huh," I said. Then I just posed for pictures and kept my mouth shut. I wasn't going to say or do another goddamn thing until my advisers showed up and started advising.

Well, of course, the people panicked. Pleen told me to expect that, but I had figured it out for myself. We've seen too many movies about visitors from space. Sometimes they come with a message of peace and universal brotherhood and just the inside information mankind has been needing for thousands of years. More often, though, the aliens come to enslave and murder us because the visual effects are better, and so when the nuhp arrived, everyone was all prepared to hate them. People didn't trust their good looks. People were suspicious of their nice manners and their quietly tasteful clothing. When the nuhp offered to solve all our problems for us, we all said, sure, solve our problems—*but at what cost?*

That first week, Pleen and I spent a lot of time together, just getting to know one another and trying to understand what the other one wanted. I invited him and Commander Toag and the other nuhp bigwigs to a reception at the White House. We had a church choir from Alabama singing gospel music, and a high school band from Michigan playing a medley of favorite collegiate fight songs, and talented clones of the original stars nostalgically re-creating the Steve and Eydie Experience, and an improvisational comedy troupe from Los Angeles or someplace, and the New York Philharmonic under the baton of a twelve-year-old girl genius. They played Beethoven's Ninth Symphony in an attempt to impress the nuhp with how marvelous Earth culture was.

Pleen enjoyed it all very much. "Men are as varied in their expressions of joy as we nuhp," he said, applauding vigorously. "We are all very fond of human music. We think Beethoven composed some of the most beautiful melodies we've ever heard, anywhere in our galactic travels."

I smiled. "I'm sure we are all pleased to hear that," I said.

"Although the Ninth Symphony is certainly not the best of his work."

I faltered in my clapping. "Excuse me?" I said.

Pleen gave me a gracious smile. "It is well known among us that Beethoven's finest composition is his Piano Concerto No. 5 in E-flat major."

I let out my breath. "Of course, that's a matter of opinion. Perhaps the standards of the nuhp—"

"Oh, no," Pleen hastened to assure me, "taste does not enter into it at all. The Concerto No. 5 is Beethoven's best, according to very rigorous and definite critical principles. And even that lovely piece is by no means the best music ever produced by mankind."

I felt just a trifle annoyed. What could this nup, who came from some weirdo planet God alone knows how far away, from some society with not the slightest connection to our heritage and culture, what could this nup know of what Beethoven's Ninth Symphony aroused in our human souls? "Tell me, then, Pleen," I said in my ominously soft voice, "what *is* the best human musical composition?"

"The score from the motion picture *Ben-Hur,* by Miklos Rózsa," he said simply. What could I do but nod my head in silence? It wasn't worth starting an interplanetary incident over.

So from fear our reaction to the nuhp changed to distrust. We kept waiting for them to reveal their real selves; we waited for the pleasant masks to slip off and show us the true nightmarish faces we all suspected lurked beneath. The nuhp did not go home a week from Monday, after all. They liked Earth, and they liked us. They decided to stay a little longer. We told them about ourselves and our centuries of trouble; and they mentioned, in an offhand nuhp way, that they could take care of a few little things, make some small adjustments, and life would be a whole lot better for everybody on Earth. They didn't want anything in return. They wanted to give us these things in gratitude for our hospitality: for letting them park their mother ship on the Mall and for all the free refills of coffee they were getting all around the world. We hesitated, but our vanity and our greed won out. "Go ahead," we said, "make our deserts bloom. Go ahead, end war and poverty and disease. Show us twenty exciting new things to do with leftovers. Call us when you're done."

The fear changed to distrust, but soon the distrust changed to hope. The nuhp made the deserts bloom, all right. They asked for four months. We were perfectly willing to let them have all the time they needed. They put a tall fence all around the Namib and wouldn't let anyone in to watch what they were doing. Four months later, they had a big cocktail party and invited the whole world to see what they'd accomplished. I sent the secretary of state as my personal representative. He brought back some wonderful slides: the vast desert had been turned into a botanical miracle. There were miles and miles of flowering plants now, instead of monotonous dead sand and gravel sea. Of course, the immense garden contained nothing but hollyhocks, many millions of hollyhocks. I mentioned to Pleen that the people of Earth had been hoping for a little more in the way of variety, and something just a trifle more practical, too.

"What do you mean, 'practical'?" he asked.

"You know," I said, "food."

"Don't worry about food," said Pleen. "We're going to take care of hunger pretty soon."

"Good, good. But hollyhocks?"

"What's wrong with hollyhocks?"

"Nothing," I admitted.

"Hollyhocks are the single prettiest flower grown on Earth."

"Some people like orchids," I said. "Some people like roses."

"No," said Pleen firmly. "Hollyhocks are it. I wouldn't kid you."

So we thanked the nuhp for a Namibia full of hollyhocks and stopped them before they did the same thing to the Sahara, the Mojave, and the Gobi.

———

On the whole, everyone began to like the nuhp, although they took just a little getting used to. They had very definite opinions about everything, and they wouldn't admit that what they had were *opinions*. To hear a nup talk, he had a direct line to some categorical imperative that spelled everything out in terms that were unflinchingly black and white. Hollyhocks were the best flowers. Alexander Dumas was the greatest novelist. Powder blue was the prettiest color. Melancholy was the most ennobling emotion. *Grand Hotel* was the finest movie. The best car ever built was the 1956 Chevy Bel Air, but it had to be aqua and white. And there just wasn't room for discussion: the nuhp made these pronouncements with the force of divine revelation.

I asked Pleen once about the American presidency. I asked him who the nuhp thought was the best president in our history. I felt sort of like the Wicked Queen in "Snow White." Mirror, mirror, on the wall. I didn't really believe Pleen would tell me that I was the best president, but my heart pounded while I waited for his answer; you never know, right? To tell the truth, I expected him to say Washington, Lincoln, Roosevelt, or Akiwara. His answer surprised me: James K. Polk.

"Polk?" I asked. I wasn't even sure I could recognize Polk's portrait.

"He's not the most familiar," said Pleen, "but he was an honest if unexciting president. He fought the Mexican War and added a great amount of territory to the United States. He saw every bit of his platform become law. He was a good, hardworking man who deserves a better reputation."

"What about Thomas Jefferson?" I asked.

Pleen just shrugged. "He was O.K., too, but he was no James Polk."

My wife, the First Lady, became very good friends with the wife of Commander Toag, whose name was Doim. They often went shopping together, and Doim would make suggestions to the First Lady about fashion and hair care. Doim told my wife which rooms in the White House needed redecoration, and which charities were worthy of official support. It was Doim who negotiated the First

Lady's recording contract, and it was Doim who introduced her to the Philadelphia cheese steak, one of the nuhp's favorite treats (although they asserted that the best cuisine on Earth was Tex-Mex).

One day, Doim and my wife were having lunch. They sat at a small table in a chic Washington restaurant, with a couple of dozen Secret Service people and nuhp security agents disguised elsewhere among the patrons. "I've noticed that there seem to be more nuhp here in Washington every week," said the First Lady.

"Yes," said Doim, "new mother ships arrive daily. We think Earth is one of the most pleasant planets we've ever visited."

"We're glad to have you, of course," said my wife, "and it seems that our people have gotten over their initial fears."

"The hollyhocks did the trick," said Doim.

"I guess so. How many nuhp are there on Earth now?"

"About five or six million, I'd say."

The First Lady was startled. "I didn't think it would be that many."

Doim laughed. "We're not just here in America, you know. We're all over. We really like Earth. Although, of course, Earth isn't absolutely the best planet. Our own home, Nupworld, is still Number One; but Earth would certainly be on any Top Ten list."

"Uh-huh." (My wife has learned many important oratorical tricks from me.)

"That's why we're so glad to help you beautify and modernize your world."

"The hollyhocks were nice," said the First Lady. "But when are you going to tackle the really vital questions?"

"Don't worry about that," said Doim, turning her attention to her cottage cheese salad.

"When are you going to take care of world hunger?"

"Pretty soon. Don't worry."

"Urban blight?"

"Pretty soon."

"Man's inhumanity to man?"

Doim gave my wife an impatient look. "We haven't even been here for six months yet. What do you want, miracles? We've already done more than your husband accomplished in his entire first term."

"Hollyhocks," muttered the First Lady.

"I heard that," said Doim. "The rest of the universe absolutely *adores* hollyhocks. We can't help it if humans have no taste."

They finished their lunch in silence, and my wife came back to the White House fuming.

That same week, one of my advisers showed me a letter that had been sent by a young man in New Mexico. Several nuhp had moved into a condo next door to him and had begun advising him about the best investment possibilities (urban respiratory spas), the best fabrics and colors to wear to show off his coloring, the best holo system on the market (the Esmeraldas F-64 with hex-phased Libertad screens and a Ruy Challenger argon solipsizer), the best place to watch sunsets (the revolving restaurant on top of the Weyerhauser Building in Yellowstone City), the best wines to go with everything (too numerous to mention—send SASE for list), and which of the two women he was dating to marry (Candi Marie Esterhazy). "Mr. President," said the bewildered young man, "I realize that we must be gracious hosts to our benefactors from space, but I am having some difficulty keeping my temper. The nuhp are certainly knowledgeable and willing to share the benefits of their wisdom, but they don't even wait to be asked. If they were people, regular human beings who lived next door, I would have punched their lights out by now. Please advise. And hurry: they are taking me downtown next Friday to pick out an engagement ring and new living room furniture. I don't even *want* new living room furniture!"

Luis, my secretary of defense, talked to Hurv about the ultimate goals of the nuhp. "We don't have any goals," he said. "We're just taking it easy."

"Then why did you come to Earth?" asked Luis.

"Why do you go bowling?"

"I don't go bowling."

"You should," said Hurv. "Bowling is the most enjoyable thing a person can do."

"What about sex?"

"Bowling *is* sex. Bowling is a symbolic form of intercourse, except you don't have to bother about the feelings of some other person.

Bowling is sex without guilt. Bowling is what people have wanted down through all the millennia: sex without the slightest responsibility. It's the very distillation of the essence of sex. Bowling is sex without fear and shame."

"Bowling is sex without pleasure," said Luis.

There was a brief silence. "You mean," said Hurv, "that when you put that ball right into the pocket and see those pins explode off the alley, you don't have an orgasm?"

"Nope," said Luis.

"*That's* your problem, then. I can't help you there, you'll have to see some kind of therapist. It's obvious this subject embarrasses you. Let's talk about something else."

"Fine with me," said Luis moodily. "When are we going to receive the real benefits of your technological superiority? When are you going to unlock the final secrets of the atom? When are you going to free mankind from drudgery?"

"What do you mean, 'technological superiority'?" asked Hurv.

"There must be scientific wonders beyond our imagining aboard your mother ships."

"Not so's you'd notice. We're not even so advanced as you people here on Earth. We've learned all sorts of wonderful things since we've been here."

"What?" Luis couldn't imagine what Hurv was trying to say.

"We don't have anything like your astonishing bubble memories or silicon chips. We never invented anything comparable to the transistor, even. You know why the mother ships are so big?"

"My God."

"That's right," said Hurv, "vacuum tubes. All our spacecraft operate on vacuum tubes. They take up a hell of a lot of space. And they burn out. Do you know how long it takes to find the goddamn tube when it burns out? Remember how people used to take bags of vacuum tubes from their television sets down to the drugstore to use the tube tester? Think of doing that with something the size of our mother ships. And we can't just zip off into space when we feel like it. We have to let a mother ship warm up first. You have to turn the key and let the thing warm up for a couple of minutes, *then* you can zip off into space. It's a goddamn pain in the neck."

"I don't understand," said Luis, stunned. "If your technology is so primitive, how did you come here? If we're so far ahead of you, we should have discovered your planet, instead of the other way around."

Hurv gave a gentle laugh. "Don't pat yourself on the back, Luis. Just because your electronics are better than ours, you aren't necessarily superior in any way. Look, imagine that you humans are a man in Los Angeles with a brand-new Trujillo and we are a nup in New York with a beat-up old Ford. The two fellows start driving toward St. Louis. Now, the guy in the Trujillo is doing 120 on the interstates, and the guy in the Ford is putting along at 55; but the human in the Trujillo stops in Vegas and puts all of his gas money down the hole of a blackjack table, and the determined little nup cruises along for days until at last he reaches his goal. It's all a matter of superior intellect and the will to succeed. Your people talk a lot about going to the stars, but you just keep putting your money into other projects, like war and popular music and international athletic events and resurrecting the fashions of previous decades. If you wanted to go into space, you would have."

"But we *do* want to go."

"Then we'll help you. We'll give you the secrets. And you can explain your electronics to our engineers, and together we'll build wonderful new mother ships that will open the universe to both humans and nuhp."

Luis let out his breath. "Sounds good to me," he said.

Everyone agreed that this looked better than hollyhocks. We all hoped that we could keep from kicking their collective asses long enough to collect on that promise.

When I was in college, my roommate in my sophomore year was a tall, skinny guy named Barry Rintz. Barry had wild, wavy black hair and a sharp face that looked like a handsome, normal face that had been sat on and folded in the middle. He squinted a lot, not because he had any defect in his eyesight, but because he wanted to give the impression that he was constantly evaluating the world. This was true. Barry could tell you the actual and market values of any object you happened to come across.

We had a double date one football weekend with two girls from another college in the same city. Before the game, we met the girls and took them to the university's art museum, which was pretty large and owned an impressive collection. My date, a pretty elementary ed. major named Brigid, and I wandered from gallery to gallery, remarking that our tastes in art were very similar. We both liked the Impressionists, and we both liked Surrealism. There were a couple of little Renoirs that we admired for almost half an hour, and then we made a lot of silly sophomore jokes about what was happening in the Magritte and Dali and de Chirico paintings.

Barry and his date, Dixie, ran across us by accident as all four of us passed through the sculpture gallery. "There's a terrific Seurat down there," Brigid told her girlfriend.

"Seurat," Barry said. There was a lot of amused disbelief in his voice.

"I like Seurat," said Dixie.

"Well, of course," said Barry, "there's nothing really *wrong* with Seurat."

"What do you mean by that?"

"Do you know F. E. Church?" he asked.

"Who?" I said.

"Come here." He practically dragged us to a gallery of American paintings. F. E. Church was a remarkable American landscape painter (1826–1900) who achieved an astonishing and lovely luminance in his works. "Look at that light!" cried Barry. "Look at that space! Look at that air!"

Brigid glanced at Dixie. "Look at that air?" she whispered.

It was a fine painting and we all said so, but Barry was insistent. F. E. Church was the greatest artist in American history, and one of the best the world has ever known. "I'd put him right up there with Van Dyck and Canaletto."

"Canaletto?" said Dixie. "The one who did all those pictures of Venice?"

"Those skies!" murmured Barry ecstatically. He wore the drunken expression of the satisfied voluptuary.

"Some people like paintings of puppies or naked women," I offered. "Barry likes light and air."

We left the museum and had lunch. Barry told us which things on the menu were worth ordering, and which things were an abomination. He made us all drink an obscure imported beer from Ecuador. To Barry, the world was divided up into masterpieces and abominations. It made life so much simpler for him, except that he never understood why his friends could never tell one from the other.

At the football game, Barry compared our school's quarterback to Y. A. Tittle. He compared the other team's punter to Ngoc Van Vinh. He compared the halftime show to the Ohio State band's Script Ohio formation. Before the end of the third quarter, it was very obvious to me that Barry was going to have absolutely no luck at all with Dixie. Before the clock ran out in the fourth quarter, Brigid and I had made whispered plans to dump the other two as soon as possible and sneak away by ourselves. Dixie would probably find an excuse to ride the bus back to her dorm before suppertime. Barry, as usual, would spend the evening in our room, reading *The Making of the President 1996.*

On other occasions Barry would lecture me about subjects as diverse as American Literature (the best poet was Edwin Arlington Robinson, the best novelist James T. Farrell), animals (the only correct pet was the golden retriever), clothing (in anything other than a navy blue jacket and gray slacks a man was just asking for trouble), and even hobbies (Barry collected military decorations of czarist Imperial Russia. He wouldn't talk to me for days after I told him my father collected barbed wire).

Barry was a wealth of information. He was the campus arbiter of good taste. Everyone knew that Barry was the man to ask.

But no one ever did. We all hated his guts. I moved out of our dorm room before the end of the fall semester. Shunned, lonely, and bitter, Barry Rintz wound up as a guidance counselor in a high

school in Ames, Iowa. The job was absolutely perfect for him; few
people are so lucky in finding a career.

If I didn't know better, I might have believed that Barry was the
original advance spy for the nuhp.

When the nuhp had been on Earth for a full year, they gave us
the gift of interstellar travel. It was surprisingly inexpensive. The
nuhp explained their propulsion system, which was cheap and safe
and adaptable to all sorts of other earthbound applications. The
revelations opened up an entirely new area of scientific speculation.
Then the nuhp taught us their navigational methods, and about the
"shortcuts" they had discovered in space. People called them space
warps, although technically speaking, the shortcuts had nothing to
do with Einsteinian theory or curved space or anything like that.
Not many humans understood what the nuhp were talking about,
but that didn't make very much difference. The nuhp didn't understand the shortcuts, either; they just used them. The matter was
presented to us like a Thanksgiving turkey on a platter. We bypassed
the whole business of cautious scientific experimentation and leaped
right into commercial exploitation. Mitsubishi of La Paz and Martin
Marietta used nuhp schematics to begin construction of three luxury
passenger ships, each capable of transporting a thousand tourists
anywhere in our galaxy. Although man had yet to set foot on the
moons of Jupiter, certain selected travel agencies began booking
passage for a grand tour of the dozen nearest inhabited worlds.

Yes, it seemed that space was teeming with life, humanoid life
on planets circling half the G-type stars in the heavens. "We've
been trying to communicate with extraterrestrial intelligence for
decades," complained one Soviet scientist. "Why haven't they responded?"

A friendly nup merely shrugged. "Everybody's trying to communicate out there," he said. 'Your messages are like Publishers
Clearing House mail to them." At first, that was a blow to our racial
pride, but we got over it. As soon as we joined the interstellar
community, they'd begin to take us more seriously. And the nuhp
had made that possible.

We were grateful to the nuhp, but that didn't make them any easier to live with. They were still insufferable. As my second term as president came to an end, Pleen began to advise me about my future career. "Don't write a book," he told me (after I had already written the first two hundred pages of a *A President Remembers*). "If you want to be an elder statesman, fine; but keep a low profile and wait for the people to come to you."

"What am I supposed to do with my time, then?" I asked.

"Choose a new career," Pleen said. "You're not all that old. Lots of people do it. Have you considered starting a mail-order business? You can operate it from your home. Or go back to school and take courses in some subject that's always interested you. Or become active in church or civic projects. Find a new hobby: raising hollyhocks or collecting military decorations."

"Pleen," I begged, "just leave me alone."

He seemed hurt. "Sure, if that's what you want." I regretted my harsh words.

All over the country, all over the world, everyone was having the same trouble with the nuhp. It seemed that so many of them had come to Earth, every human had his own personal nup to make endless suggestions. There hadn't been so much tension in the world since the 1992 Miss Universe contest, when the most votes went to No Award.

That's why it didn't surprise me very much when the first of our own mother ships returned from its 28-day voyage among the stars with only 276 of its 1,000 passengers still aboard. The other 724 had remained behind on one lush, exciting, exotic, friendly world or another. These planets had one thing in common: they were all populated by charming, warm, intelligent, humanlike people who had left their own home worlds after being discovered by the nuhp. Many races lived together in peace and harmony on these planets, in spacious cities newly built to house the fed-up expatriates. Perhaps these alien races had experienced the same internal jealousies and hatreds we human beings had known for so long, but no more. Coming together from many planets throughout our galaxy, these various peoples dwelt contentedly beside each other, united by a single common aversion: their dislike for the nuhp.

Within a year of the launching of our first interstellar ship, the population of Earth had declined by 0.5 percent. Within two years, the population had fallen by almost 14 million. The nuhp were too sincere and too eager and too sympathetic to fight with. That didn't make them any less tedious. Rather than make a scene, most people just up and left. There were plenty of really lovely worlds to visit, and it didn't cost very much, and the opportunities in space were unlimited. Many people who were frustrated and disappointed on Earth were able to build new and fulfilling lives for themselves on planets that until the nuhp arrived, we didn't even know existed.

The nuhp knew this would happen. It had already happened dozens, hundreds of times in the past, wherever their mother ships touched down. They had made promises to us and they had kept them, although we couldn't have guessed just how things would turn out.

Our cities were no longer decaying warrens imprisoning the impoverished masses. The few people who remained behind could pick and choose among the best housing. Landlords were forced to reduce rents and keep properties in perfect repair just to attract tenants.

Hunger was ended when the ratio of consumers to food producers dropped drastically. Within ten years, the population of Earth was cut in half, and was still falling.

For the same reason, poverty began to disappear. There were plenty of jobs for everyone. When it became apparent that the nuhp weren't going to compete for those jobs, there were more opportunities than people to take advantage of them.

Discrimination and prejudice vanished almost overnight. Everyone cooperated to keep things running smoothly despite the large-scale emigration. The good life was available to everyone, and so resentments melted away. Then, too, whatever enmity people still felt could be focused solely on the nuhp; the nuhp didn't mind, either. They were oblivious to it all.

I am now the mayor and postmaster of the small human community of New Dallas, here on Thir, the fourth planet of a star known in our old catalog as Struve 2398. The various alien races we encountered here call the star by another name, which translates into "God's Pineal." All the aliens here are extremely helpful and charitable, and there are few nuhp.

All through the galaxy, the nuhp are considered the messengers of peace. Their mission is to travel from planet to planet, bringing reconciliation, prosperity, and true civilization. There isn't an intelligent race in the galaxy that doesn't love the nuhp. We all recognize what they've done and what they've given us.

But if the nuhp started moving in down the block, we'd be packed and on our way somewhere else by morning.

A Cabin on the Coast

GENE WOLFE

Gene Wolfe won his first Nebula for the novella "The Death of Doctor Island" and a second for his novel The Claw of the Conciliator *(part of the* Book of the New Sun *tetralogy). He is also the recipient of the World Fantasy Award, the John W. Campbell Award, and the Rhysling Award for science fiction poetry. His novel* Peace *received the Chicago Foundation Award for Literature. Wolfe recently won the French Prix Apollo for* The Citadel of the Autarch *(the last novel in the* New Sun *quartet). Other novels include* The Fifth Head of Cerberus *and* The Devil in a Forest.*

"A Cabin on the Coast" was a Nebula Award finalist for 1984. It's a haunting short story with a provocative theme, written with a style comparable to that of the finest American writers.

It might have been a child's drawing of a ship. He blinked, and blinked again. There were masts and sails, surely. One stack, perhaps another. If the ship were really there at all. He went back to his father's beach cottage, climbed the five wooden steps, wiped his feet on the coco mat.

Lissy was still in bed, but awake, sitting up now. It must have been the squeaking of the steps, he thought. Aloud he said, "Sleep good?"

He crossed the room and kissed her. She caressed him and said, "You shouldn't go swimming without a suit, dear wonderful swimmer. How was the Pacific?"

"Peaceful. Cold. It's too early for people to be up, and there's nobody within a mile of here anyway."

"Get into bed, then. How about the fish?"

"Salt water makes the sheets sticky. The fish have seen them before." He went to the corner, where a showerhead poked from the wall. The beach cottage—Lissy called it a cabin—had running water of the sometimes and rusty variety.

"They might bite 'em off. Sharks, you know. Little ones."

"Castrating woman." The shower coughed, doused him with icy spray, coughed again.

"You look worried."

"No."

"Is it your dad?"

He shook his head, then thrust it under the spray, finger-combing his dark curly hair.

"You think he'll come out here? Today?"

He withdrew, considering. "If he's back from Washington, and he knows we're here."

"But he couldn't know, could he?"

He turned off the shower and grabbed a towel, already damp and a trifle sandy. "I don't see how."

"Only he might guess." Lissy was no longer smiling. "Where else could we go? Hey, what did we do with my underwear?"

"Your place. Your folks'. Any motel."

She swung long golden legs out of bed, still holding the sheet across her lap. Her breasts were nearly perfect hemispheres, except for the tender protrusions of their pink nipples. He decided he had never seen breasts like that. He sat down on the bed beside her. "I love you very much," he said. "You know that?"

It made her smile again. "Does that mean you're coming back to bed?"

"If you want me to."

"I want a swimming lesson. What will people say if I tell them I came here and didn't go swimming?"

He grinned at her. "That it's that time of the month."

"You know what you are? You're filthy!" She pushed him. "Absolutely filthy! I'm going to bite your ears off." Tangled in the sheet, they fell off the bed together. "There they are!"

"There what are?"

"My bra and stuff. We must have kicked them under the bed. Where are our bags?"

"Still in the trunk. I never carried them in."

"Would you get mine? My swimsuit's in it."

"Sure," he said.

"And put on some pants!"

"My suit's in my bag, too." He found his trousers and got the keys to the Triumph. Outside the sun was higher, the chill of the fall morning nearly gone. He looked for the ship and saw it. Then it winked out like a star.

That evening they made a fire of driftwood and roasted the big greasy Italian sausages he had brought from town, making giant hot dogs by clamping them in French bread. He had brought red supermarket wine, too; they chilled it in the Pacific. "I never ate this much in my life," Lissy said.

"You haven't eaten anything yet."

"I know, but just looking at this sandwich would make me full if I wasn't so hungry." She bit off the end. "Cuff tough woof."

"What?"

"Castrating woman. That's what you called me this morning, Tim. Now *this* is a castrating woman."

"Don't talk with your mouth full."

"You sound like my mother. Give me some wine. You're hogging it."

He handed the bottle over. "It isn't bad, if you don't object to a complete lack of character."

"I sleep with you, don't I?"

"I have character, it's just all rotten."

"You said you wanted to get married."

"Let's go. You can finish that thing in the car."

"You drank half the bottle. You're too high to drive."

"Bullshoot."

Lissy giggled. "You just said bullshoot. Now *that's* character!"

He stood up. "Come on, let's go. It's only five hundred miles to
Reno. We can get married there in the morning."

"You're serious, aren't you?"

"If you are."

"Sit down."

"You were testing me," he said. "That's not fair, now is it?"

"You've been so worried all day. I wanted to see if it was about
me—if you thought you'd made a terrible mistake."

"We've made a mistake," he said. "I was trying to fix it just now."

"You think your dad is going to make it rough for you—"

"Us."

"—for us because it might hurt him in the next election."

He shook his head. "Not that. All right, maybe partly that. But
he means it, too. You don't understand him."

"I've got a father myself."

"Not like mine. Ryan was almost grown up before he left Ireland.
Taught by nuns and all that. Besides, I've got six older brothers and
two sisters. You're the oldest kid. Ryan's probably at least fifteen
years older than your folks."

"Is that really his name. Ryan Neal?"

"His full name is Timothy Ryan Neal, the same as mine. I'm
Timothy, Jr. He used Ryan when he went into politics because
there was another Tim Neal around then, and we've always called
me Tim to get away from the Junior."

"I'm going to call him Tim again, like the nuns must have when
he was young. Big Tim. You're Little Tim."

"O.K. with me. I don't know if Big Tim is going to like it."

Something was moving, it seemed, out where the sun had set.
Something darker against the dark horizon.

"What made you Junior anyway? Usually it's the oldest boy."

"He didn't want it, and would never let Mother do it. But she
wanted to, and I was born during the Democratic convention that
year."

"He had to go, of course."

"Yeah, he had to go, Lissy. If you don't understand that, you don't understand politics at all. They hoped I'd hold off for a few days, and what the hell, Mother'd had eight with no problems. Anyway, he was used to it—he was the youngest of seven boys himself. So she got to call me what she wanted."

"But then she died." The words sounded thin and lonely against the pounding of the surf.

"Not because of that."

Lissy upended the wine bottle; he saw her throat pulse three times. "Will I die because of that, Little Tim?"

"I don't think so." He tried to think of something gracious and comforting. "If we decide we want children, that's the risk I have to take."

"*You* have to take? Bullshoot."

"That both of us have to take. Do you think it was easy for Ryan, raising nine kids by himself?"

"You love him, don't you?"

"Sure I love him. He's my father."

"And now you think you might be ruining things for him. For my sake."

"That's not why I want us to be married, Lissy."

She was staring into the flames; he was not certain she had even heard him. "Well, now I know why his pictures look so grim. So gaunt."

He stood up again. "If you're through eating . . ."

"You want to go back to the cabin? You can screw me right here on the beach—there's nobody here but us."

"I didn't mean that."

"Then why go in there and look at the walls? Out here we've got the fire and the ocean. The moon ought to be up pretty soon."

"It would be warmer."

"With just that dinky little kerosene stove? I'd rather sit here by the fire. In a minute I'm going to send you off to get me some more wood. You can run up to the cabin and get a shirt, too, if you want to."

"I'm O.K."

"Traditional roles. Big Tim must have told you all about them. The woman has the babies and keeps the home fires burning. You're not going to end up looking like him, though, are you, Little Tim?"

"I suppose so. He used to look just like me."

"Really?"

He nodded. "He had his picture taken just after he got into politics. He was running for ward committeeman, and he had a poster made. We've still got the picture, and it looks like me with a high collar and a funny hat."

"She knew, didn't she?" Lissy said. For a moment he did not understand what she meant. "Now go and get some more wood. Only don't wear yourself out, because when you come back we're going to take care of that little thing that's bothering you, and we're going to spend the night on the beach."

When he came back she was asleep, but he woke her carrying her up to the beach cottage.

Next morning he woke up alone. He got up and showered and shaved, supposing that she had taken the car into town to get something for breakfast. He had filled the coffeepot and put it on before he looked out the shoreside window and saw the Triumph still waiting near the road.

There was nothing to be alarmed about, of course. She had awakened before he had and gone out for an early dip. He had done the same thing himself the morning before. The little patches of green cloth that were her bathing suit were hanging over the back of a rickety chair, but then they were still damp from last night. Who would want to put on a damp, clammy suit? She had gone in naked, just as he had.

He looked out the other window, wanting to see her splashing in the surf, waiting for him. The ship was there, closer now, rolling like a derelict. No smoke came from its clumsy funnel and no sails were set, but dark banners hung from its rigging. Then there was no ship, only wheeling gulls and the empty ocean. He called her name, but no one answered.

He put on his trunks and a jacket and went outside. A wind had smoothed the sand. The tide had come, obliterating their fire, reclaiming the driftwood he had gathered.

For two hours he walked up and down the beach, calling, telling himself there was nothing wrong. When he forced himself not to think of Lissy dead, he could only think of the headlines, the ninety seconds of ten o'clock news, how Ryan would look, how Pat—all his brothers—would look at him. And when he turned his mind from that, Lissy was dead again, her pale hair snarled with kelp as she rolled in the surf, green crabs feeding from her arms.

He got into the Triumph and drove to town. In the little brick station he sat beside the desk of a fat cop and told his story.

The fat cop said, "Kid, I can see why you want us to keep it quiet."

Tim said nothing. There was a paperweight on the desk—a baseball of white glass.

"You probably think we're out to get you, but we're not. Tomorrow we'll put out a missing persons report, but we don't have to say anything about you or the senator in it, and we won't."

"Tomorrow?"

"We got to wait twenty-four hours, in case she should show up. That's the law. But kid—" The fat cop glanced at his notes.

"Tim."

"Right. Tim. She ain't going to show up. You got to get yourself used to that."

"She could be . . ." Without wanting to, he let it trail away.

"Where? You think she snuck off and went home? She could walk out to the road and hitch, but you say her stuff's still there. Kidnapped? Nobody could have pulled her out of bed without waking you up. Did you kill her?"

"No!" Tears he could not hold back were streaming down his cheeks.

"Right. I've talked to you and I don't think you did. But you're the only one that could have. If her body washes up, we'll have to look into that."

Tim's hands tightened on the wooden arms of the chair. The fat cop pushed a box of tissues across the desk.

"Unless it washes up, though, it's just a missing person, O.K.? But she's dead, kid, and you're going to have to get used to it. Let me tell you what happened." He cleared his throat.

"She got up while you were still asleep, probably about when it started to get light. She did just what you thought she did—went out for a nice refreshing swim before you woke up. She went out too far, and probably she got a cramp. The ocean's cold as hell now. Maybe she yelled, but if she did she was too far out, and the waves covered it up. People think drowners holler like fire sirens, but they don't—they don't have that much air. Sometimes they don't make any noise at all."

Tim stared at the gleaming paperweight.

"The current here runs along the coast—you probably know that. Nobody ought to go swimming without somebody around, but sometimes it seems like everybody does it. We lose a dozen or so a year. In maybe four or five cases we find them. That's all."

The beach cottage looked abandoned when he returned. He parked the Triumph and went inside and found the stove still burning, his coffee perked to tar. He took the pot outside, dumped the coffee, scrubbed the pot with beach sand and rinsed it with salt water. The ship, which had been invisible through the window of the cottage, was almost plain when he stood waist-deep. He heaved the coffeepot back to the shore and swam out some distance, but when he straightened up in the water, the ship was gone.

Back inside he made fresh coffee and packed Lissy's things in her suitcase. When that was done, he drove into town again. Ryan was still in Washington, but Tim told his secretary where he was. "Just in case anybody reports me missing," he said.

She laughed. "It must be pretty cold for swimming."

"I like it," he told her. "I want to have at least one more long swim."

"All right, Tim. When he calls, I'll let him know. Have a good time."

"Wish me luck," he said, and hung up. He got a hamburger and more coffee at a Jack-in-the-Box and went back to the cottage and walked a long way along the beach.

He had intended to sleep that night, but he did not. From time to time he got up and looked out the window at the ship, sometimes visible by moonlight, sometimes only a dark presence in the lower night sky. When the first light of dawn came, he put on his trunks and went into the water.

For a mile or more, as well as he could estimate the distance, he could not see it. Then it was abruptly close, the long oars like the legs of a water spider, the funnel belching sparks against the still-dim sky, sparks that seemed to become new stars.

He swam faster then, knowing that if the ship vanished he would turn back and save himself, knowing, too, that if it only retreated before him, retreated forever, he would drown. It disappeared behind a cobalt wave, reappeared. He sprinted and grasped at the sea-slick shaft of an oar, and it was like touching a living being. Quite suddenly he stood on the deck, with no memory of how he came there.

Bare feet pattered on the planks, but he saw no crew. A dark flag lettered with strange script flapped aft, and some vague recollection of a tour of a naval ship with his father years before made him touch his forehead. There was a sound that might have been laughter or many other things. The captain's chair would be aft, too, he thought. He went there, bracing himself against the wild roll, and found a door.

Inside, something black crouched upon a dais. "I've come for Lissy," Tim said.

There was no reply, but a question hung in the air. He answered it almost without intending to. "I'm Timothy Ryan Neal, and I've come for Lissy. Give her back to me."

A light, it seemed, dissolved the blackness. Cross-legged on the dais, a slender man in tweeds sucked at a long clay pipe. "It's Irish, are ye?" he asked.

"American," Tim said.

"With such a name? I don't believe ye. Where's yer feathers?"

"I want her back," Tim said again.

"An' if ye don't get her?"

"Then I'll tear this ship apart. You'll have to kill me or take me, too."

"Spoken like a true son of the ould sod," said the man in tweeds. He scratched a kitchen match on the sole of his boot and lit his pipe. "Sit down, will ye? I don't fancy lookin' up like that. It hurts me neck. Sit down, and 'tis possible we can strike an agreement."

"This is crazy," Tim said. "The whole thing is crazy."

"It is that," the man in tweeds replied. "An' there's much, much more comin'. Ye'd best brace for it, Tim me lad. Now sit down."

There was a stout wooden chair behind Tim where the door had been. He sat. "Are you about to tell me you're a leprechaun? I warn you, I won't believe it."

"Me? One o' them scamperin', thievin', cobblin' little misers? I'd shoot meself. Me name's Daniel O'Donoghue, King o' Connaught. Do ye believe that, now?"

"No," Tim said.

"What would ye believe, then?"

"That this is—some way, somehow—what people call a saucer. That you and your crew are from a planet of another sun."

Daniel laughed. " 'Tis a close encounter you're havin', is it? Would ye like to see me as a tiny green man wi' horns like a snail's? I can do that, too."

"Don't bother."

"All right, I won't, though 'tis a good shape. A man can take it and be whatever he wants, one o' the People o' Peace or a bit o' a man from Mars. I've used it for both, and there's nothin' better."

"You took Lissy," Tim said.

"And how would ye be knowin' that?"

"I thought she'd drowned."

"Did ye now?"

"And that this ship—or whatever it is—was just a sign, an omen. I talked to a policeman and he as good as told me, but I didn't really think about what he said until last night, when I was trying to sleep."

"Is it a dream yer havin'? Did ye ever think on that?"

"If it's a dream, it's still real," Tim said doggedly. "And anyway, I saw your ship when I was awake, yesterday and the day before."

"Or yer dreamin' now ye did. But go on wi' it."

"He said Lissy couldn't have been abducted because I was in the same bed, and that she'd gone out for a swim in the morning and drowned. But she could have been abducted, if she had gone out for the swim first. If someone had come for her with a boat. And she wouldn't have drowned, because she didn't swim good enough to drown. She was afraid of the water. We went in yesterday, and even with me there, she would hardly go in over her knees. So it was you."

"Yer right, ye know," Daniel said. He formed a little steeple of his fingers. " 'Twas us."

Tim was recalling stories that had been read to him when he was a child. "Fairies steal babies, don't they? And brides. Is that why you do it? So we'll think that's who you are?"

"Bless ye, 'tis true," Daniel told him. " 'Tis the Fair Folk we are. The jinn o' the desert, too, and the saucer riders ye say ye credit, and forty score more. Would ye be likin' to see me wi' me goatskin breeches and me panpipe?" He chuckled. "Have ye never wondered why we're so much alike the world over? Or thought that we don't always know just which shape's the best for a place, so the naiads and the dryads might as well be the ladies o' the Deeny Shee? Do ye know what the folk o' the Barb'ry Coast call the hell that's under their sea?"

Tim shook his head.

"Why, 'tis Domdaniel. I wonder why that is, now. Tim, ye say ye want this girl."

"That's right."

"An' ye say there'll be trouble and plenty for us if ye don't have her. But let me tell ye now that if ye don't get her, wi' our blessin' to boot, ye'll drown—hold your tongue, can't ye, for 'tis worse than that—if ye don't get her wi' our blessin', 'twill be seen that ye were drownin' now. Do ye take me meaning?"

"I think so. Close enough."

"Ah, that's good, that is. Now here's me offer. Do ye remember how things stood before we took her?"

"Of course."

"They'll stand so again, if ye but do what I tell ye. 'Tis yerself that will remember, Tim Neal, but she'll remember nothin'. An' the truth of it is, there'll be nothin' to remember, for it'll all be gone, every stick of it. This policeman ye spoke wi', for instance. Ye've me word that ye will not have done it."

"What do I have to do?" Tim asked.

"Service. Serve us. Do whatever we ask of ye. We'd sooner have a broth of a girl like yer Lissy than a great hulk of a lad like yerself, but then, too, we'd sooner be havin' one that's willin', for the unwillin' girls are everywhere—I don't doubt but ye've seen it yerself. A hundred years, that's all we ask of ye. 'Tis short enough, like Doyle's wife. Will ye do it?"

"And everything will be the same, at the end, as it was before you took Lissy?"

"Not everythin', I didn't say that. Ye'll remember, don't ye remember me sayin' so? But for her and all the country round, why 'twill be the same."

"All right," Tim said. "I'll do it."

" 'Tis a brave lad ye are. Now I'll tell ye what I'll do. I said a hundred years, to which ye agreed—"

Tim nodded.

"—but I'll have no unwillin' hands about me boat, nor no ungrateful ones neither. I'll make it twenty. How's that? Sure and I couldn't say fairer, could I?"

Daniel's figure was beginning to waver and fade; the image of the dark mass Tim had seen first hung about it like a cloud.

"Lay yerself on yer belly, for I must put me foot upon yer head. Then the deal's done."

The salt ocean was in his mouth and his eyes. His lungs burst for breath. He revolved in the blue chasm of water, tried to swim, at last exploded gasping into the air.

The king had said he would remember, but the years were fading already. Drudging, dancing, buying, spying, prying, waylaying, and betraying when he walked in the world of men. Serving something that he had never wholly understood. Sailing foggy seas that were sometimes of this earth. Floating among the constellations. The years and the slaps and the kicks were all fading, and with them (and he rejoiced in it) the days when he had begged.

He lifted an arm, trying to regain his old stroke, and found that he was very tired. Perhaps he had never really rested in all those years. Certainly, he could not recall resting. Where was he? He paddled listlessly, not knowing if he were swimming away from land, if he were in the center of an ocean. A wave elevated him, a long, slow swell of blue under the gray sky. A glory—the rising or perhaps the setting sun—shone to his right. He swam toward it, caught sight of a low coast.

He crawled onto the sand and lay there for a time, his back struck by drops of spray like rain. Near his eyes, the beach seemed nearly black. There were bits of charcoal, fragments of half-burned wood. He raised his head, pushing away the earth, and saw an empty bottle of greenish glass nearly buried in the wet sand.

When he was able at last to rise, his limbs were stiff and cold. The dawnlight had become daylight, but there was no warmth in it. The beach cottage stood only about a hundred yards away, one window golden with sunshine that had entered from the other side, the walls in shadow. The red Triumph gleamed beside the road.

At the top of a small dune he turned and looked back out to sea. A black freighter with a red and white stack was visible a mile or two out, but it was only a freighter. For a moment he felt a kind of regret, a longing for a part of his life that he had hated but that was now gone forever. I will never be able to tell her what happened, he thought. And then: Yes, I will, if only I let her think I'm just making it up. And then: No wonder so many people tell so many stories. Good-bye to all that.

The step creaked under his weight, and he wiped the sand from his feet on the coco mat. Lissy was in bed. When she heard the door open she sat up, then drew up the sheet to cover her breasts.

"Big Tim," she said. "You did come. Tim and I were hoping you would."

When he did not answer, she added, "He's out having a swim, I think. He should be around in a minute."

And when he still said nothing: "We're—Tim and I—we're going to be married."

Dogs' Lives

MICHAEL BISHOP

Michael Bishop is that rarity among writers—a man of letters. Poet, short story writer, novelist, editor, and critic, he exudes authenticity in everything he does. Even an author as wildly different from Bishop as A. E. Van Vogt has written that "he is becoming the best science fiction writer in the world." Bishop's novels include the Nebula winner No Enemy but Time, *the satirical* Who Made Stevie Crye?, Ancient of Days, *and* A Little Knowledge. *His stories have been collected in* Blooded on Arachne *and* One Winter in Eden. *He is one of that growing number of imaginative writers who feel as at home in SF as they do in other fictions. In 1984 Bishop edited* Light Years and Dark, *a massive anthology that did much to correct the commercial overkill that too often seems to threaten SF publishing. Bishop lives in Pine Mountain, Georgia, with his family and is one of the most distinguished writers ever to convert to a word processor.*

"Dogs' Lives" originally appeared in a special SF issue of the Missouri Review *and was in the running for the final Nebula ballot. It was also selected for* Best American Short Stories 1985 *(Houghton Mifflin), a rare honor, to which Bishop responded: "I am as excited by my story's selection as I was on two past occasions when my work won Nebula awards. It also seems to me additional confirmation of the fact that one can do literate, seriously intentioned work within the SF field. And receive credit for so doing."*

All knowledge, the totality of all questions and all answers, is contained in the dog.

—Franz Kafka, "Investigations of a Dog"

I AM TWENTY-SEVEN: Three weeks ago a black Great Dane stalked into my classroom as I was passing out theme topics. My students turned about to look. One of the freshmen wits made an inane remark, which I immediately topped: "That may be the biggest dog I've ever seen." Memorable retort. Two of my students sniggered.

I ushered the Great Dane back into the hall. As I held its collar and maneuvered it out of English 102 (surely it was looking for the foreign language department), the dog's power and aloofness somehow coursed up my arm. Nevertheless, it permitted me to release it onto the north campus. Sinews, flanks, head. What a magnificent animal. It loped up the winter hillock outside Park Hall without looking back. Thinking on its beauty and self-possession, I returned to my classroom.

And closed the door.

TWENTY-SEVEN, AND HOLDING: All of this is true. The incident of the Great Dane has not been out of my thoughts since it happened. There is no door in my mind to close on the image of that enigmatic animal. It stalks into and out of my head whenever it wishes.

As a result, I have begun to remember some painful things about dogs and my relationships with them. The memories are accompanied by premonitions. In fact, sometimes I—my secret self—go inside the Great Dane's head and look through its eyes at tomorrow, and yesterday. Every bit of what I remember, every bit of what I foresee, throws light on my ties with both humankind and dogdom.

Along with my wife, my fifteen-month-old son, and a ragged miniature poodle, I live in Athens, Georgia, in a rented house that was built before World War I. We have lived here for seven months. In the summer we had bats. Twice I knocked the invaders out of the air with a broom and bludgeoned them to death against the dining-room floor. Now that it is winter the bats hibernate in the eaves, warmer than we are in our beds. The furnace runs all day and all night because, I suppose, no one had heard of insulation in 1910 and our fireplaces are all blocked up to keep out the bats.

At night I dream about flying into the center of the sun on the back of a winged Great Dane.

I AM EIGHT: Van Luna, Kansas. It is winter. At four o'clock in the morning a hand leads me down the cold concrete steps in the darkness of our garage. Against the wall, between a stack of automobile tires and a dismantled Ping-Pong table, a pallet of rags on

which the new puppies lie. Everything smells of dogflesh and gas-
oline. Outside the wind whips about frenetically, rattling the garage
door.

In robe and slippers I bend down to look at the furred-over lumps
that huddle against one another on their rag pile. Frisky, their
mother, regards me with suspicion. Adult hands have pulled her
aside. Adult hands hold her back.

"Pick one up," a disembodied adult voice commands me.

I comply.

The puppy, almost shapeless, shivers in my hands, threatens to
slide out of them onto the concrete. I press my cheek against the
lump of fur and let its warm, faintly fecal odor slip into my memory.
I have smelled this smell before.

"Where are its eyes?"

"Don't worry, punkin," the adult voice says. "It has eyes. They
just haven't opened yet."

The voice belongs to my mother. My parents have been divorced
for three years.

I AM FIVE: Our ship docks while it is snowing. We live in Tokyo,
Japan: Mommy, Daddy, and I.

Daddy comes home in a uniform that scratches my face when I
grab his trouser leg. Government housing is where we live. On the
lawn in the big yard between the houses I grab Daddy and ride his
leg up to our front door. I am wearing a cowboy hat and empty
holsters that go *flap flap flap* when I jump down and run inside.

Christmas presents: I am a cowboy.

The inside of the house gathers itself around me. A Japanese
maid named Peanuts. (Such a funny name.) Mommy there, too.
We have radio. My pistols are in the toy box. Later, not for Christmas, they give me my first puppy. It is never in the stuffy house,
only on the porch. When Daddy and I go inside from playing with
it the radio is singing: "How Much Is That Doggy in the Window?"
Everybody in Tokyo likes that song.

The cowboy hat has a string with a bead to pull tight under my

chin. I lose my hat anyway. Blackie runs off with the big dogs from
the city. The pistols stay shiny in my toy box.

On the radio, always singing, is Patti Page.

DOGS I HAVE KNOWN: Blackie, Frisky, Wiggles, Seagull, Mike, Pat,
Marc, Boo Boo, Susie, Mandy, Heathcliff, Pepper, Sam, Trixie,
Andy, Taffy, Tristram, Squeak, Christy, Fritz, Blue, Tammi, Na-
poleon, Nickie, B.J., Viking, Tau, and Canicula, whom I some-
times call Threasie (or 3C, short, you see, for Cybernetic Canine
Construct).

"Sorry. There are no more class cards for this section of 102."

How the spurned dogs bark, how they howl.

I AM FOURTEEN: Cheyenne Canyon, Colorado. It is August. My
father and I are driving up the narrow canyon road toward Helen
Hunt Falls. Dad's Labrador retriever Nick—too conspicuously my
namesake—rides with us. The dog balances with his hind legs on
the back seat and lolls his massive head out the driver's window,
his dark mouth open to catch the wind. Smart, gentle, trained for
the keen competition of field trials, Nick is an animal that I can
scarcely believe belongs to us—even if he is partially mine only
three months out of the year, when I visit my father during the
summer.

The radio, turned up loud, tells us that the Russians have brought
back to Earth from an historic mission the passengers of Sputnik
V, the first two animals to be recovered safely from orbit.

They, of course, are dogs. Their names are Belka and Strelka,
the latter of whom will eventually have six puppies as proof of her
power to defy time as well as space.

"How 'bout that, Nick?" my father says. "How'd you like to go
free-fallin' around the globe with a pretty little bitch?"

Dad is talking to the retriever, not to me. He calls me Nicholas.
Nick, however, is not listening. His eyes are half shut against the
wind, his ears flowing silkenly in the slipstream behind his aristo-
cratic head.

I laugh in delight. Although puberty has not yet completely caught up with me, my father treats me like an equal. Sometimes on Saturday, when we're watching Dizzy Dean on *The Game of the Week*, he gives me my own can of beer.

We park and climb the stone steps that lead to a little bridge above the falls. Nick runs on ahead of us. Very few tourists are about. Helen Hunt Falls is more picturesque than imposing; the bridge hangs only a few feet over the mountain stream roaring and plunging beneath it. Hardly a Niagara. Nick looks down without fear, and Dad says, "Come on, Nicholas. There's a better view on up the mountain."

We cross the bridge and struggle up the hillside above the tourist shop, until the pine trunks, which we pull ourselves up by, have finally obscured the shop and the winding canyon road. Nick still scrambles ahead of us, causing small avalanches of sand and loose soil.

Higher up, a path. We can look across the intervening blueness at a series of high falls that drop down five or six tiers of sloping granite to disappear in a mist of trees. In only a moment, it seems, we have walked to the highest tier.

My father sits me down with an admonition to stay put. "I'm going down to the next slope, Nicholas, to see if I can see how many falls there are to the bottom. Look out through the trees. I'll bet you can see Kansas."

"Be careful," I urge him.

The water sliding over the rocks beside me is probably not even an inch deep, but I can easily tell that below the next sloping of granite the entire world falls away into a canyon of blue-green.

Dad goes down the slope. Nick, as always, is preceding him. On the margin of granite below, the dog stops and waits. My father joins Nick, puts his hands on his hips, bends at the waist, and peers down into an abyss altogether invisible to me. How far down it drops I cannot tell, but the echo of falling water suggests no inconsequential distance.

Nick wades into the silver flashing from the white rocks. Before I can shout warning, he lowers his head to drink. The current is not strong, these falls are no torrents—but wet stone provides no traction and the Lab's feet go slickly out from under him. His body twists about, and he begins to slide inexorably through the slow silver.

"Dad! Dad!" I am standing.

My father belatedly sees what is happening. He reaches out to grab at his dog. He nearly topples. He loses his red golf cap.

And then Nick's body drops, his straining head and forepaws are pulled after. The red golf cap follows him down, an ironic afterthought.

I.am weeping. My father stands upright and throws his arms above his head. "Oh my dear God!" he cries. "Oh my dear God!" The canyon echoes these words, and suddenly the universe has changed.

Time stops.

Then begins again.

Miraculously, even anticlimactically, Nick comes limping up to us from the hell to which we had both consigned him. He comes limping up through the pines. His legs and flanks tremble violently. His coat is matted and wet, like a newborn puppy's. When he reaches us he seems not even to notice that we are there to care for him, to take him back down the mountain into Colorado Springs.

"He fell at least a hundred yards, Nicholas. At least that—onto solid rock."

On the bridge above Helen Hunt Falls we meet a woman with a Dalmatian. Nick growls at the Dalmatian, his hackles in an aggressive fan. But in the car he stretches out on the back seat and ignores my attempts to console him. My father and I do not talk. We are certain that there must be internal injuries. We drive the regal Lab—AKC designation, "Black Prince Nicholas"—almost twenty miles to the veterinarian's at the Air Force Academy.

Like Belka and Strelka, he survives.

SNAPSHOT: Black Prince Nicholas returning to my father through the slate-gray verge of a Wyoming lake, a wounded mallard clutched tenderly in his jaws. The photograph is grainy, but the huge Lab-

rador resembles a panther coming out of creation's first light: he is
the purest distillation of power.

ROLL CALL FOR SPRING QUARTER: I walk into the classroom with my
new roll sheets and the same well-thumbed text book. As usual,
my new students regard me with a mixture of curiosity and dispas-
sionate calculation. But there is something funny about them this
quarter.
   Something *not right.*
   Uneasily I begin calling the alphabetized list of their names:
"Andy . . . B.J. . . . Blackie . . . Blue . . . Boo Boo . . . Canicula
. . . Christy . . . Frisky . . ."
   Each student responds with an inarticulate yelp rather than a
healthy "Here!" As I proceed down the roll, the remainder of the
class dispenses with even this courtesy. I have a surly bunch on my
hands. A few have actually begun to snarl.
   "Pepper . . . Sam . . . Seagull . . . Squeak . . ."
   They do not let me finish. From the front row a collie leaps out
of his seat and crashes against my lectern. I am borne to the floor
by his hurtling body. Desperately I try to protect my throat.
   The small classroom shakes with the thunder of my students'
barking, and I can tell that every animal on my roll has fallen upon
me with the urgency of his own peculiar bloodlusts.
   The fur flies. Me, they viciously devour.
   Before the lights go completely out, I tell myself that it is going
to be a very difficult quarter. A very difficult quarter indeed.

I AM FORTY-SIX: Old for an athlete, young for a president, maybe
optimum for an astronaut. I am learning new tricks.
   The year is 1992; and it has been a long time since I have taught
freshman English or tried my hand at spinning monstrously improbable tales. (With the exception, of course, of this one.) I have
been too busy.
   After suffering a ruptured aneurysm while delivering a lecture in
the spring of 1973, I underwent surgery and resigned from the
English department faculty. My recovery took eight or nine months.

Outfitted with several vascular prostheses and wired for the utmost mobility, I returned to the university campus to pursue simultaneous majors in molecular biology and astrophysics. The G.I. Bill and my wife's and my parents footed the largest part of our expenses—at the beginning, at least. Later, when I volunteered for a government program involving cybernetic experimentation with human beings (reasoning that the tubes in my brain were a good start on becoming a cyborg, anyway), money ceased to be a problem.

This confidential program changed me. In addition to the synthetic blood vessels in my brain, I picked up three artificial internal organs, a transparent skull cap, an incomplete auxiliary skeletal system consisting of resilient inert plastics, and a pair of removable visual adaptors that plug into a plate behind my brow and so permit me to see expertly in the dark. I can even eat wood if I have to. I can learn the most abstruse technical matters without even blinking my adaptors. I can jump off a three-story building without even jarring my kneecaps. These skills, as you may imagine, come in handy.

With a toupee, a pair of dark glasses, and a little cosmetic surgery, I could leave the government hospitals where I had undergone these changes and take up a seat in any classroom in any university in the nation. I was often given leave to do so. Entrance requirements were automatically waived, I never saw a fee card, and not once did my name fail to appear on the rolls of any of the classes I sat in on.

I studied everything. I made A pluses in everything. I could read a text book from cover to cover in thirty minutes and recall even the footnotes verbatim. I awed professors who had worked for thirty-forty years in chemistry, physics, biology, astronomy. It was the ultimate wish-fulfillment fantasy come true, and not all of it can be attributed to the implanted electrodes, the enzyme inoculations, and the brain meddlings of the government cyberneticists. No, I have always had a talent for doing things thoroughly.

My family suffered.

We moved many, many times, and for days on end I was away from whatever home we had newly made.

My son and daughter were not particularly aware of the physical changes I had undergone—at least not at first—but Katherine, my wife, had to confront them each time we were alone. Stoically, heroically, she accepted the passion that drove me to alter myself toward the machine, even as she admitted that she did not understand it. She never recoiled from me because of my strangeness, and I was grateful for that. I have always believed that human beings discover a major part of the meaning in their lives from, in Pound's phrase, "the quality of the affections," and Katherine could see through the mechanical artifice surrounding and buttressing me, Nicholas Parsons, to the man himself. And I was grateful for that, too. Enormously grateful.

Still, we all have doubts. "Why are you doing this?" Katherine asked me one night. "Why are you letting them change you?"

"*Tempus fugit.* Time's wingéd chariot. I've got to do everything I can before there's none left. And I'm doing it for all of us—for you, for Peter, for Erin. It'll pay off. I know it will."

"But what started all this? Before the aneurysm—"

"Before the aneurysm I'd begun to wake up at night with a strange new sense of power. I could go inside the heads of dogs and read what their lives were like. I could time-travel in their minds."

"You had insomnia, Nick. You couldn't sleep."

"No, no, it wasn't just that. I was learning about time by riding around inside the head of that Great Dane that came into my classroom. We went everywhere, everywhen. The aneurysm had given me the ability to do that—when it ruptured, my telepathic skills went too."

Katherine smiled. "You regret that you can't read dogs' minds any more?"

"Yes. A little. But this compensates, what I'm doing now. If you can stand it a few more years, if you can tolerate the changes in me, it'll pay off. I'm certain it will."

And we talked for a long time that night, in a tiny bedroom in a tiny apartment in a big Texas city many miles from Van Luna, Kansas, or Cheyenne, Wyoming, or Colorado Springs, or Athens, Georgia.

Tonight, nearly seventeen years after that thoughtful conversation, I am free-falling in orbit with my trace-mate Canicula, whom I sometimes call Threasie (or 3C, you see, short for Cybernetic Canine Construct). We have been up here a month now, in preparation for our flight to the star system Sirius eight months hence. Katherine has found this latest absence of mine particularly hard to bear. Peter is a troubled young man of twenty, and Erin is a restless teen-ager with many questions about her absent father. Further, Katherine knows that shortly the *Black Retriever* will fling me into the interstellar void with eight other trace-teams. Recent advances in laser-fusion technology, along with the perfection of the Livermore-Parsons Drive, will no doubt get us out to Sirius in no time flat (i.e., less than four years for those of you who remain Earthbound, a mere fraction of that for us aboard the *Black Retriever*), but Katherine does not find this news at all cheering.

"*Tempus fugit,*" she told me somewhat mockingly during a recent laser transmission. "And unless I move to Argentina, Nick, I won't even be able to see the star you're traveling toward."

In Earth orbit, however, both Canicula and I find that time drags. We are ready to be off to the small Spartan world that no doubt circles our starfall destination in Canis Major. My own minute studies of the "wobble" in Sirius's proper motion have proved that such a planet exists; only once before has anyone else in the scientific community detected a dark companion with a mass less than that of Jupiter, but no one doubts that I know what I am doing.

Hence this expedition.

Hence this rigorous though wearying training period in Earth orbit. I do not exempt even myself, but dear God how time drags.

Canicula is my own dark companion. He rescues me from doubt, ennui, and orbital funk. He used to be a Great Dane. Even now you can see that beneath his streamlined cybernetic exterior a magnificent animal breathes. Besides that, Canicula has wit.

"*Tempus fugit,*" he says during an agonizingly slow period. He rolls his eyes and then permits his body to follow his eyes' motion: an impudent, free-fall somersault.

"Stop that nonsense, Threasie. See to your duties."

"If you'll remember," he says, "one of my most important ones
is, well, hounding you."

I am forty-six. Canicula-Threasie is seven.

And we're both learning new tricks.

I AM THIRTY-EIGHT: Somewhere, perhaps, Nicholas Parsons is a bona
fide astronaut-in-training, but in this tributary of history—the one
containing me now—I am nothing but a writer projecting himself
into that grandiose wish-fulfillment role. I am an astronaut in the
same dubious way that John Glenn or Neil Armstrong is a writer.
For nearly eleven years my vision has been on hold. What success
I have achieved in this tributary I have fought for with the sometimes
despairing tenacity of my talent and a good deal of help from my
friends. Still, I cannot keep from wondering how I am to overcome
the arrogance of an enemy for whom I am only a name, not a
person, and how dangerous any visionary can be with a gag in the
mouth to thwart any intelligible recitation of the dream.

Where in my affliction is encouragement or comfort? Well, I
can always talk to my dog. Nickie is dead, of course, and so is
Pepper, and not too long ago a big yellow school bus struck down
the kindly mongrel who succeeded them in our hearts. Now we
have B.J., a furrow-browed beagle. To some extent he has taken
up the slack. I talk to him while Katherine works and Peter and
Erin attend their respective schools. B.J. understands very little of
what I tell him—his expression always seems a mixture of dread
and sheepishness—but he is a good listener for as long as I care to
impose upon him; and maybe when his hind leg thumps in his
sleep, he is dreaming not of rabbit hunts but of canine heroics
aboard a vessel bound for Sirius. In my capacity as dreamer I can
certainly pretend that he is doing so . . .

A SUMMER'S READING, 1959: *The Call of the Wild* and *White Fang*
by Jack London. *Bob, Son of Battle* by Alfred Oliphant. Eric Knight's
Lassie Come Home. Silver Chief, Dog of the North by someone
whose name I forget. *Beautiful Joe* by Marshall Saunders. *Lad, a*

Dog and its various sequels by Albert Payson Terhune. And several others.

All of these books are on the upper shelf of a closet in the home of my mother and stepfather in Wichita, Kansas. The books have been collecting dust there since 1964. Before that they had been in my own little gray bookcase in Tulsa, Oklahoma.

From the perspective of my thirty-eight or forty-sixth year I suppose that it is too late to try to fetch them home for Peter or Erin. They are already too old for such stories. Or maybe not. I am unable to keep track of their ages because I am unable to keep track of mine.

In any event, if Peter and Erin are less than fourteen, there is one book that I do not want either of them to have yet. It is a collection of Stephen Crane's short stories. The same summer that I was blithely reading London and Terhune, I read Crane's "A Small Brown Dog." I simply did not know what I was doing. The title lured me irresistibly onward. The other books had contained ruthless men and incidents of meaningless cruelty, yes, but all had concluded well: either virtue or romanticism had ultimately triumphed, and I was made glad to have followed Buck, Lassie, and Lad through their doggy odysseys.

The Crane story cut me up. I was not ready for it. I wept openly and I could not sleep that night.

And if my children are still small, dear God I don't even want them to *see* the title "A Small Brown Dog," much less read the story itself.

"All in good time," I tell myself. "All in good time."

I AM TWELVE: Tulsa, Oklahoma. Coming home from school, I find my grown-and-married stepsister's collie lying against the curbing in front of a neighbor's house. It is almost four in the afternoon, and hot. The neighbor woman comes down her porch when she sees me.

"You're the first one home, Nicholas. It happened only a little while ago. It was a cement truck. It didn't even stop."

I look down the hill toward the grassless building sites where twenty or thirty new houses are going up. Piles of lumber, Sheetrock, and tar paper clutter the cracked, sun-baked yards. But no cement trucks. I do not see a single cement truck.

"I didn't know what to do, Nicholas. I didn't want to leave him—"

We have been in Tulsa a year. We brought the collie with us from Van Luna, Kansas. Rhonda, whose dog he originally was, lives in Wichita now with her new husband.

I look down at the dead collie, remembering the time when Rhonda and I drove to a farm outside Van Luna to pick him out of a litter of six.

"His name will be Marc," Rhonda said, holding him up. "With a *c* instead of a *k*. That's classier." Maybe it was, maybe it wasn't. At the time, though, we both sincerely believed that Marc deserved the best. Because he was not a registered collie, Rhonda got him for almost nothing.

Now I see him lying dead in the street. The huge tires of a cement truck have crushed his head. The detail that hypnotizes me, however, is the pool of gaudy crimson in which Marc lies. And then I understand that I am looking at Marc's life splattered on the concrete.

At supper that evening I break down crying in the middle of the meal, and my mother has to tell my stepfather what has happened. Earlier she asked me to withhold the news until my father has had a little time to relax. I am sorry that my promise is broken, even sorrier that Marc is dead.

In a week, though, I have nearly forgotten. It is very seldom that I remember the pool of blood in which the collie's body lay on that hot spring afternoon. Only at night do I recall its hypnotizing crimson.

175 YEARS AGO IN RUSSIA: One night before the beginning of spring I go time-traveling—spirit-faring, if you like—in the mind of a Great Dane who once stalked into my classroom.

I alter his body into that of a hunting hound and drop him into the kennels on the estate of a retired Russian officer. Hundreds of my kind surround me. We bay all night, knowing that in the morning we will be turned loose on an eight-year-old serf boy who yesterday struck the general's favorite hound with a rock.

I jump against the fence of our kennel and outbark dogs even large than I am. The cold is invigorating. My flanks shudder with expectation, and I know that insomnia is a sickness that afflicts only introspective university teachers and failed astronaut candidates.

In the morning they bring out the boy. The general orders him stripped naked in front of his mother, and the dog-boys who tend us make the child run. An entire hunting party in full regalia is on hand for the festivities. At last the dog-boys turn us out of the kennels, and we surge across the estate after our prey.

I am the first to sink my teeth into his flesh. I tear away half of one of his emaciated buttocks with a single ripping motion of my jaws. Then we bear the child to the ground and overwhelm his cries with our brutal baying. Feeble prey, this; incredibly feeble. We are done with him in fifteen minutes.

When the dog-boys return us slavering to our kennels, I release my grip on the Great Dane's mind and let him go foraging in the trashcans of Athens, Georgia.

Still shuddering, I lie in my bed and wonder how it must feel to be run down by a pack of predatory animals. I cannot sleep.

APPROACHING SIRIUS: We eight men are physical extensions of the astrogation and life-support components of the *Black Retriever*. We feed on the ship's energy; no one must eat to stay alive, though we do have delicious food surrogates aboard for the pleasure of our palates. All our five senses have been technologically enhanced so that we see, hear, touch, smell, and taste more vitally than do you, our brethren, back on Earth.

Do not let it be said that a cybernetic organism sacrifices its humanity for a sterile and meaningless immortality. Yes, yes, I know. That's the popular view, but one championed by pessimists, cynics, and prophets of doom.

Would that the nay-sayers could wear our synthetic skins for only fifteen minutes. Would that they could look out with new eyes on the fierce cornucopian emptiness of interstellar space. There is beauty here, and we of the *Black Retriever* are part of it.

Canicula-Threasie and the other Cybernetic Canine Constructs demonstrate daily their devotion to us. It is not a slavish devotion, however. Often they converse for hours among themselves about the likelihood of finding intelligent life on the planet that circles Sirius.

Some of their speculation has been extremely interesting, and I have begun to work their suggestions into our tentative Advance Stratagem for First Contact. As Threasie himself delights in telling us, "It's good to be ready for any contingency. Do you want the tail to wag the dog or the dog to wag the tail?" Not the finest example of his wit, but he invariably chuckles. His own proposal is that a single trace-team confront the aliens without weapons and offer them our lives. A gamble, he says, but the only way of establishing our credibility from the start.

Late at night—as we judge it by the shipboard clocks—the entire crew gathers around the eerily glowing shield of the Livermore-Parsons Drive Unit, and the dogs tell us stories out of their racial subconscious. Canicula usually takes the lead in these sessions, and my favorite account is his narrative of how dog and man first joined forces against the indifferent arrogance of a bestial environment. That story seems to make the drive shield burn almost incandescently, and man and dog alike—woman and dog alike—can feel their skins humming, prickling, with an unknown but immemorial power.

Not much longer now. Sirius beckons, and the long night of this journey will undoubtedly die in the blaze of our planetfall.

I AM FIFTEEN: When I return to Colorado Springs to visit my father the year after Nick's fall from the rocks, I find the big Labrador strangely changed.

There is a hairless saddle on Nick's back, a dark gray area of scar tissue at least a foot wide. Moreover, he has grown fat. When he greets me, he cannot leap upon me as he has done in past years.

In nine months he has dwindled from a panther into a kind of heartbreaking and outsized lap dog.

As we drive home from the airport my father tries to explain:

"We had him castrated, Nicholas. We couldn't keep him in the house—not with the doors locked, not with the windows closed, not with rope, not with anything we tried. There's always a female in heat in our neighborhood and he kept getting out. Twice I had to drive to the pound and ransom him. Five bucks a shot.

"Finally some old biddy who had a cocker spaniel or something caught him—you know how gentle he is with people—and tied him to her clothesline. Then she poured a pan of boiling water over his back. That's why he looks like he does now. It's a shame, Nicholas. A goddamn shame."

That summer lasts an eternity.

TWENTY-SEVEN, AND HOLDING: Behind our house on Virginia Avenue there is a small self-contained apartment that our landlord rents to a young woman who is practice-teaching. This young woman owns a mongrel bitch named Tammi.

For three weeks over the Christmas holidays Tammi was chained to her doghouse in below-freezing temperatures. Katherine and I had not volunteered to take care of her because we knew that we would be away ourselves for at least a week, and because we hoped that Tammi's owner would make more humane arrangements for the dog's care. She did not. She asked a little girl across the street to feed Tammi once a day and to give her water.

This, of course, meant that Katherine and I took care of the animal for the two weeks we were home. I went out several times a day to untangle Tammi's chain from the bushes and clothesline poles next to her doghouse. Sometimes I fed her, sometimes played with her, sometimes tried to make her stay in her house.

Some days it rained, others it sleeted. And for the second time in her life Tammi came into heat.

One night I awoke to hear her yelping as if in pain. I struggled out of bed, put on a pair of jeans and my shoes, and let myself out the back door.

A monstrous silver black dog—was it a Great Dane?—had mounted Tammi. It was raining, but I could see the male's pistoning silhouette in the residual glow of the falling raindrops themselves. Or so it seemed to me. Outraged by the male's brutality, I gathered a handful of stones. Then I threw.

I struck the male in the flank. He lurched away from Tammi and rushed blindly to a fenced-in corner of the yard. I continued to throw, missing every time. The male saw his mistake and came charging out of the cul-de-sac toward me. His feet churned in the gravel as he skidded by me. Then he loped like a jungle cat out our open gate and was gone. I threw six or seven futile stones into the dark street after him.

For a week this went on. New dogs appeared on some nights, familiar ones returned on others. And each time, like a knight fighting for his lady's chastity, I struggled out of bed to fling stones at Tammi's bestial wooers.

Today is March the fifth, and this morning Katherine took our little boy out to see Tammi's three-week-old puppies. They have a warm, faintly fecal odor, but their eyes are open and Peter played with them as if they were stuffed stockings come to life. He had never seen anything quite like them before, and Katherine says that he cried when she brought him in.

I AM AGELESS: A beautiful, kind-cruel planet revolves about Sirius. I have given this world the name Elsinore because the name is noble, and because the rugged fairness of her seascapes and islands calls up the image of a more heroic era than any we have known on Earth of late.

Three standard days ago, seven of our trace-teams descended into the atmosphere of Elsinore. One trace-team remains aboard the *Black Retriever* to speed our evangelical message to you, our brethren, back home. Shortly, we hope to retrieve many of you to this brave new world in Canis Major.

Thanks to the flight capabilities of our cybernetic dogs, we have explored nearly all of Elsinore in three days' time. We divided the planet into hemispheres and the hemispheres into quadrants, and each trace-team flew cartographic and exploratory missions over its assigned area. Canicula and I took upon ourselves the responsibility of charting two of the quadrants, since only seven teams were available for this work, and as a result he and I spotted and made contact with the indigenous Elsinorians.

As we skimmed over a group of rugged islands in a northern sea, the heat-detecting unit in Canicula's belly gave warning of this life. Incredulous, we made several passes over the islands. Each time we plummeted, the sea shimmered beneath us like windblown silk. As we searched, up-jutting rocks flashed by us on every side, and Canicula's heat sensors confirmed that sentient beings did indeed dwell in this archipelago.

At last we pinpointed their location.

My trace-mate hovered for a time. "You ready to be wagged?"

"Wag away," I replied.

We dropped five hundred meters straight down and settled gently into the aliens' midst: a natural senate of stone, open to the sky, in which the Elsinorians carry on the simple affairs of their simple state.

The Elsinorians are dogs. Dogs very like Canicula-Threasie. They lack, of course, the instrumentation that so greatly intensifies the experience of the cyborg. They are creatures of nature who have subdued themselves to reason and who have lived out their apparently immortal lives in a spirit of rational expectation. For millennia they have waited, patiently waited.

Upon catching sight of me, every noble animal in their open-air senate began wagging his or her close-cropped tail. All eyes were upon me.

By himself Canicula sought out the Elsinorians' leader and immediately began conversing with him (no doubt implementing our Advance Stratagem for First Contact). Nor did Canicula require the assitance of our instantaneous translator. He and the alien dog shared a heritage more fundamental than language. I stood to one side and waited for their conference to conclude.

"His name translates as Prince," Canicula said upon returning to me, "even though their society is democratic. He wishes to address

us before all the assembled senators of his people. Let's take up a
seat among them. You can plug into the translator. The Elsinorians,
Nicholas, recognize the full historic impact of this occasion, and
Prince may have a surprise or two for you."

Having said this, 3C grinned. Damned irritating.

We took up our seats among the Elsinorian dogs, and Prince
strolled with great dignity onto the senate floor. The I.T. System
rendered his remarks as several lines of nearly impeccable blank
verse. English blank verse:

> Fragmented by the lack of any object
> Beyond ourselves to beat for, our sundered hearts
> Thud in a vacuum not of our making.
> We are piecemeal beasts, supple enough
> To look upon, illusorily whole;
> But all this heartsore time, down the aeons
> Illimitable of our incompleteness,
> We have awaited this, your arrival,
> Men and Dogs of Earth.
>   And you, Canicula,
> We especially thank for bringing to us
> The honeyed prospect of Man's companionship.
> Tell your Master that we hereby invite
> His kinspeople to our stern but unspoiled world
> To be the medicine which heals the lesions
> In our shambled hearts.
>   Together we shall share
> Eternity, deathless on Elsinore!

And so he concluded. The senators, their natural reticence overcome, barked, bayed, and bellowed their approval.

That was earlier this afternoon. Canicula-Threasie and I told the
Elsinorians that we would carry their message to the other trace-
teams and, eventually, to the people of Earth. Then we rose above
their beautifully barbaric island and flew into the eye of Sirius, a
ball of sinking fire above the sea.

Tonight we are encamped on the peak of a great mountain on one of the islands of the archipelago. The air is brisk, but not cold. To breathe here is to ingest energy.

Peter, Erin, Katherine—I call you to this place. No one dies on Elsinore, no one suffers more than he can bear, no one suffocates in the pettiness of day-to-day existence. That is what I had hoped for. That is why I came here. That is why I sacrificed, on the altar of this dream, so much of what I was before my aneurysm ruptured. And now the dream has come true, and I call you to Elsinore.

Canicula and I make our beds on a lofty slab of granite above a series of waterfalls tumbling to the sea. The mist from these waterfalls boils up beneath us. We stretch out to sleep.

"No more suffering," I say.

"No more wasted potential," Canicula says.

"No more famine, disease, or death," I say, looking at the cold stars and trying to find the cruel one upon which my beloved family even yet depends.

Canicula then says, "*Tempus?*"

"Yes?" I reply.

"*Fug it!*" he barks.

And we both go to sleep with laughter on our lips.

TWENTY-SEVEN, AND COUNTING: I have renewed my contract for the coming year. You have to put food on the table. I am three weeks into spring quarter already, and my students are students like other students. I like some of them, dislike others.

I will enjoy teaching them *Othello* once we get to it. Thank God our lit text does not include *Hamlet*: I would find myself making hideous analogies between the ghost of Hamlet's father and the Great Dane who haunted my thoughts all winter quarter.

I am over that now. Dealing with the jealous Moor again will be, in the terminology of our astronauts, "a piece of cake."

Katherine's pregnancy is in its fourth month now, and Peter has begun to talk a little more fluently. Sort of. The words he knows how to say include *Dada*, *juice*, and *dog*. *Dog*, in fact, is the first word that he ever clearly spoke. Appropriate.

In fifteen years—or eleven, or seventeen—I probably will not be able to remember a time when Peter could not talk. Or Erin, either, for that matter, even though she has not been born yet. For now all a father can do is live his life and, loving them, let his children— born and unborn—live their own.

"Dog!" my son emphatically cries. "Dog!"

The Eichmann
Variations

GEORGE ZEBROWSKI

George Zebrowski's nearly fifty stories have appeared in many original anthologies, as well as in The Magazine of Fantasy & Science Fiction, New Worlds, Amazing Stories, Isaac Asimov's Science Fiction Magazine, Popular Computing, and the Bertrand Russell Society News. His novels include Macrolife, The Omega Point Trilogy, Sunspacer (a Books for the Teen Age selection), and The Stars Will Speak. The Monadic Universe collects his best stories from the 1970s. He has edited six anthologies, ten volumes in Crown's Classics of Modern Science Fiction series, and is also an editor of the Bulletin of the SFWA. Two books about his work are forthcoming from Borgo Press.

"The Eichmann Variations" was a short story Nebula Award finalist for 1984.

The beast must die;
and the man as well;
one and the other.

—Brahms, Songs

O Germany—
Hearing the speeches that ring from your house
　　one laughs.
But whoever sees you, reaches for his knife.

—Bertolt Brecht

And just as you supported and carried out a policy of not wanting
to share the earth with the Jewish people and the people of a number
of other nations—as though you and your superiors had any right
to determine who should and who should not inhabit the world—
we find that no one, that is, no member of the human race, can be
expected to want to share the earth with you. This is the reason,
and the only reason, you must hang.

—*Hannah Arendt,*
Eichmann in Jerusalem

1.

I learned the details after the war. Jewish scientists had been
gathered in America to create a vengeance weapon against us. It
happened very much in the way described in those fantastic American pulp magazines that von Braun was always reading (he kept
up his subscription through a neutral country once the war started).
A team of physicists got together at a secret desert laboratory and
concocted the atomic bomb out of decades-old theories.

I didn't believe that Berlin, Munich, and Dresden had disappeared completely until I saw the *Life* magazine photos published
after the formal surrender in 1946. By then I had been for some
months in the Argentine, living quietly, hoping to finish out my
life in solitude.

The Japanese had avoided atomic attack by surrendering shortly
after their agents reported the magnitude of the blasts in Europe. I
don't blame myself for being skeptical; who would have believed
such a story, especially after our bad experience with the V-2 wonder
weapons? Always too expensive and impractical, Speer had complained, who knew something of engineering as well as financial
planning.

I watched the Jews build their Israel for twenty years, growing in
power and prestige, until it dominated the Middle East. Everybody

loved them, but how could it be otherwise? Their first miracle, the Manna Machine, took sand and through certain physico-biological manipulations of basic patterns produced edibles of any kind, as well as any other physical object or resource. Solar Power was endless, so the machine ran without stop, giving away as much stomach support as Israel's neighbors demanded. I read about it in *Reader's Digest.*

The world fell into a stupor of peace as the Semites gifted the planet with their easy solutions. But it was all on the surface; these magicians would just as easily have worked for our Fuehrer if he had courted them, if their very existence had not been such a blinding abomination. We were too zealous in our convictions. Since it is in the nature of the lower orders to go where they are welcome, these sorcerers would have built for us the greatest bakeries in Europe, and our armies would have marched to victory on the bread transubstantiated from the raw material of the underfolk.

Now, with their stomachs satisfied and their homeland secure, they began to refine their tastes for revenge. I was captured in 1961, as I was strolling by the seashore, and taken to Jerusalem aboard a luxurious submarine. It seems that their Maimonides Mentality, a sophisticated artificial intelligence that also plans economies, had finally been able to predict where I might be found, on the basis of elaborate probabilities and shabby scraps of gossip. It had taken a picture of my footsteps, as well as my bald head, from a satellite.

A world benefiting so greatly from Israeli science and technology looked the other way when I was kidnapped. Nazis were merely a strange and rare form of humanity collected by their Jewish benefactors, for private reasons.

2.

Ten gallows.

They die by metric count, these scarecrows who wear my face. Each morning I am duplicated ten times and forced to watch the execution.

The faces seem puzzled as they stare at me. Who am I? they wonder, knowing full well who they are. Why am I not with them on the block? Do they all have my memories? Or are they blank die cuts, wearing my wrinkles? They are innocent, even if they remember what is in my brain.

What can I care for my doubles?

I imagine rushing forward to mingle with them, thus denying my captors the satisfaction of seeing the original perish, except as the hidden member of a group. Any one of us will answer to being the original, except that the Doppelgängers are innocent!

Why? How can that be?

Because they did not exist when my so-called crimes were committed! Only the pattern of specific memories is guilty. I will not rush among my doubles; I do not wish to die anonymously.

They force me to watch as the bodies are fed into the fusion torch, which consumes utterly, leaving only a gas from which basic elements can be reclaimed. What we could have done with that! The final solution would have been completed by 1941.

3.

The point of killing your racial enemies lies in denying them their future, the embodiment of their children. The stream of history is diverted, given a different character than it might have had; but now cultures live or die where once individuals of unconscious species clashed for glorious possession of plain, sea, forest, or sky.

They are manlier, these scientific Jews; they are not fearful of wielding power. Once they were constrained and cowardly; a good number were homosexual. What did they know of true freedom, they who would not dare do what was in their hearts? A true man listens to the abyss, to the inner song that the Fuehrer knew so well. A few years after the war I read that some of the survivors were developing nostalgia for the war, for the death camps, for slavehood.

4.

This morning, one year after my imprisonment, I dreamed of a pit. A huge, dark beast came into it on all fours. Its skin was sandpapery, gray-black, covered with sores. It stood up on all fours and spoke to the crowd pressing in around the guard rail.

"The world is not mine," it said as the crowd drew back, horrified by its massive body. "This my father taught me, that the world is not mine." The voice was soft, cultivated, threatening.

The crowd gasped and whispered, and moved closer to observe the tragic, apelike face.

"They captured it at the headwaters of the Amazon," someone said. "It's descended from giant tree otters."

I didn't want to look into the beast's eyes. The lights in the arena flickered. It grew dark.

"You see," the same voice said, "it's not really intelligent. A very kind, sensitive man taught it that speech, but it's nothing but a kind of mimicry . . ."

I watched the beast out of the corner of my eye. The creature was watching me; it knew I was there.

I woke up and yearned to see the sun; there was no time in my cell.

5.

Today, one of my brothers visited me.

"How goes it?" the image asked.

"And you?"

He shrugged. "I have your thoughts and memories, innocently. They explained, as if confessing their crime. I feel that what we did, what you and I remember doing, is a bad dream from which I have wakened."

"Have they told you that you will die?" I asked, staring into my own eyes.

He smiled. "I'm a sample. I'll work for them. They want me to labor on a farm, even though they no longer till the soil. I'll make public speeches of repentance. You and I know exactly what they wish to hear. They will not kill me."

"Traitor," I whispered.

"To what? Do you want me to die with the puppets that torment you? They'll only get another to walk in your shadow."

"But you are me!"

He nodded and touched my hand. "I would have been if they had not explained. The facts of my origin have absolved me. Don't you see? I've been forgiven."

"But they might be lying! You didn't think of that, did you? I might be you and you me!"

"But I'm not," he said serenely. "My brother, imagine if you were given the chance to undo what you have done, or to learn that you did not do it. Imagine that you are merely a copy of the flesh and memory of one who did, but that your flesh was born only a few days ago. Imagine."

He was glad not to be me, and I knew how he felt, how I would have felt to have been him.

"You are only a bit of me that has stepped aside, not escaped."

"I'll be honest with you," he replied. "Our pattern is guilty, in so far as it contains certain beliefs, but only the pattern at a specific moment in time is physically guilty. It doesn't matter that I would have acted as you did. I am implicated, certainly, through no choice of my own, but not physically guilty. Get it through your head, I wasn't there."

He got up and gazed at me as if I were a child who would never learn.

6.

The Fuehrer spoke to me that night. Adolf, his voice said, you never understood the deepest reasons for killing the Jew, only that they were to be hated and butchered. You could not imagine in your ordinary soul, as I knew, the inner need to return Germany to another age.

I woke up and realized that my tormentors had poisoned my memory of the Fuehrer; his echo was beginning to reproach me.

But I know now that they cannot punish me; their rope is too feeble a thing, their puppet show no match for my camps and ovens and endless trainloads of flesh.

I have won. And even if they should hang me, it will not be enough. The cowards! They do not even put hoods over my faces to hide the truth!

7.

They are not going to tell anyone what they are doing with me. I am the subject of an experiment in physico-biological duplication. Their psychologists claim that it will reveal to them hitherto unplumbed depths of human nature; the facts of historical guilt, the honesty of vengeance, the essential weakness and banality of evil, will stand naked before their gaze.

I have begun to wonder if I am the original Eichmann at all. They won't answer that question. In their secret hearts they hope that I will prize the possibility that has been created for me, of a self swept clean, made innocent. There will always be an Eichmann for them to study, long after I am gone; they can't bring themselves to kill me completely. They need a sample of my evil.

8.

They came today to explain.

"To kill you once," the gray-haired spokesman said, "would have been a blot on memory. All agree concerning the inadequacy of such a punishment."

"How many of me have you killed?" I asked.

"Ten per hour, these years . . . it will be six million one day."

I spat on the floor in front of him. "It's no punishment for me, you fools!"

"We're trying," he said.

"No one can punish me!" I shouted in triumph.

"Or forgive you," he said softly, "no matter what contortions we impose upon the living fact."

"You're no better than me."

"There was little heroism in the camps, Mr. Eichmann, only a confrontation with a human nature that we had thought tamed within ourselves. You have only yourself to blame."

"Your vengeance will be my victory."

"Perhaps. I have already admitted the inadequacy. You are being punished because it will happen nowhere else. All punishment is futile, I suppose. That is why those of us who have no faith in it as a deterrent or corrective have readopted an eye for an eye." He sighed deeply. "It is the best we can do, anyone can do. Six million German flesh for six million Jewish. German flesh created by our conscience, from our soil and the sunlight of God, Mr. Eichmann."

I stared at him and answered, "Innocence in your eyes is not the prize you think. I repudiate nothing."

He shrugged. "I understand. It is the only way you can still dirty us. That is why in your case justice must be very personal. I will kill you myself, Mr. Eichmann, next Monday."

9.

"Another set of ravings?" the gray-haired man asked.

"Yes," the young doctor replied.

"Do they differ?"

"Not much. The language changes, but it's the same."

"File them in sequence."

"How long can we go on?" the doctor asked.

"Indefinitely, even if it's useless. Our sample may still not be large enough to reveal the angelic core of the human being. We must give him enough chances. I still can't quite accept that the raging beast is more . . . than a vestige in each of us."

"We should kill the original and be done with it," the doctor said.

The gray-haired man sighed and shook his head. "His guilt would flee from the world and we would forget. We must relieve it with punishment, but we can never let it die."

"But the doubles—"

"They're innocent, of course, in a technical sense, but they carry the guilty pattern just the same. His guilt cannot be duplicated, but it is passed on. The new generations of Germans are not guilty, but they inherit past crimes socially, like it or not. He says it himself— the pattern is guilty."

"But we, the children of victims, have now created our own, permanent victim," the doctor insisted.

"He lives in all humanity," the gray-haired man said. "Our punishment, at worst, merely matches his crime."

"We are always better than the worst," the doctor whispered. "What would they think, those who died in the Holocaust?"

The old man looked at his hands, as if he had just discovered them. "It's been said that in the Holocaust reality for the first time exceeded the imagination. And for a time afterward imagination retreated and hid, to ready something that would give it back its own."

"Nuclear war?"

"Our fear restrains us, Doctor, but I suppose reality will always have the last word—unless we learn to make angels of ourselves."

"Shall we stop then?"

"No—that would waste all that has gone before. He will live and he will die. Maybe we'll learn something yet."

"But how can you even hope?"

"If even one variation repents, I'll destroy the original and close down the project."

10.

My neck holds a sympathetic crick this week. Muscle tension from watching my flesh and blood dying day by day. In the evenings they show me a museum of details from individual lives—photos, letters, drawings, bits of clothing. They push these sentiment-laden moments into my brain. They want me to feel, psychosomatically, that my body, my life, is joined to others; that one's brother or sister or neighbor is morally identical to one's self through these petty details.

But I can only record that my tormentors have failed. I have overcome the uncertainty of whether I am a copy or not—by finding the small tattoo with which they have marked me . . . on my elbow. The horror of being innocent even as I embrace my guilt has left me.

It follows, therefore, that I am myself, and they are using duplicates to make further copies while holding me separate. My alternates are only animated garbage, mere echoes. For what can they be punished? How can they be me, if they are innocent?

I cannot be copied.

Poems

There is no Nebula Award for poetry, but the Rhysling Awards are the closest thing to it, named as they are for the wandering blind singer in Nebula Grand Master Robert A. Heinlein's famous story "The Green Hills of Earth." The awards are presented each year by the membership of the Science Fiction Poetry Association. The only awards of their kind, they honor excellence in speculative poetry (science fiction and fantasy) written during the preceding year. The awards were established, along with the association, by Suzette Haden Elgin in 1978. Past winners have included Gene Wolfe, Sonya Dorman, Michael Bishop, Robert Frazier, Thomas M. Disch, Ursula K. Le Guin, and Alan P. Lightman.

The following are the newest winners for best short and long poems. Helen Ehrlich is an American poet whose work has been published in The Lyric, Star*line, and Velocities #4. "Love Song to Lucy" and "Lucy Answers" first appeared in Science 83. (Lucy is, of course, the name given to the remains discovered in Africa of what may be a human ancestor.) Joe Haldeman is the multi-award-winning author of The Forever War, Worlds, Worlds Apart, and other novels. "Saul's Death" first appeared in Omni.

Two Sonnets

HELEN EHRLICH

Love Song to Lucy

Three million times your bones have swept around
The sun since last your warm brown foot walked here
Upon the veldt. The hills, the lake, were dear

To you, and morning flowers, and each sweet sound
Of bird. In meadows where you played were found
The beasts that fed and clothed you—life's career.
And so you lived, until one day in fear
You died, and never knew you would astound
A future race. What waves of time beyond
Your ken evolved your sires, and ours, and sent
You here to us upon this destined shore,
Where we, your seed, have found you and respond
In awe? You speak in tomes you never dreamt—
A parent-link to all that lies before.

Lucy Answers

Your turn will come—time upon time your bones
Will also sweep the sun, and from the clay
Strange creatures, on a far and stranger day,
With eye and hand the primal mind disowns,
Will find you there among the silvered stones—
Will lift you, brush the ancient years away
And sift your possibilities the way
You do with me, in hushed and puzzled tones.
Your seed will seek his sire in mark and line
And try to mold your face, as you mold mine.
Yet I knew not you'd issue forth from me,
Nor can you penetrate his mystery.
As silence holds all future time at bay,
So tides will turn and sweep him, too, away.

SAUL'S DEATH:
Two Sestinas

JOE HALDEMAN

1.

I used to be a monk, but gave it over
Before books and prayer and studies cooled my blood,
And joined with Richard as a mercenary soldier.
(No Richard that you've heard of, just
A man who'd bought a title for his name.)
And it was in his service I met Saul.

The first day of my service I liked Saul;
His easy humor quickly won me over.
He confided Saul was not his name;
He'd taken up another name for blood.
(So had I—my fighting name was just
A word we use at home for private soldier.)

I felt at home as mercenary soldier.
I liked the company of men like Saul.
(Though most of Richard's men were just
Fighting for the bounty when it's over.)
I loved the clash of weapons, splashing blood—
I lived the meager promise of my name.

Saul promised that he'd tell me his real name
When he was through with playing as a soldier.
(I said the same; we took an oath in blood.)
But I would never know him but as Saul;
He'd die before the long campaign was over,
Dying for a cause that was not just.

Only fools require a cause that's just;
Fools and children out to make a name.
Now I've had sixty years to think it over
(Sixty years of being no one's soldier.)
Sixty years since broadsword opened Saul
And splashed my body with his precious blood.

But damn! we lived for bodies and for blood.
The reek of dead men rotting, it was just
A sweet perfume for those like me and Saul.
(My peaceful language doesn't have a name
For lewd delight in going off to soldier.)
It hurts my heart sometimes to know it's over.

My heart was hard as stone when it was over;
When finally I'd had my fill of blood.
(And knew I was too old to be a soldier.)
Nothing left for me to do but just
Go back home and make myself a name
In ways of peace, forgetting war and Saul.

In ways of blood he made himself a name
(Though he was just a mercenary soldier)—
I loved Saul before it all was over.

2.

A mercenary soldier has no future;
Some say his way of life is hardly human.
And yet, we had our own small bloody world
(Part aches and sores and wrappings soaking blood,
Partly fear and glory grown familiar)
Confined within a shiny fence of swords.

But how I learned to love to fence with swords!
Another world, my homely past and future—

Once steel and eye and wrist became familiar
With each other, then that steel was almost human
(With an altogether human taste for blood).
I felt that sword and I could take the world.

I felt that Saul and I could take the world:
Take the whole world hostage with our swords.
The bond we felt was stronger than mere blood
(Though I can see with hindsight in the future
The bond we felt was something only human:
A need for love when death becomes familiar).

We were wizards, and death was our familiar;
Our swords held all the magic in the world.
(Richard thought it almost wasn't human,
The speed with which we parried others' swords,
Forever end another's petty future.)
Never scratched, though always steeped in blood.

Ambushed in a tavern, splashing ankle-deep in blood;
Fighting back-to-back in ways familiar.
Saul slipped: lost his footing and our future.
Broad blade hammered down and sent him from this world.
In angry grief I killed that one, then all the other swords;
Then locked the doors and murdered every human.

No choice, but to murder every human.
No one in that tavern was a stranger to blood.
(To those who live with pikes and slashing swords,
The inner parts of men become familiar.)
Saul's vitals looked like nothing in this world:
I had to kill them all to save my future.

Saul's vitals were not human, but familiar:
He never told me he was from another world:
I never told him I was from his future.

Science Fiction Films
of 1984

BILL WARREN

Bill Warren is the author of the well-received Keep Watching the
Skies!, *an exhaustive reference work on SF films released in the U.S.
from 1950 through 1962. A second volume is scheduled. His stories
have appeared in* Worlds of Fantasy *and* Amazing Stories. *Warren,
a researcher for Hollywood Film Archive, is a film critic who knows
SF and SF film and can tell when the two forms don't knock each
other out.*

A couple of years ago, *Blade Runner* was expected to usher
in an era of adaptations of SF novels. But despite a lavish production,
a genuine contemporary star (Harrison Ford), and a star director
(Ridley Scott), the film was a financial flop. The fate of *Dune*, in
many ways *the* SF movie of 1984, was thus very closely tracked by
the businessmen who run Hollywood.

Hollywood executives these days generally don't come from a
movie-oriented background; they tend to be accountants, lawyers,
bankers, even newspaper tycoons—and their attitudes are shaped by
concerns completely foreign to the people who actually make the
films. Although he was talking about network television, what pro-
ducer-writer Allan Katz had to say on this subject in the *Los Angeles*

Times is worth quoting, since it applies equally well to movie executives: "Many of the most important creative decisions . . . are made by people who have never invented a character, never written any dialogue, never plotted a scene in their lives. . . . They have a tremendous problem seeing that it's the soul of something like M*A*S*H that made it work. They're like somebody who sees a guy run a four-minute mile wearing red shorts [who] then thinks red shorts are the key to running a four-minute mile."

Studio executives undoubtedly felt that the failure of *Blade Runner* could have been due to its having been based on a novel by a mere (feh!) science fiction writer like Philip K. Dick. After all, director Ridley Scott had a legitimate SF film hit, *Alien*, and Harrison Ford was one of the stars of the *Star Wars* series. (And neither *Alien* nor the *Star Wars* films were based on novels.) The studio types probably didn't want to consider that perhaps the style of marketing was a factor in the failure of *Blade Runner*. So what is another variable? The source material . . .

Even though *2010*, the film, is based on a Real Science Fiction Book by Arthur C. Clarke, than whom SF writers don't get any Realer, movie executives saw the film as a movie version of a best-seller (which is how the book was sold). It is more like *The Godfather* or *Gone with the Wind* than *Blade Runner* or even *Dune* (that novel became a best-seller *eventually*). This may seem like splitting hairs, but the hairs are being split by the big-money boys.

The year 1984 was bracketed by adaptations of famous novels in the genre: *Dune* at the end, and at the beginning, the peculiarly titled *Greystoke: The Legend of Tarzan, Lord of the Apes*. Between lay a variety of mostly unsurprising films, but overall the quality of SF movies in 1984 was remarkably high. Except for *2010* and, to a lesser degree, *The Ice Pirates*, there weren't any major clunkers solidly within the SF genre. And three low-budget films, *Android*, *The Brother from Another Planet*, and *Night of the Comet*, were skillfully made and very entertaining.

Two were wildly eccentric, oddball concoctions that won cult and (for the most part) critical approval if not popular followings:

Repo Man and *The Adventures of Buckaroo Banzai: Across the 8th Dimension* are among the strangest films ever released by major studios.

There are many rumors floating around Hollywood as to how such a bizarre movie as *The Adventures of Buckaroo Banzai* came to be filmed, but the most plausible is that Fox was earnestly searching for another series concept to replace *Star Wars*. This didn't happen with *Banzai*, which failed to catch on with audiences. Very few, after all, could have been expecting this bizarre mixture of pulp adventure, SF, spoof, satire, and hip comedy, with an invasion-epic plot and a punk-new-wave-camp style.

Banzai was the first film directed by W. D. Richter, who scripted, among other films, the fine remake of *Invasion of the Body Snatchers* as well as the interesting Frank Langella *Dracula*. *Banzai* was written by Earl Mac Rauch; in interviews, Richter said that he and Rauch had been working on the concept for at least ten years.

The story is amazingly hard to follow, but I don't think Richter and Rauch were interested in narrative coherency; they were after a style, an approach, and in those terms succeeded. *Banzai* looks and sounds like no other film, and its casual, mocking attitude somehow brings all the separate strands together while leaving most viewers behind.

Buckaroo Banzai (Peter Weller) is a latter-day Doc Savage, with a group of fellow young scientists (who also perform as a rock group) who team up to battle peril and menace. This time, they find themselves involved with evil orange aliens from the eighth dimension and good black aliens watching us from orbit.

John Lithgow is immensely entertaining as Dr. Emilio Lizardo, who in his own experiments with the eighth dimension got mixed up with orange alien bad guy Lord John Whorfin. (All the aliens are named John.) The plot includes travel through solid matter, an impending nuclear war, a sneaky government official, Orson Welles, aliens disguised as people, and a race against time. *Banzai* ends with a rather snazzy battle between organic-looking spacecraft whizzing around in the clouds.

In addition to these bizarre details—another one has the black aliens disguising themselves as Rastafarians—the movie has a sense of good fun; it's relaxing, oddly enough. If Richter as director isn't quite up to the demands of the script, he still seems confident with the sophisticated material. This is one of those films where you need to surrender yourself to its flow. Those who insist that movies must always make full logical sense won't enjoy *Buckaroo Banzai*. They don't know what they're missing. Not all of it works, but what does, works well.

In *Repo Man*, the SF elements are even odder and are simply part of the movie as a whole, rather than major elements in and of themselves. The central idea that concerns us is a 1964 Chevy Malibu with something very weird in the trunk (perhaps two dead aliens): whoever opens the trunk is blasted into vapor by a power within.

Disaffected quasi punk Otto (Emilio Estevez) has a falling-out with his hippies-turned-Jesus-Freaks parents and hooks up with automobile repossession man Bud (Harry Dean Stanton, seedy and excellent). Eventually, Bud, Otto, and others are all in hot pursuit of the Chevy. True to the predictions of a spaced-out pal of Otto's (Tracey Walter), the aliens may not be dead. At the end, the car begins glowing and flies away with Otto and his friend.

Repo Man was written and directed by Alex Cox, a Briton living in Los Angeles, and offers amusingly raunchy views of L.A.; as J. Hoberman said in the *Village Voice* review of the film, it's set "in a milieu that's half skid row, half 7-Eleven" but still manages to be fresh and anything but depressing, despite robberies, murders, and other deaths. Cox has a unique viewpoint and seems to be sneering at rampant consumerism much of the time. Sometimes it's hard to see just what Cox intended, but it's a novel film and takes SF material in new directions.

Some films simply imitated what had gone before, tossing various components into a stew of ripped-off ideas. According to Kevin Thomas in the *Los Angeles Times*, the Italian-French coproduction *After the Fall of New York* (filmed in 1983 as *2099: The Fall of*

New York) was a "surprisingly entertaining and imaginative" combination of elements from *The Road Warrior, Escape from New York,* and *Knightriders.*

After a nuclear war, the leader (Edmund Purdom) of a group of survivors in Alaska recruits the head of a gang of motorcyclists to go to New York and bring back the only known fertile woman. Manhattan is held by the villainous Euracs, who dress like knights and ride white horses and also conduct genetic experiments. Thomas found the film had "a scrappiness that inspires a kind of amused affection." It *is* above average for a junk-apocalypse film, though not actually a good film.

Another Italian movie, filmed as *I nuovi barbari* (The new barbarians), was released in the U.S. as *Warriors of the Wasteland,* and was another postholocaust thriller in the mold of *The Road Warrior.* In 2019, various groups try to find the source of mysterious radio signals, hoping civilization may still exist somewhere. The story pits lone warrior Skorpion against motorized Templars, led by One. Helped by another lone warrior (American actor Fred Williamson), Skorpion eventually conquers One and teams up with a band of religious nomads.

Again, according to U.S. reviewers, this was a shade better than one would expect from such a blatantly imitative film. But the *Monthly Film Bulletin* (a fine publication of the British Film Institute) considered it "abysmal" and added that "it would be totally indigestible . . . were it not for the inevitable absurdities that mark the gulf between inspiration and arrogantly inadequate execution."

Another European import, yet another postholocaust story, was something else: France's *Le dernier combat,* an imaginative, intelligent, and often funny story about getting along in a wiped-out world. Shot in black and white, this assured film, directed by Luc Besson, is perhaps a bit longer than it should be, but is stylish and suspenseful; we care about the characters. It has no dialogue. Whatever the nature of the world catastrophe (never explained), it left people voiceless. However, the story never loses coherency and is engrossing throughout. The film is a low-budget effort that never suffers from its lack of capital. Unlike virtually all other postholo-

caust stories—and there are now enough to constitute a minigenre—
Le dernier combat has a great deal of humor, sensitivity, and insight.
It shows that imagination and intelligence can be applied to the
most hackneyed of premises.

So does the careful, realistic *Iceman*. This was a big-budget film
from Universal that, though based on a questionable premise, con-
vinces us of its reality while we watch. It's the first two-thirds of an
outstanding movie. Unfortunately, writers Chip Proser and John
Drimmer get themselves into a corner and can't get out: their ending
seems like last-minute desperation and is unsatisfactory. Before that,
though, director Fred Schepisi and several good actors, particularly
John Lone, the Iceman of the title, provide fascinating entertainment.

The plot sounds like it wandered in from the 1950s (or even
earlier; Houdini himself made a silent movie with a similar idea):
a Neanderthal man is found frozen in Arctic ice and revives when
thawed. But *Iceman* goes a long way toward proving that any tired
plot can be given new life and vitality by the right kind of treatment
and with the right actors in key roles.

The well-designed film's major virtue is in making the Iceman a
rounded, believable character, not a Noble Savage, a monster, or
just a lot of grunts and groans. Rather coyly, he's called Charlie,
because that's what anthropologist Stanley Shepard (Timothy Hut-
ton), who's found his ultimate dream, thinks the Neanderthal's
name sounds like. How lucky that it didn't sound like "fireplug."

Charlie is the most believable primitive man in the history of
motion pictures. He's a heartbreaker, a character for whom it's
almost impossible not to feel deep sympathy, which makes the
strange ending so unsatisfactory. John Lone, a Hong Kong–born
stage actor, is splendid as Charlie. There are many flaws in *Iceman*,
but it is a brave and daring film.

On the other hand, *Red Dawn* takes an equally venerable SF
idea—the invasion of the U.S. by hostile foreign powers—and fails
on all levels, especially in the area of conviction.

John Milius has directed several good films; his *Dillinger* was
fresh and lively, and *The Wind and the Lion* is a near classic. Even

Conan the Barbarian has much to recommend it. But when Milius, very conservative politically, makes films on topics he cares passionately about, he seems to lose all his filmmaking skills. *Big Wednesday* was an ode to his beloved surfing but was a pompous, silly mess. And *Red Dawn*'s jingoistic fantasy of a Communist invasion of the U.S. is so rabidly macho, so fanatically and unquestioningly pro-gun and desperately antiforeign as to seem the dreamings of a fourteen-year-old far-right-wing gun freak who likes to drink hot blood.

Early in the film occurs a scene that's a litmus test for your response to the rest of the movie. The Soviets have parachuted Cuban and Russian troops into a small Rocky Mountain city and have been busily gunning down the startled populace, which is barely able to fight back. The camera comes in for a closeup of a bumper sticker on a pickup: "If They Want My Gun, They Will Have to Pry It From My Cold, Dead Fingers." Pan down to cold, dead fingers clutching gun; Russian boot clamps down on wrist, Russian hand pries gun from fingers. Now if you find that exciting, a brilliant concept and innovative filmmaking, you probably liked *Red Dawn*. I laughed at that shot, and I didn't like *Red Dawn*.

It isn't so much that I disagree with the sentiments of the film; I often disagree with themes in films I like. It's that Milius and cowriter Kevin Reynolds seem to have discarded all good ideas they ever had about structure, logic, and characterization. The exposition is so poor that a new character, before being quickly killed off, is literally dropped into the story (by parachute) just to tell the band of teenage freedom fighters what's going on elsewhere.

The central characters are pathetically unbelievable; there is, in fact, virtually no characterization anywhere in the film. The model was apparently World War II movies, but even in the most obvious of those, we could quickly differentiate among the members of the platoon. Here, it's virtually impossible.

Besides trying to make a fast buck (which it was successful at), *Red Dawn* apparently sought to provide a cautionary, if scaremongering, tale for Americans, but it's pretentious and inane, confused and confusing, as well as platitudinous. (Stoicism is once again equated with courage.) Milius, by the way, throws a few sops to liberals: the first victim is a black school teacher (the only black character in the film), and the Cuban commander eventually grows weary of combat. But those are merely gestures, and feel like it. The film is nonsensical.

So is *The Ice Pirates*, ready for release in June 1983, but held back until March 1984. Perhaps they thought it would improve with age. Stewart Raffill directed from a script he and Stanford Sherman cowrote, and the movie starred Robert Urich, Mary Crosby, Michael D. Roberts, and good old John Carradine. Set in a standard future and revolving around a water shortage, it deals with pirates who steal from the rich and give to the poor. There are some space battles, a princess, and a scene in a bar—sound familiar?—but according to *Variety*, nothing works. The reviewer called it "a dim-witted, slow-moving space spoof. . . . [It's] ultimately disturbing in its contempt for the audience's intelligence." When I caught up with it, I found it not as bad as some claim, though it compromises reasonable material into a hopeless jumble.

Another film that sat on the shelf for a long while—I saw it in early 1983—was finally called *Slapstick of Another Kind*. It was altered between the time I saw it and when it was finally released; some narration by Orson Welles was added to imply that the strange twins in the film were fathered by an alien.

Written and directed by young Steven Paul, the movie was based on Kurt Vonnegut's novel *Slapstick*, hardly his best work. Ugly twins, a boy and a girl, are born to millionaires Caleb (Jerry Lewis) and Letitia Swain (Madeline Kahn). The twins, presumed to be morons, are sequestered in a mansion where they obligingly pretend to be what everyone thinks they are, because that's what they think is expected of them. Actually, they are geniuses (and are also played by Lewis and Kahn in mild makeup), but only when together. The plot also involves miniaturized Chinese and friendly aliens.

Slapstick of Another Kind is well intentioned but inept in all departments. Paul's screenplay meanders and is at once too jokey and too serious. He manages to keep Lewis in check most of the time but also prevents him from being funny. The actors who come

off best include John Abbott, Pat Morita, and (director) Samuel
Fuller. Mostly this boring film is a seriously misfired satire; it failed
to gather any audience and soon vanished.

Sheena also beat a hasty retreat, with just cause. Words fail me
when I try to describe in just what low esteem I hold Lorenzo
Semple, Jr., who cowrote Sheena with David Newman, who's not
much better. Semple has written a few good films; his script for
Never Say Never Again was okay, and he didn't do badly with Pretty
Poison or The Super Cops. But Sheena is a comic-book fantasy with
SF elements.

To make a film like this properly requires a sophisticated approach, a conscious suspension of scorn: the writers and director
(here, John Guillermin) have to be willing to understand the power
of this kind of simplistic tale, and to work with the material, not
against it, even when spoofing it. The creators have to have an
understanding of the value of such fantasies, to realize they are a
part of the mythology of our race.

Semple, however, seemed determined to show he is not taken in
by this and to show us, the audience, the contempt with which he
regards this material. He must not only write down to it, he must
also make patronizing fun of it. He knows he's intellectually superior
to what he sees as irredeemable garbage and so cannot write SF or
fantasy without jeering at it. Proof? He created the "Batman" TV
series and wrote the scripts for the most recent Flash Gordon and
King Kong.

Granted, with a limp actress like Tanya Roberts in the lead, there's
hardly any way that Sheena would have been much less silly even
if it had been well made, but it could have been smart-silly rather
than stupid-silly. However, the three cynics, Newman, Semple,
and Guillermin, did their job too well: audiences thought they were
idiots who simply made a bad movie rather than Hollywood sharpies
trying hard to show they're above this sort of thing. Sheena trashed
its material and, ultimately, trashed itself.

Greystoke: The Legend of Tarzan, Lord of the Apes made some
errors, but it played fair with its premises and approached the ma-

terial seriously. It was entertainment for the whole family, treating the story with respect.

Greystoke was a daring undertaking. For years, writer (and recently director) Robert Towne worked on an adaptation of the first Tarzan novel by Edgar Rice Burroughs and expected to direct the picture. But at the ultimate moment, he was removed, and the script was rewritten by Michael Austin. (The credited cowriter, P. H. Vazak, is Towne's pseudonym.) It was directed by Hugh Hudson, who earlier directed *Chariots of Fire*.

Like Hudson's previous film, *Greystoke* isn't just a fable, it's a look into our past and contrasts corrupt civilization with rough but honest savagery. The last half of the film is set on the lavish Greystoke estates; it is the contrast between the ordered life there that Tarzan is dropped into and his life in the jungle that fascinated Hudson.

Warner Bros. insisted that the director shorten the film. As a result, much of value seems to have been lost. As one reviewer noted, an epic should be allowed to be an epic instead of arbitrarily being reduced to fit enough screenings per day into a theater's schedule.

For some, the film was slow, but I didn't find it so; some disliked it intensely, apparently judging it by preconceived notions of what *their* Ultimate Tarzan Movie should be, rather than by the intent of the actual film. As an adaptation, it's about as close to Burroughs as "Hill Street Blues" is to "Car 54, Where Are You?" My liking and respect for Burroughs are such that I have almost everything he wrote, but I don't have any complaints about this adaptation, even though it most emphatically is not a close adaptation. I wasn't expecting one. It's a compromise; some values were lost, and some were gained. *Greystoke* is a romantic, haunting drama about the duality of man, and on that level, it works well.

Other adaptations in 1984 varied in quality. The new version of George Orwell's *Nineteen Eighty-Four* is about as good a film version of that novel as possible. As was not the case with the earlier version, the makers of the new film imaginatively refused to *add* imagination to Orwell's novel. In fact, at the end there's a smug little announcement that the film was shot in the same places and on the same dates that Orwell specified.

The movie was written and directed by Michael Radford, who makes a very impressive debut. A friend of mine pointed out that the film maintains the same steady pace from beginning to end. That's a matter of the old principle: the way a thing is said is a part of what is being said. The pace is part of the theme. You aren't going to get out of *this* 1984 alive; that bootheel smashing a human face forever will rise and fall at an unvarying rate.

Nineteen Eighty-Four is a dry, careful rendering of the novel; the technology in the film is available to us today, including television sets that watch you. It's a 1948 vision of a bleak 1984. As a result of this adherence to the book's reality, we first realize that Orwell's prediction was true about the Soviet Union (or at least about the Soviet Union we are told exists); later, we uncomfortably realize that many of Orwell's evils exist in our *own* country, here in 1984. But then, that was the novel's goal.

In one sense, of course, it was not a novel at all; it was a treatise. The world of *Nineteen Eighty-Four* is a debater's world, not intended to be a real world; it's a grimly purposeful satire and so is difficult to turn into drama. But as satire both the novel and the new film succeed very well indeed.

John Hurt was an excellent choice for Winston Smith. He already looks haunted, furtive, and cowardly, but intelligent and resigned: a timid dreamer. He's drawn, worn, frightened; we can believe him on any plane the film presents: as the questioner, the diarist, the sad customer of whores, the clandestine lover, and, finally, the man who has caved in, believes 2 + 2 = 5, and loves Big Brother. It's a fine performance. Hurt gives us more characterization than Orwell provided, and he fulfills Radford's excellent script.

As Julia, Suzanna Hamilton is outstanding. In the novel, she's a cipher, but she comes to life in the film. She's passionate, arrogant, and naive; Hamilton makes us believe that Julia believes she hates purity and wants everyone to be corrupt.

As O'Brien, in what was to be his last film role, Richard Burton turns in a precisely modulated performance. He's careful, quiet, and avuncular, even while torturing Smith on the well-used torture devices. Somewhere, Burton hid the great natural warmth he always had and gives us an icy, dead, intelligent O'Brien.

Director Radford literalizes Orwell's ideas, gives them visual reality, brings them to life: the complete domination by the government, the subservience of the people, the fear and dread, the corruption of the language. He's helped by excellent photography by Roger Deakins and imaginative production design by Allan Cameron.

The film of *Nineteen Eighty-Four* is grim, depressing, cheerless—but it had to be.

On the other hand, *Firestarter* is also rather cheerless, but it didn't need to be. Like *Nineteen Eighty-Four*, it's a close adaptation of a novel. Unfortunately, the novel was not one of Stephen King's best. It was primarily a replay of *Carrie*, with a younger protagonist having different powers, and a clichéd involvement of a government agency. The screenplay by Stanley Mann and direction by Mark L. Lester manage to capture King's mood, tone, and plot, but following the plot gives us an aimless, illogical film.

Lester's direction is placid, unimaginative, lacking in drive and momentum, except in the scenes of the girl using her powers. The story is pretty flashy, though: as a result of genetic experimentation on her parents, eight-year-old Charlie (Drew Barrymore) can start fires with her mind. She and her father (David Keith) are fleeing that clichéd government agency but end up in its fiendish clutches. Also, there's a huge, scarred Indian hit man (George C. Scott), who passionately plans to kill Charlie.

Firestarter has good action scenes: a group of government men are fricasseed; brick walls and even water explode into flame. At the wowser of a climax, Charlie flings fireballs about and roasts everyone in sight.

The major virtue here is Drew Barrymore, who almost makes Charlie believable. Martin Sheen seems to be having a good time as the pleasant, evil head of the government agency, but his part is underwritten. Scott and Freddie Jones are hammy; David Keith is okay.

Some people loathe *Firestarter*, and it wasn't much of a money-maker, but those who blame the filmmakers entirely are mostly aiming their ire at the wrong target, as even Stephen King thinks this was a good adaptation of one of his novels. He's right. The flaws with the film are mostly straight from the book.

Another adaptation arrived near the end of the year. Arthur C. Clarke was offered a great deal of money to write a sequel to *2001: A Space Odyssey*. The disappointing novel that resulted violated the basic premise of *2001*. In both the book and the film of *2001*, very clearly the Starchild was the next step in human evolution; that was the story. But in his novel *2010*, Clarke unwisely discarded that idea in favor of a lesser one: the Starchild is nothing more than a cosmic messenger boy. And in Peter Hyams's ghastly film of *2010*, it isn't even that. The Starchild is on screen for maybe five seconds and serves no function.

2010 was written, produced, directed, *and* photographed by Hyams; maybe he overextended himself. Because so much depended on the success of the film, it has a most peculiar air about it: smug desperation. It's an ugly, boring, trivial film, even worse than Hyams's *Outland*, but tries so hard to be winning and endearing that some are fooled by the energy alone. So much goes into trying to make us feel a sense of wonder that some viewers responded favorably. I suspect a second viewing will be dismaying. Comparing the film with Stanley Kubrick's *2001* is pointless: they weren't made for the same audiences. (Insiders tell me that the target audience for *2010* was a fourteen-year-old boy who hadn't seen the original film.)

The science is grotesque. While I'll accept sound-in-space in space operas like *Star Wars* or *Star Trek*, I will not in a film that purports to be hard science. In *2010*, rockets roar, wires twang, and spaceships clank. Jupiter seems to be photographed in time-lapse photography: storms zip around the planet's bulging middle at what must be 100,000 mph. Gravity (or its equivalent) varies at the director's whim. In a centrifuge aboard the Soviet ship, pens suddenly float just to illustrate a point—while the people remain fixed in one place. A spaceship outruns the speed of light.

Dramatically, the film is hackneyed. In bed, a husband and wife embrace, and Hyams cuts to a shot of crashing surf. The tough Soviet spaceship captain (Helen Mirren) and the dashing Heywood Floyd (Roy Scheider, overacting) have been at odds through much of the film, but finally they sit down and talk about their kids and everything is hunky-dory. (This is not in the novel.)

There is a Funny American (John Lithgow, disappointing) and a Funny Russian named Max (Elya Baskin) who wears a Funny Hat; they become Funny Friends. Neither *is* very funny, though Baskin comes nearer than Lithgow.

The dialogue is strictly TV-sitcom banal. Everyone speaks in preposterously "sharp" lines. The characters are two-bit impersonations of characters. There's bogus suspense and a muddled ending.

I suppose the idea was to offset what many saw as the "lack of humanity" in *2001*, but to approach it that way begs a central question. People were *supposed* to seem dehumanized in *2001*; it wasn't an accident. But instead of "warm characters" in *2010*, Hyams gives us bomber-crew clichés.

Maybe I was asking too much. Hyams has always been a bad director of actors and a very bad, illogical writer; he can handle action scenes very well indeed, but this film has none. His plotting in *Outland* and *Capricorn One* was idiotic; why should I have expected anything better from him here? But surely even he could have avoided the scene in which Baskin removes his faceplate, takes a deep breath, then announces that there is oxygen. And he didn't need to add the hackneyed international tension subplot to Clarke's clean narrative.

The film is dark, cramped, crowded. Scenes are awash in garish oranges and heavy browns; everything is angular and harsh. There's no grace to the picture, no beauty, no clarity. (Hyams even floods scenes aboard a sealed spaceship with his traditional fog.) Instead of the awe and mystery that permeated *2001*, Hyams gives us a trite, we're-all-brothers-under-the-sun(s) message. *2010* was made for those who didn't understand *2001*, to produce in them an "Oh, now I get it" reaction. They can have it.

Android was a heck of a lot cheaper and a heck of a lot better. This cheeky, intelligent little film has been achieving a well-deserved reputation wherever it plays. It was finished in 1982 but not released theatrically until 1984. Director Aaron Lipstadt, working from a script by James Reigle and Don Opper, created a quirky picture, set on a space station, about an android who dreams.

Mad scientist Dr. Daniel (Klaus Kinski, wonderful as always) is busy constructing various types of androids, including the skinny Max 404 (played very well by cowriter Opper), who is curious about Earth. He learns some of what he wants to know by watching old movies, occasionally wearing a fedora in imitation of Jimmy Stewart.

A group of fleeing criminals takes refuge at the space station, much to the delight of Max and the initial annoyance of Dr. Daniel. The scientist decides to use the bioelectrical force of criminal Maggie (Brie Howard) to bring to life his ultimate creation, the android Cassandra (Kendra Kirchner). Complications arise when Max is attracted to Maggie and the criminals decide to use this affection.

The plot of *Android* is of no great concern, although it is ingenious and interesting. It's the acting and directing that make the film the special low-budget treat that it is. The movie was coproduced with Roger Corman, who gave up on it later; the filmmakers bought it back from him. Corman should have known better. This is a lively, entertaining picture, with many great moments—a fully realized vision.

So is *The Brother from Another Planet*, also a low-budget film (though it has a good deal of location shooting). Writer-director John Sayles, who wrote several good exploitation films, such as *The Howling*, returns to that kind of story, with a different perspective. An alien lands on Earth, clearly a fugitive, and seeks shelter in Harlem. He happens to be black (though he has strange, taloned feet) and cannot talk at all. He caroms from event to event, befriended by several people because of his innate sweetness (and ability to fix machines). He's pursued by two villainous aliens, the Men in Black. These two jokers, played for effective comedy, turn up from time to time with a fresh idea for each appearance; the tall, funnier one is Sayles himself.

The movie doesn't have a strong plot line, and probably could have used one. The black alien, portrayed extremely well by Joe Morton, is a hapless innocent who rather quickly fits into the new culture he encounters. A kind of plot turns up in the last third of the film, as he becomes involved with the drug scene, but it doesn't add much to the movie.

Sayles rings several variations on the themes of stranger-in-a-strange-land and disguise. Two naive white college kids happen into the Harlem bar where the alien hangs out. They're apprehensive but surprised and pleased to have a good time. The alien falls in love with a singer (Dee Dee Bridgewater) who, when she takes him home, removes her finery—on stage, she's in disguise, too.

As a director of his own material (this is his fourth film), Sayles has yet to learn enough about narrative structure, but he does everything else so well, especially dialogue and characterizations, that this is a much less serious failing than it would be in films by lesser talents.

Another low-budget success was *Night of the Comet*. The basic idea sounds unimpressive and imitative: a comet passes Earth for the first time in millennia, and unfortunately almost everyone who is out in the open is reduced to red dust. Those who were somehow shielded survive, but some of *those* become flesh-eating zombies.

The movie rises above this instantly, by means of sharp, witty dialogue, good characterizations, and plenty of suspense. The zombies are just background characters; we see only one kill somebody, and the other one we see, in full zombie form, is a little kid who chases the leading actor around a house. The movie is *really* about Valley Girls at the End of the World.

Writer-director Thom Eberhardt demonstrates a nervy cleverness and energy. He's not afraid to use effective scary stuff, but his emphasis is on the characters, who are delightful. The heroines are sisters Regina (Catherine Mary Stewart) and younger Samantha (the adorable Kelli Maroney, who spends most of the film in a cheerleader's outfit). They're Vals, all right, teenage girls from the San Fernando Valley, but there's no exaggeration in their characterizations; they're also smart, tough survivors. Their Green Beret daddy, presumably a comet casualty, taught them survival and fighting skills. Both know martial arts and how to handle weapons—but are still Vals. Trying out a machine gun, Samantha pouts when it jams. "Daddy would have gotten us Uzis," she complains.

The film is so funny, fresh, and inventive that many have declared it a comedy, but it's really not. It's a serious adventure film with much humor. The situations are dangerous and frightening; the girls are in real danger, and Samantha dies several times.

It's such a pleasant surprise to find a relatively nonviolent but action-packed low-budget SF movie these days, and 1984 gave us several of them. I hope that Thom Eberhardt, John Sayles, and Aaron Lipstadt return to the genre again. For such inexpensive films, each of theirs is a major achievement.

So, in its fast-paced slickness, was *The Terminator*. This unexpected smash hit, directed by James Cameron from a script he wrote with Gale Anne Hurd, took America by storm in the last quarter of the year. The distribution company, Orion, surely didn't expect this film to do so well; probably no one did.

The plot is clever but elementary. From a future in which scattered, embattled human survivors are pitted against domineering machines, Kyle Reese (Michael Biehn) comes to our time in search of Sarah Conner (Linda Hamilton), who is very important to the future. Also arriving from the future, just before Kyle, is a Terminator (Arnold Schwarzenegger), an android killing machine. It has human flesh and blood over a steel skeleton and is here with one purpose: to kill Sarah Conner.

The film is sassy and speedy, with sizzling car chases, awesome shoot-outs, explosions, and other spectacles, including a scary climax of the Terminator, reduced to a metal skeleton, still doggedly after Sarah.

Cameron shows himself a force to be reckoned with, and Schwarzenegger, in his sophisticated, funny portrayal of the punk-looking Terminator, proved to those last few doubters that he's a genuinely good actor.

I suspect we will be flooded with Italian imitations of *The Terminator* in the next few years; it's that distinctive and that imitable. (And some think the movie itself is an imitation. It strongly resembles some episodes of "The Outer Limits," especially Harlan Ellison's "Soldier," although there are elements of his "Demon with a Glass Hand" as well. Ellison also noticed the similarities and turned to a lawyer for a plagiarism suit, settled out of court. TV and video cassette prints of the film now have a credit line acknowledging Ellison's works.)

Similar to *The Terminator* and almost as good was Michael Crichton's *Runaway*, arriving in the Christmas batch of SF films. The exhilarating action scenes are so much fun that it's a shame Crichton has to stop them from time to time to engage in limp dialogue. The film bubbles with new ideas—both cinematically and in the area of real SF speculation—entertainingly presented. However, the writer-director's ear for dialogue, his characterizations, and his ideas of logic hover around the level of a bad comic book.

Still, I got a bang out of this tale of industrial and household robots going berserk, with only Tom Selleck (as a cop on Runaway patrol) between us and the accidentally murderous machines. As this is the near future, these robots are simply nonanthropomorphic machines, intelligently designed advances on the industrial robots now in use the world over. In fact, some of the machines seen in the film really are such robots.

The bulk of the story, such as it is, deals with the efforts of evil, wealthy mad scientist Luther (not, you'll notice, Lu*thor*) trying to get the plans for some nasty robotic components. The story line is muddled, however, and needn't concern us.

Most of the picture dazzles. The set pieces of Selleck and his pals battling robots are designed and executed with exciting and amusing verve by the team of Crichton, editor Glenn Farr, and cinematographer John A. Alonzo. There are stunning scenes with cameras following guided-missile bullets even down pipes, and small, freeway-traveling killer robots *under* cars.

Selleck is fine, as is the rest of the cast; rock band Kiss member Gene Simmons makes a villain so nasty you know he's the bad guy the minute you see him. But this really isn't an actors' film. Despite numerous faults, *Runaway* is a pleasing, fast-paced action picture with more ideas than any five ordinary movies.

On the other hand, *Star Trek III: The Search for Spock* has little that's new except the clever means of using the Genesis Planet from *Star Trek II* to revive Spock. *Star Trek III* should be prefaced by a warning: "For Trekkies Only." They should have been delighted, and, by all reports, they were. The old gang is back together; there are moments of familial poignance and direct references to the series (tribbles are glimpsed, for instance), and much camaraderie. But this film is inferior to the two that preceded it.

Producer Harve Bennett provided a thin, undeveloped story line that would barely have passed muster for an hour-long TV show. The film's antagonist was another Klingon, Captain Kruge, who doesn't live through the film. This is a shame; he's the best thing about it and would have made a great continuing villain. Kruge was played by the witty, distinctive Christopher Lloyd, who also graced *Buckaroo Banzai*.

The movie was directed by Leonard Nimoy but was not a promising debut for Spock the director. The emotions of everyone seem banked, cold, repressed; they've all been turned into Vulcans. Nimoy muffs the death of Kirk's son so badly that at first it seems like a trick, as if he'll turn up again later. Scenes lack tension and spark, and the staging is dull. It's nice that Nimoy has ambitions beyond acting, but he's more fun as an actor, although in that capacity his few scenes here are pompous.

Though a lesser entry in the *Star Trek* series, it was profitable; because of behind-the-scenes wrangling, though, there is apparently going to be quite a wait for *Star Trek IV*. I want to see how Kirk is going to explain to the Federation why he blew up the *Enterprise*.

Another imitative film was *The Last Starfighter*, but it was a cheerful, pleasant movie and deserved to do better than it did. The story wasn't much and gave lumpy evidence of successive rewrites. Our young hero (Lance Guest), recruited by means of testing on a video arcade machine, becomes a skillful space pilot and saves the galaxy. The plot has him return to Earth twice, for no good reason, giving the movie's rhythm a misstep. There's a robot duplicate of the hero, and though Guest is amusing as the copy, it's an unnecessary detail.

The biggest pleasure of *The Last Starfighter* was in the actors, the dialogue, and some of the situations. As Centauri the interstellar con man, Robert Preston is pretty much Harold Hill from *The Music Man*, but he's still a delight. He's not quite as lovable as you might expect, but that works to the film's advantage. Even at the end, you're not quite sure if you can trust him. Dan O'Herlihy is splendid as the lizardy navigator.

The Last Starfighter is one of the great wish-fulfillment movies of recent years. At the end, after defeating the alien armada, the hero not only returns in triumph to Earth but is seen in his fancy Starfighter uniform by all his friends and neighbors, and he takes his girlfriend off to space with him. Talk about bringing it all back home. Nick Castle directed from a screenplay by Jonathan Betuel, and with the exceptions noted, both did fine jobs.

One final note: the special effects are realistic and exciting, and they were *entirely* computer generated. Now anything can be filmed.

Some of the imagination that made *The Last Starfighter* so much fun within its familiar plot would have helped *Dreamscape*. Its imagination lay in the wild premise, but after that, it was worked out in very commonplace terms. The script by David Loughery, Chuck Russell, and director Joe Ruben never engages the intellect, even while the emotions are occasionally caught by the action.

A technique has been devised by kindly scientist Dr. Novotny (the ubiquitous Max von Sydow) enabling those with ESP abilities to enter the dreams of others. This is hard to swallow, especially when the dreams we see in the film are basically unimaginative, except for the nightmare of one little boy.

The U.S. president (Eddie Albert) has been having dreams of nuclear annihilation, screaming nightmares that are affecting his waking hours. Telepath Alex (Dennis Quaid) is assigned to enter the president's dreams and help him. But the usual twisted government official (more credible here because he's played by Christopher Plummer) hires a psychotic telepath, the gleefully evil Tommy (David Patrick Kelly), to kill the president by murdering him in his dreams.

Dreamscape takes too long to set up the premise, which isn't

worth setting up in the first place, but it's still a reasonably entertaining film. It will probably look best on television.

The Philadelphia Experiment was originally scheduled to be a
Sunn Classics–like documentary on the destroyer that supposedly
vanished during radar testing in World War II, then reappeared.
Joe Dante was assigned to direct a few years ago; before leaving the
project, he came up with several new story ideas, many of which
were retained and expanded on by writers William Gray and Michael Janover. Stewart Raffill's direction is plodding, methodical,
and, for all that, quite interesting.

In the finished film, the ship vanishes but falls into a time stream,
or something, transporting sailors David (Michael Pare) and Jim
(Bobby Di Cicco) to the present, where similar experiments are
being conducted again. All this leads to a big crisis in time, the
potential destruction of the universe, and more pursuit by the government, although this time the government is only wrong, not
villainous. It was good summer escapism, but despite several good
sequences, little more.

A few other SF films came and went rather swiftly, some despite
reasonably good reviews, such as Impulse. The film, which stars
Tim Matheson, Meg Tilly, and Hume Cronyn, begins with an
intriguing premise: people in a small town start going haywire.
Unfortunately, this behavior is unimaginatively blamed on hazardous waste. At least the ailment has an interesting effect: it strips
away inhibitions, and people act on their private fantasy impulses.
Reviewers considered the film promising but generally felt that the
promise was betrayed before the end. Impulse was written by Bart
Davis and Don Carlos Dunaway and directed by Graham Baker. I
found it to be well-produced, competently acted, but badly con-
ceived.

C.H.U.D. stands for Cannibalistic, Humanoid, Underground
Dwellers (and "something else," several reviewers said). It too deals
with hazardous wastes, nuclear this time, which transform bums
who live in New York sewers into gooey monsters that feed on the
unchanged. Surprisingly, very good actors turned up in this, including John Heard and Daniel Stern. According to most reviewers,

C.H.U.D., like *Impulse*, was above average. Lawrence Van Gelder, in the *New York Times*, said that "in the category of horror films, it stands as a praiseworthy effort." The film was written by Parnell Hall and directed by Douglas Cheek.

Many have been predicting that the next new batch of directors will arise out of rock videos. *Electric Dreams* is one of the first features to be directed by a graduate of videos, Steve Barron. Some complained about the movie's fragmentation. Rusty Lemorande's overly cute script is about a home computer getting real smart (from spilled champagne) and falling in love with a pretty cellist, who mistakes the computer's attentions for those of its owner, Michael. Soon Michael and the cellist fall in love, and Edgar the computer gets jealous. Edgar (voice by Bud Cort) gives some hints of villainy, but the film ends on an upbeat note. It's a glitzy but empty science-fantasy variation on *Cyrano de Bergerac*.

Massive Retaliation, written by Larry Wittenbert and Richard Beban, was directed by Thomas A. Cohen. It deals with the efforts of a group of survivalists to gather at a survival center during the first few hours of an impending nuclear war. The film did not receive favorable reviews and played almost nowhere but the festivals.

There were are fewer made-for-television SF movies than usual in 1984. Among this scant number was *Airwolf*, a blatant imitation of *Blue Thunder*, dealing as it did with a superhelicopter. However, the series of *Airwolf* that resulted lasted longer than the series of *Blue Thunder* itself.

Late in the year, Lucasfilm produced the TV movie *The Ewok Adventure*, a Star Wars–universe tale about a group of the teddy-bear-like heroes of *Return of the Jedi* helping some human children save their parents from the clutches of a monster. Reviewers felt director John Korty did about as well with the material as could be expected.

At the end of the year, a flock of theatrical SF films crowded into theaters. Along with the already-discussed *Nineteen Eighty-Four*, *2010*, and *Runaway*, we were given *Supergirl*, *Starman*, and *Dune*.

In the U.S., *Supergirl* is about fifteen minutes shorter than the version shown overseas; perhaps as a result, it's fast-paced and, actually, more fun than I was expecting. It's astoundingly silly in some ways, especially at the beginning. Directed by Jeannot Szwarc, *Supergirl* is a strange mixture of the idiotic and the inspired, with inspiration, of a sort, taking over once the parameters of the story are established.

Supergirl (Helen Slater) has come to Earth in search of the power source of her native Argo City, a missing "omegahedron" that's a kind of do-anything machine. It falls into the hands (and clam dip) of Selena (Faye Dunaway), a carnival magician with dreams of ruling the world. Supergirl has to get the gadget back from Selena, whose powers increase by leaps and bounds.

The movie is far more spoofy than the Superman films and much more entertaining than *Superman III*. Slater is charming both as Supergirl (Superman's cousin) and as her alter ego, Linda Lee (Clark Kent's cousin). But the greatest fun comes from Dunaway, a howl as the frowzily elegant Selena. She chomps up the scenery as she did in *Mommie Dearest* and is even funnier here: this is a fine actress enjoying herself slumming in a silly role.

Starman is the film Columbia made because the studio thought it would outgross *E.T.*. (Columbia had passed on Spielberg's film.) *Starman* is an idiot's delight of an SF movie, made for those who don't care about logic, either scientific or storytelling. Directed by John Carpenter, *Starman* is an interstellar love story combining elements of *It Came from Outer Space*, *E.T.*, *Bonnie and Clyde*, and *It Happened One Night*.

An alien spaceship encounters Voyager and accepts its invitation to visit. The shuttle craft is shot down at once by the government, 1984's favorite villain (which, considering the implications of the date, may be appropriate). The stranded alien—never seen—clones a body from a fragment of hair and grows it to manhood. The result is Jeff Bridges, the recently deceased husband of Karen Allen, who is naturally surprised to find her dead husband, naked and smiling, in her living room. Eventually, she agrees to drive the alien/human to his Arizona rendezvous, and they fall in love as they travel.

Although *Starman* is reasonably entertaining, it's unimaginative and literal. Fortunately, the leads are outstanding: Jeff Bridges rises above the flaws in the script to create a charming personality, and I have never seen Karen Allen better. If the film works at all—and it does—it is largely due to the performances of these two and of Charles Martin Smith as a sympathetic exobiologist.

There were the typical silly failings: the alien knows many things about us but has never heard of stoplights or food. He can start machines and even bring the dead back to life. He's arrived from fairyland, not a rational, believable alien world. As usual in such unimaginative stories, the aliens may be ahead of us technologically, but they have lost some important values that we retain: love and stuff like that. Still, *Starman* is basically pleasing.

Finally, there was *Dune*. Based on Frank Herbert's magnum opus, it was worked on for three and a half years and was almost a full year in production. Director-writer David Lynch seems an odd choice to helm this $40 million production; his only previous films were the bizarre cult favorite *Eraserhead* and the sturdy, touching *Elephant Man*. Considering that Lynch had never read the novel when he was hired to film it, it's a bit surprising that his only real fault lay in being *too* faithful to the material. Herbert's novel probably should have been two or more films, or much of what Lynch includes should have been done away with. It's such a dense story that more time was needed to tell it fully.

But in collaboration with a talented array of technicians, especially production designer Anthony Masters and photographer Freddie Francis, Lynch has created the first truly unique big-budget SF film since *2001*, and perhaps a masterpiece. It is not a conventionally exciting film; the action scenes seem remote and hasty, as if Lynch weren't really interested in them, but his grasp of the epic qualities of the story is sure and masterful.

Most of *Dune* takes place *inside*, not on the expansive planet of Arrakis. It is a tale of palace intrigue and betrayal; in fact, in its hermetically sealed way, it's another telling of Joseph Campbell's *monomyth*.

Lynch concentrates on the details of the intrigues and the interactions of the characters; he supplies voice-over thoughts for almost everyone, an extremely rare technique but here almost demanded, and certainly useful. He doesn't dwell on the opulent sets, although there are many of them, and they are gorgeous; after all, these people don't gaze at the sets in rapture, they simply live in them.

Perhaps the best way to judge the film of *Dune*—and perhaps the novel as well—is to consider it a historical epic, more comparable to *Lawrence of Arabia* or *Cromwell* than to *Star Trek* or *Blade Runner*. It is an epic, but it is an epic of human interaction; the film takes over half an hour just to establish who everyone is.

The performances vary in quality. José Ferrer, as the Emperor, seems strangely lifeless; Freddie Jones is as hammy as ever; Max van Sydow and Silvana Mangano, though good, barely get a word in. On the other hand, Kyle MacLachlan, as Paul Atreides, is very good; handsome enough to be a hero, he is also able to make believable Paul's change from an intelligent if callow youth to a messiah. Jurgen Prochnow as Duke Leto, Paul Smith as Rabban, Dean Stockwell as Dr. Yueh, and Everett McGill as Silgar are all fine.

Several performers are outstanding, such as Sting as Feyd Rautha. He's a grinning, asexual villain, exuding energy and hatred. Brad Dourif as the mentat De Vries seems like a genuine creature from another world: his eyes are always wide, he mutters to himself, and he has developed an entire range of novel gestures for the role. The most exuberant performance is Kenneth McMillan's as Baron Harkonnen, a villain's villain: omnisexual, bloated, diseased and quite happy about it. He literally and figuratively sails over the heads of most of the performers and comes exuberantly to life.

For those who are captured by Lynch's intricate, careful spell and who admire his daring, *Dune* is one of the most rewarding SF films ever made. In years to come, it will be regarded as a classic.

I was one of the few singing the praises of *Dune*. Harlan Ellison liked it, and so did *Newsweek* and scattered people here and there. But SF fans as a group, the public as a whole, and the vast majority of critics disdained the film, and it was a colossal failure at the box office. It was already on videotape by June 1985. There's an interesting aspect to the failure of *Dune*: well before it was released, the advance word was very poor. The advertising for the movie was unimaginative, and, to a degree, the film was simply dropped into the marketplace with little of the promotion that such films usually get. There are rumors that the half-hearted sell of *Dune* was deliberate; the deal for the film had been made between Dino De Laurentiis and an administration at Universal different from that which headed the studio when the film was finally ready for release. And to make the previous administration look bad, the film was not promoted properly. As I said, this is only a rumor—but studio executives are quite capable of that sort of thing.

If nothing else, the box-office bonanzas of *Ghostbusters*, *Splash*, *Gremlins*, and *Indiana Jones and the Temple of Doom* prove that there's still a market for *fantasy* films. (Most audiences make little distinction between SF and fantasy.) Eventually even Hollywood executives will know that.

Although many of the science fiction films of 1984 were well above average, it was not a watershed year. It did, however, have the distinction of being a make-or-break time for large-budget SF movies that are *not* part of a series. As the year drew to a close, one picture in particular, *Dune*, was considered a stalking-horse for the future of movies adapted from written science fiction. It fell on its face commercially, and this may be fatal for SF novels-into-films for a long time to come. No other major novels have been announced as films, with the semi-exception of *Battlefield Earth*. SF films are still popular, but for the foreseeable future they will almost always be based on original screenplays.

APPENDIXES

SFWA, the Guild

NORMAN SPINRAD

Norman Spinrad is a past president of SFWA. His best-known novels are The Void Captain's Tale, Bug Jack Barron, *and* The Iron Dream. *He has won the Prix Apollo and the Jupiter Award and has been a multiple Nebula and Hugo award nominee. His stories and novels have appeared in a dozen languages.* Child of Fortune *is his latest novel. Spinrad was born in New York City and now lives in Los Angeles.*

The following article is an unusually complete and concise statement of what SFWA is all about.

While to readers of this book and others in the series of Nebula Awards anthologies published under the aegis of the Science Fiction Writers of America, Inc., the SFWA may sometimes seem to exist primarily to honor the works of its own members by awarding the Nebulas, to the over seven hundred members of the organization throughout the world the SFWA is primarily a trade guild and the

Nebula Awards almost peripheral, though of course it never seems that way when the awards banquet is held.

But the SFWA was not founded to award the Nebulas, and indeed the Nebulas and these award anthologies were instituted as much to help finance SFWA's other activities as to honor the best works of the year in the field.

For while SFWA is emphatically *not* a union—indeed while the very word "union" is anathema to many of even its most militant members—since its inception in 1965 the organization has performed most of the services of a union and more, demonstrating just how much a writers' organization can do to protect, promote, and defend the rights of its members without the necessity of formal and legal unionization. Indeed, today the SFWA is generally recognized by the publishing industry and by other writers' organizations as the most effective guild of writers in the United States, bar the Writers Guild of America, which *is* a legally recognized union with the right to strike and picket.

So in what ways does the SFWA function as a guild and how does it do it?

To begin with, the organization provides continually updated information on book and magazine markets in the United States—and, to the extent possible, elsewhere—in the "Market Reports" published in the SFWA *Bulletin* and the SFWA *Forum*. These market reports tell the membership who is buying what and what the going rates are, relying not only on what editors are *saying* but also on information supplied by the membership as to what they are *doing*.

The SFWA contracts committee has drawn up model paperback and hardcover contracts, as well as a model anthology contract and a model royalty statement. While no publisher has as yet signed either of the SFWA model book contracts, they serve as standards for members (particularly newer writers) to use in evaluating the justice and equity of contracts that they are offered. From time to time, the contracts committee publishes evaluations and ratings of actual publishers' contracts.

Similarly, while no publisher has as yet adopted the SFWA model royalty statement, it serves to inform the relative novice as to what information a publisher should provide, and some more experienced SFWA members have succeeded in writing clauses into their book contracts requiring the publisher to supply upon written request the information called for in the SFWA model royalty statement.

The SFWA model anthology contract, on the other hand, represents generally-agreed-upon industry standards and *has* been used by anthologists in the field, including, of course, the editors of SFWA's own Nebula Awards anthologies.

Which brings us to one of the main sources of SFWA's success. Unlike most other writers' organizations, the membership of SFWA is not confined to writers alone but includes most of the active editors of science fiction, quite a few publishing executives, academics, critics, and of course most of the anthologists, many of whom are also writers. (Libraries can also join, as institutional members.) Because of this, there is a certain solidarity between the writers and the editors, and moral suasion is often sufficient to redress grievances. Most editors, and many publishers, would not care to lose the respect of their fellow SFWA members.

For example, early on in the history of the SFWA, the organization was able to get a publisher to pay royalties to J. R. R. Tolkien after it had taken advantage of a technicality that had thrown *Lord of the Rings* into the public domain to publish the trilogy without paying the writer. While this was entirely legal, it was the consensus of the SFWA that it was not *moral*, and the publisher was persuaded to pay Tolkien on moral grounds alone.

Alas, not all grievances between writers and publishers are so easily settled by appeals to morality or standards of honorable conduct, and SFWA, of necessity, has established a standing grievance committee.

The grievance committee consists of a chairman and four members covering the areas of books, short fiction, foreign publication, and nonprint media. Members with a payment problem or other grievance against an editor, publisher, or producer first write privately to the appropriate member of the grievance committee, who then tries to settle the matter quietly out of public print, with the unstated threat that failure to settle in a gentlemanly manner may eventually result in public exposure in the *SFWA Forum* (which circulates only to members) or, in extreme and generalized instances, in the *SFWA Bulletin* (which is available to anyone by subscription and is carried in many libraries).

If this doesn't work, and particularly if the grievance in question turns out upon investigation to be generalized, then the matter is raised in public in a grievance committee report in the *Forum*, and the "Market Report" also apprises other writers of the situation.

If public exposure doesn't work either, SFWA retains legal counsel to advise its members and also to write some preliminary letters to the miscreant, though actual suit must, at least at this writing, be paid for by the individual member.

And while SFWA is not legally empowered to call for boycotts or strikes or to throw up picket lines, certain collective actions *can* be and *have* been taken in extreme situations. SFWA pressure has been instrumental in getting a book publisher to modify a particularly unjust contract, and SFWA has audited a publisher whose royalty statements and payments were particularly abusive, extracting large sums of money for members and persuading the publisher in question to mend its ways. SFWA once suspended publication in a certain magazine as an acceptable credential for membership because of a serious grievance, which was eventually resolved.

SFWA is now in the process of tackling the whole question of late royalty payments. The organization has adopted a payments-guideline policy and a series of steps to be taken in case of systematic violation by any publisher, up to and including possible legal action.

SFWA was instrumental in causing the abrogation of a packaging agreement between a major science fiction publisher and a major agent in the field because of the question of conflict of interest. It continues to monitor and deal with developments in the new gray area of "sf packagers" and the effects of this new structure in the industry upon the interests of writers.

If all of this sounds somewhat militant and confrontational, well, it *is*. Of all the existing writers' organizations (save the Writers Guild of America), *including*, to date, the recently established National

Writers Union, the SFWA has by far done the most to protect the economic rights and interests of its member writers, and this cannot always be done by sweetness and light alone.

But as a guild and to some extent a trade organization, SFWA also performs certain cooperative functions vis à vis the publishing industry and its members.

SFWA has established an arbitration procedure whereby disputes between members or between members and publishers or editors may be settled by mutual agreement.

SFWA publishes an annual directory of its membership, available at a fee to interested parties, so that publishers, editors, anthologists, producers, and other professionally interested parties may contact writers or learn who their agents are. The directory also furnishes the addresses and phone numbers of most of the agents in the field.

The organization also has a speakers bureau that attempts to secure speaking engagements for science fiction writers on the one hand and gives schools and organizations seeking science fiction speakers a central point of contact on the other.

There is a circulating book plan allowing hardcover publishers to circulate books to members, and SFWA also provides computerized mailing labels free to publishers who wish to promote their books by sending copies to the membership. SFWA also has its own publicity bureau through which members may get out press releases free of charge on their own newsworthy activities.

Finally, the SFWA once even aided an incarcerated member in securing parole from prison.

While SFWA's hard-nosed attitude toward grievances and abuses has accomplished much, the unusual solidarity among its writer, editor, and publisher members is at least as responsible for the unique success of this quite unusual writers' organization. It is commonly held that most writers are solitaries, that they hardly ever talk to each other, remain secretive about their advances and royalties, feel jealous and competitive toward their fellows, and generally regard editors as the enemy. But the great strength of the Science Fiction Writers of America rests in great measure upon the fact that through SFWA the writers see the editors as colleagues, that information circulates among the membership with what is viewed in certain quarters as amazing speed, that writers will frequently commend the work of other writers to editors and the virtue (or lack thereof) of editors to fellow writers. Better than a union, the SFWA is the professional organization of the science fiction industry and community, ready, willing, and quite able to raise its fist when need be, but just as ready, willing, and able to hold out a helping hand.

About the
Nebula Award

The Nebula Awards are voted on, and presented by, active members of the Science Fiction Writers of America. Founded in 1965 by Damon Knight, the organization's first president, the SFWA began with a charter membership of 78 writers; it now has over 800 members, among them most of the leading writers of science fiction.

Lloyd Biggle, Jr., the SFWA's first secretary-treasurer, originally proposed in 1965 that the organization publish an annual anthology of the best stories of the year. This notion, according to Damon Knight in his introduction to *Nebula Award Stories: 1965* (Doubleday, 1966), "rapidly grew into an annual ballot of SFWA's members to choose the best stories, and an annual Awards Banquet." The trophy was designed by Judith Ann Lawrence from a sketch made by Kate Wilhelm; it is a block of lucite in which are embedded a spiral nebula made of metallic glitter and a specimen of rock crystal. The trophies are handmade, and no two are exactly alike.

Since 1965, the Nebula Awards have been given each year for

the best novel, novella, novelette, and short story published during the preceding year. An anthology including the winning pieces of short fiction and several runners-up is also published every year. The Nebula Awards Banquet, which takes place each spring, is held in alternate years in New York City and on the West Coast; the banquets are attended by many leading writers and editors and are preceded by meetings and panel discussions.

The Grand Master Nebula Award is given to a living author for a lifetime's achievement in science fiction. This award is given no more than four times in a decade. Nominations for the Grand Master Award are made by the President of the SFWA and are then voted on by the past presidents, the current officers, and the current Nebula Awards Jury. The Grand Masters, and the years in which they won, are Robert A. Heinlein (1974), Jack Williamson (1975), Clifford D. Simak (1976), L. Sprague de Camp (1978), Fritz Leiber (1981), and Andre Norton (1983).

The 1984 Nebula Awards Ballot

Novel

Frontera by Lewis Shiner (Baen Books)
The Integral Trees by Larry Niven (Del Rey Books)
Job by Robert A. Heinlein (Del Rey Books)
The Man Who Melted by Jack Dann (Bluejay Books)
* **Neuromancer** by William Gibson (Ace Books)
The Wild Shore by Kim Stanley Robinson (Ace Books)

Novella

"**The Greening of Bed-Stuy**" by Frederik Pohl (*he Magazine of Fantasy & Science Fiction*, July 1984)
"**Marrow Death**" by Michael Swanwick (*Isaac Asimov's Science Fiction Magazine*, Mid-December 1984)
* "**PRESS ENTER ■**" by John Varley (*Isaac Asimov's Science Fiction Magazine*, May 1984)
"**A Traveler's Tale**" by Lucius Shepard (*Isaac Asimov's Science Fiction Magazine*, July 1984)

"**Trinity**" by Nancy Kress (*Isaac Asimov's Science Fiction Magazine,*
October 1984)
"**Young Doctor Eszterhazy**" by Avram Davidson (*Amazing,* No-
vember 1984)

Novelette

"**Bad Medicine**" by Jack Dann (*Isaac Asimov's Science Fiction
Magazine,* October 1984)
* "**Bloodchild**" by Octavia E. Butler (*Isaac Asimov's Science Fiction
Magazine,* June 1984)
"**The Lucky Strike**" by Kim Stanley Robinson (*Universe 14,* Dou-
bleday)
"**The Man Who Painted the Dragon Griaule**" by Lucius Shepard
(*The Magazine of Fantasy & Science Fiction,* December 1984)
"**Saint Theresa of the Aliens**" by James Patrick Kelly (*Isaac Asimov's
Science Fiction Magazine,* June 1984)
"**Trojan Horse**" by Michael Swanwick (*Omni,* December 1984)

Short Story

"**The Aliens Who Knew, I Mean, Everything**" by George Alec
Effinger (*The Magazine of Fantasy & Science Fiction,* October
1984)
"**A Cabin on the Coast**" by Gene Wolfe (*The Magazine of Fantasy
& Science Fiction,* February 1984)
"**The Eichmann Variations**" by George Zebrowski (*Light Years and
Dark,* Berkley)
* "**Morning Child**" by Gardner Dozois (*Omni,* January 1984)
"**Salvador**" by Lucius Shepard (*The Magazine of Fantasy & Science
Fiction,* April 1984)
"**Sunken Gardens**" by Bruce Sterling (*Omni,* June 1984)

Special Award

Ian and Betty Ballantine

The winners were announced, and the awards presented, at the Nebula Awards Banquet held at the Warwick Hotel in New York City on May 4, 1985.

* Winners

Past Nebula
Award Winners

1965

BEST NOVEL:	*Dune* by Frank Herbert
BEST NOVELLA:	"The Saliva Tree" by Brian W. Aldiss
	"He Who Shapes" by Roger Zelazny (tie)
BEST NOVELETTE:	"The Doors of His Face, the Lamps of His Mouth" by Roger Zelazny
BEST SHORT STORY:	" 'Repent, Harlequin!' Said the Ticktockman" by Harlan Ellison

1966

BEST NOVEL:	*Flowers for Algernon* by Daniel Keyes
	Babel-17 by Samuel R. Delany (tie)
BEST NOVELLA:	"The Last Castle" by Jack Vance
BEST NOVELETTE:	"Call Him Lord" by Gordon R. Dickson
BEST SHORT STORY:	"The Secret Place" by Richard McKenna

1967

BEST NOVEL:	*The Einstein Intersection* by Samuel R. Delany
BEST NOVELLA:	"Behold the Man" by Michael Moorcock
BEST NOVELETTE:	"Gonna Roll the Bones" by Fritz Leiber
BEST SHORT STORY:	"Aye, and Gomorrah" by Samuel R. Delany

1968

BEST NOVEL:	*Rite of Passage* by Alexei Panshin
BEST NOVELLA:	"Dragonrider" by Anne McCaffrey
BEST NOVELETTE:	"Mother to the World" by Richard Wilson
BEST SHORT STORY:	"The Planners" by Kate Wilhelm

1969

BEST NOVEL:	*The Left Hand of Darkness* by Ursula K. Le Guin
BEST NOVELLA:	"A Boy and His Dog" by Harlan Ellison
BEST NOVELETTE:	"Time Considered as a Helix of Semi-Precious Stones" by Samuel R. Delany
BEST SHORT STORY:	"Passengers" by Robert Silverberg

1970

BEST NOVEL:	*Ringworld* by Larry Niven
BEST NOVELLA:	"Ill Met in Lankhmar" by Fritz Leiber
BEST NOVELETTE:	"Slow Sculpture" by Theodore Sturgeon
BEST SHORT STORY:	No Award

1971

BEST NOVEL:	A *Time of Changes* by Robert Silverberg
BEST NOVELLA:	"The Missing Man" by Katherine MacLean
BEST NOVELETTE:	"The Queen of Air and Darkness" by Poul Anderson
BEST SHORT STORY:	"Good News from the Vatican" by Robert Silverberg

1972

BEST NOVEL:	*The Gods Themselves* by Isaac Asimov
BEST NOVELLA:	"A Meeting with Medusa" by Arthur C. Clarke
BEST NOVELETTE:	"Goat Song" by Poul Anderson
BEST SHORT STORY:	"When It Changed" by Joanna Russ

1973

BEST NOVEL:	*Rendezvous with Rama* by Arthur C. Clarke
BEST NOVELLA:	"The Death of Doctor Island" by Gene Wolfe
BEST NOVELETTE:	"Of Mist, and Grass and Sand" by Vonda N. McIntyre
BEST SHORT STORY:	"Love Is the Plan, the Plan Is Death" by James Tiptree, Jr.
BEST DRAMATIC PRESENTATION:	Soylent Green

1974

BEST NOVEL:	*The Dispossessed* by Ursula K. Le Guin
BEST NOVELLA:	"Born with the Dead" by Robert Silverberg
BEST NOVELETTE:	"If the Stars Are Gods" by Gordon Eklund and Gregory Benford
BEST SHORT STORY:	"The Day Before the Revolution" by Ursula K. Le Guin
BEST DRAMATIC PRESENTATION:	*Sleeper*
GRAND MASTER AWARD:	Robert A. Heinlein

1975

BEST NOVEL:	*The Forever War* by Joe Haldeman
BEST NOVELLA:	"Home Is the Hangman" by Roger Zelazny
BEST NOVELETTE:	"San Diego Lightfoot Sue" by Tom Reamy
BEST SHORT STORY:	"Catch That Zeppelin!" by Fritz Leiber
BEST DRAMATIC PRESENTATION:	*Young Frankenstein*
GRAND MASTER AWARD:	Jack Williamson

1976

BEST NOVEL:	*Man Plus* by Frederik Pohl
BEST NOVELLA:	"Houston, Houston, Do You Read?" by James Tiptree, Jr.
BEST NOVELETTE:	"The Bicentennial Man" by Isaac Asimov
BEST SHORT STORY:	"A Crowd of Shadows" by Charles L. Grant
GRAND MASTER AWARD:	Clifford D. Simak

1977

BEST NOVEL: *Gateway* by Frederik Pohl
BEST NOVELLA: "Stardance" by Spider and Jeanne Robinson
BEST NOVELETTE: "The Screwfly Solution" by Raccoona Sheldon
BEST SHORT STORY: "Jeffty Is Five" by Harlan Ellison
SPECIAL AWARD: *Star Wars*

1978

BEST NOVEL: *Dreamsnake* by Vonda N. McIntyre
BEST NOVELLA: "The Persistence of Vision" by John Varley
BEST NOVELETTE: "A Glow of Candles, a Unicorn's Eye" by Charles L. Grant
BEST SHORT STORY: "Stone" by Edward Bryant
GRAND MASTER AWARD: L. Sprague de Camp

1979

BEST NOVEL: *The Fountains of Paradise* by Arthur C. Clarke
BEST NOVELLA: "Enemy Mine" by Barry B. Longyear
BEST NOVELETTE: "Sandkings" by George R. R. Martin
BEST SHORT STORY: "giANTS" by Edward Bryant

1980

BEST NOVEL: *Timescape* by Gregory Benford
BEST NOVELLA: "The Unicorn Tapestry" by Suzy McKee Charnas
BEST NOVELETTE: "The Ugly Chickens" by Howard Waldrop
BEST SHORT STORY: "Grotto of the Dancing Deer" by Clifford D. Simak

1981

BEST NOVEL:	*The Claw of the Conciliator* by Gene Wolfe
BEST NOVELLA:	"The Saturn Game" by Poul Anderson
BEST NOVELETTE:	"The Quickening" by Michael Bishop
BEST SHORT STORY:	"The Bone Flute" by Lisa Tuttle*
GRAND MASTER AWARD:	Fritz Leiber

1982

BEST NOVEL:	*No Enemy but Time* by Michael Bishop
BEST NOVELLA:	"Another Orphan" by John Kessel
BEST NOVELETTE:	"Fire Watch" by Connie Willis
BEST SHORT STORY:	"A Letter from the Clearys" by Connie Willis

1983

BEST NOVEL:	*Startide Rising* by David Brin
BEST NOVELLA:	"Hardfought" by Greg Bear
BEST NOVELETTE:	"Blood Music" by Greg Bear
BEST SHORT STORY:	"The Peacemaker" by Gardner Dozois
GRAND MASTER AWARD:	Andre Norton

* This Nebula Award was declined by the author.